Stolen

Deborah Moggach

D1354217

ARROW

This edition published in the United Kingdom in 1999 by
Arrow Books

5 7 9 10 8 6 4

Copyright © Deborah Moggach 1990

The right of Deborah Moggach to be identified as the author of this work has been
asserted by her in accordance with the Copyright, Designs and Patents Act, 1988

First published in the United Kingdom in 1990 by William Heinemann

Arrow Books Limited
Random House UK Limited
20 Vauxhall Bridge Road, London, SW1V 2SA

Random House Australia (Pty) Limited
20 Alfred Street, Milsons Point, Sydney, New South Wales 2061, Australia

Random House New Zealand Limited
18 Poland Road, Glenfield
Auckland 10, New Zealand

Random House South Africa (Pty) Limited
Endulini, 5a Jubilee Road, Parktown 2193, South Africa

Random House UK Limited Reg. No. 954009

A CIP catalogue record for this book is available from the British Library

Papers used by Random House UK Limited are natural, recyclable products made
from wood grown in sustainable forests. The manufacturing processes conform
to the environmental regulations of the country of origin

Printed and bound in Norway by
AIT Trondheim AS

ISBN 0 7493 0974 1

*For Roger, Cheryl
and all the cast and crew.
And especially for Tara,
who started it all.*

PART ONE

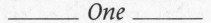 *One*

There's a woman in the next seat. She's Pakistani and she has this little boy with her. After take-off he brought out his colouring book; now he's filling up a cow with purple. I must have been staring at him, because he turns and stares back. He looks as solemn as a businessman; my son looked like that, once.

I don't talk on these flights, not usually. I can't read much, either. So I've put on my headphones but it's the same humour loop as last time, the Frank Muir one. His voice gets on my nerves. I switch past the pop music – batter-batter-thump, can't stand it, not today – then the classical, but it's something with a violin and my throat swells. I pull off the headphones.

The woman turns to me politely. 'Is this your first visit to Karachi?'

I shake my head.

'You've been there before?'

I nod. 'I was married to a Pakistani, you see,' I reply. 'Long ago.'

I went to this evening class, once a week, to learn French. I first spotted him in the canteen. He was sitting all alone, reading. It was 1968, the year of my suede miniskirt. Remember the sixties, when everybody wore suede and nobody got it cleaned? I didn't, anyway. Remember those Moroccan jackets that smelt of dead goats? They *were* dead goats. I wore musk oil, then. It was supposed to turn men into animals.

The next week I saw him again: a dark, handsome Pakistani. He had blue-black, shiny hair. I saw him through the glass, through the classroom door. I checked the list; they were doing Romantic Poetry in there. I was on my way to my French Conversation, which wasn't conversation at all, it meant talking into a tape. Outside it was a stormy night: branches knocked at the windows as I sat in my booth.

'Je m'appelle Marianne. J'ai dix-huit ans.'

The wind whistled in the phone wires. I didn't know anything then. Well, you don't when you're eighteen. I can hardly recognize myself. It's nearly twenty years since I first saw Salim, back in Ashford, Kent, where I was born and brought up.

I was living at home, then, and working at the Coach and Horses.

'He's all . . . smouldering,' I said to Sonia, who ran the pub. We were laying out ashtrays. 'He's got these big treacly eyes like Omar Shariff.'

'What's the rest of him like?'

'Slim – '

'Don't!'

'Lovely, tight little bum – '

'Don't!'

Bill, her husband, shouted across to us: 'Get a bloody move on.'

She looked at him coldly. 'Look at that lovely, tight little gut.'

He pointed upstairs. 'And Zara's crying.'

She ignored him. Their marriage was breaking up, but he didn't know that then. Sonia was screwing a plumber called Humphrey. She was my boss but she was also my friend: she told me everything. She was thirty-five; she seemed so experienced.

'What am I going to do?' I asked.

'Drop your books. It's an old trick but it always works.'

'I haven't got any books. We've got language booths.'

She straightened up, and looked at me. 'Marianne!'

The next week I waited, outside his classroom door. My arms were loaded. People clattered past me, down the corridor – old dears from How to Write Romantic Fiction, tired-looking blokes who were bettering themselves.

Through the glass door his class was rising. I was wearing my angora sweater from Etam. When he came out I loosened my arms and the books fell on to the floor.

It worked. Everyone else pushed past, but he bent down.

He picked up a book. '*One Hundred Great Chicken Dishes*', he read.

'I'm doing French Conversation,' I said, blithe as anything.

In the canteen he introduced himself: Salim Siddiqi. We pushed along our plastic trays, one coffee on each. At the till he put both our cups on to his tray, and paid.

'We've been doing William Wordsworth,' he said.

'We did him at school.'

'I think he's one of your most wonderful lyric poets. Who do you like?'

'Bob Dylan,' I said. 'His lyrics are fab.'

We sat down. He was wearing a blue shetland wool sweater and jeans – and, oh, his eyes! You're supposed to hold a man's eyes with a steady gaze, sort of challenging, it said so in *Honey*.

'I haven't seen you around,' I said. 'You know, around here.'

'I've only been in England since three months. You've heard of Karachi?'

I hadn't a clue where it was, but I nodded. I was watching his mouth as he talked. All over my body, my skin prickled with lust and curiosity. My God, he was gorgeous. I've always liked dark, dangerous-looking men.

He said that his family lived in Pakistan. That's where Karachi was. His father owned a construction company and he knew the chairman of Cormorant Homes, here in Ashford. So Salim had come here to work. He worked in a sales office, out on one of the new estates. Ashford's full of new estates. His eyes were like a deer's, two deep pools. He said he was here for just a year, not only for work experience but to see a bit of England, go to the theatre, all that. He was obviously ever so cultured. He had a cousin in London, he said. He seemed to have bits of family all over the place – Montreal, New York – they must be dead rich. He said he lived in digs with a landlady who made him watch *Coronation Street* with her.

'Sounds a gas,' I said.

'A gas?'

I was looking at his hands and imagining them under my angora sweater. They were beautiful hands – delicate, tapering, with fine black hairs.

We talked for ages. The other people seemed miles away, and when I looked up there was only one person left and the canteen was closing. With a clatter, the grille came down over the serving hatch. We both jumped. He smiled at me.

'Fancy choosing Ashford,' I said. 'You must be daft.'

'I didn't know anything about England,' he said. 'I thought it would all look like a Constable painting.' I wondered what his skin would taste like, if I ran my tongue over it. 'I must say, I did expect the odd dreaming spire.'

'You'll have to make do with Allied Carpets,' I said. 'See, it's a London overspill town, which means they got all the ugliest people to come and live here. It's a dump. Wish I could get out. High spot of my childhood was spitting competitions in the bus shelter.'

He laughed. 'I'm getting quite fond of it.'

'You didn't grow up here. Anyway, you haven't met my parents.'

'I'd like to.'

There was a silence. I looked at the skin on my undrunk coffee, and pushed some biscuit crumbs into a pyramid.

'Aunty Hilda's coming round to tea,' said my mum.

'*Elle est un cochon.*'

'Wendy's starting her Pitman's in September. That young lady's doing very well for herself.'

'*Wendy est une vache grosse.*' I was sitting in the kitchen, eating Rice Krispies.

'She'll be getting engaged to Terence soon, I expect,' said my mum.

'*Je l'aime. Je veux faire l'amour avec lui.*'

'What's that?'

'We've got to be cosmopolitan,' I said. 'One day they're going to build a tunnel to France. Kent'll be full of Froggies.'

'It's not the French I mind about; it's all the other lot getting in. Catch me being prejudiced, but take our newsagents.'

'*Je vais coucher avec lui. O la la.*'

'Don't be pert.'

I grew up in this terraced house, just behind the Ashford freight depot. They were small, mean houses, streets of them. I was dying to get away.

I used to smoke joints in my bedroom, listening to Radio Caroline. My bamboo wallpaper pulsed; outside, the backs of all the other little houses swelled and shrank, as if they were breathing. 'Overspill' made me giggle. Anything made me giggle. A haze of smoke hung across my Animals poster. How pasty they looked now, like boys next door – even Eric Burdon, the wicked one. They held their guitars like toys. I thought of Salim meeting my parents, and how my mother would talk too much, her usual reaction to shock. To anything, actually. My dad would compliment him on his English. Very good for an Arab. He'd probably expect him to have a camel tied up outside. My only daughter! he would think. So pure, so blonde, so English.

That made me giggle harder. I coughed, batting at the veil of smoke, breaking it up.

Salim came to the Coach and Horses, flinching at the smoke. The jukebox was playing Frank Ifield, remember him? *I remember you-hoo*. It was an old number, even then. Sonia had painted eyelashes for me, Twiggy-like, with a felt-tipped pen. Sixties spiderwoman, we all did it in those days.

I can't remember what we said. Salim drank Britvic orange juice and looked out-of-place. I supposed alcohol was against his religion. With him there, the other customers looked more beery and leery. My boss Sonia, with her seen-it-all, leathery face, looked somehow blowzier.

He looked up at the beamed ceiling, with its nicotine stains; he looked at the horse brasses. 'It's charming,' he said. 'It reminds me of an Agatha Christie book.'

I nodded. 'We had a knifing last week.'

'I just meant – I expect Miss Marple to come through the door.'

'You'll be lucky,' I laughed.

I stood behind the bar, pulling pints, feeling flushed and artificial. I felt I was performing on a stage. Tonight he wore a sports jacket; somehow, it made him look even more exotic.

Somebody put on the Stones. 'I won't be off till eleven!' I shouted over the din.

'You look beautiful,' he said.

I turned away to the shelves of mixers, so he couldn't see me blush. I had never met anybody like him before. He was like an interesting new cocktail – gentlemanly, but laced with something so fiery and dangerous that it only hit you later.

'You'll try anything new,' whispered Sonia, as she measured out a Gordons.

'Isn't he tasty,' I whispered.

She nodded. 'Just watch out.'

'What do you mean?'

The guitar swooped, the drums thudded. Beyond the bar, someone guffawed.

'He's not like us,' she said.

'Thank God.'

At that point I didn't have a clue what she was talking about. Nor, I think, did she.

We started going out together, me and Salim, in a shy way.

He hardly touched me, those first few weeks. I thought there must be something wrong with me. I ached for him, my ribcage hurt, I lost weight. I had never felt like that before, not with anybody else, not quite like that. Perhaps it was the sexual frustration. Most of the time I'd had to fight blokes off, struggling in the back of their Fords or their delivery vans, bumping into their spare petrol cans and steaming up the windows. Sometimes there wasn't much of a struggle at all. But Salim was different.

My skin felt tight and burning. I couldn't sleep. I wanted him, more and more. When I pictured his face, my insides clenched. Perhaps he was shy, I thought, because I was an

English girl. Perhaps it was his religion. I knew by now that he was a Muslim, and that they were strict about sex.

I washed the cigarette smoke out of my hair – pubs make you stink – and I sprayed myself with Je Reviens, classier than musk. Sometimes he took me out after work. We went to the Curry Paradise in Ashford High Street, which was the only place that stayed open late. It was deep red, like a womb, and we sat there till long after midnight while the sitar musak played and the waiter cleared his throat. Salim told me about his *ayah* – his native nanny – and how he and his sister would creep out when she dozed and steal mangoes from the next-door tree. He seemed to have grown up with a lot of servants – a cook-bearer, a *mali* who did the garden, except they called it a compound. His talk was full of strange words, strange vegetables and unpronounceable names. Perhaps I'd never reach him. His foreignness inflamed me, but sometimes I panicked. Perhaps they did it differently there, and when we got into bed I wouldn't know how. He was more than dark, he was a black void. I wanted to close my eyes and step into him. I wanted him to close over me.

Three weeks went by. He had a car, a Morris 1100. We drove out into the countryside, into places I'd never been before. The radio played; he liked classical stuff and I pretended I did. We walked hand-in-hand through the woods, blameless as the Start-Rite advert. Around us, the birds sang. He asked me what sort they were but neither of us knew anything about natural history. Then he spread his jacket on the grass and we lay down and stroked each other's faces. Sometimes we brought sandwiches but we weren't hungry. We just lay there for hours, kissing, our legs locked around each other. I got to know his body through his clothes. We must have broken all the records. I explored his mouth as if it was a new country, though the rest of the territory was forbidden. I was wearing jeans. Trembling, he ran his hand down my thigh, and then he pushed me away and sat up.

'What's the matter?' I asked.

'I mustn't.'

'Why not?'

'I respect you,' he said. Then he paused. 'I love you too much.'

I didn't dare tell him I'd been on the Pill since I was sixteen. Even *I* wasn't that stupid.

The only person I could talk to was Sonia. She was the only person who had met him, and that made us closer. She was like a mother-figure to me, much better than my real mum. I remember one October day, waiting with her at a bus stop. She'd had an auburn rinse. She wasn't beautiful, but she looked game; she looked ready for anything. She was going to meet her boyfriend, and I'd promised to collect her daughters from school.

I was talking about Salim, as usual.

'Bet he thinks you're a virgin,' she chortled. 'Ho ho.'

'Keep your mouth shut or I'll throttle you.'

'You really fancy him, don't you?

I couldn't answer because, just then, her bus came round the corner.

She looked at her watch. 'Now remember, fetch Zara and Kirsty at three-thirty, and I'm at the dentist.'

'Having your holes filled,' I said. 'What would Bill do if he found out?'

'Kill me.'

'Is it worth it?'

She smiled. 'You *are* young, ducky, aren't you?'

The bus arrived. Suddenly she looked radiant. She sprang in, flashing a smile at the conductor, at everybody.

She was right. I was too young to understand any of it, then. Adultery, Islam. All the words were just names to me, more foreign than my French. I was young and feckless, a bleached blonde in my white cowboy boots. I probably looked a bit of a scrubber, now I think about it, though I didn't think much about anything, then. I was just a child of the sixties, eager for sensations, eager to get away from home, itching for something foreign and exciting. And along came Salim, my handsome Pakistani. I hadn't a clue what I was letting myself in for. Not in those days. I just knew that when he touched me, I shuddered.

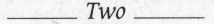

Two

The little boy has fallen asleep, just like that, as if somebody has switched him off inside. He lies loose-jointed across his mother's lap. His hair is dark and damp; it's crowded in here, and stuffy. These flights always seem to be full of kids, behaving more obediently than British ones.

My son and daughter were dark, too. Are dark. Nobody would guess they had an English mother.

All these years; all these flights. Sometimes I've sat in the toilet for hours, while somebody rattles the door.

'Yesterday I parked in your street,' said Salim. We were sitting in his car. It was some weeks later. He was stroking the back of my hand. 'I waited for you to come out of your house.'

'Did I?'

He shook his head. 'You weren't there. Or if you were, you never came out.'

'You just sat there?'

He nodded. 'I thought of you growing up, all the years I've missed. Me in Karachi, you in England. My heart ached. I thought of you on your bicycle – did you have a bike? You and your friends I'll never know.'

'Did you really?'

'I even went to your post office. Around the corner. I just stood there. Well, in the end I bought some stamps. I just wanted to be where you'd been.'

I smiled. 'You daft thing.'

'I can't sleep,' he said. 'I didn't know it would feel like this.'

I kissed him, and rubbed my face against his shoulder. 'Nor did I.'

They're serving breakfast now. I can hear the rattle of the trolley. The little boy stirs and wakes. The stewardess passes me a tray with a PIA omelette on it. The woman cuts up her son's for him, and butters his croissant. Outside, the sun is blinding bright. It had been raining in England.

She holds her cup, her little finger crooked, and turns to me. 'You said your husband's from Pakistan?' she asks.

I nod. 'From Karachi.'

'When did you get married?'

'Years ago. In 1969.' I sip my coffee. 'Twenty years ago.'

'We're getting married.'

'Come again?' asked my dad.

'Me and Salim. We're getting married.'

It was a Sunday morning that winter. I had just come down to breakfast. Outside stretched our garden, a shanty-town of sheds. There had been a frost. Dad's chrysanths had died, slimily. Their heads hung lolling from their stakes, like a row of executions.

My mum sat in her housecoat, waxy-faced. 'You can't.'

'When are you planning this?' asked dad.

'Next month.'

'Next month! What's the hurry?'

'But you can't!' said mum.

'Why not?'

'Are you, you know?' she asked.

'No.'

'What's the hurry then?' She stared at me. 'You can't!'

'Why not?'

'He's not – well, he's not – '

'What?'

'One of us.'

'Thank God.'

'You know what I mean!' she said. 'What's got into you?'

'Nothing.'

'Listen, love . . .' said dad.

Mum said: 'You planning on having kids?'

'Hope so,' I said.

'They'll be darkies! My own grandchildren!'

'All right, Dot,' said dad. He turned to me. 'Look, why don't you wait a bit . . .?'

'We don't want to wait.'

'He'll take you away!' cried mum.

'He wants to live here,' I said. 'He doesn't want to go back, his family's going to blow their top. He loves England – weird as that might seem when there's people like you calling him . . .'

'She's upset!' said dad.

'My only daughter!' wailed mum. 'He'll be locking you up – '

'Mum!'

'How many wives he planning on having?'

'Oh, five or six,' I said. 'But he says I'll always be his favourite.'

'Don't talk to your mother like that.'

'What're we going to tell people?' wailed mum.

'Tell them not to worry,' I said. 'He's fully housetrained.'

She leant across the table. 'He been giving you drugs?'

'He doesn't even *drink*.'

'Even the Beatles have. That Paul, he looked so dependable.'

I said: 'You haven't even asked if I love him.'

'Everybody loves him,' she said. 'He's got the nicest face.'

'Who?' asked dad.

'Not John, of course,' she said. 'Paul. Of course, they went to India, too. To the Maha-whatsit. Them and their granny specs.'

'All right, Dot,' he said.

I lined up the cruet, parallel to my placemat. I hadn't got this right, but how could I have done it? It made me sad, that I couldn't love them enough. Now that I was going to leave them they looked older and dumpier. I was the child of their middle-age and they had never quite learnt how to be parents. They had never, once, read me a story.

I had always escaped to other people. Salim and I weren't going to be like that. I wanted him so much, just then, that I thought I was going to be sick.

'I love him,' I said. 'He loves me. You don't understand anything.'

'Your mother's a wonderful woman.'

I turned to him. 'So why do you spend all your time out there, then?' I pointed to his shed, where he kept his radio. He had a whole row of sheds. 'If it's so wonderful, why do you spend your whole time out there, talking to all those other berks about what MPGs their Cortinas do?'

'Marianne!' said mum.

'You'd move your bed out there,' I said, 'if you could get it in.'

'That's no way to speak to your father!'

I swung round, to her. Perhaps I was feeling uneasy about the whole thing, even then. That's why I was being so obnoxious. 'You just sit in front of the TV all day talking to Jimmy Saville. What's happened to you two? What've you got to crow about?'

My father rolled himself another cigarette. He had this old tin, from his army days. He never threw anything away, that's why he had to build so many sheds. I was the only thing that was leaving.

'We just want the best for you,' he said.

'He *is* the best!' I said. 'He's the most decent bloke I've ever met. You've no idea. He's not like the others.'

'You can say that again,' said mum.

My dad looked at me through the smoke. 'He know about them?' he asked. 'The others?'

'No!'

'He know about your sojourn in a squat?'

'Don't you dare!'

'He know about your little operation?'

'No!'

My dad paused. 'Does *he* know what he's letting himself in for?'

I didn't reply. Outside, the wind blew and all the brown, dangling pom-poms shook their heads.

We were married in January, three months after we had met. The sun shone and the air was splinter-sharp. I breathed in lungfuls of it as we stood on the steps of the Ashford Register

Office. Confetti from an earlier wedding blew around my high heels. Salim gripped my arm; we squinted into the sun for the photographer.

My parents were putting a brave face on it. Indoors, my mother had cried, but now she looked stout and skittish in a mustard suit she'd bought specially. Salim's cousin from London, Aziz, was charming her. He designed record covers. He was a smoothie, with long curling locks. He wore a denim suit and a paisley shirt; he was trendier than Salim. Apparently, up in London, all the dolly birds were after him.

Sonia's kids threw confetti all over themselves and shrieked with pleasure. Kirsty, who's a grown woman now, was still in her pushchair then. Bill was pissed, as usual. I clung to Salim's arm. He was wearing a morning suit; he looked debonair and very handsome. I was so proud of him. I'd caught him talking in Urdu to Aziz; it was probably to do with his parents, who had refused to fly over. Bugger them, I thought. I knew Salim was giving up a lot to stay in England with me, but this was our day and I'd never seen them. I hadn't even spoken to them on the phone. All I possessed was their name, Siddiqi. I'd had a jolt when I wrote it down in the register, but perhaps every bride feels that her new name is foreign and strange.

And, of course, I possessed their son too. But they hadn't given him to me; they thought I had stolen him. They'd probably got a marriage for him all arranged.

Salim stood beside me, stiff and suave as a shop dummy. He tensed for the photo; I had never seen him so solemn. I wore white, which, in the circumstances, wasn't inappropriate. We still hadn't made love; he hadn't come inside me, though I'd made love to the rest of him, down to his snowy underpants. He had a wonderful body, slender and surprisingly hairy. A rock-hard bum. I felt a pang for all the women in Kent, that they wouldn't be having him tonight in a big double bed in the SeaView Hotel, Dover.

I smiled dreamily at the passing traffic. We were a small party on the steps that day. My Aunty Ivy, who was killed in a car crash two years later, dabbed at a tear. But she used to cry at *Mrs Dale's Diary*. My Uncle Eric, who later emigrated to

Australia, took a film of us. At the reception he held up cardboard placards with silly remarks on them; we waved and grimaced at his whirring camera. I've still got the film, somewhere. There are some things you can't bear to throw away.

Salim and I spent 1969 in bed. That's how it seemed, anyway. John and Yoko did, too – remember their love-ins? But I hardly registered them. I hardly registered anybody but Salim. The Kray brothers were put into jail, Brian Jones drowned, and I wandered through the daylight hours in a dream, my face burning from the scrape of Salim's skin, from his face rubbing against mine, my limbs heavy and warm. Salim was a wonderful lover, even better than I had hoped, because you never quite know, do you? Not quite.

We had moved into a top-floor flat in Talacre Road, near the shopping precinct, and to the outside world we carried on as usual. I went to work at the Coach and Horses, I sat in the bus, I went to Sainsbury's. But all that seemed unreal and automatic, as if I was watching myself on Uncle Eric's film. I was waiting to get into bed. It was at night that Salim and I woke up, naked between our sheets. It was strange – I did feel truly married. I had no idea I would feel like this, or if other couples did. They couldn't, could they? Nobody could. This was our secret.

Salim aroused me, passionately. His body answered mine, we unlocked each other; his dark skin inflamed me, but yet it was familiar; it was a darkness inside me; he reached there with his mouth and his cock – oh, his cock – and with his warm hands that ran over my body, moulding me to him just as I moulded him to me, pulling him in. I loved the peppery smell of his sweat; I licked his armpits and nuzzled in his groin.

Neil Armstrong landed on the moon. 'The surface is like a fine powder.' His voice crackled as he bounced, weightlessly. 'It has a soft beauty all its own, like some desert.' But everything else seemed just as distant; I missed the wonder of this giant step for mankind. I was too self-absorbed, too Salim-absorbed. Mick Jagger stood up in Hyde Park, in a dress, and recited Keats to thousands of hippies. It just made me realize that Salim knew much more about poetry than I did; he loved Keats too. I got him to read me some in a Wimpy Bar.

It was like that then. It really was. I can remember it, just.

There was fighting in Belfast, as always. People were killed who would have been middle-aged now. But while the streets burned, Salim and I were making love. Once or twice we made love all night, falling apart damply to the sound of the milk-float rattling in the street below. Next day he said he snoozed at his desk; my thighs ached so much I could hardly stand. Perhaps it was his religion which made him so ardent – he had been pent-up all those years. He was twenty-three when we married and he said there had only been two other women – a divorcee who ran a boutique in some Karachi hotel and a Parsi girl who did voice-overs for commercials and who was game for anything.

I didn't know, then, how important his religion was to him. I didn't know anything. We never ate pork; that was about the only Muslim thing we did. He said he was supposed to pray five times a day but that he hardly ever did, nowadays.

'Why?' I asked. He just shrugged. 'Is it because of me?' I asked. He shook his head.

I think he did pray sometimes, in the bathroom. When I came in I found the candlewick bathmat aslant across the lino. I didn't know where Mecca was but maybe it was pointing in the right direction.

Despite my mum's forebodings he didn't have any other funny habits, except gargling. Early in our marriage I heard this strangled noise in the bathroom and came hurrying in, thinking he was ill.

'What're you doing?' I asked, laughing. 'Training for the Ashford Bus Shelter Spitting Marathon?'

He straightened up, affronted. 'It's our custom.'

'Ours?'

'Mine. All Muslims do it. It's to clear the passages.'

'Well, this is an old English custom.' I goosed him from behind, making him jump, surprising his face in the mirror.

I was blind, not to see trouble ahead. I suppose that deep

17

down I wanted something to happen. I had grown up rebellious, you see. I was the first girl in the third form who learnt how to smoke properly, inhaling. Once, for a dare, I'd not worn any knickers for a week. I was the first girl in my class who knew what a blow-job was, and the second to try it (not that successfully, in fact, but I persevered). Aged fifteen, I used to hang around rock gigs. My first roadie, an overweight bloke with crushed-velvet hipsters much, much too small for him — remember those buttocks in the sixties? He taught me how to roll a joint and to roll on a condom, both with one hand. I loved telling my girl friends, shocking them. That's why I did it, I suppose, to shock. And if you knew Ashford, which I wouldn't recommend, then there was nothing more shocking than to set up house with a Pakistani.

'Wotcha, Ali Baba,' some blokes shouted out once, when Salim and I were walking to the launderette. I recognized one of them. He called out: 'Does it rub off at night?'

I turned to Salim and grabbed him. I slid my hands under his sweater and kissed him deeply, lasciviously, running my hands over his body, his hips, his crotch.

'Don't!' he whispered, pulling my hand away. 'Don't, Marianne!'

My heart was thudding but I just laughed. When I looked round, the row of them was leaning against the wall watching us.

There were very few Asians in Ashford then — in fact, there still aren't. Just a couple of newsagents, and the people who ran the Curry Paradise. It was a town full of ugly, pasty Brits. That was partly what made Salim so attractive in the first place. It was pure animal magnetism, with shock-value thrown in. But nobody realized that in fact he was much better-educated than me, rather than the other way round. It was me who had brought him down in the world. He came from a cultured family. He knew more about Britain than I did; he'd read George Bernard Shaw's plays and Churchill's stuff; our shelves sagged with his books. He liked Indian music but he liked Bach and things too — I didn't know anything about either of them. He bought a record with Yehudi Menuhin and Ravi Shankar playing together, violin and sitar, East and West mingling eerily, answering each other and twining together like we did in bed.

But when people looked at Salim they just thought, *immigrant*. One night he lay, naked, between my legs. I was hot and wet for him. He licked my neck; he eased himself in.

'Let one in,' he murmured, smiling, 'and they'll all come.'

I knew there might be trouble ahead, but in those early months I didn't care. We stayed in the flat together, we hardly ever went out or saw anybody else. When I had to go to work I missed him, I physically ached for him. In fact, I cut my evenings to three a week and made up the hours at lunchtimes. Our flat, cramped and cosy, was all we needed. Opposite, down in the road, there was a corrugated-iron chapel run by Seventh Day Adventists. Its placard told us: *JESUS SAVES YOU*. Sometimes it was changed to *JESUS IS WATCHING YOU*. But neither Salim nor I, for our different reasons, took any notice. We didn't need his prophet or mine. In those early days we were everything to each other. I couldn't bear him leaving me, it was like Elastoplast tearing off my skin; we even went to the launderette together, would you believe? Stepping into the open street, we felt bruised; we flinched at the cars.

Once in bed, he had an itch on his back and he asked me to scratch it. 'Lower' he said. 'To the left.' Suddenly I panicked, that I couldn't find the right place. I wanted to be under his skin, to *be* him.

I wanted to batter at him, to let me in.

Looking back, that year seemed like one long honeymoon. We lay in bed; he rubbed my feet between his because mine were always colder, and we talked about our childhoods. His seemed hot and sunny and full of cousins. There were green parrots in the trees, he said. There were banyan trees, he said, and tamarisks, and something else I couldn't pronounce. I told him how it was always raining and how I hid in my dad's shed, the one with his weedkillers in it, and read my comics.

Sometimes he questioned me about later things, his voice

edgy, but I said that there was nobody important. He was jealous and possessive but it wasn't too bad at first. Needless to say, I kept my mouth shut. In a way, I wasn't lying. He had made me feel a virgin again, the first time we slept together. It was only later that I started remembering the other men.

None of this was too bad at first. Sometimes he got angry, but it was mostly about the pub. I used to brush my teeth when I got home in the afternoon, so he couldn't smell the booze. I had given up wearing my bra-less T-shirts, too; I wasn't an idiot. But he still didn't like it.

'Why do you have to work there?' he asked again, one afternoon.

'I like it.'

'Men full of drink, looking at you.'

'Looking?'

'You know how.'

'They don't.'

'How many of them did you know before you met me?'

'None,' I said.

'Who was that man the other day, when I came in?'

'He used to be at school with me.'

'Nothing else?'

'No.'

'You swear?'

'Yes!'

He looked out of the window. 'I hate you being there.'

'What else can I do? Any suggestions?'

'You could . . .'

'Could what?'

He pushed his hands through his hair. 'I just wish you didn't, you wouldn't . . .'

'It's my job, to be nice to people. To look nice. That's what I'm paid for.'

'I can support you.'

'I don't want you to! I like it.'

He sighed, and gave up. He was tolerant of my decadent Western ways, then. There was a lot of goodwill between us in those days, as well as lust. We wanted our marriage to work, partly because nobody else thought it would.

And so the year went by. *Chappaquiddick*, they said on the TV news, but in my dreamy state it sounded like a distant squawk, like Donald Duck squawking.

And anyway, the few arguments we had – about the pub, about me working – they all came to a natural end because, by Christmas, I was pregnant. And when Yasmin was born I gave all that up.

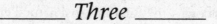 *Three*

Was I a good mother? Eighteen years I've had to think about that. Again and again I've gone over those early years, but I still can't answer that question. I don't even know if I was a normal mother. 'JESUS KNOWS YOU', said the sign. If He knew, why didn't He tell?

When something terrible happens, it muddles up everything that happened before. You can't think straight. For instance I can't see Aunty Ivy clearly now, as she was. The week before she was killed she came round to tea. In my memory this isn't just any old tea, it's the Last Tea. The last bit of shortbread. When she kissed Bobby goodbye it was the Last Kiss. His nappy was wet; when she went out of the door there was a damp patch on her hip. Now it seems like an omen.

How can I tell what I was really like? First Yasmin was born (Yasmin Elizabeth). Then, eighteen months later, I had Bobby (Robert Jamil, to make it quits: one Pakistani name each).

I stayed at home to look after them. It was difficult, in a top-floor flat. Double buggies had just come in, those double pushchair things you got at Mothercare, and I pushed the babies through the Ashford streets, which had suddenly grown kerbstones everywhere. I manoeuvred them into the bus and came home laden with plastic bags – babies need so much blooming stuff, don't they? I hung the bags over the pushchair handles and when I lifted out the kids, the whole thing tipped up in the hallway. Our flat was festooned with drying clothes; like Aunty Ivy, my hip was permanently damp from carrying the little buggers from one room to another. Sometimes, when it was cold outside, it took so long to get them zipped into their clothes that by the time we were ready to go out it was time to come back home again. Or they wanted to go to the toilet. Sometimes I wanted to scream. Sometimes I counted down the hours to bedtime, like an astronaut waiting for take-off.

I refused to put away my high heels – I had some pride – and I tottered up and down our three flights of stairs. But I didn't get so many wolf-whistles now. Salim and I didn't get any sleep, either. The kids did. They went out like a light the moment I strapped them into their buggy, they slept soundly all the way, their anorak hoods lolling, they slept like the boy near me now, but the moment we got back home they woke up, yelling.

Sometimes I screamed at them, as I said. Sometimes I felt like hitting them. But I was just a kid myself, I wasn't prepared for motherhood. Who is? Nobody knows what it's like until it hits them.

And I did love them, I really did. I loved them fiercely. I would have strangled anyone who tried to harm them. I squeezed my babies tight, dancing with them to Radio 1. The Troggs sang '*Wild Thing*' and I turned up the volume, loud, and pressed my face into Bobby's hair. The dirty cups rattled as we swooped around the kitchen, double-time to the grinding beat, the pelvic-thrusting beat, until Mrs Tewson downstairs banged on the ceiling with her broom. Oh, their hair smelt so wonderful. Their skin.

Yasmin was a sedate little baby; Bobby was a terror. Salim was intensely proud of them, especially Bobby. They both resembled him – dark, liquid eyes, blue-black hair. They looked more adult and sophisticated than English babies. Their skin was nearly as dark as his, especially Bobby's, and sometimes when I bathed them my pale, freckly arms gave me a surprise, as if it was my own body that didn't belong to me. They didn't feel separate; they were mine, all mine. And they were much more attractive, naked, than the other mottled babies at the clinic. People used to look at them in their pushchair, then look at me. I felt racy and interesting. Sexier, somehow. Their brown bodies were the breathing result of our lovemaking, our hot nights. They were little Salims for me to fondle.

Sometimes people looked at us oddly. One woman once asked if they were adopted. 'I do admire you,' she said. 'You're doing a great job.'

The old colonel from the Coach and Horses, one of the regulars, used to greet them in the street with a boozy '*Salaam, aliecum!*' He used to be in the army, in India.

Just once or twice, kids were rude to them. Once, someone called out 'Nigger fucker' to me. But there wasn't a lot of that – not nearly as much as Salim pretended, later. He lied about that.

I suppose we brought them up as English, really. The only Pakistani thing I did was to learn how to cook terrific curries, but that was because I'd always loved them. The traditional evening's entertainment in Ashford was to get pissed and then go and have a vindaloo and taunt the waiters.

Salim would come in from work and taste a bit, sucking it off the spoon. Then he'd go to the fridge. He had such a sweet tooth – he was always buying the kids ice cream and then eating it all himself. He had a passion for tea shops and Battenburg cake, that disgusting pink and yellow thing with marzipan around it.

'Nobody eats that anymore!' I said.

'I do,' he said, munching away. 'You think I'm staying in England because of you?' He smiled, and shook his head. 'It's so I can eat lots and lots of Battenburg cake.'

He still worked for Cormorant Homes, flogging houses to couples like us. On Thursday evenings he went to photography classes. He sent photos of the kids back to his parents. Perhaps they had softened a bit, because he used to chat on the phone to his sister, Aisha, in Karachi. Sometimes he spoke to them, but I couldn't tell the difference because it was all in Urdu. Once, his mother even sent us two little outfits, little pyjama-suit things for the kids, one green and one maroon, with fancy stitching around the hems.

'They're traditional,' said Salim. '*Shalwar-kamize*. Aren't they pretty?'

They were hideous – sort of shiny nylon stuff which I knew would run in the wash. Luckily, they were the wrong size, anyway.

It seems odd, now, in the light of what happened, that I didn't know more about his family. I had spoken to his sister once or twice, and she sounded all right. She had an educated voice. But he didn't talk about them much, and after he'd been on the phone I felt irritable because I hadn't understood a word and he'd seemed so foreign when he was talking in Urdu. They were probably jealous of me, too – the wicked English girl who had stolen their only son. He gestured differently, when he was on the phone; apart from the gargling it was the only time when he seemed like a Pakistani. I heard the word '*Abba*', like the Eurovision Song Contest winners, but he said it was the word for 'father' out there, everyone used it.

When the children were small he flew to Karachi a couple of times to visit his parents, so they must have had some sort of truce. He wanted to be a good son; he didn't want to distress them. But he never asked me to go with him.

'Are you ashamed of me?' I asked him once.

'Why should I be?'

'You'd have a much better time if you were living out there. You wouldn't have to sit in an office flogging all those crummy houses – '

'They're not crummy!' he said. 'They're first-class workmanship – '

'Just to pay the rent. If you went back to your family, you'd be rich.'

'I don't give a damn.'

It was romantic, wasn't it? It was like a story I got out of the Children's Library, *The Sheik and the Cow-girl*. He gives up his kingdom to marry her and live happily ever after. In her case, however, she turned out to be a princess. Lucky bitch. Still, I did have my lurex sweater. That glittered a bit.

Families were different in Muslim countries, according to Salim. They were much closer, everything revolved around the home. You were obedient to your parents. But he had broken away, he'd rebelled. It must have been painful for him but he didn't like to talk about it. In some ways, he was more stiff-upper-lip than the British.

It was a shock for him, too, the way I talked about my parents.

'Why don't you show them any respect?' he asked.

25

'Because I don't respect them. Do you?'

'That's not the point. They're your parents.'

'They've hardly been parents at all. They're bloody hopeless.'

English family life was a shock to him. The papers were full of scandal, drugs and divorce. He said: 'We're not going to be like that, are we?'

'Of course not,' I said. 'We love each other.' I stroked his face. 'Don't we?'

Sonia was an omen, but I didn't see that at the time. It was late one rainy, November night when the doorbell rang. I got out of bed and ran downstairs.

Sonia stood there, drenched. She had a black eye. Zara and Kirsty were with her, looking skinny as weasels.

'Can they stay the night with you?' she asked. 'I don't think they should be at home right now.'

When they woke up, Yasmin and Bobby were thrilled to find Sonia's daughters, two huge sleeping-bag caterpillars, on their floor. They idolized them; they thought it was some sort of game.

Sonia's marriage broke up messily and violently. The police were called to the pub, twice, and Sonia moved in with her daughters to a flat nearby where they had to barricade the door. Bill called her a whore and a slut and tried to get custody of the kids, waylaying them outside school and hammering on the door of the flat in the small hours. Sonia's current boyfriend was a keep-fit fanatic called Trevor. Despite his muscles, however, he was an emotional cripple and melted away at the first sign of trouble.

Sonia sat in my kitchen, wreathed in cigarette smoke. 'Men!' she said. 'They're all bastards.'

Salim came home from work, and stumbled over an empty Cinzano bottle.

'Screw the lot of them,' she said. 'Hi, Salim.'

'Where are the children?' he asked, coughing.

I indicated the lounge. 'In there, watching *Dr Who*.'

When I went in, later, he was sitting with his arms around Yasmin and Bobby. The TV glowed blue on their faces. Bobby was sucking the disgusting old bit of blanket he carried around with him everywhere; he called it his 'chinsel'.

'Just get that woman out of here,' said Salim.

It couldn't happen to us, could it? That autumn the ground shifted under my feet. I felt uneasy, but I admired Sonia too – for breaking loose rather than mouldering on, year after year, like my parents. She was a new and enthusiastic convert to Women's Lib, which was just starting up. She cropped her hair short and wore dungarees like a farmworker. She told me I looked like a Barbie doll. She said I should stop pleasing men, I should start pleasing myself. Released from captivity, she was in terrific spirits, full of vim and vigour. She put up a poster in her lounge: *If They Can Send One Man to the Moon, Why Can't They Send Them All?*

'Up with Germaine Greer!' she shouted. 'Down with bloody men! Down with bloody cystitis!'

We were crouched on her balcony, trying to burn her bras. We'd lit a fire in her baking tray.

'Good riddance, Charnos Uplift.' She flung it in. 'Good riddance, Playtex Underwired.'

I looked in the tray. 'They're just sort of shrivelling.'

Zara got up from watching the TV and came over. 'What's that funny smell?' she asked.

'My past,' said Sonia.

After a long and bitter battle Sonia's divorce came through. It was the spring of 1975. She got custody of the kids and Bill got access. This was the first time I'd heard those words 'custody' and 'access' applied to people I knew. It was like reading the word 'emphysema' and then finding your granddad has it. Bill was allowed to have the girls on alternate weekends, but if he didn't return them, if he tried to keep them, he would be taken to court. Sonia didn't trust him but at least it was fixed. She said we'd all go out and have a drink.

Salim was tiling the bathroom – the kids splashed so much that the walls were rotting. I sat on the lid of the toilet.

'Tracey'll babysit,' I said. Tracey lived on the ground floor.

'I told you, I've got to finish this. I've only got the weekend.'

I gazed at his back view as he crouched behind the basin. He was doing a tricky bit. There was a smear of yellow on his overalls, from when he'd leant against the kitchen doorframe. We'd painted the kitchen together, but that was before we had the kids. I tried to remember what it had been like to make love without being interrupted by a baby waking up.

'Salim, please come.'

'You go.'

'No. I won't go if you don't.'

'Don't be silly,' he said.

'I don't want to.'

'Don't mind me,' he said. 'I'd rather be here with the kids.'

'Please come. We never go out.'

He turned round, bent under the sink's waste-pipe. 'Marianne, you don't understand. People aren't quite so hysterically witty when one's drinking pineapple juice. Especially *her* friends.'

'Let's go out alone, then. We'll just say hi and go off together. Like we used to, remember? Candlelight, soft music . . .' I smiled. 'You can touch me up under the table, if you want.'

Salim sighed. 'All right then.'

'Don't sound so thrilled.'

'I said all right, do, let's,' he said.

'Don't bother!'

'I said all right.'

'Oh, get on with your fucking tiles!'

By the next year I was feeling itchy and restless. By now Yasmin had started infants' school and Bobby went to playgroup twice a week. I missed them, ridiculously, when they left me in the mornings. Watching them charging into the buildings, chattering with the other kids, my heart ached. Bobby suddenly looked so small and defenceless in his blue dungarees, forging his way in the world without me. I'd cut his hair, and his little ears stuck out. From now on, so many things were going to happen to them and I could do nothing to help them. Not in the hours they were away from me.

But I felt liberated, too. Suddenly I had time to myself. I rebleached my hair and sauntered around Ashford like a prisoner on day-release. I wasn't like some of the women I met at the clinic; I hadn't let myself go. But I'd been engulfed by nappies and needs and little, persevering fingers pulling my sweaters out of shape.

Bruce Springsteen's hoarse voice belted out from Ed's Record Mart. I swung my hips and inspected myself in the window as I passed. I could still fit into the same size jeans as before, if I held my breath when I zipped them up. My breasts were still firm. I was only twenty-six. I'd done my post-natal exercises, the pelvic ones, to keep me tight inside. When I cross-questioned Salim, prodding him for an answer, he said I was just as good as before. I still felt like a girl really, but fuller and fruitier. I went to Dolcis and bought myself a pair of red, high-heeled boots, dead tarty. A bloke delivering fridges whistled at me. But when I got back home I hid the boots at the back of the cupboard.

Salim was funny about my clothes. He loved me looking sexy just for him, with the door closed. He went up to London once and came back with some wonderful underwear for me, from Selfridges. He loved me dressing up in it – black stockings, suspenders, the lot – and lying ready for him in bed. He liked to pull the thongs of my corset thing so tight that my skin bulged; he licked the exposed flesh of my thighs and nuzzled me like a dog. He turned me over like a parcel and breathed Urdu oaths into my ears. When he finally came into me his face darkened; he loved watching me. I loved him for that.

But he hated me flaunting myself; he hated other men looking at me, though sometimes this inflamed him for later. Since the kids, he'd become more possessive and oriental. I wasn't just his wife; I was a mother. I should be staying home, devoting myself to the children and washing the floor with Flash. In the daytime I should be looking demure and doing my duty.

Sometimes I felt we didn't know each other at all. Sometimes he seemed like a headmaster.

*

I had to get out of the house. I enrolled at a driving school and took lessons. Sonia had set herself up in catering, working from her flat. She had contracts with three new firms who had moved into our area. She had always been a foodie, though the word wasn't invented then; I just called her greedy. She wanted me to help her and she'd put a down-payment on a van. I pictured us careering around Kent together, loaded with *vol-au-vents*. At least I could meet people; I'd forgotten how to talk to a grown-up.

'You talked to Salim yet?' she asked one afternoon. I'd bumped into her in Bejam's, where she was doing a bulk-buy.

I shook my head. 'I know what he'll say.'

'That's marriage in a nutshell. *I know what he'll say*.' She flung bags of peas into her cart. 'Look, Marianne, it's your life too.'

'This bloke from his office, he's left his wife. He's run away to Ramsgate with a manicurist.'

'What's that got to do with it?'

'Salim thinks it has.'

'He wants to lock you up.' She hurled in some brussels sprouts. 'They've got it all their own way, haven't they.'

'Who?'

'Men. Especially where he comes from. When they want to get rid of a wife all they have to say is "I divorce you" three times.'

'Do they?'

'Don't you know anything?'

Sonia was better-educated than me. She'd been to a convent.

The Cormorant Homes office was on the outside of Ashford, on one of their new estates. The day I passed my test I drew up outside with a flourish, and rushed in.

Salim was sitting at his desk. He half-rose when I came in. I flung my arms around him.

'I've passed!'

'You haven't!' He looked pleased and embarrassed. I had my arms around his neck. I kissed him; we bumped against his chair. Malcolm, the other salesman, grinned at us.

Salim moved me away. 'You've been celebrating?'

'Only a tiny one. Come on.' I turned to Malcolm. 'Can I take him for a spin?'

'But . . .' Salim paused.

'Go on, mate,' said Malcolm. He turned to me. 'Third time lucky, eh? How did you do it?'

'Oh, just a quick knee-tremble with the tester. It's OK, we didn't break the speed limit.'

Outside, Salim opened the car door for me. 'What did you say?'

'Nothing. Just a joke.'

'I didn't hear it. What did you say?'

'Nothing.' I kissed him, and got into the car.

We drove down the Folkestone road, towards the sea. The gears crashed as I changed into fourth. It was exhilarating. 'Hythe 6' said the sign. I'd never noticed signs before; now they seemed to have been put up especially for me.

For the first mile or so Salim sat, his knuckles clenched. Then he looked out of the window. There were banked-up storm-clouds ahead, and a golden light lay over the fields.

'Remember when I used to read you Wordsworth?' he said. 'Earth hath not anything to show more fair.'

'Isn't that the bit you're going to build on?' I took my hand from the wheel and pointed.

'What?'

'Over there.' I pointed to the fields. 'Your new estate.'

There was a silence. Then he said: 'Why do you spoil it?'

I didn't reply.

'What's the matter with you?' he said. 'Why do you spoil things?'

The road curved; my packet of fags slid across the dashboard.

'You've been very strange lately,' he said.

I indicated right, and swerved out to pass a tractor.

We parked above Folkestone, on the downs. Below us stretched the town, sprawling. Beyond it glittered the sea. The clouds were heavier now. A ferry, leaving for France, caught the last of the sun. In the sudden silence there was a rumble of thunder.

'Anything's possible now!' I said. 'There's France, there's the world.'

'What do you mean? Where do you want to go?'

'I've never been anywhere,' I said.

I took out a cigarette, and hesitated. He hated me smoking in the car.

'You've got us,' he said. 'You've got our home.'

'I know.'

'What else do you want?'

'I don't know,' I said.

There was a silence. I watched the ferry; it was so small I felt I could lean out of the car and push it with my finger. The wind blew; I shivered and wound up the window.

'I used to be a romantic too,' he said.

'You still are.' I turned to him. 'Aren't you?'

'Aren't you?'

I smiled at him. '*Je t'adore. Tu es le plus beau homme du monde.*'

'What's that? Another of your jokes?'

'No. I said: You are the dishiest man in the world.'

Salim paused. Then he said: '*Agar tum mujhe chorogi, main tumhe maar doonga aur phir apney aap ko.*'

'What's that mean?'

'If you ever left me, I'd kill, first you, and then myself.'

I sat very still. I put the cigarette back in the packet. Suddenly, drumming on the roof, the rain began.

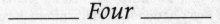

Four

I should have seen the signs. *Salim* should have seen the signs.

When we lived in the flat we were young, with kids. We lived in a hugger-mugger way that sometimes exasperated Salim – he wasn't that tidy, but I was a real slut. I mean, what was the point of cleaning when it all got dirty again? But we were bound together by the children, and we still found each other attractive; sometimes it seemed to be wearing thin, sometimes it died altogether, but it could still flare up, the old animal magnetism.

I remember one afternoon. I was cooking a chicken curry, stirring the joints around in the spices, standing in a haze of frying, when Salim came home from work. I was doing the odd job for Sonia by now and I'd been out all day; the kids were still with a babyminder who lived two doors down the road.

I'd put Bob Dylan's *Bringing It All Back Home* (still my favourite) on the stereo. Salim came in.

'There's a parcel for you,' I said. 'From Karachi.'

I pointed to the brown-paper package. He undid it and pulled out a shirt. I wiped my hands and came over to look.

'It still seems weird,' I said, 'to know a man with a tailor.'

'My mother sent it. My family has used him for years, his stitching is superb.'

I lifted out a shirt, and giggled.

'What's the matter?' he asked.

'Very Brian Poole and the Tremeloes.'

'What do you mean?'

'The collars!' I chortled.

He looked hurt.

'No, honest,' I said. 'They're lovely. Dead sixties.' I grabbed the shirt, and rushed out to the bedroom.

When he came in, I'd taken off my clothes and put on the

33

shirt. I stood in front of the mirror, wearing nothing but the pink shirt, my white high-heeled slingbacks and my frilly briefs. Remember that poster 'It Looks Even Better On a Man'?; I was trying to be like that. I bunched my hair up on top of my head and swayed to Bob's harmonica, coming from the other room.

Salim watched me in the mirror. I watched him, and smiled. I swayed my hips. His face darkened; I watched his eyes, moving up and down me. Suddenly he stepped nearer. I felt his hand on my thigh. It moved up; his finger slid under the lace.

'You harlot.' His face was pressed against my hair; I felt his warm breath.

Suddenly, roughly, he pulled the shirt off my shoulders. The buttons popped off, one by one. He pushed me on to the bed, unzipping his trousers.

'Salim!'

He hurt; he pulled my briefs off, scraping the skin on my thighs.

'Ouch!' I cried; he was hurting my arms. 'Hey, what about the kids? They'll be back soon.'

He didn't care. His cock nudged against me, and pushed. I was too dry; I cried out, but soon his hands were moving over my breasts, warming me up, opening me. I drew my legs up around him, wrapping him tightly, pulling him in. We rolled over, and over again, landing on the floor with a thump, pulling the bedclothes with us. Something clicked in my brain, he plunged me into blackness; I was blind, my mouth blurred with his, after all these years he could still work this magic on me.

We bumped against the chest of drawers. I came, wave after wave, each spasm more intense and sweeter than the last, God knows what she was thinking downstairs, and finally he came. He cried out in Urdu, some word I'd never understood, it always gave me a shock to hear that.

We lay there, panting. He had moved me so much that my face was wet with tears. We lay there, exhausted, on the musty-smelling rug.

At last he raised his head and kissed my damp hair. 'Don't you ever fool around with me,' he said.

I smiled. 'If I promise to, can we do it all over again?'

He smiled down at me. 'Little harlot.'

'That hurt.' I rubbed my arm. 'Anyway, if you get fed up with me you can always marry another one. How many are you allowed? I've forgotten.'

He sat up. 'Don't ever say that!'

'Why?'

'Since the moment I met you – '

'I thought somebody else would pick up my books instead,' I said.

'I knew you would be mine till we died.'

I stared at him in silence. Bob Dylan had long since stopped. Then I struggled to my feet. 'I'm getting dressed.'

Later that night, when the children were in bed and he was having a bath, I sewed the buttons back on the shirt. As I was doing it, my eye caught an open book on his desk. It was his Koran.

I picked it up and read the page:

And say to the believing women, that they cast down their eyes and guard their private parts, and reveal not their adornment save such as is outward, and let them cast their veils over their bosoms, and not reveal their adornment save to their husbands, or their husbands' fathers, or their sons, or their husbands' sons or their brothers, or their brothers' sons, or their sisters' sons, or their women, or what their right hands own, or such men as attend them, not having sexual desire, or children who have not yet attained knowledge of women's private parts.

I put the book down slowly, and went back to my sewing. From the bathroom I heard the muffled thump of the geyser, lighting.

In 1977 we moved into a new house in one of the Cormorant Homes estates, on the edge of Ashford. Salim had had his eye on these houses as they were being built, that was why we'd waited so long for one. They were three-bedroomed and came in a choice of three styles. He chose Tudor because it reminded him of a picture postcard he'd kept, of Stratford-on-Avon. He'd been there once, to the theatre, to see *Othello*. He was fascinated by that play and could recite bits by heart.

'"Oh, beware, my lord, of jealousy,"' he'd told me once in the Inglenook Tea Shoppe:

> '"It is the green-eyed monster which doth mock
> The meat it feeds on; that cuckold lives in bliss
> Who, certain of his fate, loves not his wronger;
> But, O, what damned minutes tells he o'er
> Who dotes, yet doubts, suspects, yet strongly loves."'

The old biddies at the next table gave us a funny look.

He'd set his heart on this house, 12 Harebell Close. The other streets were called Poppy, Clover, and so on – to commemorate all the meadow flowers, I suppose, that this estate had obliterated. He liked it because, from the bathroom window, you could just see the hills of his beloved South Downs. Just. If you stood right to one side and craned your neck. The houses were ever so close together.

People change, when they move house. Or perhaps they've been changing slowly all the time, but you only notice it against the new walls. As I said, I didn't see the signs.

In the old flat we muddled along, with the kids. Sometimes we almost seemed like kids ourselves. But when we moved, Salim grew up. Or his older self was waiting in the wings. He didn't seem like a lover anymore; he became a parent. A ratepayer.

Oh, that's not quite it. I can't find the word. I'll just tell you about one Tuesday, soon after we moved in. The day he didn't notice my new sweater. I'd been collecting the kids from school – Yas was seven now, and Bobby nearly six. On the way back, we stopped at C&A. It was a sunny afternoon, I'd just collected my family allowance; I was itching for something new to wear.

I remember standing in the communal changing-room, surrounded by teenage girls. Music thumped out, the Bee Gees (yuk). I was trying on sweaters.

'Mum,' whined Yas. 'Come on!'

I looked at the teenagers, frowning, then back to myself. I was ten years older than any of them, and it showed. I wasn't bad-looking – nice big eyes, pouty mouth – but in the harsh light I could see the tiny wrinkles between my eyebrows. I held my breath, pressed in my stomach, and looked at myself from the side.

'Mum . . .'

One of the girls was trying on a gorgeous sweater. You should have seen it – white and fluffy, with this low, cutaway back. Dead alluring. I darted back into the shop and found one on the rails.

I tried it on. It was sensational. Elvis came on, 'Jailhouse Rock', one of my favourites, and I started jiggling my hips to the beat. Then I crossed my arms in front and caressed my back, so it looked like somebody else was doing it.

'Mum!' said Yasmin, embarrassed.

'Used to love doing this,' I laughed. 'We did it at school.'

'They're all looking!'

'You're talking to a bona fide ex-raver here,' I said. 'I once stood in a lift with Bill Wyman.'

'I want to go home,' said Bobby.

I looked at my two children – Yasmin, a slip of a girl in her stripey T-shirt; Bobby chubbier and fidgety. His round belly bulged above his waistband; his top and bottom half never seemed to join, I was forever hitching up his trousers.

Suddenly I swooped down on him, picking him up in my arms and hugging him tightly. I kissed his plump cheek and his soft black hair; he smelt of plasticene and boiled sweets.

When we got back Salim was in the kitchen, unpacking boxes. I came in, wearing the new sweater.

'Like it?' I asked.

He glanced up briefly; he looked flustered. He pointed to a

pile of saucepans. 'Everything's upside-down, those bloody removal men. These were in the bathroom.'

I twirled round in front of him but he didn't notice. He looked at his watch.

'They'll be here in a minute,' he said.

'Salim!'

'What?'

'Nothing'.

Our new neighbours, Jill and Alan, were coming to tea. We sat in our half-furnished lounge, politely nibbling shortbread. Salim gestured towards the window.

'Solid hardwood frames, that's what counts. And look at the depth of those skirtings.'

Alan smiled. 'You don't have to sell it to us, old chap. We've already bought one.'

'I hope you'll like living here,' said Jill. She had sallow skin and a new perm. 'All the neighbours are very pleasant.'

'Lots of new jobs and people coming in to this part of Kent,' said Alan.

'Getting pretty cosmopolitan,' said Jill. There was a silence. She cleared her throat. 'And the gardens are a big plus.'

'So where're you from originally, Salim?' asked Alan.

'Pakistan. I only came over for a year. But . . . well, I stayed.'

Alan glanced at me, and smiled. 'Don't blame you.'

Jill shot him a look.

I suddenly had a vision of us living here for the rest of our lives. We'd moved into a proper house now. This was it. No turning back. Sitting there in our through-lounge, red-brick out front, red-brick out back, I felt panic-struck.

'I'll get some hot water,' I said.

Salim followed me into the kitchen.

'Cosmopolitan!' I hissed.

'She didn't mean it like that' he said.

'Actually, I think she fancied you.'

'Really?' he asked.

'Search me why.'

38

'What do you mean?' he demanded.

'Only joking.' I ruffled his hair. 'How are we going to get rid of them?'

Luckily, Sonia rescued us. A few minutes later she burst into the lounge, with her daughters. She looked flustered.

'Hi, Salim! Hi, Marianne!' She dumped a bottle of champagne on the table.

I introduced her to our new neighbours. 'Salim's just been showing them our skirting-boards,' I said.

'Hey, it looks even bigger with your furniture in!' she said.

'My firm built these,' said Salim, gesturing around at the house.

'Ah' she cried. 'That's why the doorknob came off in my hand!'

I giggled. Salim darted out to the front door.

Kirsty started whining. 'Don't want to go to dad's.'

'Well, you've got to,' said Sonia.

'It's boring!'

'I found a condom in his drawer,' said Zara.

'Bully for him,' said Sonia.

Salim came back.

'Didn't mean it,' she said. She paused. 'Listen, can I ask you a favour? Gloria's not turned up.' Gloria helped her in the catering business.

'I'll come and help!' I said, getting up.

'We must be toddling, anyway,' said Alan.

Sonia turned to Salim. 'I'm desperate. Do you mind?'

He paused. 'Of course not.'

'We won't be long,' she said. 'It's only a finger buffet.'

I laughed. 'As opposed to the whole arms and legs.'

I grabbed my bag and gave Salim a kiss.

'Sorry, sweetheart. There's some stuff in the fridge.' I paused. 'Well, I think there is.'

The four of us started for the door. Alan got to his feet. 'I can see you're going to liven the place up!' he said.

Outside, Sonia's van waited for us: 'Taste Buddies: Functions, Banquets, Private Contracts.' I leapt into it, like a child being released from school.

*

Despite the sudden space I felt more closed-in than I'd ever felt in the flat. I suppose the flat wasn't ours, so there was no reason to do much to it. But now I had no excuse.

Salim scattered grass seed over the raw mud of our garden, I did help him with that. But he wanted to put up shelves and fitted cupboards; he wanted to do up the third bedroom for Bobby so that the kids didn't have to sleep together. He spent all his weekends working on the house; every hammer-blow seemed to be sealing us in. We'd lost our old playfulness, our sudden bouts of passion. I felt restless and bored. All Sundays I listened to the whirr of his Black and Decker. The kids couldn't play in the garden because of the grass seed; they couldn't play in their room because he was trying to assemble their incredibly complicated bunks. I had to take the children out, driving them to playgrounds and pushing them on the swings in the whistling wind.

When someone does up a house he makes everybody else feel in the way. And they feel guilty, too. And resentful. We hadn't made love for weeks. Our bedroom was simply a place whose wallpaper we couldn't agree on. At night I lay awake, heating myself up with memories, remembering other men coming into me and rerunning my most exotic old locations – the back of a bus in a lay-by, *en route* to Hastings (he was a conductor); various rural settings, complete with nettles; my dad's home-brewing shed at five in the morning, the blue morning light iluminating the flagons.

In the weekdays I had to endure my neighbour, Jill. Her daughter, Emily – a little old lady – had become friends with Yasmin. Under Emily's influence Yasmin had become insufferably prim. They kept telling me not to smoke.

'I see you're a reader,' said Jill, looking at the bookshelves. We were having tea one afternoon, while the two little girls swapped hairslides in the corner.

'They're not mine,' I said. 'They're Salim's.'

'Emily loves reading, don't you, poppet? Always got her nose in a book. It's so important, isn't it?'

'Oh, I just chain the kids to the TV,' I said.

'Pardon?'

'I said, would you like some tea?'

In the kitchen I stubbed my toe on Bobby's trike. I hopped, yelping. The floor was littered with the dismembered limbs of his Action Man and the sink was full of last night's dirty dishes. Gazing out at the garden I remembered that day, months before, when I had worn my new sweater. I thought, bitterly: He would have noticed me if I'd been a plank of bloody shelving pine. There's a moment in a marriage when something shifts. A tiny moment, maybe, but afterwards things aren't quite the same. You only realize it later, sometimes years later. One of those moments was when I had stood in the kitchen, wearing my new sweater, unnoticed. Something died, then. I realize it now.

The grass grew. We bought a lawnmower and Salim mowed the lawn. On Saturdays you could hear the lawnmowers, all down the gardens, whirring away behind the wooden fences. It seemed daft that we couldn't borrow each other's. We bought a guinea-pig and the kids called him Toulouse, for some reason. We probably looked content enough; we did what everybody else did. I worked part-time for Sonia, and Salim didn't make too much fuss.

That summer we went to France a couple of times, on the ferry — Folkestone was only ten miles away, it didn't take long to get there. My spirits lifted when we left the house; Salim improved, too. We went to Boulogne and I bought stuff for Sonia at the hypermarket — brie, camembert, mange-tout peas which had just come into fashion.

On the way back I stood on the windy deck with the children and Salim took photos of us. Behind us were the White Cliffs of Dover, bright in the sunshine. We larked around; we were suddenly carefree that day. I borrowed a sailor's hat, or perhaps it was the purser's, he was standing nearby — I borrowed it and put it on Salim's head.

'Aye, aye, captain.' I saluted him. He looked like someone in Gilbert and Sullivan. 'Can I come up to your fo'c's'le and look at your radar equipment?'

I snapped his photo. He smiled. 'Would you do me the honour of dining with me tonight, at my table?'

I leered at him. 'Depends what's for afters.'

'Come here, kids,' he said, posing them with him.

'Come on, smile,' I said.

'I've always wanted to build a boat,' he said. 'I wanted to sail to the Seychelles and gut fish with my penknife.'

I chanted: 'He shails to the Say-sells – he sails to the Shay . . .' I gave up. I'd drunk a whole carafe of wine at lunch.

'What?' he asked.

'Didn't you ever do that?'

He shook his head.

'Big smile,' I said. I snapped them once, twice.

We had our moments. But most of the time Salim was busy and I was restless. I didn't admit it, of course, but I was starting to be bored with him.

I remember one Sunday in September. We'd been in the house nearly a year, and his cousin Aziz had come down from London for lunch. Cricket stumps had been set up in the garden and they were starting to play a game with the kids. I hung around, half-heartedly; I couldn't stand cricket.

After the first wicket or whatever Aziz asked Salim something in Urdu. I heard the word 'Karachi'; Aziz was going out there for a visit. I think he was trying to persuade Salim to go there, too, to visit his parents, because Salim replied sharply to him.

Then he turned to Bobby. 'You should've seen Aziz when we were kids. He was a terror. Once, we were on the beach and he bowled with such a roar, like this . . .' He flailed his arms. 'I ran away, like a bat out of hell.' He looked at his cousin. 'My God, he was a bully. Always telling me what to do.'

Then he lifted up Bobby suddenly, and held him upside-down. Bobby kicked his legs like a beetle, shrieking with pleasure.

Just then Sonia arrived.

'Hi,' she said. 'The door was open.'

I went into the kitchen with her. She rummaged in her carrier bag and brought out some sandwiches.

'Herewith, the remains of our Assistant Head Masters' Annual Buffet.' She inspected the sandwiches. 'No smoked salmon left, the swine.'

I looked out of the window into the garden. With Aziz there my family suddenly looked like a foreign family and nothing to do with me. I wondered if Salim was missing his parents. Despite our new home I suspected that his love-affair with England was suffering from strain. For instance, a rival property company in Ashford was converting an old church into flats. They looked ever so stylish – luxury apartments with galleried lounges. I remembered joking to him, how they could put a font in the bathrooms. But he was shocked. 'How bloody spiritually bankrupt can you get?' he demanded. Catch a Muslim turning a mosque into maisonettes.

Sonia and I laid out the sandwiches for tea. 'We shouldn't be doing this,' she said. 'It's your Sunday too.'

'I don't mind,' I said.

'He'll be putting you into a veil soon.'

'Sonia!'

'Would you like one of those sort of sheets, with a little hole in front for your eyes?'

'Oh yes, please!' I said, sarcastically.

'He can just poke the food in three times a day.' She fetched another plate. 'At St Agnes, we had to wash underneath a sheet, so nothing rude showed.'

'Didn't have much effect, did it?'

'Only because I'm hooked on confession,' she said. 'Cheaper than a shrink – anyway, I like it when I get to a good bit and he sits very still.'

I laughed. 'He must look forward to you.'

She nodded. 'Guilt's like mustard. Once you've got the taste for it, everything seems bland. Still, you wouldn't know.'

'No,' I said. 'I wouldn't.'

There was a silence. Out in the garden Bobby made a run, cheered on by Salim. Yasmin searched for the ball under the guinea-pig hutch. Up above, the sky was a blameless blue.

Sonia poured us out some more wine. We watched the two men. They wore jeans and T-shirts.

'Tasty, aren't they?' she said.

I nodded.

'Salim's not put on any weight.'

'He doesn't drink, that's why.'

She took a sip of her wine. 'Nice and slim. Nice little bums. I could do with a quick bunk-up with that Aziz.'

'Really?'

She nodded. 'It's been six weeks. I'm starting to hyperventilate whenever I see a cucumber.'

I laughed. 'You really fancy him?'

'Just for one night, mind. You should just use a man for his body. Much less disappointing, in the long run.' She drained her glass. 'You've been very quiet lately.'

'Have I?'

She looked out of the window. 'He's changed, hasn't he? Since the kids. Got more . . . Salim-ish.'

I didn't reply. I watched my husband. He had stopped playing; he was inspecting a bit of lawn that was wearing thin already.

Then I said: 'I'd do anything for a man who made me laugh.'

She looked at me. 'Anything?'

I nodded.

And a few months later I did.

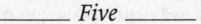

Five

You've probably guessed what happened. It was bound to, wasn't it? Sooner or later. It was just a question of when. In fact, I'm surprised, now, that it took so long.

Why didn't he see the signs? Why didn't we move away from our boring estate full of boring housewives, away from our boxy little house I couldn't keep clean? Why didn't we escape in time? When I first saw Salim I thought we would escape. He looked so exotic and so out-of-place; he would lift me up and sweep me off somewhere so unlikely that I wouldn't be able to recognize myself. He would take me to the places I dreamed about at night.

Instead, nine years later, we had ended up in Ashford DIY Mart choosing wallpaper. Quarrelling about it, in fact.

Perhaps, wherever he had taken me, it would have happened. In the end.

It all began in April 1978. Salim and I were in bed; he was half-asleep but I hadn't had a chance to speak to him earlier; the kids had been around.

'Sonia phoned today,' I said. 'You know she's getting these premises in Ashford, a proper place for Taste Buddies?'

'Mmm.'

'She's asked me to join her.'

'But you have.'

'I mean, more.' I looked at the glow of the street lamp through the curtains. 'I could use my French. She's just got this contract with an engineering firm, something to do with the Channel Tunnel.'

There was a pause. 'You want to work full-time?' he said. 'Is that what you're getting at?'

'Not all the time . . .'

'You're short of money?'

'Not really, . . .'

'I don't earn enough?' He sat up.

'That's not the point,' I said.

'I can't support my own family?'

'No! I mean, yes!'

He switched on the light. I looked at his chest, black with hairs. He always slept naked; he never seemed to get cold.

'What have I done wrong?' he asked.

'Nothing!'

'What's wrong with me?' he asked.

'What do you mean?'

'I know I could be doing something better than this,' he said. 'But what can I do about it?'

'It's nothing to do with that!' I said.

'And what about the children?'

'Even Bobby's at school now. I can fit it in. I've spoken to mum . . .'

'Ah!' he said. 'You've got this all arranged . . .'

'No. I just . . .'

'You don't speak to me first,' he said.

'I am, now!'

'You don't love our children?'

'Of course!' I said. I stared at him, gripping my nightie around my neck. 'I'd die for them. But you don't have to be with them all day. For Christ's sake, you were brought up by an *ayah* and you're always saying how wonderful that was . . .'

'Marianne!' he shouted. 'You know nothing about it!'

I stared at him. 'What do you mean?' I paused. 'Please. Don't make a fuss. Not this time . . .'

He sat there in the pool of light, propped against the pillows. There was a daisy pattern on the pillows; I looked at their little blobs of yellow. Then he switched off the light and turned away from me.

Sonia and I went up to London to sign the lease. Mum had looked after the kids – it was the Easter holidays – and Salim was going to pick them up after work.

We were in high spirits, Sonia and me. I'd borrowed her black suit and done up my hair, to look businesslike. We

46

arrived back at Ashford Station, triumphantly. My dad worked for British Rail; he was there, taking the tickets. I think I even hugged him.

'We've got it!' I said. 'We've got the shop!'

'What's that?' he asked; passengers pushed past us.

'We even came back First Class,' I said.

Sonia laughed. 'She means, nobody *caught* us in First Class.'

'You did what?' he said.

We clattered away down the corridor in our high-heeled boots.

When I got back home, Salim was upset. Apparently, my mum had dozed off and he'd had to search for the kids in dad's sheds. He'd found them, eventually, in the wine-brewing one, playing with the tubes and corks. When Yasmin was with her brother she could be quite mischievous.

'There could have been a terrible accident!' he said. The children were in the lounge, watching TV. We were standing in the kitchen, both in our business suits. 'All those weedkillers and sickles and God knows what.'

'But mum's perfectly capable . . .'

'She's not! She's getting deaf!'

'Well, I'm not, so don't yell at me . . .'

'They should've been with you, where they belong,' he said.

'Look, Salim. Women do this now. It's 1978. If I was here all day, listening to Jill telling me one more time about Emily's wide vocabulary, I'd be locked up in a loony bin and *then* who'd look after the kids?'

'Bringing up children is the most important job in the world.'

'Then why aren't men doing it?' I demanded. 'Know why? Because if they did, they'd go round the bend.'

Salim looked at me. 'What's happening to you?' he said.

I glared at him. 'You're starting to sound like my father.'

Sonia's catering premises was an empty shop near the centre of Ashford. On one side was a minicab firm, and on the other was a Ladbrokes. Back home, Salim listened to *Any Questions*

47

and painted the bedroom; meanwhile, at the shop, Sonia and I listened to Radio 1 and painted the walls crimson.

For some reason I enoyed it more than decorating the house; it seemed a different process altogether. I remember coming back home one night, elated, when *Top of the Pops* was on. I grabbed Bobby and danced with him round the room, holding him tight, burying my face in his hair. Then I dumped him down and twirled with Yas, faster and faster. I'd taken her to *Saturday Night Fever*; we swivelled our hips like John Travolta. I turned the volume up.

A moment later Salim came down the stairs. The music must have been too loud. Yasmin turned the TV down and we all stood there awkwardly.

There was a pause. Then he said, sadly: 'No, do go on.'

But we didn't.

With the help of some of Sonia's cronies we did up the place in two weeks. Various old boozers from the Coach and Horses even dropped in; it was nice to see them again. An ancient geezer called Alf, permanently afflicted with the DTs, painted the woodwork with a trembling brush. Sonia bought a catering oven, a socking great thing, on the HP, and some second-hand freezers from a wholesale fishmongers which had gone bust. Soon we were in business.

I remember coming home one day, late. Salim had made the kids hamburgers. He said to me, wistfully: 'You seem to be cooking for everybody, nowadays, except your own family.'

Half-joking, I said: 'My family doesn't pay me.'

'That's Sonia talking. You're getting more like her every day.'

'I'm not.'

He turned away. 'You've got so hard.'

They've taken away our breakfast trays – oh, hours ago. It seems hours ago, but now I look, twenty minutes have passed. Perhaps my watch has stopped. The plane seems to have stopped; it's so steady that I can hardly believe we are still in the air. Outside the window the clouds are way below us, white and quilted. You can buy cotton-wool like that. Yasmin once pulled all of mine out of its plastic bag, to make a bed for her glass animals.

Around me, people have settled down for the long haul. The man across the aisle has taken off his glasses, ready to listen to this story that I'm telling nobody.

I'll have to start, now. And tell you about Terry.

May 7 was Sonia's birthday, that's why I came to work in my white, fluffy sweater with the cutaway back, the sweater I hadn't worn for months. We were going for a drink at lunchtime, to celebrate.

I arrived at work early. We had a busy day ahead – an annual dinner to prepare for the Association of Sanitary Inspectors. Sonia was on the phone. I can remember everything, clear as yesterday. She'd pulled her hair back with a rubber band; she had her specs on, and she was writing something down. I think she was speaking to the laundry about tablecloths.

I dumped down my shopping – I'd picked up some last-minute things from the greengrocers. I took off my jacket and hung it up. I was just going to get my apron when Terry came in.

He was a driver with the minicab firm next door. 'Our vending machine's on the blink again, hint hint,' he said. 'Subtle, aren't I?'

I nodded. 'Like a sledgehammer.'

I turned to put on the kettle.

'Wow,' he said. 'Go on, I dare you, wear it the right way round.' Eyebrows raised, he was looking at my sweater.

'I spent a whole month's family allowance on this,' I said.

'At last!' he cried. 'A woman with the right priorities. I've been searching for one all my life.'

'You really like it?' I asked.

He nodded. 'You look absolutely gorgeous.'

'Honest?'

He grinned. 'The only woman in Ashford who can stop the traffic in both directions.'

I blushed, and turned away. I'd seen Terry once or twice –

he'd popped in to say hello when we moved in, and I'd nipped next door to borrow their phone book. He was in his late thirties, I suppose; I never found out. He wasn't that good-looking, really – he had a sort of rubbery, humorous face and twinkly eyes.

I spooned in the Nescafé. He sat down on the work surface beside me and picked up an endive I'd just unpacked.

'Ah, a Kevin Keegan perm!' he said.

'It's endive.'

'Endive?'

'You don't know anything, do you?' I said.

He took a radish, and popped it into his mouth. 'Nope. I come from a poor, deprived background.'

'That's no excuse. So do I. We had an outside toilet.'

'We didn't even have a toilet,' he said. 'We didn't even have a TV. We used to sit around, looking at our framed rent arrears.'

'Rent arrears? We didn't even have a house.'

'Nor did we,' he said hastily. 'Just pretending.'

I started washing the salads. 'Ah, but the community spirit,' I said.

'*Hancock's Half Hour* . . .'

'*Ron and Eff* . . . who *was* she?'

'June Whitfield.' He drank his coffee.

'Mmm . . . cars with little indicators that flipped up . . .'

'Somewhere to park . . .'

'Spam fritters . . .'

'Woodies . . .'

'Loose sweets' I said.

'Loose women . . .'

'Old policemen,' I said.

'Young Beatles . . .'

'Playtex girdles,' I said.

He groaned. 'Playtex girdles . . .'

He had spotted a bag of grapes. He took some out and started eating them.

'Know something?' he said.

'What?'

'I used to be a front bloke. Boring, conventional.' He paused. 'That was before I saw your back.'

I turned round, from the sink. 'Really?'

'Really.'

He grinned at me, and went on eating the grapes. Outside, a car hooted. It seemed to come from miles away. I looked at him.

'You always take things that don't belong to you?' I asked.

'Yep.' He took another grape.

There was a silence.

'Well, you shouldn't,' I said.

I turned away, abruptly, and put on my apron. I only realized, then, that Sonia had long since come off the phone. She was busy dismembering chickens. Her knife thumped once, twice, as she chopped off the claws. I jumped.

Just then, one of the other blokes looked in at the door.

'Terry!' he called. 'You free to go to Whitstable?'

So Terry drained his coffee, and left.

When I got in that night, Salim was catching up with his paperwork. He was playing his beloved Billie Holliday; he'd become keen on her mournful songs and had recently bought a boxed set of her records.

I went upstairs and sat in the bathroom for a long time before he came up. I sat there on the edge of the bath, amongst the plastic, lidless bottles of bubble bath and the single, chewed-looking socks, amongst the litter of our family life. I looked at my face in the mirror. After the dinner, Sonia and I had seen off her birthday with the last of the Mouton Cadet '72, and I was a bit tipsy. I lifted my hair and pressed it against my face; it smelt of cigarette smoke. I pushed it back and looked at my eyes, my mouth.

I thought how, one day, my kids would grow up and leave me. One day I was going to die.

What was going to happen, before that? What was going to happen, in between?

When Salim climbed into bed I put my arms around him and

kissed him, desperately. I squeezed my eyes shut and stroked his upper arm, goosebumpy at the back.

He just mumbled in surprise, and stroked my hair.

We had a lovely day, me and Salim and the children, the next Saturday. It was suddenly hot, almost like summer. We had a picnic on a hill near Aldington, a village not far from us. They're building an industrial estate there now, part of the Ashford Expansion Scheme, but then it was still unspoilt. We were all still unspoilt.

The kids played in the grass and picked buttercups. I hope they remember that; I've never asked them. Below us stretched Romney Marsh, a mysterious, flat expanse. Its dykes, straight as rulers, glittered in the sun. Beyond was the far hump of Dungeness Power Station, hazy in the distance, and beyond that, the Channel. I'd made sandwiches with some chicken, left over from a Countrywomen's Guild luncheon. I thought: We should just sit here, in the sunshine, and never go home.

Salim laced up one of Bobby's plimsolls, which had come undone. He told him how he'd stolen the mangoes; Bobby liked to hear this again and again; '. . . so our bearer told me, if I stole them again, a big black bird would come down from the tree . . . whoosh, like this . . .' he flapped his arms, 'and gobble me all up.'

Bobby ran off and jumped from one ant-hill to another. The sheep huddled in the corner of the field, watching him. Another family was walking across the grass; I heard the shouts of their kids. I gazed down at the trees, whose names Salim and I still didn't know; they were misted with their new green leaves.

I pulled off my T-shirt and lay face-down on the grass, smelling the earth. The sun warmed my skin.

I closed my eyes and thought about Terry. A moment passed; then I murmured to Salim: 'Have I got a nice back?'

There was a pause; he must have turned to look at me. Then he flung my T-shirt over me and said: 'For God's sake, Marianne! There's other people here!'

I wish he hadn't said that. I do wish it.

*

Weeks passed. Terry dropped in for coffee most days. He leant against the work counters, nicking prawns and cracking jokes. Sometimes he told me about his weird customers. The Kent countryside looks so blameless, doesn't it? But you wouldn't believe what people got up to. At some point or other, a minicab came into it. He always seemed to be ferrying people around at four in the morning, and seeing things he shouldn't in his rearview mirror.

'Isn't anybody married anymore?' I asked him.

He wasn't. He had an ex-wife, and a daughter called Gail. His ex ran a bric-à-brac shop in Sandwich; he used to commiserate with her, on the phone, about her new boyfriend.

'It's much better than being married,' he said. 'But then, most things are. Marriage, my darling, darling, is the maximum of loneliness and the minimum of privacy.'

He knew some of my old mates, and we gossiped about them – Cheryl, who I used to go on double-dates with, and who'd since married a vet; a greaser called Spike, who'd had a Harley Davidson. He'd now reverted to his real name, Norman, and he sold computer software. Terry had even gone to my old primary school, but years before me. We reminisced about the toilets. I told him things Salim never knew.

At some point that month, I can't remember when, Salim took the kids up to London. I was supposed to go with them, we'd planned it some time before. But Gloria, a dumpy school-leaver who sometimes helped Sonia, got tonsilitis so I was roped in for a dinner.

I remember that Saturday evening for two reasons. One was that Sonia's van had broken down yet again, and we had to hire a minicab from next door to cart the stuff. I realized, suddenly, how I longed for the driver to be Terry. It was half-past five, and I was sealing cling film around our *noisettes de veau* when the door opened. I went on, wrapping the dishes with extra concentration. But when I turned round it was another driver, Stan. My heart was pounding. That made me realize how stupidly I had hoped. In fact, my palms were so sweaty that the cling film clung to them. It always does, of course, but you know what I mean. I was sure Terry was free; why hadn't he come? Couldn't he be bothered?

The other thing concerned Salim. The plan was for him to take the kids to Buckingham Palace and Horseguards Parade. He was ever so patriotic, much more than me – in fact, I'd never been to either of those places in my life.

When I got back from the dinner that night, Salim was sitting in front of the TV. It was showing wrestling so I knew something was wrong. He never watched wrestling.

I kissed him, and stumbled across him on to the sofa. The room swayed, slightly; they'd kept plying me with drinks.

'Three hundred pissed chartered surveyors,' I said 'not a pretty sight.'

'Why did you leave us?' he said. His voice sounded strange.

'I told you, I had to.' I ruffled his hair. 'How was London?'

'Fine.'

'Kids behave themselves?'

He nodded.

'Please don't be angry.'

'I'm not,' he said.

'You are.'

'I'm not!'

'You're all huffy.'

'I'm not!'

I shrugged. I just thought he was sulking.

The next day I asked Yasmin what had happened in London. She was washing her two favourite teddies in the bath, except most of the water seemed to be on the floor.

'We were in a Wimpy Bar,' she said. 'And then daddy took us away.'

Later, much later, I heard what had happened. Two berks had sat next to Salim and the kids. They'd started sniffing their hamburgers and saying how horrible they smelt. 'Must be the cat food,' they said, 'The Kit-e-Kat. Know why?' they said to each other. They grinned at my family. 'Pakis. Makes 'em feel at home.'

Salim had got up, and taken the children out.

He didn't tell me till later. If only he had told me things. If only he hadn't been so bloody *British*.

The next evening I went into the children's bedroom. Salim was reading to them from *Winnie the Pooh*, one of his favourite books.

'"What's the matter?" asked Piglet. "It's a very funny thing," said Bear, "but there seem to be two animals now . . ."'

Salim stopped.

'Go on' said Bobby.

'"This – whatever-it-was – has been joined by another – whatever it is . . . Would you mind coming with me, Piglet, in case they turn out to be Hostile Animals . . ."'

He stopped. He hadn't seen me, standing in the doorway. He just sat there, stroking Bobby's hair.

If only I'd noticed things about Salim. I never really understood what it must have been like for him, in England.

On the other hand, he could have noticed things about me. Like that bloody sweater.

As I said, we both should have noticed. And we both paid for it, later.

Six

The summer began, hot and sultry. Our lawn had worn away, so Salim turfed it with carpet squares of grass. They soon curled up, browning at the edges. They never really grew in.

Had we really settled down for life? It sounds so final, doesn't it? At night the other houses seemed to draw in even closer. Hot and restless, I stood at the window while Salim slept. The street lamp gleamed on the mullioned windows opposite. I looked across at the family saloons, already dewy, parked in all those driveways. How obediently people drove home each night, back to their own front doors. Did they really want to? Was this really it?

At night there was a dog that barked, far away. It must have been beyond our estate, right out in the country. I felt I was the only person in the world who was hearing it. Our lightbulb hung from the ceiling; I still hadn't got around to buying a shade. In fact, I never got around to buying one.

I stood there, stroking my breasts. I touched my nipples under my nightie. Salim lay in bed, sleeping. We had been married nine years. Once, long ago, my mouth had gone dry when he'd simply brushed past me.

I loved the kids, of course, more than anything on earth. Sometimes I sat in their bedroom, amongst the scattered toys, and listened to their regular breathing as they slept. I knelt beside them and smelt the fragrance of their hair — it smelt different, nowadays, from the way it had when they were babies. I knew I was a bit feckless with them sometimes, and impatient too, but they were my joy — more and more so, as they grew. When they were tiny I'd loved them, but they'd driven me round the bend. Now, I was really starting to enjoy them. Bobby was six and Yas was eight. She was starting to try on my make-up with me; she could be all superior and prissy, but when we were alone with our tubes and blushers we got quite giggly. She put on my foundation, but it was too chalky for her skin, she looked like a clown. She imitated the long face I pulled when I put on my mascara. I'd never known I'd done it; Salim had never told me. The kids told me all sorts of things now.

Bobby was very masculine, a real little boy. But he still had to have his chinsel. What he liked was to sit on my knee, sucking his horrible old bit of blanket, while we watched TV. He'd had his blanket for years, it was all holey now. When I'd taken them to playgroup, in their double buggy, he'd sucked it until we were in sight of the building and then he'd gestured me to stop. He'd get out, leaving his beloved chinsel behind, disowning it, and march on ahead so that all the other kids could see him being grown-up. He was as proud and independent as his dad. But he didn't fool me.

I loved them so much, but there I was, falling in love with another man. I did try to resist Terry, for a long time. I tried, I really did. But not enough.

Late in June – I can remember the exact date – Sonia and I had a wedding to do. There was a lot of preparation involved, so I was leaving early.

I remember everything about that morning. It had rained in the night and now it was warm and misty; beyond our neighbours' houses, the hills were invisible in the haze. I remember pausing at the mirror in the hall and looking at my face. Salim was putting stuff into his briefcase.

'I'm getting these little lines!' I cried, pointing to my forehead. 'I'm getting wrinkles!'

But Salim wasn't listening. 'Bobby!' He called. 'Have you taken my calculator again?'

When I got to the shop Sonia was on the phone. 'Holy shit,' she was saying. 'You sure?' She turned to me. 'Can't use the van. The whole bleeding gearbox's gone now. Pop in next door, could you, and order a cab for ten o'clock.'

I went into the minicab office. It was empty except for Terry, who was sitting underneath the pin-ups reading the *Daily Express*. He jumped up and embraced me.

'Morning, sweetness!' he cried, and held me back to inspect me. 'Dawn-picked!'

'Don't feel it. Can you take us to the Willesborough Community Hall at ten?'

'Sure.'

Sonia had taught me a lot about baking – I could even do choux pastry by now. But neither of us could tackle wedding cakes so we had hired an old pro called Mrs Dobson to do them for us. Long ago she'd worked at the Grand Hotel in Brighton. She'd delivered us this three-tiered job, complete with pillars. Terry and I took it to the community hall in his car. His cassette played some Country and Western song: 'My little darlin', my sweetness, I'm leavin' you, dear . . . the place that I'm goin', you don't want to hear . . .' On either side of the road the puddles flashed in the sun. We sang along to the tune, our voices yodelling.

When we got to the hall, Sonia was already unpacking the food. It was a large room with a piano against the wall and a barman laying out glasses. For some reason, we were all in high spirits. It often happened during preparations for a do, partly because we were being paid and partly because we didn't have to sit through it ourselves, being bored out of our minds. That's one of the nice things about the catering business.

I took the cakes out of their cardboard boxes, and Terry helped me set them up between their pillars. There was a little plaster bridegroom and bride. I tried to stand them up on top of the cake, but they kept falling over; their feet were too small. They lay on the icing like war casualties. Terry and I got the giggles. Sonia had to come over and rescue the happy couple, propping them up unsteadily against each other. The bride fell over again.

'Just nerves.' Terry held up the plaster bride, looking at her. 'Isn't it, love?'

Just then, across the room the barman started playing the piano. He was terrific, really good. It was old ragtime stuff.

Suddenly Terry grabbed me and we started dancing around the hall. He held me tightly, grinning at me, as we swooped round and round; the room had a surprisingly springy wooden

58

floor. The corrugated-iron roof span; I gasped, laughing. His breath was in my ear, his body pressed against mine. I hadn't danced with anybody except my kids for years; Salim didn't dance.

'Ready?' Terry whispered. He spun me round, my feet skimming the floor. We twirled like tops, fused together. When he steered me into a sort of glide, my legs melted.

Just as suddenly, the music stopped and the barman went back to work. Hot and sweaty, Terry and I faced each other.

We were still in each other's arms. For a long moment we didn't speak. Then he pushed a strand of hair off my face, tenderly. I turned away, and went back to work.

The reception was in full swing. Sonia and I stood in the kitchenette, scraping food off plates. From the hall came a roar of laughter and applause. People clap at anything, at a wedding.

'Isn't he gorgeous?' said Sonia.

'Who?'

'The best man. He asked for my phone number. I said, work or home?'

'What?' I wasn't really listening.

'I asked him, work or home? He said work. But that doesn't mean anything, does it? He probably thinks I'm married.'

I pointed to the chicory salad. 'Shall we keep this?'

She nodded. 'Philistines,' she said. 'Still, waste not, want not.' She started washing up a bowl. 'They made short work of the coronation chicken. As per usual.'

Next door, the hall was suddenly hushed, for the toast.

'So let's raise our glasses,' said a voice, 'and wish all future happiness to Sue and Gordon.'

Sonia scraped some rubbish into the bin. 'Poor sods,' she said.

The guests had left, and I was packing the last of the stuff into boxes. Sonia had gone back. From the hall, I heard the barman whistling 'Coming Through the Rye'.

Terry came into the kitchen. I was folding a tablecloth; I turned away from him.

'What's up, sweetheart?' he said.

'Nothing.'

'What is it?' He took the tablecloth from me. I wiped my eyes.

'I don't know,' I said.

'It's weddings, isn't it?'

I didn't reply. He put his arms around me.

'Should've seen my mum at mine,' he said.

'Should've seen mine.'

'Bet mine had more to cry about than yours.'

I smiled, shakily. He stroked my cheek with his finger. 'That's better.'

There was a pause. Over in the sink, a tap dripped.

'First time I saw you,' he said, 'you were in your painting gear, and you had your hair done up in those silly little red combs.'

'You remember?' I said. I gazed at the floor.

He nodded. 'Every little bit.'

I paused. 'I didn't think . . . well, people noticed anymore.'

'That's a shame,' he said gently. 'Did they used to?'

I nodded. 'I suppose so. Once.'

He put his finger under my chin and raised my head. 'Don't cry,' he said.

'I'm not.'

'You're ever so beautiful.'

'Am I?'

He nodded. 'And you've got the sexiest elbows in Southeast England.'

I smiled, a little.

'Been wanting to tell you for weeks,' he said.

'Have you?'

He nodded. 'Haven't you noticed?'

'You've always looked like a fast worker to me,' I said.

There was a pause.

He said: 'In this case it's different, isn't it?'

He knew I was married, of course. He'd even seen Salim, once or twice, when I was being dropped off at work.

60

I nodded. Outside, a car revved up. It was probably the barman leaving. Exhaust fumes came through the window.

'Stop looking at me like that!' I said.

'I'm not.'

'I'm very happy, see? So you can shut up!'

I turned away and started shoving the tablecloth into our laundry bag. 'We'd better get this stuff into the car,' I said.

'Rightiho' he said. 'I'll take you back.'

There was a silence. Outside, the car engine had long since faded away. I stood still, gazing at the folds of tablecloth. Then I turned round to face him.

'Don't take me back!' I said.

Four little words. Five, if you count the punctuation mark. What the hell.

We drove out into the countryside, fast. He reversed the car up a rutted track. The back seat was full of catering stuff, so we stumbled out into the bracken. I don't know if we were laughing or deadly serious. A bit of both, I think.

In fact, it wasn't so enoyable, that first time. It was just something we had to do, and there wasn't much time. We pulled off most of our clothes and yanked each other on to the ground. It was incredibly uncomfortable – bumpy and damp. We were just – well, desperate, I guess. I kept my eyes shut while his skin moved up and down against mine. Greedily, I dug my hands into his buttocks, pulling him into me. I was salivating for him like a dog. His unknown cock felt stout and eager; I refused to look at it that first time; I locked a muscle in my head, jamming my brain so I couldn't think about anything at all except our straining bodies. Some insect stung me. I was stuck in some sort of rut, under him, and I could hardly move. It was a bit of a farce, really. I was hopeless. When it was over we burst out half-laughing, half-sobbing on each other's shoulders.

Back in the car I tried to brush the tangles out of my hair. 'Hurry!' I said. 'Faster!' I was starting to feel horribly guilty; a sort of delayed shock. It rose in my throat like vomit.

*

It was quarter to four. The children had come out of school fifteen minutes ago. Terry negotiated the Ashford traffic, weaving in and out of cars, hooting his horn at a lorry and pulling out, with an inch to spare, as a bus thundered towards us. A picture flashed through my mind: I was lying in hospital, bandaged, and paralysed from the waist down. On one side of me sat Salim and on the other sat the children, but none of them was holding my hand.

'Left here!' I yelled. Terry swerved the car left, down the road towards the school. It was three-fifty. Gripping the dashboard, I remembered other cars I'd seen breaking the speed limit. Now I knew why they did it. The occupants had just committed adultery too. I had joined a vast and invisible club, a club for real grown-ups; ten minutes' thrashing in the bracken and I had stepped from one life into another. I could never go back, now. It was like losing my virginity but much, much more terrifying.

Terry squealed to a stop at the corner of the street. We kissed each other quickly and he drove off. I ran up to the school gates. The playground was empty. My heart stopped. Perhaps Salim knew? Perhaps he'd collected the kids and was waiting for me at home?

Then I saw them. They were sitting together on the bench behind the climbing-frame – one red sweater and one blue. They jumped up and ran over to me.

'Where have you been?' asked Yasmin.

'Why are you late?' demanded Bobby.

I took their hands; at one of the classroom windows, their teacher was watching us. We walked towards the gate.

'Where've you *been*?' asked Yasmin.

I couldn't bear to lie to my kids. I learnt to later, but not that first time. Anyway, I didn't have to reply, because Yasmin pulled me to a halt.

'What's that?' she asked.

'What's what?'

She was looking at the back of my sweater. 'You've got stuff all over you.'

'Come on!'

As we walked along the street, she pulled bits of bracken and burrs off my sweater.

'Don't,' I said, trying to pull them off myself.

'I got a nosebleed today,' said Bobby.

We stood at the bus stop. I was wearing a skirt that day, and my legs were bare. As the bus came round the corner, I felt the warm liquid from Terry trickle down the inside of my thigh. I stood there, holding Yasmin's hand.

So that was how it started. I held off, for the next few days, but I couldn't resist him. He seduced me with his jokes and his familiarity. He seduced me by chatting; Salim never chatted, just talked. I felt I'd known Terry all my life. I know it seems a funny thing to say about a lover, but he seemed like the brother I'd always wanted. We could have been brought up together. Despite the passion and the guilt, we were basically chums. We counted each other's moles; we sat up in bed and compared the number of creases in our stomachs. (Five – T; three – M). I jeered at him because he was putting on weight; he was fleshier than Salim, and not nearly as good-looking. He was really quite a plain bloke, but somehow that didn't matter. He made me laugh.

All that came later. I'll tell you about the second time because it was worse, really. We'd planned it, you see. It wasn't an impulse; it was premeditated.

He said he had a flat above Unwins off-licence. It was only three streets away from Taste Buddies. We made a date to meet there, Thursday evening.

I felt so guilty that I spent the whole afternoon turning out the kitchen cupboards and scrubbing them. When Salim came back from work he stopped in the doorway, and stared.

'My God,' he said. 'What's all this?'

'Just, you know . . . it was such a mess.' My voice was bright.

'The lounge looks nice too.'

I climbed to my feet. 'Shall I get you some tea?'

'Gosh.' He looked around. My heart felt squeezed. I turned away, and spoke to the kettle.

'Er, Salim. You know I'm doing this dinner party tonight?'

'Mmm.'

'For this woman. She's entertaining some foreign clients.'

'You told me,' he said.

'Japanese. I think they're setting up some electronics factory.'
I was giving him too much information; my voice sounded as
artificial as a newsreader's.

'Anyway, we've got to serve and everything, so I may be
back a bit late.'

'I know. You said.'

I fetched the tea bags. 'I probably won't be back till late.'

'Don't worry. I'll put the kids to bed. I'll read them *Babar the
Elephant*. I used to love it.'

I turned round, suddenly. 'You're so nice!' I said.

'Now you say it.' He smiled.

In the bathroom, I shaved my legs. Somebody rattled the door.

'Mum!' called Yasmin. 'What're you *doing*?'

'Coming!' I called, gaily.

I took my diaphragm out of its case and inserted it. I closed
its case; it clicked like a pistol shot. Then I put it back into the
mirrored cabinet and closed the door carefully. He'd never
check to see if my diaphragm was there. Why should he?

Bobby stood in his pyjamas, sucking his chinsel. I was just
about to leave when Salim came out of the kitchen.

'You look nice,' he said.

'Do I?'

'You watch out for those Japs.'

I frowned. 'What?'

'Japanese.'

'Oh. Yes.'

He smiled. 'Can't trust these foreigners.'

I tried to smile back. Salim turned to Bobby, and gently took
the chinsel out of his mouth.

'Big boys don't need this anymore.'

'It's my chinsel!' wailed Bobby.

'You're a big boy now.'

'Bye,' I said abruptly, and hurried out to the car. I drove off at high speed, like a criminal.

'I'll have to charge you mileage, mind,' said Terry. We were lying in his bed, sleepy and affectionate. We'd been smoking a joint; I picked shreds of tobacco out of his belly button.

'How far then?'

'Oh, sixty miles.'

'Bighead,' I said. 'More like twenty.'

'Let's call it quits at forty-five.'

I climbed on top of him. 'And you'll be expecting a tip on top of that?'

'Yep.'

But we were both too exhausted to move.

'Grunt, grunt,' he said. 'Groan, groan.' He moaned, pretending to climax. 'Aah . . . that's better.'

I rolled off. 'Any previous owners?'

He smiled at me. 'None that counted.'

I kissed him. 'Don't let me fall asleep.'

'You're the most terrific kisser in Kent,' he said.

'Apart from you, that is.'

He nodded, smugly. 'Apart from me.'

He got up and fetched us a can of McEwans each, and his fags. He had a horrible flat, clothes all over the place. I'd never met anybody as sluttish as me before. His mantelpiece was cluttered up with stuff; he was the sort of bloke people sent silly cards to, and candles shaped like penises.

'Nobody ever lights those candles, do they?' I said. 'It's never the moment, somehow.'

He climbed back into bed. I tried to look at his watch, but he covered it up.

'It's all right,' he said.

'What's the time?'

'Ssh.'

'How long have we got?' I asked.

He shook his watch; it didn't work properly. 'A bit. Don't think about it.' He lit a cigarette for me. 'Now what did you give them?'

65

I recited: 'Avocado mousse, *boeuf wellington* and *crème brûlée*.'

'Excellent. Top of the class.'

There was a silence. Then he turned to me. 'I didn't mean this to happen. Honest. Not like this.'

'Nor did I.'

We lay there for a moment. Then I said: 'Oh, let's stay here for ever!'

Salim had left the lounge light on for me. I unlocked the front door and tiptoed in. There were the signs of a family evening – the *Babar* book; Bobby's Robot King which Salim must have reassembled, yet again; the newspaper opened at the TV page. Salim had doodled squiggles down the margin. I sat down heavily in the armchair.

I must have sat there for a long time. I had one more cigarette, and finally went upstairs. I paused at the doorway to the children's room. Salim must have tidied it up with them, that was the only way to do it. It looked nice.

Yasmin was sleeping, curled up on her side, as she always did; I just saw her dark hair. Perhaps they all know what I've done, I thought. Perhaps they've left me, and there's just puppets there, and I'll never see my children again.

I went up to her. She was there, breathing innocent breaths. Bobby's chinsel had fallen onto the floor. I picked it up and put it gently back into his hand. He started sucking it in his sleep, with little moist sounds, his jaw working.

Then I sat in the empty bedroom for a while. It had been painted by now, but Bobby hadn't moved in yet. It was becoming the clutter room, full of DIY stuff and the Styrofoam shapes from the packing case of Salim's new stereo. We hadn't put in any curtains yet. Outside was a square of sky. There was a milky patch of cloud, where the moon must be. Far away, the dog barked. It went on and on.

I lit another cigarette, but then I thought Salim might wake up and smell the smoke so I stubbed it out in a paint-tin lid. The blisters of paint were hard by now. I wondered when Bobby was going to move into the room, and what was going to happen to us.

In the end I had to go to bed. I undressed and lay beside Salim, not touching him. I lay there, stiff-limbed, my eyes open. Even the lightbulb, hanging from the ceiling, seemed to be watching me with its glassy eye.

'He must be blind,' said Sonia. 'You're lit up like a frigging lightbulb.'

'Am I?' I asked, alarmed. It was three weeks later. We were peeling tomatoes for a chicken dish. I'd told Sonia we should just use tinned ones, but she'd been horrified. She was a perfectionist.

'You radiate sexual gratification. Or happiness.' She paused. 'Same thing, really.'

I gazed down at the empty skins. 'I don't know what to do.'

'Enjoy it!'

'I feel terrible.'

'Just be careful then,' she said. 'I'm a bit of an expert in these matters.'

'If Salim found out, he'd kill me,' I said. 'He's got an awful temper.' I slid my knife across the board and the skins fell into the bin. 'Sometimes I feel I don't know him at all.'

'That's what made him attractive in the first place.'

I looked up at her. 'I did love him.'

'Listen, ducky. You were ever so young. You were dying to get away from home. Along came Salim, on went the old musk oil and you were a gonner.' She took my tomatoes. 'I think the rot set in when he joined the Consumers' Association.'

'I'm frightened,' I said.

'Old Sonia's here, with her inexhaustible supply of alibis. He must think we're ever so successful, all those dinners. He'll be buying shares in us soon.'

'I'm frightened.'

I was frightened. You know what it's like in a small town. Now I'd met Terry I kept seeing him everywhere – waiting outside the station, driving around the street, coming out of Burger

Heaven at lunchtime. Suddenly Ashford seemed cramped and dangerous.

Salim was promoted to sales manager and one day he went up to London for a meeting. I waited on tenterhooks. What would happen if Terry picked him up from the station? Just seeing my face, Salim would know the truth.

The summer holidays started and things got more complicated. I had a couple of babyminders on tap, and there was always my mum, but I had to make up lies for them, too. I felt I was jumping from log to log, in a stormy sea, and one day a log would shift – just slightly – and I'd fall in. I had to juggle work, too. Sonia liked Terry but I couldn't let her down. I had to snatch an hour with Terry, here or there – in his flat, in the countryside.

One afternoon Salim arrived unexpectedly to pick me up from work. I was rolling out pastry and Terry was sitting beside me like a husband, eating leftover syllabub and filling in his pools coupon.

'Salim!' I cried, jumping up. 'What a surprise!'

Terry jerked his head up; I saw him out of the corner of my eye.

Sonia, as usual, came to our rescue. She took off her oven gloves, sauntered across to Terry and kissed him.

'Listen, darling,' she said. 'I won't be ready for half an hour. Why don't you wait in the pub?'

As we got into the car Salim said: 'Same old Sonia.'

I nodded as I climbed in.

'Always had a funny taste in men,' he said.

I thought I'd be able to manage it. I'd two-timed blokes often enough in the past. But this was entirely different. You've no idea what adultery's like until you suddenly find yourself in the thick of it, and then it's too late. There's children involved, and a husband. There's a whole family. And you know you should mind about them more than anything in the world. You do, of course.

At the time it really did seem worth it, though it's hard to see that now. But I was so happy, those summer weeks.

Terribly happy. Terry was so silly, we had such fun together, I felt so alive. Neither of us had to quarrel over what the kids could watch on the TV, or feel resentful that we had to clear up all their stuff. Terry used to post me silly notes through the letterbox at Taste Buddies, so I would find them when I arrived at work. He made up rude recipes for me, using body parts. Once he presented me with a VAT invoice for all the things we'd done the day before, stamped with the official Ashford Radio Cabs stamp – sex, tea, buttered toast, a joint. He totted them all up, and added depreciation for his own body and mine. It sounds silly now; it *was* silly.

We experimented with sex like teenagers. It wasn't as intense as it had been with Salim, in the early days, but it was fun. We were mates, with this strong attraction. I think I was in love with him, really. I thought so then.

One day I'd left the kids with mum and stolen a couple of hours with Terry in his flat. It was very hot, and we'd ended up having a bath together. We'd tried to do it again in the bath – amazingly enough, neither of us ever had before – but we couldn't get into the right position: we kept slipping and sliding and banging against the taps (well, I did), and we ended up soaked. When I collected the kids and took the bus home, my hair was still damp (Terry didn't possess anything as civilized as a hair-dryer). The car was parked outside our house. I stopped dead.

'Daddy's home!' cried Bobby, running up to the door. He was very close to his father, more so than Yasmin.

I followed slowly. All of a sudden, I felt naked. Had anybody seen us? If so, where? When?

Salim was in the lounge, just putting down the phone.

'I thought we'd go out for a drink tonight,' he said.

My throat tightened. 'What?'

'Lorraine says she'll babysit.'

An hour later we were sitting in the garden of the Three Tuns, a pub in a village near us. I watched Salim carrying the two glasses, weaving his way back towards me through the tables.

He was wearing his blue, open-necked shirt; he'd had his hair cut that day, it made his ears look vunerable. I willed him not to sit down; not to say anything.

He sat down and passed me my vodka and tonic. When I lifted it, he said: 'Marianne, there's something I want to talk about.'

I stared at him. 'What?'

'It's time we had a talk.'

I took out my cigarettes. 'Talk?'

'I think you know what it's about.'

'What do you mean?'

'It's about us.'

What had I left lying around the house? What had he found? My mind raced.

'We ought to discuss it, you know,' he said.

Had he looked in the bathroom cabinet? He couldn't have overheard any phone calls; Terry had never phoned the house.

'Now we're settled,' he said.

I lit my cigarette. 'What do you mean?'

'I mean, having another child.'

I raised my eyes. It seemed like an hour passed; in fact, it was a split-second. I tried to let out my breath without him hearing.

'We always said we shouldn't wait for ever,' he said.

'Look, Salim. Let's not talk about it now.'

'But you never want to talk about it.'

'I'm just so busy . . .' I said.

'I know, but . . .'

'I mean, this is something I've always wanted to do.'

'But you're always grumbling,' he said.

'Everybody grumbles about their job,' I said.

'You're always saying you're worked off your feet . . .'

'That's why people get married,' I said. 'To have somebody to grumble to.' I paused. 'Look, let's talk about it in a bit. Can we?'

He turned away and looked at the ducks on the pond. Some kids were throwing them whole slices of bread. I didn't think about Salim – what he wanted, what he felt. I just sat there, feeling my heartbeat return to normal, and I thanked God I hadn't been found out. I'd never communicated with God until I started committing adultery.

'We met at evening classes' I told Terry. 'He'd just arrived from Pakistan, he comes from ever such a posh family. He wasn't planning to say here long, then. He was studying poetry – Pope and all that.'

'Pope, eh? What team does he play for?'

I nudged him. 'Shut up. Anyway, so I fell for him . . .'

'OK, OK, cut that bit.'

'But it's never been like this.' I stroked his chest. He wasn't nearly as hairy as Salim.

'I saw him yesterday,' he said. 'At the next petrol pump, filling up his car.'

'Did he see you?'

Terry shook his head. 'Doesn't know who I am, does he?' He paused. 'Seems strange, you being married to a bloke like him.'

'What do you mean?'

'You know.' He shrugged.

'Oh.' I looked at his curtains; there was a splinter of sunshine between them. 'He never really felt foreign, till I met you.'

I had to go away on holiday. We went to the Brittany coast for a week. I ached for Terry; my chest hurt, I missed him so much. Once or twice I managed to slip away to a phone box near the beach. The first time I said I was going to the toilets, but then the kids said they wanted to go too, so we had to find a real one. It was miles away. The next time I just sidled away, clutching my handbag against my swimsuit. But just as I put in my francs Yasmin came up and banged on the glass, so I had to pretend I was phoning Sonia. It was awful, lying to my kids, but I did it automatically now.

I lay on the beach, tanning myself for Terry. I closed my eyes and listened to the waves lapping; I pictured him pulling off my T-shirt when I got back, and gasping with lust. In the evenings we went to little restaurants along the coast and I drank too much *vin ordinaire*. The kids got whiney and restless.

72

Salim and I made them eat up their *poulet frites*. We talked about the weird German couple at our *pension*; we spread out our Michelin map – Salim was hopeless at map-reading, and I had to do it. I felt so guilty that I kept over-reacting, saying how nice, how interesting, let's go there, do, let's!

Inflamed by the sun and sand, Salim grew ardent at night. After all, that was the point of holidays, wasn't it? I'd felt like that too, in the past. It was so sad, because now I had to pretend. Most nights he wanted to make love, and I either pretended I had a sunburn or – worse, much worse – I squeezed my eyes shut and put my treacherous arms around him and stroked his cock and slid my tongue into his mouth. I pretended I was a prostitute and he was a client, or I was a go-go dancer and he'd stepped out of the audience and pulled aside my G-string and we started fucking on stage, with businessmen watching us and getting all aroused. The men were dark; I'd always fantasized about black blokes. I became juicy then, and gasped and faked my pleasure. Honest, I don't think Salim noticed the difference. Afterwards, I felt more desolate than I'd ever felt in my life. What had happened to us? What was I going to do?

At least I never pretended he was Terry.

When I got back to England Terry had a faint tan too – from sitting outside the minicab office on his plastic chair, watching the passing talent. He made me admire it.

'Not as good as his, though,' he said, edgily. He was jealous of Salim, of course – he always had been – but now he said I looked all flushed and sexually gratified.

'Don't be daft,' I said. 'That's sunburn.' I had this pale delicate skin. I was so desperate to see Terry that I'd left the kids alone for an hour – surely they'd be all right? I'd told them that Sonia was on holiday too, and that I was watering her plants. Terry had parked around the corner and we'd sped off. I wondered if any net curtains were twitching. 'I love you, nitwit,' I said. 'I've missed you so much. Oh, what are we going to do?'

'Do you want to leave him?' he asked.

I couldn't reply.

When I got home the children were exactly where I'd left them, watching TV.

'You've been ages,' said Yasmin.

Emily's birthday party was in mid-August, and I took Yasmin to Folkestone to buy her a dress. It was a blue, frilly one. She twirled round in front of the mirror while the assistant watched.

'I can see *somebody's* been away for their hols,' said the assistant, an old dear with grey hair. She just thought Yasmin was tanned.

Yas spun round and round, looking at her reflection. I rememberd that fateful day at C&A, when I'd spun around, admiring myself in that sweater. It was only eighteen months ago, amazingly enough. It seemed that decades had passed. Everything had changed.

'My daddy says I can go to aerobics classes,' said Yasmin.

'Very nice,' said the assistant.

'When I'm nine. He's going to buy me a leotard.'

'What a nice daddy.'

'He's going to take me there in his car.'

I was standing, looking at the rack of children's dresses – puffed sleeves, full skirts, lace and smocking and net. They were squashed up together, waiting for somebody's daughter to choose them.

Suddenly they blurred and swam. I realized that I was crying.

Emily's house was just down the road. Balloons were tied to the front door. When the party was over I went to fetch Yasmin. I stopped, and froze. Terry's minicab was parked outside her front door, and he was sitting inside it. No mistake – Ford Granada, with tassels down the back window.

I walked past him casually and just gave him a glance. He winked back. When I came out of the house, with Yas, another mother and daughter were getting into his car.

I hurried across the street, back to my house. Amongst the other cars revving up I heard the sound of his – I knew it so well, like the voice in a crowd of somebody you love. Fumbling with my key, I heard him driving past me, a few yards away. I felt so exposed; my front door felt so flimsy.

'He's getting suspicious, I'm sure he is. He asked me where I was going this afternoon.'

'What did you say?' asked Terry.

'A textured-soya cookery demonstration. Then he asked where.'

September began, heavy and thundery. No rain came to water our carpet squares of grass. The kids went back to school. This should have made it easier for Terry and me, but I was filled with unease. The old, carefree days were over; the whole thing was getting serious.

Perspiring and edgy, Sonia and I stirred our cooking pots in our cramped premises. Would the weather never break?

'He was awake last night,' I said. 'I was lying there, in bed, and when I turned he was looking at me. I nearly had a heart attack.'

Sonia dipped her finger in the sauce and sucked it. 'Think he knows something?'

I shook my head doubtfully.

'What're you going to do if he finds out?'

'He won't! He can't!'

'You want to leave him for Terry?' she asked.

'I don't know!' I cried.

We've hit some turbulence. Ping: *Fasten your seat-belts*. The pilot's voice has just come on: 'Would passengers please return to their seats.'

Next to me, the Pakistani woman wakes her son and clunks him into his seat-belt. The cabin starts bucking, as if it's being punched underneath with a giant fist. The stewardess walks down the aisle, staggering to one side and then the other, balancing herself on an arm-rest. She smiles down at us, checking we're buckled up.

'What's happening?' asks the little boy.

75

I've closed my eyes. It's hard, what happens next. It's hard to tell you.

On Thursday, September 13, I'd spent the afternoon with Terry. He dropped me off near the kids' school, and I fetched them as usual. For some reason I was feeling happier that day, more light-hearted. The sun was shining at last. I swung the children's arms. They chattered to me but I wasn't really listening. I was rerunning everything Terry and I had just done, like a video in my head. The bus arrived and we jumped on it. I had no premonitions at all.

Even when I saw our car parked outside the house, I had no inkling that anything was wrong. I just presumed that Salim had come home early; they were building Phase Three of our estate, and I presumed he'd been showing some customers around and decided to pack it in early.

We bounded up the path. The front door was open. I was going through to the kitchen when I stopped. Salim was sitting in the lounge.

'Go upstairs,' he said to the children.

Yasmin stared. 'Why have we got to go upstairs?'

'Go up to your room.'

'But Daddy . . .'

'*NOW*!' he bellowed.

The children backed away, alarmed. Behind me, I heard them scuttling up the stairs.

I didn't move. Salim still didn't get up. He said, quite calmly: 'Where were you this afternoon?'

'At work.'

'You're lying.'

'What?'

'I've been there,' he said.

My throat closed up. 'I was out. Shopping.'

Salim stood up. I moved back, against the wall. 'Who is he?' he asked. His voice was low.

'What?'

'I said, Who is he?'

'Who is who?' I stuttered.

76

'Don't lie,' he said. 'Whore.'

I stared. 'What do you mean – '

'Where is your diaphragm?'

I paused. 'What?'

His voice rose. 'Where is your diaphragm, whore?'

'Ssh!'

'You don't want your children to know that their mother is a slut?'

'Salim – '

'Who is the man?'

I burst into tears. 'Don't!'

'Or is it men?'

'No!'

He stepped closer to me. 'How many? Tell me . . .'

'No!'

'How many?' he bellowed.

'It's not true!'

'Three? Four?'

'No!'

'Five? Six?'

'*No*!'

'Seven?'

'*No*!' I screamed. 'One!' I cowered against the wall. 'It's only one!'

Salim moved closer. 'Only one' he said, sarcastically.

We stood there, frozen. Then I moved behind the settee.

'May I ask how long has this been going on?' he said.

'Not long!'

'How long?' he asked.

'Three months.'

'Three months' he said. 'Where?'

'Salim – '

He grabbed me. 'Where, slut?' He started shaking me.

'Don't!' He was hurting me.

'Where? Here?'

'No!' I screamed.

'In my house?'

'No!'

'In my bed?'

'*No*!' I shouted. 'Not here!'

He started hitting me, slapping me across the face. 'You're disgusting!' He snarled. I could hardly recognize his face.

I managed to disentangle myself and rushed upstairs. The children were standing on the landing, staring. I grabbed their hands.

'Come on!' I said. 'Quick!'

'What's daddy doing?' asked Yasmin.

'Come on!'

Bobby grabbed his chinsel and we hurried downstairs. Salim was standing in the lounge, still as stone. He didn't move when we rushed past to the front door.

I bundled the children into the car, and we drove off.

Eight

I took the children to Sonia's flat. We clattered up the stairs, and when I rang the bell she opened the door at once.

'I've been trying to ring you,' she said. 'He came round . . .'

'It's too late,' I said.

'Oh, Jesus.' She put her arms around me.

'Can we stay here tonight?'

'Sure.' She turned to the children, her voice bright. 'Hi, kids! Zara and Kirsty are watching TV.' She ushered them into the lounge. Then she took me into the bedroom, closing the door behind us.

She sat me down on the bed. I was trembling so much that my teeth were chattering. I didn't know what the sound was, at first.

'How did he find out?' she said.

'I don't know.'

'Does he know who Terry is?'

I shook my head.

Suddenly, I felt freezing cold. My guts turned to liquid. I jumped up and rushed into the bathroom.

Later, I learnt what had happened. A few weeks earlier I had bought Terry a watch, because his had finally packed up. The woman who had sold it to me, at the jeweller's, she'd gone to look round the show house in Phase Three and Salim had given her his card. She had recognized the name, and asked him if he'd liked the watch I'd bought for him. She'd said I'd spent ages choosing it.

I tried to comfort the kids. I said we'd had a row but it was going to be all right. Bobby didn't seem too upset, but Yasmin asked questions. What were we quarrelling about? Why did we have to stay at Sonia's?

79

'What's a diaphragm?' she asked. Kirsty opened her mouth to answer, but I shut her up.

They went to bed, in sleeping-bags on the floor of the girls' room. They both fell asleep surprisingly quickly; perhaps they were exhausted by it all.

'Remember when we came to you?' whispered Sonia, gazing at the two shapes on the floor. 'When Bill and I had that fight?'

We went into the lounge and she poured me some more brandy. 'And look at us now,' she said. 'We're OK. Honestly, ducks, whichever way it goes, you'll survive.'

I went over to the window and looked down into the street, for the hundredth time.

'Come and sit down,' she said.

'He's going to come here, I know he is. He must know where I've gone.' I sat down and gazed at our overflowing ashtray. I still felt numb. 'What shall I do?'

'Lie low.'

'What do you think he's doing?'

'Maybe he's gone to a friend's,' she said.

'He hasn't got any friends.' I drank the brandy. 'I don't know what he's going to do. I don't *know* him. You should've seen his face. I didn't recognize him. He terrifies me, Sonia!'

'Don't worry. You're safe here.'

Just then, the doorbell rang. We froze.

'Christ!' I said.

'Get into the kitchen!' she hissed.

I got up. 'Tell him I'm not here!'

'How can I?' she said. 'Your car's outside.'

The doorbell rang again, twice.

'What're you going to say?' I asked.

Sonia hesitated. She took a breath, then she went to the door. I hid in the kitchen.

I heard her opening the door, and then her voice. She sounded surprised.

'What're you doing here?' she said.

A strange man's voice answered. 'Thought you were coming for a drink. I've been bloody waiting since nine.'

I stepped out of the kitchen. There was a bloke I'd never seen before standing in the doorway.

'Hello,' he said.

'Sorry, Les,' said Sonia. 'Look, I'll give you a ring tomorrow.'

'OK,' He shrugged. She gave him a quick kiss, and he left.

She came back into the lounge. We looked at each other, then we sat down heavily on the settee. She reached for the brandy bottle and refilled our glasses. It was the first time I'd ever seen her hands shake. For some reason, that alarmed me more than anything.

I don't know what time we went to bed, but it was late. Sonia was already in bed when I went to the window, for the last time, and looked down into the street. There was an empty space now. Our car had gone.

The next morning Sonia and I dropped the kids off at school. Yasmin had made a fuss about wearing the same clothes as the day before, but that seemed to be the only thing that really bothered her. I tried to be as calm as they were. Perhaps it was all going to blow over. He'd got it out of his system now. I'd tell him that the thing with Terry was over – I'd broken it off, I was so sorry, it hadn't meant anything, I loved him, Salim, really. He would forgive me, in the end. It might take a week or two, but I'd win him round.

At that point I couldn't really think about Terry and me. I was too frightened. Besides, he wasn't around. He'd gone off to Norway for a week with two of his mates. The ferry took two days and they were going to have a mega-piss-up. That's why I had seen him the day before, to say goodbye. Except now it seemed to have happened a hundred years ago.

Sonia drove me up to my house. There was no car outside. We went in. No sign of Salim. I phoned his office. Malcolm answered.

'No,' he said.' He's not in today. He said he had to take the day off, urgent business or something.'

I put the phone down. We fed the guinea-pig and went off to work. I couldn't think what else to do. Besides, we had to pick up a salmon for a boardroom lunch, and do some shopping.

At three-thirty I fetched the children from school. I remember standing at the gates with the other mothers. I knew some of them, of course; I'd even taken the kids to tea at their houses. Today they looked separate from me. They looked responsible and married. I stood apart from them, feeling grubby and dislocated. Just one night away from home and you can feel like an outcast. Jill was there, as usual. I looked at her plain, bland face and tried to imagine her fucking in the bracken. I tried to picture Alan hitting her and calling her a whore. Sometimes she had her car and offered me a lift home but today was Friday, thank God, Emily's Suzuki-violin class. I thought of them all going back to their houses and opening their front doors without a care in the world. Their biggest problem was what to watch on TV that night.

There was the sound of voices, and the children ran out of the school doors towards us. Bobby's two-day-old T-shirt was stained by now. It was one of those Mr Men ones. Mr Greedy. Yasmin came up to me and took my hand. She pressed against my jeans.

'Are we going home?' she asked.

'Have you stopped quarrelling?' said Bobby, severely.

'I don't want to stay at Sonia's' said Yasmin.

'We're going home,' I said.

We walked towards the bus stop. There was a low bit of wall that Bobby always walked on; so did I, sometimes, when I was in a good mood. But today he walked docilely beside me, sucking his blanket.

And that was the last time I ever took them home from school.

The car was parked outside our house now. I unlocked the door, and let the children in first. Salim was in the lounge, sitting at his desk. He was wearing his business suit. He glanced up, and smiled at them. They both drew back, suddenly shy. He didn't look at me.

82

I gave the kids some lettuce, from work. 'Give it to Toulouse' I said. They went into the garden.

There was a silence.

'Would you like some tea?' I asked.

'Not just now, thank you.' He went on sorting out some papers.

'Are you all right?' I asked.

He didn't reply. I cleared my throat.

'Look, Salim. It's finished now. I'm terribly sorry, but it's all over . . .'

'Marianne!' He glared at me, indicating the garden. 'Have you got no sense of decency?'

He had altered. I can't say how, exactly; it was too subtle. If I saw the old Salim I would spot the difference, like standing two identical twins side by side. My Uncle Eric's face changed, just slightly, when his wife died.

'We must talk,' I said. 'Please.'

He looked at his watch, and shifted his papers again. I felt as if I'd committed some disgusting crime and was waiting to be charged.

'What time does *Blue Peter* come on?' he said.

'In half an hour.'

He closed the bedroom door behind us. Downstairs there was the penny-pipe *Blue Peter* theme tune. And then the three presenters' cheery greeting. Salim stood at the window and I stood on the other side of the bed. Between us lay the expanse of bedspread.

'I take it you want a divorce?' he said.

'Salim, we can't just . . .'

'I said, I take it you want a divorce?'

I paused. 'Do you?'

'Of course. I've made some preliminary arrangements.' He looked out of the window. His voice was horribly formal. 'I've found somewhere to live, and I move there on Monday.'

I stared. 'But Salim – '

'Don't worry. Until then I shall sleep on the settee – '

'I didn't mean that!'

He turned round. 'I expect you, over the weekend, to behave yourself in front of the children – '

'Of course! But – '

'It's not a great deal to ask. Do you think you could manage that?'

'But what are you – '

'In my opinion,' he said, 'though obviously not yours, the children are our first concern – '

'Of course they are!'

'So I suggest we keep everything as pleasant as possible over the next two days – '

'Salim! – '

'I've spoken to my lawyer, and I would advise you to make an appointment with yours – '

'I haven't got a lawyer!' I cried. 'You know that!'

'That's all I have to say.'

He moved forward and paused, to go past me. I sprang back, as if I'd been stung. He went out of the bedroom, and down the stairs.

A few moments later I came down. He was sitting on the settee with the kids, watching *Blue Peter*.

'What a nice dog' he was saying.

'Haven't you seen it?' said Yasmin. 'They always have it.'

I'll never forget that supper. We sat at the table in our usual places. Salim asked the children what they'd done at school. They answered him politely. Once or twice I caught them exchanging glances. Yasmin looked at me, then back to her father. I'd been crying, and I probably looked a bit weird because all my mascara had come off.

When Salim had finished he dabbed at his mouth with his serviette, like a spinster. I could hardly recognize him by now.

'Thank you,' he said to me. 'That was delicious.' He looked at my plate. I hadn't eaten anything. 'You didn't like it?'

There was a pause. Then he got to his feet. 'Bedtime, children!' he said in an odd, hearty voice. He turned to me. 'I'll sleep downstairs tonight, dear. I think I've got a cold coming on.'

He held out his hands to the children. Bobby went with him obediently, but Yasmin paused at the door.

'Will you come up and say goodnight?' she asked me.

It's hard to describe the weekend that followed. Every now and then I thought that if I pinched myself perhaps I would wake up and realize it was all just a nightmare.

Salim was very strange. I caught him looking at me once or twice, but most of the time he acted as if I wasn't there, except for our terrible, polite meals when he talked to me with a sort of elaborate courtesy, as if he was a bit surprised to find me in his house but determined to make the best of it. He acted as if I was a complete stranger. His manners were perfect; it was so chilling. And yet he looked bright-eyed, and sort of hectic. I wondered who was going mad, him or me?

He never touched me, of course. Our house had never seemed so small. But he was very attentive with the kids, like a parody of a father. Most weekends he was busy fiddling with his carpentry or recording his records on to cassettes or catching up with his paperwork. But now he played with them, and even drove them to the pet shop to get some sawdust, and helped them clean out the guinea-pig. Upstairs, on the Saturday evening, I heard him asking Yasmin which were her favourite dolls.

I didn't have any suspicions, then. I just thought he was devoting himself to them so he could avoid talking to me. Maybe he was trying to shame me, by showing me what a good and caring parent he was compared to their wicked mother. But it made me uneasy, and the kids too.

'Isn't mummy going to bath me?' I heard Bobby say.

His jovial voice replied: 'I expect mummy has better things to do.'

I stayed out of his way. It was so painful, to see him like this. Perhaps he was being odd because he was so unhappy. He was spending all this time with the children because it was our last weekend together, as a family, and he wanted to make the most of it. I didn't know if he had told them that he was

85

moving out, and I didn't dare ask. We couldn't talk about things like that anymore.

Just once or twice, something puzzled me. On Saturday afternoon I was upstairs, tidying the children's room. I couldn't think what else to do – what else could I do? I found some old clothes that they'd outgrown, and I was just stuffing them into a carrier bag when Salim passed the door. He stopped and stared.

'What're you doing?' he demanded, his face blazing.

'Nothing,' I stuttered. 'Just some old clothes.'

He rushed in, grabbed the bag and looked at it. Then he seemed to recover himself. He gave it back to me, muttered something and left the room.

Another time I was lying on the bed. It was Sunday afternoon and I felt paralysed with misery. The kids were out in the street, playing. I heard the extension ping; he must have lifted the receiver downstairs. It was at this point that I decided to get up. I had to get out of the house; I felt suffocated.

When I went downstairs he was talking on the phone, his voice low. When he saw me he stopped in mid-sentence and replaced the receiver, quickly. I didn't say anything. I couldn't say anything personal to him, like 'Who was that?' We weren't familiar enough, now.

'I'm just going for a walk,' I said. At the time I presumed he was making some call about his new flat and he didn't want me to listen because it wasn't my business; he wanted to keep it separate.

I should have seen the signs. But everything was so creepy, they hardly showed. In the evenings he read to the children. I heard his voice in their bedroom.

'Ho ho ho!' he thundered, in his hearty voice. 'The giants are coming!'

Then he'd come out, and call politely to me.

'Would you like some tea, dear? I'm just putting on the kettle.' He'd never called me 'dear', in ten years.

He spent the evening downstairs. I don't know what he did. Sometimes I heard the TV. Once the children had gone to bed I stayed upstairs. By some unspoken agreement I never saw his sleeping arrangements. By the time I came downstairs in the morning he'd rolled up his sleeping-bag and put it neatly in the corner. Oh, I hated that sleeping-bag. Once, when he wasn't there, I kicked it across the carpet and knocked over our lamp.

The children were uneasy, too. We were edgy, like horses which can sniff an approaching thunderstorm even though the sky is blue. On the Monday morning Bobby didn't want to go to school.

'Come along, darling.' I had to half-pull him to the door.

He took his chinsel out of his mouth. 'Where're you going?'

'Only to work,' I said. 'We've got a big do on today, I've got to hurry.'

'Don't go!' he said.

Salim was standing at his desk. He was dressed for work, but he hadn't gone yet. This surprised me slightly. Was he really going to work, and moving into the flat later? Or was he pretending he was going to work, so the kids weren't alarmed? He couldn't have told them he was moving out, yet. I thought he was leaving it a bit late. Were they just going to come back from school and find him gone?

He didn't offer to give us a lift, and I couldn't ask. But he did kiss the children, lovingly.

'Have a good time at school, darlings,' he said. 'Don't be naughty.'

He held them tight, first Yasmin and then Bobby, as if he was going away and wouldn't be seeing them for a long time.

We took the bus. At the school gates Bobby started crying.

'Don't want to go!' he wailed.

It was unusual for him to cry in full view of his mates. His best buddy Darren stopped and stared, but his mother hustled him away.

'I'll see you at half-past three,' I said. 'It's all right.'

Yasmin said: 'You can't take your chinsel to school, baby.'

'Leave him alone!' I snapped.

'Don't go away!' said Bobby.

'I'll just be at work, darling. It's not far.'

'Bye,' said Yasmin, and took his hand.

They walked across the playground, towards the school doors. I hurried away; I didn't even watch them go in.

Taste Buddies was in turmoil. We had a Rotary Club banquet that night, and we were behind schedule. Sonia had brought in two other assistants and we kept bumping into each other.

For the first hour or so I hardly had a moment to think about my marriage, which was ending so shockingly quickly. Everything had collapsed, like a shaky stone wall which had been given one little push. Suddenly it was just a heap of stones, and I could hardly remember what it had looked like when it was standing.

'It's terrifying,' I said to Sonia. 'He's being so polite!'

'At least he's not getting pissed and beating you up.'

'It's so weird. He's being so reasonable. He says he won't take any furniture or anything.'

'That's just to make you feel guilty. You wait till he gets his solicitor's claws into you.'

'I don't want a divorce!'

'He won't even discuss it?' she asked.

'Something's wrong,' I said.

Gloria was trying to defrost prawns, for the prawn cocktail. She was holding a frozen plastic square of them under the hot tap. Lynne was chopping up mushrooms for the *boeuf en daube*.

'Perhaps I should phone the school,' I said to Sonia. 'Bobby seemed so upset. He knows something's wrong, they both do, but nobody's told them anything.'

'The béchamel!' she yelled, shoving me towards the saucepan. The sauce was rising like a blister.

I stirred the sauce; I sorted the cutlery. Whenever I thought about phoning, the phone rang.

'Where're the bloody lemons?' shouted Sonia.

The phone rang again. Five more people were expected at the banquet, they'd got the numbers wrong.

I tried to light a cigarette but my hands were wet; in that job your hands were always either wet or oily. I started slicing the beef but the knife kept slipping; I couldn't concentrate. After a moment I realized that I was throwing the gristle back into the meat bowl and the pieces of meat into the rubbish bin.

'Hell, forgot the paprika!' said Sonia, who was beating her special mayonnaise. Lynne ran out to buy some. I picked the meat out of the bin. When I next looked at the clock it was eleven-thirty.

'When's Terry coming back from Norway?' Sonia asked.

'Thursday night.'

'Unless Salim gets to him first,' she said, beating vigorously.

'He doesn't know who he is!'

'Only joking.'

I tossed the meat pieces in the flour. Some of them fell on to the floor.

'I'm going to take them out after school,' I said, picking up the slices of beef and putting them back into the bowl. 'We'll go to the Wimpy and I'll explain it all to them. That their dad's moving out, but they'll see him at weekends.'

Sonia poured some cooking wine into two tumblers. 'Get that into you,' she said. She looked at her bowl. 'Holy shit, it's curdling!'

Then we found that half the broccoli was yellow, and I had to run out for some more, to the greengrocers round the corner. By the time I got back Sonia was on the phone to the laundry, because the linen still hadn't arrived. I knew I should be making a phone call, but I'd forgotten what it was.

Lynne was slicing the oranges wrong, in chunks, and I had to rescue them and start again. I felt ill with nerves. What was Salim doing now? Had he really gone to work or was he at home, packing his suitcases? What would I find when I got back home? An empty house? There was something wrong, something I hadn't understood. He had worked out some plan, I was sure of it.

'Maybe he's going to tell me he's changed his mind,' I said. 'I'll get back home and it'll be my things he's packed. He'll chuck me out of the house and change the locks.'

'Darling, they're still full of pips.'

'He called me a whore! I thought he was going to kill me!'

The phone rang, just then. It was the laundry.

'They can't find the tablecloths!' called Gloria. Sonia darted across, and grabbed the receiver.

As I trimmed the pith off the oranges it suddenly swept over me, the enormity of it all. Our lives were changed for ever. Overnight, our family had collapsed. There was no going back now. Yasmin and Bobby had become children of a broken home. They had lost their parents; now they just had a mother and a father. They'd be like Sonia's daughters, packing up their pyjamas into carrier bags, forgetting things they needed for school the next day, moaning that it was boring at dad's. Or mum's. Salim couldn't look after them, he didn't even know about Yasmin's ear drops. And how was I going to manage? Who was going to have the car? Somebody would have to buy another fridge, and another bed. Another hoover.

'We'll have to sell the house!' I wailed to Sonia. I nearly added: I'll have to live in a flat like yours. It was on the main Willesborough road, without a garden. Where could the children play? What about Emily, Yasmin's best friend? Who was going to have the guinea-pig?

'Don't cry, sweetie.' Sonia put her arm around me. 'Or save it till later.'

Later. I looked at the clock. It was nearly three.

'I forgot to phone!' I said. 'I forgot to phone the school!'

'If Bobby was really unhappy they would've phoned you,' she said. 'Anyway, you're going there in half an hour.'

'I suppose so,' I said doubtfully.

'Slosh some kirsch over those oranges,' she said.

The school was only three streets away. I hurried along the verge of the road. It was much chillier today; there was the smell of autumn in the air. A lorry thundered past, windily. I half-stumbled, in my slingbacks. I hadn't picked up my jacket that morning, I'd been too keen to get out of the house.

I tottered along the grass, shivering. For the first time in my life I was dreading seeing my own kids. I'd have to answer their questions. Whatever waited for us at home, it was bound to be painful for them. They would suffer, and none of it was their fault.

I went round the corner. There was the knot of mothers, as usual, plus a few dads. The kids hadn't come out yet. I stood a little apart. I couldn't speak to any of them, that day. I stood near the ice-cream van; it rumbled behind me, filling the air with diesel fumes. I shivered in my T-shirt and jeans. Would Salim buy a washing machine? Somebody would have to tell him to turn the kids' Smurf T-shirts inside out, or else the transfer would wash off.

Then I heard the kids' voices, laughing and shrieking. The children spilled out of the school doors, a blur of colours, red, yellow, tartan. The mothers moved forward; the kids ran across the playground towards them. I scanned their faces, looking for Yasmin and Bobby. Behind me, the ice-cream van struck up its tune, 'Boys and Girls Come Out to Play.'

A moment or two passed. Some of the bigger kids were coming out now. They greeted their mothers. Behind me, I heard car doors slam and engines revving up. The lollipop lady was shepherding families across the street, on their way back home.

I moved nearer the school, into the playground. Maybe their classes hadn't come out yet. But just then I saw Emily and Stacey; they were already with their mothers, and ready to go home.

'Would you like a lift?' asked Jill.

I jumped. 'No, thanks,' I said. I couldn't face her today. 'I'm taking them shopping.' Then I remembered – no, I was taking them to the Wimpy Bar. Where was I going to take them? We didn't really have a home anymore.

Darren had come out by now, and the other kids from Bobby's class. When I looked around there was only a handful of parents left. The children were still coming out, but just in a trickle now. I looked at my watch. It was three-forty.

Behind me, the ice-cream tune tinkled. 'The moon is shining bright as day.' A bunch of kids stood at it, buying lollies. More children were collected, and walked away down the road.

Five minutes passed. The last remaining mother, a beaten-up-looking woman with two little boys, left.

91

I was all alone. When I turned round, the lollipop lady had gone.

It was ten to four. Suddenly I crossed the playground and rushed into the school. Bobby's classroom was through the hall, on the left. I went up to the door and looked in.

His teacher was there. She was just switching off the lights. Otherwise the classroom was empty.

I rushed in. 'Where's Bobby?' I said.

'Oh, Mrs Siddiqi. Hello.'

'Where's Bobby?'

She stared. 'Bobby?'

'Where is he?'

'But he's gone,' she said.

I stood still. 'What?'

'His father took him to the dentist. Oh, hours ago.'

'*What*?'

'Before lunch. Didn't you know?'

I rushed out, across the hall. Yasmin's classroom was empty too.

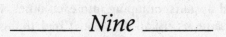

Nine

I ran out of the school. The bus was disappearing round the corner. I had to wait for the next one, and it was four-forty by the time I arrived at the estate. Panting, I ran down Meadow Road and into Harebell Close. Our car wasn't there.

I let myself in. The house was empty. I could sense it the moment I stepped into the lounge.

'Yasmin?' I called. 'Bobby?'

There was nobody in the garden. The back door was locked. I dashed upstairs, into the children's bedroom.

'Yasmin!' I yelled. '*Bobby*!'

Then I ran downstairs and phoned Sonia.

'They aren't here!' I cried.

'What?'

'The kids!'

'What do you mean, pet?' I heard the clatter of saucepans.

'Salim took the kids out of school,' I said. 'He came before lunch, he said he was taking them to the dentist. I don't know where they've gone!'

A quarter of an hour later I heard Sonia's van arriving. She rushed into the house.

'Is he at work?' she asked.

'I've just phoned. He hasn't been in all day!'

'Don't panic' she said. 'Here, have a Kleenex.' She passed me a tissue. 'Is there a note?'

I shook my head.

'He's probably just taken them to look at his new flat,' she said.

'In the middle of school?'

'Perhaps he's taken them out for a treat. Or something.'

'He's taken them away!' I cried.

'How do you know?' she said. 'Have you searched their room?'

I hadn't done anything.

We rushed upstairs, bumping into each other. The bedroom looked the same as usual. At least, I had thought so. Sonia started pulling open drawers. I opened the cupboard.

Inside, it was emptier. Some of their things had gone. I swung round and stared at the chest of drawers. The drawers weren't completely empty, but there was less stuff in them, fewer knickers and T-shirts.

I scrabbled in the back of the cupboard, looking for Yasmin's overnight bag, a two-tone nylon thing. It wasn't there.

Wildly, I scanned the room. When I'd tidied it up, during the weekend, I'd put all their teddies and dolls in a row along the top of the chest of drawers. Now that I looked, some of them were missing – Bobby's rag hippo, Yasmin's best doll, Candy. There were gaps; the other toys leant against each other. *What's your favourite doll?* he'd asked.

Sonia and I stared at each other, then we darted next door. I opened Salim's side of the cupboard. It was nearly bare. Just a few things hung there – his painting overalls, a jacket he hadn't liked once he'd bought it, a dated suit. Otherwise, there was a row of empty coathangers. His two suitcases had gone.

I remember that moment when I closed his cupboard door. I couldn't move. Sonia must have been speaking to me.

She put her hand on my arm. 'Marianne!' she said. 'Marianne! Where's his passport?'

We were downstairs now. I was opening his desk and scrabbling through the little cubbyhole, where he kept the passports.

I turned to Sonia. 'It's gone.'

'His passport?'

I nodded. The blood had drained from my body.

'What about yours?' she was asking.

I clawed through, and found mine. I took it out.

'Are the kids on yours?' she asked.

I nodded.

'That's OK then,' she said. 'Thank God.'

94

Then I said: 'They're on his too.'

'What?'

'They're on his passport. He was going to take them to Karachi, remember? But Bobby got whooping cough.'

It was then that it hit me. I started crying again – dry, hacking sobs, as if I was being sick. Sonia put her arms around me holding me tightly. I lay against her like a log. I remember how she smelt – of garlic and shampoo.

Suddenly the doorbell rang. We froze. Then I disentangled myself and rushed to the door.

I opened it. Emily stood there.

'Can Yasmin come and play?' she asked.

I stared at her. 'What?'

'Can Yasmin – '

'Sorry,' I said. 'Not now.'

Sonia must have poured us a drink. I felt numb, and utterly blank. She lit me a cigarette.

'Now, let's think straight,' she said. 'Where could he have taken them? Who are his friends?'

'I told you. He hasn't got any friends.'

'What about Aziz?'

'What?'

'His cousin, in London,' she said. 'Perhaps he's gone there. What's his phone number?'

'I don't know.'

'Where does he live?' she asked.

'I don't know!'

'Not even the area?'

'No!' I cried. 'We'll never find him!'

'Ssh. Now, calm down.' She looked at her watch. 'He'll still be at work, anyway. It's only half-past five. Where's his office?'

'Some design thing. What's it called . . .'

'Come on, ducky,' she said. 'Think!'

'Hi, Aziz!' Sonia said, on the phone. Her voice was bright. 'It's Sonia here, remember? Fine, how are you? Er, I'm just trying to get hold of Salim. I've got a bit of business to put his way.'

She listened. 'What? Oh, no . . . I was just wondering – I thought he was going up to London today.' She listened. 'Never mind. Thanks.'

She put the phone down. 'Hasn't seen him for weeks.'

'You sure?'

She shook her head. 'He's lying. Devious bastards.'

'We've got to phone the ports! Phone the airport!'

'What can we do?'

'Stop them!' I shouted.

'How long have they had?'

'Six hours,' I said.

'How do you phone a port?' she said. She started scrabbling through her handbag. 'We'll phone the police.'

She found her address book and looked up the number of the police station. She dialled. We waited. The phone rang and rang.

'Bloody police station,' she said. 'Remember when my handbag got nicked? They all go off somewhere and – oh, polish their handcuffs or something.'

I grabbed the phone from her.

'What're you doing?' she asked.

I dialled 999. Somebody answered.

'Police, please,' I said. After a moment, a man's voice came on the line. 'Yes, there's been an incident,' I told him. 'It's 12 Harebell Close. Yes. Hurry!'

I put down the phone.

'What about the banquet?' I asked, abruptly.

'It's OK. Gloria's mother's helping out.'

I don't remember what happened before the police came. They might have taken five minutes, or half an hour. I don't think I moved. I suppose I was in shock. I'd never had a particularly chummy relationship with the police, but now I longed for them to arrive. The whole thing had suddenly become official, which was a terrifying thought. But at least it would be taken out of my hands. It was like falling ill, and lying very still until the ambulance comes.

I can't remember how many cigarettes I smoked. It was getting dark, and we hadn't closed the curtains. The first thing

I remember was blue light, flashing in the lounge, and then the doorbell ringing.

Two policemen came in. The lounge looked small with them standing in it. One of them took out his notebook. He licked his finger childishly, like a TV cop, as he turned the page. The whole thing was unreal.

I must have been talking because he was asking me about it all over again. He was the taller one, with a baby face. 'Young policemen,' I'd giggled, with Terry.

'Now, let me get this straight,' he said.

'My husband has taken my children,' I repeated.

'What gives you cause – '

'I told you,' I said. 'We had a fight. He came to the school today – '

I started crying again. I heard Sonia's voice, from far off.

'He's taken his passport and their clothes,' she explained. 'He's obviously taken them out of the country.'

'He's stolen them!' I bellowed.

'He's been gone since lunchtime,' she said. Her voice sounded clipped and thin, not like Sonia at all. She must be frightened too. This made it worse. 'They could be anywhere by now.'

'All we can do at this point, Mrs, er, Siddiqui, is to put out a search for the missing car. If you can give me details?'

'But we'll be too late!' I cried.

He looked at his notebook. 'If we find, er, Yasmin and Robert, then you can take proceedings to make them wards of court.'

'You've got to stop them!' cried Sonia. She turned to me. 'Look, Marianne, you wait here in case the phone rings. I'll go down to the police station.'

Suddenly, I was alone. The house had never felt so empty. I sat there for a while. Outside, the street lamp came on. It bathed the lounge in cold, orange light, like a stage set. The phone sat there like a dead thing.

Just then I jumped up. Leaving the front door open, so I could hear the phone, I ran next door and rang the bell. My neighbour, Margaret, opened the door.

'Hello,' she said.

'Have you seen Salim and the kids?'

She laughed. 'Lost them, have you?'

'What? Er, they went out this afternoon, and they're not back yet. Have you seen anything?'

'Typical men!' she said. 'Never tell you where they're going, do they? Derek's just like that – '

'Have you seen anything?'

'No.' She looked at me. 'Something wrong?'

'No,' I said quickly, and went back to my house.

The street was empty; all the children had gone in now. Back in the lounge, I closed the curtains and put on the lights. I wanted it to look cosy for them. I sat down and waited. It was seven o'clock. They hadn't gone far, I was sure of that. He would phone me, his voice thin and hostile. Or he might let me suffer for a bit longer and phone tomorrow. He'd taken them to a bed and breakfast, somewhere along the coast. They'd walk along the beach, in the morning, and then he wouldn't have a clue what to do. He'd buy them fish and chips and they'd come back after lunch. The children would be missing me. He wouldn't want to see them upset.

Or else he'd taken them to London. Aziz knew a lot of people in the Pakistani community. They had flats in Kensington, or houses in the suburbs.

Salim would camp the night with somebody's aunty, in Cricklewood or Croydon. He'd pour out his story and get a lot of sympathy – poor Salim, the cheated husband. That's what happened when you married an English girl. The children would watch TV and ask where I was. He wouldn't stay there long – two days at the most. Stupid of me, to panic. He just wanted to scare the shit out of me.

I drank a tumbler of Cinzano. When I looked at the clock it was quarter to eight. Just then the phone rang. I jumped.

I rushed over and grabbed it, fumbling with the receiver.

'Hello?'

'Can I speak to Courtney?' said a voice.

'Who? What?'

98

I put the phone down. I sat down again, my heart thudding. The sudden silence pressed in, as if I was under water.

What must they be thinking? What was he telling them? They must be getting anxious by now.

Sonia was right. He'd just taken them out for a meal. He needed to explain everything to them. He'd packed their clothes, just to give me a shock. He wanted to hurt me, like I'd hurt him. They'd be back soon, full of knickerbocker-glories.

I dashed up to their room and tidied their beds. I closed the curtains and put on their beside light.

Outside in the street, I heard Sonia's van arriving. It had a special rattle. She rang the doorbell and I ran downstairs.

'Any news?' I asked.

She shook her head.

'Have they found the car?'

'Not yet.'

'I bet he's in London,' I said. 'He's just trying to scare me.'

Zara and Kirsty were with her. They had their sleeping-bags. They darted to the TV; they had been in the middle of some programme.

Sonia had brought along a bottle of gin and some tonics. We sat down and she poured them out.

'That's what he was doing on Friday,' I said. 'Making all the arrangements.'

'He'll probably come home tomorrow with his tail between his legs.'

'Christ,' I said. 'I wish I could *do* something!'

'Look, he's not going to do anything that'd harm the kids.'

'He hates me,' I said. Suddenly I was sure that he'd taken them abroad. 'Don't you see? He hates me!'

The phone stayed silent. We drank the gin and smoked. Sonia went out, later, and came back with a takeaway. It was Chinese.

We sat in the kitchen. I couldn't eat anything; my throat had closed up.

'Go on, have a spring roll,' she said. 'At least I didn't buy Indian.'

When we went back into the lounge, the girls had taken out Bobby's toy box. They were pushing a jeep across the floor.

'Put that away!' snapped Sonia.

'It's all right,' I said. 'Honest.'

'It's a bit babyish, anyway.' Zara put it back into the box.

'Go on, bed!' said Sonia.

'But, mum . . .'

'Go on!'

'Do we have to go to school tomorrow?' asked Kirsty.

'Why the hell not?'

'Don't shout at them,' I said. 'Please.'

She turned to her daughters. 'Of course you have to go to school,' she said, more gently. 'Go on, upstairs.'

The girls climbed to their feet, reluctantly.

Sonia turned to me. 'Do you mind them sleeping there?'

'Where?' I asked.

She pointed upstairs. 'In their bedroom.'

'What? Oh. It doesn't matter.'

She poured me another drink. 'Run out of tonic,' she said.

The phone didn't ring. We went to bed, at some point. Sonia steered me into the bathroom as if I were an invalid, and made me do my teeth.

'Mustn't let our standards slip,' she said.

She was trying to cheer me up, but her voice came from a long way off. I was suddenly terribly tired. She undressed me and put me into bed. Then she climbed in beside me.

'Any more of this,' she said, 'and people'll start talking.'

I must have fallen asleep, because it was dark when I heard the noise. I'd been beside a river, and Bobby's voice came from behind some reeds. I heard a thump. I knew, suddenly, that he was in a rowing boat, and he hadn't got any oars, and it was bumping against the bank as it drifted off, further down the water.

I got out of bed and hurried across the grass. It felt like carpet, under my bare feet. And then the cold knob was in my hand and I opened the door.

It was dark; they lay there. One of them had knocked the bedside lamp on to the floor. Yasmin always slept in the bottom bunk. I knelt beside her, and smelt her hair. Different from when she was a baby. I stroked it; how short it was now!

And then, of course, I woke up, and realized I'd been stroking Zara.

It was very early when the phone started ringing. I must have got back into bed, because I was leaning over Sonia's sleeping body and it was already light outside.

'Mrs Siddiqui? This is Sergeant Thomas, from Ashford Police Station here. We've found your car.'

'Where is it?'

'In the car park at Folkestone. By the ferry terminal.'

Ten

'I knew something like this would happen,' said my mum.

I stared at her. 'Like this?'

'Knew it would end badly,' she said.

'For Christ's sake!'

It was an hour or so later, that morning. 'Remember that day at Hastings, when he blew his top? You were wearing that little bikini, your itsy-bitsy-teeny-weeny one. You were only engaged then – remember? – and that other bloke . . .'

'I remember,' I said.

'I thought he was going to have a fit,' she said. 'He went so strange. Didn't talk to you for days.' She sighed. 'When it comes down to it, they're not the same as us – '

'Oh, shut up!' I said.

She took out her hearing-aid and fiddled with it.

'It's making that weeing noise again,' she said.

'Look, can you two just wait here, in case the phone rings?' Sonia asked.

'What did you say?' said mum.

'In case the phone rings,' dad told her.

I got up, slowly, and put on my jacket. I had a terrible headache.

'You OK?' Sonia asked me.

'I know what I'll say to him,' said my dad.

'Don't say anything!' I told him. 'Just find out where they are. Say I'll come and collect them, wherever they are! Say I'm not angry. You understand?'

He nodded. 'Those poor little kiddies. What'll they be thinking?'

Sonia drove me to Folkestone in her van. It wasn't far – about twelve miles. I'd learnt to drive along this stretch of road but

102

now it looked like enemy territory. We didn't speak. I felt as if I'd come unstitched inside.

We drove to the ferry terminal, and into the car park. Salim and I had parked here before, when we'd taken a day-trip to France. Sonia cruised down the aisles, rows of cars on either side of us. Their windscreens flashed in the sun. And then I saw ours.

At various times my hopes had soared, and then plummeted. Now it hit me, all over again. I couldn't pretend anymore.

Sonia helped me out of the van. I saw her looking at me anxiously. I approached the car hesitantly, as if it was wired up with a bomb. Sonia unlocked it for me and we looked inside.

There was nothing, of course, no clues. It was as messy as usual — when it came to cars, Salim was surprisingly untidy. Empty crisp packets and sweet wrappers; one of Bobby's socks; discarded stickers from Pay 'n' Display car parks.

'Maybe they've gone to France,' I said, at last.

'I told you. A man like Salim won't have a clue what to do with two kids. *Cherchez la mère*. They always go back to them, the spineless bastards.'

'But his mother's in *Karachi*,' I said. I pointed to the car. 'Why's it not at the airport?'

'To put you off the scent,' she replied. 'Or . . .' She stopped.

'Or what?'

'Never mind,' she said.

'*What*?'

She paused. 'Or to trick the kids.' She turned back to her van. 'When I see him, Marianne, I'm going to tear his eyes out.'

I drove back, following Sonia's van as if I was blind. Then she drove on to work, and I went home.

My mum was dozing on the sofa. Dad was nowhere to be seen. I went into the kitchen; he was in the garden, talking over the fence to Derek, my next-door neighbour.

I went back into the lounge and shook my mother awake.

'Any phone calls?' I asked.

'Pardon?' She blinked.

'You've been asleep!' I cried. 'The phone might have rung!'

'Haven't heard anything,' she said.

'Are you sure?'

'I can hear perfectly well, when I take this blessed thing out.' She adjusted her hearing-aid, again. 'Things would've been different if you'd stayed at home. Hadn't gone gadding about. Wasn't good for your marriage.'

'Oh, shut up!'

'I always knew – '

'You don't know anything about it!' I shouted.

'You and your boyfriend.'

There was a silence.

'What?' I asked.

'I know you've been carrying on,' she said. 'Known it for weeks. All this time I've been looking after the kiddies.' She looked at me. 'You've been a very silly girl.'

When they'd gone I sat there, numb. I simply didn't know what to do. If I left, the phone would ring, I knew it would.

It was still only ten-thirty. Time seemed to have stopped. I sat on the settee. Tuesday morning. What would they be doing at school? Maybe I should go there and look through the gates? Yasmin and Bobby would be there, playing as usual. They'd be dressed in the clothes they wore yesterday; they'd come bounding up to the gate, like puppies: *Mum, what're you doing here? What's wrong?* I'd closed my eyes and dreamt it all. The whole thing had been a missed beat, a hiccup in our lives. It was like dozing off in the afternoon; you think you've been asleep for hours, but then you wake up and see that everybody's still doing what they had been doing before. I dreamt it all up, because I felt so guilty.

I opened my eyes. Ten-forty. Suddenly, I got up, locked up the house and drove to London.

I'd never driven in heavy traffic before. Cars kept hooting at me; a red bus reared up behind me like a cliff. I got lost trying to find Tottenham Court Road, and ended the wrong way up a one-way street. A taxi flashed its lights at me and I knew my phone was ringing.

A delivery lorry backed out in front of me; I jammed on my

brakes. People filed past in front of my bonnet, turning to stare at me. Somewhere, a police siren wailed.

I reversed down a road and found myself in another one-way street. I must have been blocking the traffic, I don't know. Everybody seemed to be shouting at me. A traffic warden leant down and peered at me, mouthing words against the window: *I know where your kids are*, he was saying. *Wicked woman. I'll give you a ticket for that.*

I drove along the pavement, swerving round some parked cars, and turned left into a narrow street. Dark buildings rose up on either side. I parked on a double yellow line and ran off, looking for Whitfield Street. It was somewhere near Tottenham Court Road.

'But this is terrible,' said Aziz. 'Sit down, let me get you some coffee.'

'What did he tell you?' I asked.

'I told you. Nothing.'

'He must have said something!' My voice rose.

Aziz shrugged. It must have been lunchtime because his office was empty. It was an open-plan place, with white blinds at the windows like an operating theatre. I felt I was fighting off an anaesthetic.

'Salim's an impulsive chap,' said Aziz. 'Why do you think he came out here in the first place? He and his parents, they were – '

'Where have they gone?'

'I don't know.'

'You must know!' I said.

'Look, he adores his kids. Whatever's happened between you two, he won't let them come to harm – '

'I know you know, Aziz. Tell me, please! I've got to find them!'

'My dear, he's my cousin.'

'But they're my children!' I cried.

'I can't tell you anything,' he said. 'I'm sorry.'

'You're not sorry, you bloody hypocrite! He's gone to Karachi, hasn't he? Just tell me the address of his parents!'

'Don't you know?'

'No!' I shouted. 'They used to speak on the phone. I haven't got an address! I haven't got any bloody letters! I don't know where they bloody live!'

'This is between yourself and your husband,' he said.

'You bastard!' I started clawing at him; I pulled at his sweater.

'Marianne – '

'You're lying!' I pummelled at his chest, screaming at him. 'You lying bastard!'

He ducked away, half-smiling, shielding his face. I rushed after him, bumping against a drawing-board. Paper slid off it.

He was trying to get me to the door. His smooth, handsome face swung nearer; the room span. He was smiling at me pityingly. His arms were gripping my shoulders and he was propelling me in front of him. I struggled, scratching his hands.

One of the phones started ringing. I rushed to it. Yasmin had been trying to get through for hours.

I grabbed the receiver. 'Yas?'

A man's voice was asking if Mary had been to the printers yet. The last thing I remember was Aziz taking the phone from me, and then I was clattering down the stairs, sobbing. I made these hoarse, animal noises; they echoed in the concrete stairwell.

I must have driven home. In the afternoon I found myself sitting in my house, waiting for the phone to ring. I was sure it had rung when I was out. Where were they? What was happening to them? I physically ached for them. I had diarrhoea and kept on going to the bathroom. Once, the phone rang, but it was only my parents asking if there was any news.

Sonia came round. It was already evening, because it was dark outside. She drew the curtains and switched on the lights. She had brought along some smoked salmon but I felt too ill to eat it.

'Look, I'm taking you out for a drink,' she said.

'I can't.'

'They won't phone now,' she said. 'It's probably the middle of the night.'

106

'I can't.'

'Come on,' she insisted. 'It'll do you good. I've got to meet this bloke, anyway.'

'I've got to stay here,' I said.

She sat down. 'Well, then I'm staying.'

'Don't be daft. You've been going on about him for weeks.'

'I can't leave you,' she said.

'Go on. I'll be all right. Tell me all about it tomorrow.'

'Sure?' she asked.

I nodded.

I hadn't washed since Monday. When she left I ran myself a bath. I felt frail and brittle; I lowered myself into the water like an elderly person. I kept the door open, so I could hear the phone.

I lay in the water, looking at the empty bottle of bubble-foam that Bobby had been playing with. He had three empty bottles, in fact, lined up. Last week he'd squirted Yasmin and I had shouted at them because they got the floor wet. In the corner was a heap of their dirty clothes, beside the washing machine. Yasmin's favourite pink trousers were there, the ones like Emily's.

The bathwater was stone cold by now. I climbed out, and dressed in the clothes I had been wearing before.

Downstairs, I poured out the rest of the Cinzano and reached for my cigarettes. The packet was empty. It was twenty-five-past ten. The one thing I had to have, it was fags.

I ran out to the car and drove to the pub. I only took a minute. I opened the door. The lights dazzled me; the voices battered at me. I felt I had stepped in from outer-space. I bought twenty Benson and Hedges.

When I got back, five minutes later, I looked at the phone. I was sure it had rung. Why hadn't I taken it off the hook? Had I lost my mind?

I must have gone to sleep in Yasmin's bed, the bottom bunk. I don't remember going to bed; I was still wearing my clothes. I was dreaming I was in a plane and it was bumping through a wood, faster and faster, and never taking off. Its wings banged against the trees on either side and somebody was trying to phone the pilot; I could hear it ringing, up in the cockpit.

I heard it clearly now. It must have been ringing for ages. I rolled out of her bunk, bumping my head, and staggered into the bedroom.

The phone was there, on the bedside table. I grabbed it.

'Hello?' I said, breathlessly.

'It's Salim.'

'Salim!' I froze. 'Where are you?'

'I've been trying to get hold of you.' His voice was crackling and faint. There was a lot of static on the line. 'Been out with your boyfriend?'

'Where are you?' I yelled. 'Where are the children?'

'I've been talking to my lawyer,' he said, 'and I'll contact you again in a few days.'

'Where are the children?' I screamed.

Yasmin's voice came on the line. 'Hello, mum.'

'Yasmin! Are you all right?'

'We're fine,' she said.

'I can't hear!'

She spoke louder. 'Why aren't you here?'

'Where are you?' I yelled.

'I wish you were here,' she said.

'*Where are you*?'

Bobby's voice came on the line. 'Hi, mum.'

'Bobby, darling! Where are you? What's happening?'

'We're just having breakfast,' he said. His voice was so faint I could hardly hear him. 'We've got a cook-bearer and an *ayah*. I'm having a lovely time – '

Suddenly the line went dead. Somebody must have taken the phone from him and put down the receiver.

'Bobby!' I yelled. '*Bobby*!' I started screaming into the receiver. '*BOBBY*!'

Eleven

'I told you, love. Seven hundred.'

'But it cost £3,000,' I said.

It was the next morning. I was standing in a wire compound, full of used cars, on the Canterbury Road.

'Somebody's been playing silly buggers with these gears,' said the salesman, patting my car bonnet. He had an inflamed face; I hated him. 'And the bodywork's in a right old state, isn't it? Seen underneath?'

It was odd, being in the outside world. Everything seemed to be going on as normal. It was raining; cars passed with a hiss.

'Make it a thousand,' I said. 'You've got to!'

'I'm sorry, sweetheart.'

'Please!'

'Well . . .' He paused. Then he gave me a wink. 'I've always been a fool, where women are concerned. Especially pretty women.' He sighed. 'Oh, eight-fifty then.'

'Cash?' I asked.

He nodded.

I walked to Taste Buddies. Lorries thundered past, splashing my legs. I felt weightless. Now I knew that my children were in Pakistan, I wasn't really walking along the verge of the road at all. I didn't exist here.

Sonia was alone, filling devilled eggs.

'Hi,' she said. 'I've decided you're not having my lawyer, he ballsed-up my divorce. But I'm on the track of another one.'

'Can I take some time off?'

'Of course, honey.'

'Er, I was wondering,' I said. 'Can you lend me some money?'

'Sure. I could do a couple of hundred, but it won't go far with those bloodsuckers.'

'What?' I said.

'Lawyers. They have this meter running. Shake your hand and it's fifty quid down the drain. Then they start to refill their pipe, and you're taking out a mortgage.'

'It's not for a lawyer,' I said. 'I'm going to Karachi.'

She stared. 'You can't.'

'Have you got it here?'

'What?'

'The money,' I said.

She wiped her hands and came up to me. 'Listen, pet, you can't just go.'

'Why not?'

'We've got to suss out the legal situation – '

'Bugger the legal situation! He's stolen my children!'

'Wait till we've talked to someone,' she said.

'They're mine!'

'But you don't know anybody in Pakistan,' she argued. 'You can't even speak the language.'

I sat down. 'Christ, Sonia. I thought you'd understand. You've got kids.'

'Yeah, I wish somebody'd steal *them*.' She paused. 'Look, Marianne. What I mean is, you've got to think about *them*. What would happen to them if you went there.'

'I *am* thinking about them! What do you think they feel, stuck in another country halfway across the world?'

'I don't even know where Pakistan *is*,' she said.

I stared at the pile of eggshells. 'How *could* he?'

'He hates you. If he sees you – '

'I'll manage,' I said. 'I just need the money.'

Back home, I had one last search through the house. My hands were trembling, I kept knocking things on to the floor. There was nothing in Salim's desk, no clue as to where his parents lived. I cursed Aziz. On the top of the desk were some photos, in frames – our wedding photo, a picnic on the Downs. The clearest one of Salim was the photo I had taken on the ferry, that day when we were so happy. I wrenched it out of its frame.

Something had been stirring at the back of my mind. I ran up to the children's bedroom and rummaged in their cupboard. At the back was a pile of stuff from school.

I found Yasmin's scrapbook. It was called *All About Me*. She'd made it a few months before; I remembered her bullying us for photos.

I turned the pages, feverishly. On page three was a snapshot: *'My Granny and Granddad'*. Salim had given it to her. It showed his parents, standing outside their house in Karachi. I remembered looking at it curiously. An elderly man; a squat woman in a sari. They looked utterly alien. It had given me a jolt to realize they had brought up Salim, that this was his life before he met me.

The house was modern and white – two storeys high, with a balcony. In front was a garden, surrounded by palm trees or something, and a high white wall.

I was going to tear the photo out, but at the last moment I couldn't bear that. I took the whole book.

My mind raced. There was something else I'd forgotten, something that could be useful. What the hell was it?

I stood on the landing, clutching Yasmin's book. Outside, I heard my next-door neighbour starting up her car. It must be midday; she was going to fetch her husband from work. He always came back for his dinner. I wondered how much they knew. At odd moments, trivial thoughts like this came into my mind. It was like when somebody dies and you wonder what happened to their stuff at the dry-cleaners. I couldn't be going mad, could I, if I still wondered what the neighbours would say?

Salim's shirts. I darted to the chest of drawers, and pulled out the bottom drawer. There they were; the Brian Poole ones. Since I'd laughed at them for being old-fashioned, he had never worn them. All those years ago.

I pulled out a shirt. There was the label: *'Mohammed Ismail's Tailors. Elphinstone Street. Karachi'. My family has used them for years, their stitching is superb.*

I got a pair of scissors and cut off the label. Then I put it into

111

my suitcase, with Yasmin's book and the photo. I sat down heavily on the bed and waited for my heart to stop thumping.

I was standing in the post office, getting my family allowance. I fished out the money from under the grille, and counted it anxiously. I had known the post office man for years; he was an Asian.

'Could I have next month's too?' I asked. 'I've got to go into hospital.'

He shook his head. 'I'm sorry. You have to have a signed letter.'

I paused. 'Listen, can you help me?'

'I'm afraid you have to have a signed letter – '

'No, I don't mean that.' I fumbled in my bag, and brought out a piece of paper and a pencil. 'Could you tell me the Urdu for "Do you recognize this man?"'

'I beg your pardon?'

'The Urdu for "do you recognize this man?"'

He shook his head. 'I'm sorry,' he said. 'I come from Bengal. I don't speak Urdu.'

I paused. 'Oh. Never mind.'

I went out into the street.

I walked to the Coach and Horses. It was three-fifteen. On the way, I passed Darren's mother. She was going to school.

'Aren't you going in the wrong direction?' she said to me, smiling.

When I got to the pub the colonel was still there. He was sitting in his corner as usual. I hurried over to him.

'Make that a large Bells,' he said, holding out his glass. 'There's a dear.'

'I don't work here anymore,' I said.

'Nor you do.' He gazed at me vaguely; he was well oiled.

I sat down beside him. 'You were in India, weren't you?'

He nodded. 'Lahore, Quetta – '

'Can you help me?' I asked, quickly. 'Can you remember some Urdu?'

'You've come to the right chap, my lovely. Spoke it like a native.'

I took out my pencil and paper again. 'What's the Urdu for "Where is this house?"'

'*Syu, mera ghoda eithar la do*!'

'What's that?' I asked.

'Syce, bring me my horse!'

'House?'

'Horse,' he said. 'Syce, bring me my horse! They were all Pathans, you know. Big, strong chaps, flashing eyes – '

'No,' I said. 'I mean – '

'*Bearer, ye chai bahut thonda hai*!'

'What's that?' I asked.

'Bearer, this tea is too bloody cold!'

'I don't want that!' I cried.

'*Tum muze dhokka de pahe do*! You are swindling me, you rascal: your prices are too high!'

He stared into the distance, his eyes glazed. I gave up.

Back home, I phoned the Pakistani embassy and asked about a visa. A man answered the phone. His accent sounded like Salim's; I'd forgotten, all these years, that my husband had an accent. The man told me to hang on; I heard him talking to somebody in Urdu.

He knew who I was, he knew everything about it. He was going to forbid me to go to Pakistan. Everyone in Pakistan knew about this by now; they had closed over my children like a lid. They were whispering my name, Siddiqi, not really my name, in their foreign language. What did Pakistan look like? It was a shape on the map, to the left of India. I knew that much; a bit more than Sonia. Pakistan was a white house, with strange trees in front of it. Salim had a big family, he had told me. He had a lot of cousins. Where had they hidden my children?

The man told me I could come up the next day for a visa. He said I ought to have a cholera jab.

*

Sometime later – it must have been the same day, but dark now – I was sitting in my doctor's waiting room. I was inching through the day, moment by moment. The other people looked as if they came from another planet. I lit a cigarette.

A girl had come in and she was talking to me.

'Has Yasmin got it too?' she was saying.

She was from school. Stacey, that was it. Her mother was with her.

'What?' I said.

'Chicken pox. Is that why she's not at school?' She pulled up her jumper. 'I've got some spots too.'

'Stacey!' said her mother.

'I bet she's given it to me,' the girl said. She pointed to the doctor's door. 'Is she in there?'

'What?' I said.

'Is Yasmin in there?'

I didn't reply.

'She's got my Barbie wedding dress,' she said.

Just then the doctor's door opened and a man came out. The receptionist called me. 'Mrs Siddiqi?' she said.

On the way back, the bus passed the car dealer's pen. In the dark, the cars were spotlit like film stars. Mine was there. It had a sticker on it: 'Excellent Runner – Perfect Condition – £1,999'.

My phone was ringing. Whenever I was out of the house I heard it. My children were trying to speak to me. They wanted to ask me what was happening, they wanted me to fetch them home. How could he tear them away from me?'

My body felt raw and shivery; I felt sick all the time. That night I found myself sitting on their bedroom floor and I was making these wailing noises. They were high, like a cat's, and they went on and on. I wondered, for a moment, who could be making such a weird sound.

I had no idea, then, of the stages I was going to go through. I thought it would soon be over. I was scared shitless, of course. I was terrified of the flight, of being alone, of what I would find when I got to Karachi. But I thought it would be solved. Salim was hot-tempered but he couldn't stay angry for ever. Once I spoke to him he'd see sense. He must.

That's what I thought.

Sonia wanted to come with me, but I knew she couldn't really leave her work and her kids. Besides, she'd lent me all her money. She came round the next morning, with some paperwork, so she could sit by my phone while I went to London.

I got my visa and a plane ticket for the next morning's flight. I can't remember much about that day, Thursday. I felt like a robot. When I was walking back from Ashford station a car stopped beside me, and somebody called my name.

I turned. For a moment I didn't realize who it was.

'Hello, loveliness!' said Terry. 'I'm back!'

He jumped out of his car. I remember staring at him. All I heard was the traffic rumbling by, and there was this man, grinning at me.

He stepped towards me. 'It's me!' he said.

He tried to touch me but I pulled away.

'Hey!' he said. 'It's me, remember?' His face loomed close; he was holding my arm.

'Get away from me!' I shouted.

And then I was running down the street, towards my bus stop.

Nobody had phoned. That night I packed my things, and some of the kids' stuff. Not a lot, because I thought I'd be bringing them back home with me. I just took Yasmin's koala bear and her ear drops and one or two of Bobby's favourite toys.

Sonia stayed the night – she'd left her girls with their dad – and drove me to Heathrow Airport at dawn. We didn't speak in the van. There didn't seem anything left to say.

The departure hall was loud and dizzying. Where were all those people going? They trundled trolleyloads of suitcases. The tannoy made my stomach churn.

Sonia kissed me goodbye.

'Now tell me again,' she said. 'What've you got to go on?'

115

'A photo of Salim, a photo of his parents' house and the address of his tailor.'

'Terrific,' she said, doubtfully. 'Do you also know the Pakistani for "You lousy bastard"?'

I shook my head.

'They don't like pigs, do they?' she said. 'What about "You lousy, double-crossing piece of pork"?'

I smiled weakly.

'That's better,' she said. She took a packet of sandwiches out of her carrier bag and gave them to me. 'Smoked salmon. You can't eat that airline muck.' She gave me a half-bottle of champagne, too. 'Now, remember. Take your malaria pills and keep your pecker up.'

'I don't know what I'd have done without you,' I said.

'Don't worry, pet. You'll find them. He'll have cooled down by now.' She paused. 'Even Salim.' She kissed me again. 'Anyway, they'll be missing *Grange Hill*.'

The tannoy came on. 'This is the last call for passengers for PIA flight 147 for Kuwait and Karachi.'

'Give them my love,' she said. 'Give me a ring.'

We hugged each other.

'Good luck, darling,' she said.

I went through to passport control. When I turned round, she had gone.

Twelve

'Take my advice and steer clear of the omelette.'

There was a man sitting next to me. He was pointing to the menu that the stewardess had given us.

'I made the mistake once,' he said. 'It sort of lingered for days.' He chuckled. 'I expect they use it for their building programme, when they run out of cement.'

I sat there, trapped. Sitar musak played. The plane was full of businessmen. A lot of them were Pakistanis, like the people I'm travelling with now. Already I was in a foreign country. Now that I was on my way, I felt frightened. The last few days had passed in a haze. I hadn't really known what I was doing. Sonia had propped me up. And there had been the flurry of jabs, and packing, and scraping together the money. Suddenly, sitting there in my airline seat, I realized what I was doing. I was crossing the world to find my children. How many millions of people were there in Pakistan? I'd seen pictures of floods in India, and famine, and people swarming. How on earth was I going to find Yasmin and Bobby? I'd have to get to a hotel and stay in it all by myself. I'd never even done *that* before.

I had two photos and a scrap of material. In ten hours I would be there. How could this have happened, so suddenly? A week ago we had been a normal family.

'Allow me to introduce myself.' How long had he been talking? 'Donald Caudell.' He tried to turn in his seat – he was a big, burly bloke – and bumped my sore arm, where I'd had my jab. 'And what brings a lovely girl like you to the armpit of the Orient?'

'Oh . . . Just looking up an old acquaintance.'

'How mysterious!' he said.

'Just somebody I used to know.'

'The plot thickens! Do I smell romance in the air?'

'Do you know Karachi?' I asked.

He nodded. 'For my sins.'

'How big is it? What's it like?'

'Well,' he said, gallantly, *'you'll* have to watch out.'

'Where can I get a map?' I asked.

He laughed. 'A map?'

'Of Karachi,' I said.

'You must be joking.'

'What do you mean?' I asked.

'You've never been there before, I can see that. If we had a map, we could find our way around, couldn't we? And then we might get somewhere, and that would never do.' He paused. 'You can't get anywhere in Karachi – that's the point. I'm in pharmaceuticals; I should know.'

'How do you get somewhere?' I asked, alarmed.

'By not believing anything you hear.'

'What?'

'My dear,' he said, 'you're obviously not acquainted with the subcontinental mind.'

'I am,' I said.

'Believe me, I know these chaps.'

'So do I.'

'I don't just mean buying your newspaper from one. Take it from me, I've been around them for years, and I'll tell you one thing I've learnt.'

'What?' I asked.

'You can't trust 'em.'

I paused. 'Can't you?'

'It's not as simple as lying. That would be too easy. What they do is tell you what they think you want to hear. Quite charming, actually. Also drives you round the ruddy bend.'

Our breakfast trays arrived. Donald tucked in. I tore off a bit of croissant. It was exactly the same meal, I remember, as we've just had now.

'Do you know any Urdu?' I asked him.

'Try me.'

I rummaged under my tray for my paper and pen. 'What's the Urdu for "Do you recognize this man?"'

'Wrong! Far too simple. The answer is, "Maybe I do, maybe I

118

don't. Would you like me to recognize him?" The most useful question is this.'

'What?'

'"How much do you want? A hundred rupees? An air conditioner?"'

'What do you mean?'

He smiled. 'You do have a lot to learn, don't you?'

After breakfast a movie came on, something with Richard Dreyfuss in it. Beside me, Donald ordered tonics and produced a bottle of gin from his briefcase. I had never been on a long flight before. I thought it would never end; in fact, I didn't want it to. As the hours went on I alternated between depression and a sort of blank terror. Outside, the sunset came shockingly soon; the hours had been swallowed up, we were flying into the dark; and yet, in the plane, time seemed to stand still. I tried to read *Cosmopolitan*, but even an article about 'How Love Ends' had a photo of a beautiful model girl, in co-ordinated knits. She wasn't like me. Lunch came and went, or perhaps it was dinner. I think I sat in the toilet for a long time, so I didn't have to speak to Donald. I remember somebody rattling the door.

I don't remember much else. It's too painful. You see, I was hopeful then. It may not sound like it, but I was, underneath.

'Would passengers please return to their seats, as we are now commencing our descent into Karachi . . .'

The door was rattled again. I went back to my seat. The stewardess was trying to take Donald's glass, but he held up his hand.

'One minute,' he said. He drank. 'Might as well arrive with a full tank,' he said to me. 'Bit short on the old *chota pegs*, these chaps. Specially since what's-his-name? Zia.'

I looked out of my window. Down in the blackness, there were strings of lights.

'One more word of advice, my dear,' he said. 'Cover up those pretty arms. The men here, they're Muslims.'

'I know.'

'*Ipso facto*, they're powder kegs.' He chuckled. 'But then, that's probably why you're here.'

*

We arrived in the middle of the night. The heat was suffocating and the airport was packed with men. They stood, pressed against the glass doors, hundreds of them, jostling for a better view. What were they all doing here? They all looked like Salim. They stared at me as I went through passport control; everyone was staring. My T-shirt stuck to me; I could hardly breathe.

'Taxi, *memsahib*?'

A man pushed through the crowd.

'Change money, madam?' Another face loomed up.

Everybody seemed to be shouting; the hall echoed. I wanted Donald now, but he had disappeared.

I saw a booth; the sign said Habib Bank. I must have had my wits about me because I managed to change some money. I remember grabbing the bundle of grimy rupee notes; there seemed to be hundreds of them. Outside, the faces pressed against the glass; they were lit by the street lamps. It was chaos out there.

'Taxi, madam?' There were several men following me. I turned to one of them.

'Can you take me to a hotel?' I asked.

'No problem,' he said. He had a cloth wrapped around his head. 'I take you to first-class hotel.'

'I don't want a first-class one.'

'It's very good hotel, madam,' he said. Some of his teeth were missing.

I clung to him like a child. A porter tried to take my luggage but the taxi-driver waved him away and took it himself. As we moved forward, the crowd shuffled back. The men were dressed in loose pyjama things. I saw a boy; he looked exactly like Bobby, until I got nearer.

And then I was in the back seat of a taxi – a battered, black-and-yellow car – and we were rattling through the dark. Palm-tree trunks flashed past. There were concrete buildings on either side of the dual carriageway. Even in the moving taxi the air felt like cotton-wool. It smelt sickly-sweet, as if the whole city was rotting. I'd never smelt anything like it before. I thought of my children smelling it.

120

Sometime later we stopped outside a lobby. It said Hotel Rehana. It was two-thirty in the morning and the place was empty, except for the receptionist. He greeted the taxi-driver like an old friend and they spoke in Urdu together. Then the cabbie asked me for some money.

'Fifty rupees,' he said.

'But your meter . . .' I began.

'This is airport price, madam. Night price.'

I was too exhausted to argue. Funny to be exhausted when you've been sitting down for ten hours, but I could hardly move. Perhaps it was the heat. I paid him with the foreign notes; at least I'd managed one hurdle. He left; I heard him hawk and spit outside.

'Good morning, madam,' said the receptionist, a young bloke with oiled hair. 'You would like a single room or a double?'

'Single.'

'For how many nights?'

'I don't know,' I said.

'Your passport, please. You are here on business?'

'Sort of,' I said, giving him my passport. Suddenly I knelt down and opened my handbag. I took out the photo of Salim and gave it to him.

'Do you know this man?' I asked.

'I beg your pardon?'

'Do you recognize him?' I asked. 'His name is Salim, his family lives here.'

He looked at the photo. 'I should know this man? He comes here?'

'Not really,' I said.

He gave me back the photo. I pulled out the other snapshot.

'You don't recognize this house, do you?'

He took it. 'Where is it?'

'Here. In Karachi.'

'It is a lovely bungalow.'

'Do you recognize it?' I asked desperately. I knew it was hopeless. He was starting to look at me strangely.

He shook his head. 'There are many such bungalows in Karachi. Which part is it?'

'I don't know. Sure you've never seen it?'

'Karachi, it is expanding so fast. This is your first visit?'

I nodded.

'I hope you enjoy your stay.'

A very old porter appeared from nowhere and took my luggage to the lift. We went upstairs to the eighth floor; he opened the door of a room. The last thing I remember was lying down on the bed, fully clothed. I don't think I even washed my face.

When I woke up it was daylight. Cars hooted, down on the highway. I looked out of the window. It was already very hot. Big black birds wheeled around, slowly, in the sky; they looked like vultures. The city stretched as far as I could see. It shimmered in the heat; a brown haze of pollution lay over it. There were blocks of flats and half-built office blocks; they looked as flimsy as cardboard. There were flat-roofed houses with water tanks on top. Down on the road there was a glittering stream of cars and motor scooters and lorries. I'd never felt so lonely in my life.

I dialled reception.

'Could you give me a phone number?' I asked. 'It's Siddiqi.'

'What is the address?'

'I don't know!'

He said there were hundreds of Siddiqis in Karachi, it was the most common name. I tried a bit longer, and then I gave up.

I washed, and put on a loose blouse to cover my arms. It was half-past eight. I took the lift downstairs. The same receptionist was there. A couple of Pakistani men in business suits sat in the lobby. They eyed me curiously. I had a sudden suspicion that Salim had sent them; he couldn't have, could he? He didn't know I was coming.

I needed a cup of coffee but I couldn't face the restaurant; I could see its plastic sign above a door. I wondered how much the rooms cost here; I hadn't noticed anything the night before. One of the men lit a cigarette. Everything seemed utterly improbable.

Outside, the heat hit me. Traffic thundered past. A taxi was

122

waiting at the side of the road. For a moment I thought it was the same driver as before; everybody looked the same. I went up to him.

'Do you know Elphinstone Street?' I asked.

He half-shrugged. What did that mean?

'Can you take me there?' I asked.

He half-shrugged again. I took the tailor's label out of my bag and showed it to him.

'Do you know this tailor?' I asked.

'*Saddar*,' he said.

'What?'

'Downtown. *Saddar*.'

I waited for him to explain, but he got into the taxi and started the engine. I climbed in. The radio was playing weird, Indian-type film music; the plastic seat had a hole in it. I suddenly thought of Terry. If I'd never stepped into his cab I wouldn't be here, my jeans sticking to the seat, the fluffy ornaments jiggling as we bumped along the highway. It was stifling hot. For some reason I wasn't frightened; perhaps I was too jet-lagged. In England it was three-thirty in the morning. The little fabric label was damp in my hand.

That first morning I hardly noticed the city. I didn't dare notice how big it was. The traffic was thick; everyone seemed to be going to work. Young blokes, two to a scooter, leant down to look at me as they passed. Why did they all grin at me? People hooted their horns all the time. Sometimes we passed a donkey, tottering amongst the lorries, pulling a cartload of engine parts. I was being pulled along in a stream of humanity. Somewhere at the end of it, my children were hidden.

We stopped at a crossroads. A policeman was directing the traffic, swivelling like a ballerina. In the other cars, people stared at me. There were some women sitting in the next taxi; they were veiled in black. They peeped at me, giggling. Amongst the traffic there were three-wheeled scooter things, covered with a plastic, decorated canopy. I remembered now; they were called rickshaws. Salim had told me about them. What else had he told me? For the hundredth time I tried to remember what he'd said about his childhood, the area he grew up in, some clue as to his parents' whereabouts. But I could only remember some stories about stealing mangoes, and teasing his cook-bearer, and going to the beach with his parents. I cursed myself, again, for not listening. But then, when had he ever talked? I didn't know anything about this huge, foreign city. I hadn't even been able to buy a guide book.

We were still waiting at the intersection. Suddenly, something was pressed against the window. It was a baby, swaddled in rags. It had huge eyes, smudgy with mascara.

'*Baksheesh*,' said a woman. She tried to push her hand through the top bit of the window, which was open.

I stared, then I fumbled in my purse and took out some rupee notes. They all seemed to be tens. I gave her one; she grabbed it and sank away into the traffic, as if she were drowning.

We drove on. It seemed to take ages. On either side of us rose up concrete office blocks covered in flimsy wooden scaffolding; some of them were only half-built. 'Ajazuddin Dry Cleaning' said a shop below; 'Tiptop Photocopy House'. Buses passed in a cloud of dust; they were covered with men who clung to the roof, their clothes flapping.

And then the taxi stopped. We were in a shopping street.

'Is this Elphinstone Street?' I asked.

He half-shrugged again, and said something in Urdu. Then he said: 'Twenty rupees.'

'But . . .' The meter said ten but I was too tense to argue. I gave him a twenty-rupee note and got out. He drove off.

I stood on the pavement. There were a lot of shops, but I couldn't see a street sign. People jostled me as they passed. Men sat on the ground, selling cigarettes and shoe laces.

Just then I saw a white Mercedes stop. The driver opened the door and out stepped a Pakistani woman. She was smartly dressed.

I went up to her. 'Excuse me, do you speak English?'

'Of course.'

'What's the name of this street?'

'This street?' she asked. 'Zaibunissa Road.'

She went into a shoe shop. I looked around, helplessly. A man, sitting on a trolley, propelled himself towards me.

'*Baksheesh, memsahib,*' he whined. He had no legs. I turned away and hurried down the street.

'You want T-shirt, madam?' said a voice. '*Vogue* magazine? Step this side.'

I saw a policeman.

'Excuse me,' I said. 'Where is Elphinstone Street?'

'Elphinstone Street?'

I nodded.

'You want Elphinstone Street?'

'Yes, where is it?' My voice rose, squeakily. 'Is it near here?'

'This is Elphinstone Street,' he said.

'Here?'

But he had moved away.

'Yes, madam, you are wanting camel-skin lamp?'

'Madam, would you like carpets, please?'

'*Newsweek*?' said a boy, holding out magazines. '*Herald*?'

I pushed past them and went back to the Mercedes driver.

'Do you speak English?' I shouted at him.

He half-shrugged, like the taxi-driver.

'Where is this place?' I shouted. 'Where am I?'

He said something I couldn't understand. Just then the woman came out of the shoe shop.

'Excuse me,' I said to her. 'Somebody said this is Elphinstone Street.'

She nodded.

'Is it?' I asked.

'Sure.'

'But you said it was something else.'

A beggar came up. The woman waved him away. '*Jao!*' she said. Then she turned to me. 'Elphinstone Street is its old name, the British name. It's been changed now.' She looked at me. 'Hey, didn't we meet at the Kureishis'?'

'What?'

'Aren't you married to that chap at Grindlay's Bank?'

'What?' I said. 'No.'

'You're from England, though?'

I nodded.

'I was in London last summer,' she said. 'But it's getting so dirty, isn't it?'

'Do you know a tailors here?'

'A tailors?'

'A tailor's shop,' I said. I uncrumpled the piece of fabric. 'It's called Mohammed Ismail's.'

She paused to think. Beside us, the traffic hooted. I waited, watching her glistening red lips.

Finally she spoke. 'Ah, I know. That old place.' She pointed down the street. 'It's that side. Near the Reptile Emporium.'

I wanted to throw my arms around her. 'Thanks,' I said.

'They do beautiful handbags, and very cheap,' she said.

'What?'

'The Reptile Emporium.'

She got into her car. I hurried off in the direction she had pointed.

I couldn't find the reptile place. I crossed the next intersection and suddenly I was surrounded by vegetables. I seemed to be in some sort of bazaar. Carrots and potatoes rose up in hillocks on either side of me, and the air was thick with flies. It smelt of garbage. Men sat on the ground, selling lumps of roots. I was crushed amongst the people. I nearly stumbled into a boy, barely older than Bobby; he had a cloth laid out on the ground, with lemons on it.

'*Coolie, memsahib?*'

An old man touched my sleeve. He carried an empty basket. What did he want? What were they all saying? A man passed, bent under a yoke; on either end of it hung swaying cages of green parrots. I pushed my way through the crowd. Little boys ran after me, chattering.

I found myself in a big, dark building full of stalls. They looked like groceries. There was a man, sitting high up behind tins of Horlicks and Colemans mustard. Perhaps he spoke English.

'Where is the Reptile Emporium?' I shouted.

'You want handbags? I know a very good place.'

'I want the Reptile Emporium!' I shouted. 'Where the hell is it?'

'You know World of Saris?'

'No!'

He pointed. 'It's that way. Backside of Paradise Cinema.'

I pushed my way through the crowd, in the direction he pointed. The old man with the basket kept close behind me.

Coolie, memsahib? he muttered.

I was never going to find the tailors. I stumbled over a drain; bluish sewage seeped on to the street. I crossed a road, dodging the donkey carts, and found myself in another shopping area. There were alleys of saris, gold and tinsel, hanging like curtains: 'Ladis Dresses' said a sign. Up above, the buildings were decomposing; their wooden balconies had collapsed. This part of the city seemed older and narrower. Who lived here? And where on earth could my children be? Did they come shopping in a place like this? They only knew Sainsbury's. What did they feel? Were they frightened like me?

I told myself I wasn't frightened, of course. I had to keep going. I pushed my way along an alleyway. Men, sitting hunched at a tea-stall, stared at me. Music played from a radio. Why had I been stupid enough to marry a Pakistani? We had never understood each other. He was as strange to me as these men with their heads wrapped in turbans – no, he was worse because he wanted to kill me. Perhaps they did, too. Their heads turned in their dirty clothes.

I found World of Saris – a big, air-conditioned place – but when I turned the corner I got lost again, and found myself in a lorry park. They had weird lorries here, decorated like gypsies' caravans. Very dark men squatted in the mud, wielding spanners. Nobody wanted me here. A barefoot boy, carrying a tray of tea glasses, shouted something at me. *Ipso facto, they're powder kegs.*

They knew what I had done, that was why they were shouting. They knew I had cheated on my husband. Two of the men rose to their feet. My heart thumped. Gasping, I squeezed my way between two lorries; they had lurid paintings on their sides – a tiger snarling, a cannon exploding. I was completely lost. I ran through some churned-up mud and up an alleyway. I was in another bazaar now. Cooking pots were hung up, like aluminium fruits; they shone blindingly in the sun. The walls were spattered with red spit; a row of men squatted, urinating. I veered away and ran up another alley. Somewhere nearby, a loudspeaker was chanting something – perhaps it came from a mosque. The voice sounded strangled and high. Perhaps they'd all start saying their prayers, like Salim must have done in the bathroom. Was he praying now for me to be punished? Funnily enough, it wasn't my children I missed just then. It was Sonia.

My legs felt weak. I hadn't eaten and I must have walked for miles. It was so hot that my hair felt melted into my scalp. And then I came out into a wide street full of buses. Beside me was a row of jewellery shops, and opposite me was the Paradise Cinema.

And there was the tailors: 'Mohammed Ismail's. Tailors. Lahore, Karachi. Head Office: Rawalpindi'.

It was an old shop, with a dusty dummy in the window. I nearly got run over, hurrying across to it. But when I got to the step, I realized that it was closed. I rattled the door. It was locked.

I burst into tears.

'Yes, madam. You want sunglasses?'

A man stood beside me. He was festooned with sunglasses.

'Where are they?' I sobbed.

'What do you want?'

'Why is it shut?' I wailed.

'It is finished.'

I stared at him. 'It can't be!'

'You want tailor? Can I help you?'

'I must see this one!'

'You German?' he asked. 'American?'

'I've got to see them!'

He spat a stream of red saliva into the gutter. 'They have gone away.'

At this point, I think I sat down on the step. I couldn't even cry anymore. It was hopeless.

'You want clothes made?' he asked. 'I know a good place, all the Air France stewardesses, they go there – '

'I've got to talk to them!' I pointed to the shop. 'It's very important! Oh, shit! What am I going to do?'

He smiled. 'You ladies!'

'It's very important!'

Then he said: 'Maybe I can help you.'

'Can you?'

'The *dursiwallah*, the old man who worked here ... he is nearby.'

I climbed to my feet. 'Where?'

'He is in the small bazaar, backside of here. You want shirts, perhaps, or he makes you some slacks?'

'Where is this bazaar?'

'Please, follow me.'

He walked off, down the street. His sunglasses swung, glinting. We went back to the sari alley; I'd probably been walking around in circles.

'Hello, baby,' said a man. 'You want onyx marble?'

The sunglasses man waved him away. I stayed close to him; he was my only hope. Once or twice I nearly lost him in the crowd.

I followed him along an alley full of shoes, and another full of gaudy kids' clothes.

'This is Bohri Bazaar,' he said.

He turned left, down a narrow alleyway, sunless and stifling. Clothes hung on either side. I ducked my head, brushing past them. And then I realized that the sunglasses man had stopped.

He was standing at a stall. It was closed with a steel shutter.

'This is the tailor,' he said. 'The *dursiwallah*.' He pointed to the blank sheet of metal.

'Where is he? Where's he gone?'

He shrugged. 'Who knows, madam?'

'Is he here usually?'

'I don't know, madam.'

I started banging on the shutter. I battered it with my fists like a madwoman. I think I was shouting. I banged my knuckles against it until they were sore. He'd died. He'd shut down for ever. I would never, ever find him.

When I turned around, the sunglasses man had gone. I was surrounded by men, looking at me.

Thirteen

I woke up, bathed in light. I could hear the hum of traffic out on the Folkestone road. It must be the evening; the light was rosy-pink. Through the wall I heard a door open and close. There was the faint murmur of voices. Salim was putting the children to bed. Why was he always putting them to bed nowadays?

I heard a man's muffled voice, and then a woman laughing. Who was the woman in there? And why was the traffic so loud? I could even smell the exhaust fumes.

I wasn't inside the bed; I was lying on it, fully clothed. I gazed at the ceiling and slowly realized where I was. Hope leaked out of me.

I looked at my watch; it was six in the evening. Far away across the city, I heard that high, wailing sound again. Why were they always saying their prayers?

My inoculation plaster lay crumpled on the bedspread. Outside, against the sunset, the big black birds were still wheeling around. I had a cold shower, dressed in some clean clothes, and went down to reception. I didn't know what I was going to do. I thought: Yasmin and Bobby might be just a mile away. They might be living around the corner. Perhaps they had been to the Rehana Hotel for tea? It seemed amazing, that they had only been in Pakistan since Monday. What was it today – Saturday?

I must have been just standing there, in the lobby.

"Ullo, 'ullo,' said a voice. 'You staying here?'

Donald had walked through the door. I was ridiculously pleased to see him. He looked exhausted; there were wet semicircles under his arms.

'Did you find your mysterious friend?' he asked.

I shook my head.

'Fancy a _chota peg_? _Burra peg_, in my case.'

131

'What?'

'Drinkipoos. Maybe a spot of dinner later? I'll tell you, I could do with some sane conversation. It's taken me the whole bloody afternoon to get a bloody car.' He put on a Pakistani accent. ' "Please wait five minutes, *sahib*. Please wait ten minutes, *sahib*. *Insh'allah*, we find you nice Toyota, *sahib*." *Insh'allah* this, *insh'allah* that, *insh'allah* we'll go to the bloody moon. And this is bloody Avis! I'll tell you, my dear, getting anything done here is like swimming through very thick mulligatawny soup. Blindfolded.'

I was staring at him. 'You've got a car?'

'Pardon?'

'Did you say you've got a car?' I asked.

Five minutes later we were driving along the highway. I had the two photos on my knees. Donald gestured at the concrete office blocks.

'Not exactly your Taj Mahal, are they? A bit short on the old oriental mystery. This is the biggest, busiest, ugliest and most bloody frustrating city in the whole of bloody Pakistan. One huge bloody building site. You say you're from Ashford?'

I nodded.

'Well, this is the subcontinental version,' he said.

'It's so big,' I said. 'How does anybody find anything?'

'There's only one way to do that,' he replied, hooting at a camel cart.

'How?'

'Close your eyes and pray to the Prophet.' He patted my knee. 'It's no place for a lovely girl like you. Lucky you've got old Donald.'

I pointed to the photo of the house. 'How're we going to find this sort of place? It's going to be dark soon.'

'Suburbs here go on for miles.'

We were stuck in the traffic. He kept his hand on the horn, Pakistani-style.

'Hurry!' I said.

'Who did you say lives there?'

I paused. 'Oh, just some people I know.'

'Chairman of Burroughs Wellcome lives near here,' he said. 'Went to a barbecue there once.'

The streets were wider here. He drove more slowly. The sun was sinking in the fiery sky. His hand stayed on my knee, warm as a slab of meat. Behind high white walls I could see modern white houses. Each one was just a little bit different; I had to keep looking at my photo.

'Slower!' I said.

Through an open gate, I glimpsed a gardener – what were they called, *malis*? – hosing a lawn. Red blossoms tumbled over the walls. A car tooted its horn; a servant appeared and opened a gate for the master of the house to drive through. People were coming home from work. Lights were lit, glowing lozenges on either side of gateposts. In the wide, rutted street between the houses, a herd of goats wandered along, nibbling at dusty bushes. Even the goats were different here; they had big, ugly Roman noses. I gazed at each house in turn as we passed, driving as slowly as an undertaker.

'. . . she said she wanted a conservatory. They're all the rage in Chertsey,' said Donald. 'So, anyway, I was in the Gulf a lot last year, and each time I came home, well, there didn't seem much progress made . . . And there was always this chap hanging around, one of the chippies. You know, tight jeans with his little tape-measure fixed on the front.'

'Stop!' I yelled.

I looked at my photo. No, this house had two palm trees in front.

'Sorry,' I said.

He drove on. 'I was a bloody fool,' he said. 'Everyone knew, of course, even the neighbours. But he was half her age! To tell the truth, I thought he had the hots for my daughter.'

Just then, I saw them.

'Stop!' I shouted.

A Pakistani woman was walking along the verge of the street, away from us. She was holding Yasmin and Bobby by the hand. It was almost dark by now; I could hardly see them.

Donald jammed on the brakes and I jumped out. I ran after them; they were three blurs, gleaming in the dusk. They went

133

around a corner. I stumbled; one of my sandals had caught on something, and was half pulled off.

I wrenched my foot out of it and ran on. I rushed around the corner, past a row of bushes.

'Stop!' I yelled to them. 'It's me!'

They didn't hear. They turned in at the drive of a house. I ran after them, limping. They were halfway up the drive when I got to the gates.

'Yasmin!' I shrieked.

They still didn't hear. I saw them, bright in the porch light. The children wore pale pyjamas.

'Yasmin!' I yelled, louder.

The little girl turned and stared at me. Their mother turned.

I backed away. They weren't my kids at all.

'I'm sorry,' I said, or I think I did. I can't remember.

I walked back to the car, slowly, picking up my broken sandal on the way. By the time I reached the car it was dark; night fell so quickly. My heart was still racing.

We had to give up. It was too dark to see anything; besides, I couldn't ask Donald to drive up and down these streets all night. He drove me to a tea-stall – just some wooden tables at the side of the road. Fairy-lights were strung up in the bushes. The tea was sickly-sweet, but I was very thirsty. He turned to me. 'This is how to drink *chai*, Paki-style,' he said. He tipped the tea into his saucer and sipped. 'You know that?'

I shook my head. Listlessly, I scratched the mosquito bites around my ankles.

'You don't know much about life out here, do you?' he said.

I shook my head. I wanted to go back home, to Harebell Close, and sleep for ever.

'But you said you were married to one of these geezers,' he said. I'd told him about Salim by now. He lit my cigarette. 'It's him you're looking for, isn't it?'

I shook my head.

'There's no chance, I suppose, for poor old Donald?'

'I'm looking for my children,' I said, and burst into tears.

*

I was terribly tired but I couldn't sleep that night. Whenever I closed my eyes I heard doors opening and closing, and people whispering. Even though I was up on the eighth floor, the city seemed to be breathing in my ear. I heard every hooting car, every shout. I got up to close the window and gazed down at the thousands of lights. In one of those lit windows, behind one of them, were my children lying awake, too, missing me? I discovered an air conditioner and switched it on, but it hummed so loudly I turned it off again and lay, tossing under my sheet, while a mosquito whined around my hair. Finally I must have slept, because I heard my father looking for me while I crouched, hidden, in one of his garden sheds. Except it wasn't a shed, it was far too big, and something was stirring behind his bottles of weedkiller. I knew I mustn't look, I mustn't see what it was.

When I woke, it was early. I was very hungry. I had a shower and found some fresh clothes in my suitcase. I hadn't unpacked; everything was in the same place as when I'd arrived. How many days had I been here? Sonia's champagne was still in its carrier bag; I was saving it for when I had something to celebrate.

My room was sparsely furnished – a bed, an armchair and a twiddly, inlaid table. Outside my window there was a concrete balcony, with the same sort of twiddly Islamic shapes cut out of it, though some bits had fallen off. I stood there for a moment, gazing down on to the highway. It was another hazy, hot day. I realized that I had only been here since yesterday.

I took the lift down to the restaurant and ate some breakfast – sweetish, singed, flabby squares of toast and an omelette. There was a group of men sitting at another table; they looked jowly and pallid, like Russians. They were speaking in a guttural language I'd never heard before; they looked as if they had just flown in. Nylon curtains were closed against the sun; the room looked gloomy, as if it was under water. A bearer, wearing a cockaded turban, stood beside the domed buffet dishes; a blue flame flickered beneath them. Despite the depressing surroundings I felt full of false energy. I told myself

135

that today the tailor would be there. He must be; he was my only hope.

When I'd finished I went outside and found a taxi.

'Bohri Bazaar,' I said, bossily.

We drove off. The buildings lining the road looked more familiar today. I hated this city, yet I felt tied to its chaotic streets because, somewhere, in one of its houses, my children would be getting up for breakfast. What would they be eating?

The journey seemed much shorter today. We stopped amongst the clogged, honking buses. Alleyways, veiled with clothes, led into the rabbit warren of Bohri Bazaar. I recognized it; there was a shop on the corner selling cardboard suitcases, with fastenings made from old tins.

'Twenty rupees,' the driver said, without turning his head.

'Who do you think I am?' I said. 'Some dumb English sucker?' I paid him the nine rupees it said on the meter, bugger the lot of them, and slipped down the alleyway. Left at the shoes, right at the kids' clothes. Exactly the same clothes hung up, in exactly the same places, as the day before; it was if I'd seen them in a dream.

'You want old carpets maybe, *memsahib*? Very good price.'

I ignored everybody and blindly pushed my way through the bazaar, which was already crowded. And when I reached the tailor's stall the blind was rolled up and he was sitting there.

I stood there for a moment, dumb. I could hardly believe it. He was very old. He was squatting on the floor in front of a sewing machine. Ticker ticker, it went, very fast.

'*Salaam, memsahib*,' he said, lifting his head.

'Er, hello.'

I fumbled for the photo of Salim, and took it out of my bag.

'You know this man?' I said.

The tailor took the photo and looked at it.

'Do you know this man?' I repeated, more slowly.

He didn't reply. Minutes passed. Then he sort of shrugged, and shook his head.

'You don't?' I wailed. 'Are you sure?'

'Excuse me, he doesn't mean no.'

136

I swung round. A young bloke had stepped forward from the T-shirt booth next door.

'He doesn't mean no,' he said.

'No?'

'No.'

'What do you mean?' I asked.

'He means yes. *Gee-han*.'

'What?'

'In Pakistan, this means yes.' He half-shrugged, half-shook his head, just like the tailor. 'Confusing, isn't it? You come from Britain?'

I nodded.

'You know Huddersfield?'

'What?' I said. 'Not really.'

'I lived in Huddersfield. You know Station Road?'

I pointed to the photo. 'Does he know this man?'

The T-shirt man said something in Urdu to the tailor, who replied.

'What's he saying?' I asked.

'He says yes, his family is old customer of his.'

I stared at the tailor. 'Really?'

The T-shirt man spoke to the tailor again. I hardly dared breathe. Then he turned to me.

'He says he is making these *shalwar-kamize* for his children.'

The tailor lifted up a pair of embroidered pyjama things. They were similar to the ones the kids had been sent, years before.

The T-shirt man was talking. 'That is for the little boy,' he said.

A long moment passed. I stared at Bobby's half-finished outfit. People pushed past me but I stood there, transfixed. It was made of beige nylon.

'Can you ask him, where does the man live? The father of this boy?'

The T-shirt man spoke in Urdu. After a long pause, the tailor opened a cardboard box. It was full of visiting cards and scraps of paper. He searched through it. Shyly, I touched the cloth of Bobby's new clothes.

At that moment a boy appeared. He gave the tailor a cup of tea. The tailor said something in Urdu to the T-shirt man, who turned to me.

'He says, would *memsahib* like some tea?'

'Oh – no, thanks.'

The T-shirt man said something to the tailor, who sent the boy away. I waited. The tailor poured some tea into his saucer and sipped it. A fly settled on the rim of the cup. He waved it away. Then he turned and spat.

Finally he went back to sorting through his box. He found a card, and passed it to me. It was printed: 'Rafik Siddiqi Esq.' The T-shirt man took it from me and read out the address, even though it was printed in English.

'Residence – 55 South 4th Street, DHS.'

'DHS?' I asked.

'Defense Housing Society. A very prosperous area.'

I took out a piece of paper and my pencil and tried to write down the address, but my hand was trembling. The T-shirt man did it for me.

'You like the Kinks?' he asked.

'What?'

'That Ray Davies, he's a real minefield of talent. He's still writing songs?'

'Not really.'

He gave me the piece of paper and passed the card back to the tailor.

'Maybe you'd like a T-shirt?' he asked me. 'I can get you a cold drink.'

'No, thanks,' I said.

'Seven Up? Pepsi?'

'I must go. Is it far?'

Despite Huddersfield, the T-shirt man shrugged his head in the Pakistani manner. I paused, then I pointed to a nearby stall. It sold long, chiffon-type veils.

'I want to get one of those,' I said.

'Those?'

'That thing the women wear,' I said.

'The *dupatta*? What for?'

I fumbled in my bag again, and brought out my purse. 'I just want one.'

'Leave it to me,' he said. 'I'll get you a good price.'

He went across to the stall. I pointed out one of the veils. He spoke in Urdu to the stallholder.

He turned to me. 'They're thirty rupees, but as I am his friend he'll sell it to you for twenty.'

'Thanks,' I said.

I bought the veil and wrapped it around my head and shoulders.

'Oh, all that beautiful hair!' said the T-shirt man.

'Can you recognize me?'

He shook his head and put on a cod accent. 'You very *pukka* Pakistani *memsahib* now.'

'I don't know what I'd have done without you,' I said.

'That's OK. Just give my regards to Carnaby Street.'

'What's Urdu for "thank you"?'

'*Shoukriah*,' he said.

I practised it, and then I went across to the tailor.

'*Shoukriah*,' I said, and shook his hand. It was very thin; just a bundle of bones.

A few moments later I was back on the main shopping street. A rickshaw was parked nearby, its engine puttering.

'Can I go in this?' I asked.

'That's for poor peoples,' said the T-shirt man.

'Will you tell him the address?'

He told the driver the address, in Urdu. I climbed in; it had a narrow, plastic back seat, open to the street. I shook the T-shirt man's hand.

'*Shouk . . . shouk . . .*' I said.

'*Shoukriah*. Any time, doll.' And he disappeared into the crowd.

I held the veil across my mouth as we bounced through the traffic. The fringed canopy danced. The driver sat, hunched, in front of me; he wore a funny sort of pillbox cap. I felt exposed to the traffic, and yet disguised. Today I wore baggier trousers; perhaps nobody would recognize me. On the other hand, perhaps the kids wouldn't be there. Salim could have taken them anywhere. Then I heard Sonia's voice: *Cherchez la mère. They always go back to them, the spineless bastards.* I wished she were sitting beside me; she'd think this was a jaunt. She'd know what to do.

We weaved our way through the traffic; I clung to the rail, coughing in the exhaust fumes, as we bumped over potholes. Soon we were out of the centre of town and driving along wider streets. We were in another suburb, similar to the one I had driven through with Donald. 'East 7th Street' said a sign. Then we turned into 1st South Street.

My stomach churned. What would happen if Salim was home? What would happen if his whole family was there and I had to argue with them all? His father ran a construction company; with any luck, he would be out of the house. It was Sunday, but Donald had told me that this was a working day in Pakistan. Perhaps they would all be out.

I didn't dare think of the possibilities. I just concentrated on keeping my wits, and keeping my balance in the flimsy, jolting rickshaw.

It was mid-morning by now, and the streets were empty. A sweeper, his basket beside him, sat on the dusty verge. Some street dogs trotted past, in a pack. We passed house after house, with their high white walls and fancy ironwork gates. The whole place seemed to be asleep; it was very hot. A man pushed along a trolley of vegetables.

And then, suddenly, the rickshaw turned right. 'South 4th Street' said the sign.

I saw the house before the driver did. It was exactly like the photo imprinted on my brain. The rickshaw stopped. The driver switched off the engine.

I climbed out and stood in the street. It was absolutely silent. I hardly dared breathe.

And then I heard them.

It was Bobby's voice. He was shouting at Yasmin. I froze.

They were in the front garden, on the other side of the wall. I could hear their voices, then a squeal.

'Give it back!' shouted Yasmin.

'Shan't!'

'Give it back, or I'll tell *ayah*!'

I gestured to the driver to wait, and tiptoed to the gate. It was ajar. Through the wrought-iron I saw the driveway and the rest of the house. At the far end of the drive, at the back of the building, two servants were squatting, talking to each other. One of them – a dumpy woman in white – might be the *ayah*. They hadn't seen me arrive.

I peered around the gate. There, on the front lawn, were Yasmin and Bobby. They were wearing their English clothes – T-shirts and shorts. They had made a sort of house, with poles and a sheet. Bobby was trying to take something away from Yasmin. Somebody had plaited her hair.

I called out softly: 'Yasmin!'

They turned.

'Bobby!'

Their faces changed. 'Mum!' said Yasmin.

'Ssh!' I said.

I pressed my finger to my lips and beckoned them over. They ran up to me.

'What're you doing here?' asked Yasmin, wide-eyed.

'Quick! Come here!'

The servants still hadn't turned round. The children sidled through the open gate. I hugged them.

'Why didn't you come before?' asked Bobby.

'Ssh! Quick, we're going for a ride!'

'Where are we going?'

'Hurry!' I ushered them to the rickshaw. 'Isn't this fun?' I said, desperately.

I bundled them into the rickshaw.

'Rehana Hotel, quickly!' I said to the driver.

'Quickly is *jaldi*,' said Yasmin. '*Ayah*'s always saying it to us.'

'*Jaldi, jaldi*!' mimicked Bobby.

We were squashed together on the little plastic seat. I sat in the middle, my arms around them tightly. The driver tried to start the engine. It coughed, twice.

'*Jaldi*!' I hissed.

I'd take them back to the hotel. I had just enough money for their tickets. They were already on my passport. My eyes filled with tears; I couldn't believe my luck.

'We've got lots of cousins,' said Bobby. 'They're coming to tea today.'

'Have you missed me?' I asked.

'Yes,' said Yasmin.

The driver tried again. The engine coughed.

'Why did daddy take us away?' asked Bobby.

'He took us to Paris first, on the train,' said Yasmin.

'Oh, *jaldi*!' I wailed.

At any moment somebody would see that the kids were gone. The driver tried the engine again. This time it spluttered into life. The rickshaw jerked forward. He turned it and we started back, along the street.

'I'm here now, darlings,' I said. 'Everything's going to be all right.'

Suddenly I started laughing hysterically. The children started giggling. We clung to one another as the rickshaw bounced along the street. I glanced back at the house. Nobody had come out into the road. We'd done it!'

Just then Bobby squirmed in my arm. 'I want my chinsel,' he said.

'Don't be silly.' I said.

'I want my chinsel!' His voice rose.

'You've got me, now,' I said.

I hugged him. The whole thing had been so ridiculously simple. Tears of laughter and relief ran down my face. Yasmin rested her head on my shoulder.

'I'm glad you've come,' she said.

The rickshaw stopped at the crossroads at the end of the street. Three donkey carts were crossing, pulling carts full of building rubble. The rickshaw-driver hooted his horn impatiently.

'*Jaldi*!' I said.

Suddenly Bobby slithered from my arms, and jumped out of the rickshaw.

'Bobby!' I shouted.

142

He started running off down the street, back towards the house.

'Bobby!' shouted Yasmin.

I shook the driver's shoulders. 'Turn round!' I bellowed.

He didn't understand.

'Turn round, quick!' I shouted.

He tried to start the engine, but it had stalled. It coughed once.

'Wait here,' I said to Yasmin and jumped out. Bobby was running fast, his legs like pistons. I rushed after him.

'*Bobby*!' I yelled.

He had reached his grandparents' house. He ran in the gate. I ran after him. When I got there, he was just picking up his chinsel from the lawn.

'Bobby, quick!' I hissed.

But the *ayah* had seen us. She was running down the driveway with the other servant. She got to Bobby first. He tried to duck, but she grabbed him and held him fast.

I rushed across the lawn and tried to pull him away.

'Give him to me!' I shrieked.

Bobby yelled as I pulled him one way and the *ayah* pulled him the other. She kicked me. I punched her and she screamed.

Strong arms wrenched me back. I squirmed; the other servant wrestled with me. He was very strong. An old woman had come out of the house; she was their grandmother, I recognized her from the photo. She started yelling in Urdu.

'Give me my son!' I shrieked.

Bobby started crying. Yasmin ran through the gates and stared at us. My arms were pinioned behind my back and I was dragged, screaming, into the house.

'They're my children!' I yelled.

The front door was slammed shut behind us. The servant was a huge man; I clawed at his white uniform, but by then another servant had joined him and they dragged me upstairs. They pushed me into a bedroom and slammed the door shut. A key turned in the lock.

I rushed to the window. The lawn was empty. I tried to open the window but it had mosquito-netting over it.

'Let me out!' I shouted.

I rushed back to the door and listened. There were footsteps, and voices speaking in Urdu. Somewhere, far off in the house, I thought I heard Yasmin's voice. I heard the ping of the phone and voices jabbering.

I banged on the door. 'Yasmin! Bobby!'

Nobody came. I don't know how long it took before I heard a car – perhaps ten minutes. Outside, I heard the squeal of brakes. I rushed to the window. Salim jumped out of a car and strode towards the house.

I moved away from the window, breathing heavily. Down in the hall, I heard raised voices. Then I heard footsteps on the stairs.

The key turned in the lock, the door opened and Salim came in, followed by the servant.

'What the hell do you think you're doing?' he shouted.

I tried to push past him, but they both blocked my way.

'Give me the kids!' I shouted. 'They're mine!'

His face was dark and strange; somehow, his features had shrunk. I could hardly recognize him. He wore a business suit.

'Give them back!' I yelled.

He grabbed one of my arms and the bearer grabbed the other. I was half-dragged out of the room and down the stairs. It was like some TV film; I couldn't believe it was really happening. I screamed with pain; the servant was gripping my swollen arm, where I'd had my jab. It all happened so quickly; bump-bump, we went, down the stairs. I felt like luggage.

We were in the hall now. Outside, another car was just leaving. Bobby and Yasmin were sitting in the back seat. Their faces were pressed against the window, staring at me.

'Come back!' I shouted.

But they were driven away.

I don't know what happened then. Salim might have been talking. I was manhandled into his car, I suppose, because the next thing I knew, I was being driven back to my hotel. The bearer, or driver, or whoever he was, sat in the front seat. He seemed completely unperturbed. The back seat of the car was strewn with architectural drawings and plans; Salim must have come straight from work.

We arrived at my hotel. The man opened the door for me politely; it was hard to believe that he'd just been fighting with me. He had a big, luxuriant moustache, waxed at the tips like Terry Thomas's.

'*Sahib* will come here in half an hour,' he said.

And so I went up to my room, sat down on my bed and waited.

Half an hour later there was a knock on the door and Salim came in. There was another man with him; he had crinkly, greying hair and a briefcase.

'This is my lawyer, Mr Hussein,' said Salim.

'Where have they gone?' I shouted.

'We cannot tell you that, Mrs Siddiqi,' said the man. 'They are perfectly safe.'

'Where have you taken my kids?'

'This is their home now,' said the man.

'I'm their home!' I shouted. My throat hurt. 'They belong to me. I'm taking them back to England!'

'No, Mrs Siddiqi,' he said.

'I will!'

'That is out of the question,' he said.

I turned to Salim. 'Who is this man?'

The man cleared his throat. 'We told you. I am acting for Mr Siddiqi-*sahib* and his family.'

'You've got to let me see them'

Salim spoke. His voice was icy. 'You've upset my children.'

'They're mine too!'

'It was very distressing for them,' said Salim. 'You shouldn't have done that. Still, you weren't really thinking of them, were you?'

'You stole them! You stole my children!'

'Mrs Siddiqi – '

'Oh, shut up!' I turned to Salim. 'Get rid of him.' I turned back to the man. 'I want to talk to my husband. This is nothing to do with you, you don't know anything about it. How can you possibly understand? Get out!'

Salim turned to him. 'Now you see what I mean.'

I paused, and took a breath. We were all standing in the middle of the room. I moved over, nearer to Salim, and sat down on the edge of the bed. I pointed to the chair. He didn't move.

'Salim,' I said, more gently. 'We must talk. You and me.'

He didn't respond. With an effort, I tried to change tack. I ignored the lawyer, who stood beside the window.

'Let's go downstairs and have some lunch. Please.'

Still he didn't reply.

I paused, trying to gather my wits. I knew it was no good shouting, he would just flare up. He looked calm, but his face was shiny with sweat. There was a grubby mark down the front of his grey jacket. I wished he would sit down.

This was sickening, but I had to try it. 'Look, we loved each other once,' I said. 'Remember? Remember our flat in Talacre Road?'

He didn't reply. He looked out of the window impatiently, as if he had a more important appointment and I was keeping him waiting. I wished the other man would get out.

I swallowed, and tried again. 'We were happy then, weren't we? Remember painting our kitchen?' I looked at his profile – his straight nose, his firm chin. 'Remember the New Forest, that weekend?' I tried to smile. 'You must remember that. Remember Yasmin being born, and you read Dick Francis to me?' Still he said nothing. I paused. The air conditioner hummed. 'Darling, we're not enemies. We were husband and wife. We love our children, more than anything in the world. You know you can't do this to me. Or to them. You know that.'

There was a silence. Then Salim said, 'You are a whore.'

I stared at him.

He said, 'You are a whore and an adulteress.'

'Salim – '

'You lied and cheated – you, my wife! You said you were working; I looked after the house and the children, and all the

146

time you were . . .' He stopped. 'It's disgusting. You are a filthy woman and unfit to call yourself a mother.'

It was then, I think, that I started crying. I remember pulling a string of loo paper from my handbag. Neither man looked at me.

'I think Mr Hussein should be put into the picture, don't you?' Salim took a piece of paper out of his inside pocket. 'I have the dates here, Farooq. On August 10, she left the children with her mother, who is infirm and almost completely deaf. During that afternoon, of course, she was not at work, but committing adultery with her boyfriend.'

I stared at him. He had put on this pinched, thin voice; it was as if I had never known him.

'On September 4,' he said, looking at the piece of paper, 'our son had measles and a high fever. My wife was ostensibly preparing a dinner party for civil engineers. She returned home at two in the morning, drunk – a not unusual occurrence. There had been no dinner party, of course. She had other fish to fry.' He referred to his paper again, then looked up, as if he was addressing a courtroom. 'On June 14, she never fetched the children from school. I had to be phoned at my office by their teacher. She said she was preparing a banquet – '

'I *was* working that day!' I said. 'I remember!'

'I can go through other dates,' he said, ignoring me. 'A so-called dinner for Japanese businessmen.' He shrugged. Suddenly he seemed utterly Pakistani. 'Of course, I don't have them all. That is because I trusted her. On another occasion she left the children with a nineteen-year-old childminder who had a police record for drug-dealing and abuse – '

'I didn't know then, did I?' I said. 'She was terrific with the kids, they loved her.'

He looked at his paper again, and turned to the lawyer. 'On another occasion, June 5, she was so inebriated that she fell asleep, with the children in the house, and her smouldering cigarette set fire to the armchair – '

'It was only a little hole!' I cried. 'I'd been to Frankie's wedding.' I turned to the man. 'That's a friend of mine. He's making me sound terrible!'

'I'm telling Mr Hussein how you risked your children's safety for the sake of your own animal appetites,' said Salim.

'I didn't! I did have an affair, yes, I admitted it.' I turned to the lawyer. 'I told him it had stopped, it *has* stopped, millions of women do it, millions and millions of married men – '

'Did I?' said Salim.

'No! But it might have been better if you had. It might have made you into a human being!'

'Ah!' said Salim.

I turned to the lawyer. 'He wasn't such a wonderful father, if you really want to know. He was like a lot of men, he was always working – working in the office, working on the house, he was always somewhere else, he never had time to talk to them – '

'I was supporting my family,' said Salim. 'I was making a home for them.'

'What I did was no worse than what he did,' I said. 'It's just called marriage. Are you married?' The lawyer didn't reply. 'Every couple in the world knows what I'm talking about. He's making me sound like a criminal. *He's* the criminal! Nothing I did was anything like this. He's stolen my children!'

There was a pause. Then the lawyer spoke. 'Mrs Siddiqi, your children are now under our jurisdiction. You cannot take them out of the country. If you do so, you'll be charged with child abduction. If you remain here, you will be charged with assault.'

I stared at him. 'But – '

'Your son and daughter are now settled with their family here – '

'*I'm* their family – '

'They have their father, aunts, uncles, grandparents, cousins,' he went on. 'They are very happy here and they start school – when is it, Salim?'

'On Monday,' he said.

'But they go to school in England!' I cried.

'On Monday,' said the lawyer. 'Tomorrow.' He paused. 'You must go back to Britain, Mrs Siddiqi, find yourself a lawyer and

148

start divorce proceedings. Then we can work out terms for access.'

For a moment I thought I hadn't heard him properly. 'Access?' I said. I fumbled for another cigarette. 'I don't believe this,' I said.

Salim cleared his throat. 'Marianne,' he said. 'Let me explain something. May I tell you a story?' He paused, then he sat down on the chair. 'When I arrived in England I had such high hopes. I was young and foolish. I read you Shakespeare's *Sonnets*, remember?'

'Of course I remember,' I said.

'Did you listen? You never listened, Marianne. You just laughed at me. You put on your records, you made fun of me in front of your friends – Salim and his DIY, Salim and his Britvic orange juice.' He paused. 'You've no idea what I gave up to be with you.'

'I thought you wanted to,' I said.

'I did, once. You see, I loved England. I didn't feel a foreigner. I had my heroes to look up to. George Bernard Shaw. Even the Beatles, who made me feel alive. I left my family, whom I loved, and I came to England like . . . like a thirsty animal seeing fresh grass.'

I looked up. He wasn't looking at me. 'Why didn't you tell me then?' I asked.

'I was young, and you were a part of that. In those days.' Suddenly he got up, and turned to the lawyer. 'We must be going.'

I jumped up. 'Where are you going? Where are they?'

'They're not just your children,' said Salim. 'They're mine too.'

'Salim . . .'

He sat down again. There was a silence. I ground out my cigarette.

'You'll never understand,' he said.

'Don't go!' I pleaded.

He looked at the floor again, and spoke more quietly. 'Where was this Great Britain I had heard about? One day, I was walking with our son past the pub you worked in, and you know what happened? He slipped in some vomit and fell, grazing his knee.'

'That's not my fault,' I said.

'Last summer, I took the children to London, and in a restaurant we were racially abused.'

He told me what had happened.

'Why didn't you tell me?' I asked.

'Britain is no place for my children to grow up, now. There is Bobby, with the best education in the world, and people will still think he's a newsagent.'

'That's not true,' I said.

'You wouldn't understand,' he said. 'You'll never understand.'

'Why not?' I asked.

He looked at me. 'You're not a Pakistani.'

'*They're* not Pakistani! They're half-English, they're half mine!'

'We've never understood each other,' he said, sadly.

'We never talked,' I said. 'You were so busy.'

'*You* were so busy.' He paused. 'You said I had no time to be a father. Well, I've learnt my lesson. I'm going to be one now.'

He stood up. I grabbed him.

'That's just an excuse! You were perfectly happy in England! Come back! Come home with me! We can work something out!'

He walked to the door. The other man opened it for him.

'Wait!' I cried. 'Where are you going? Where are they? I've got to see them!'

We were out in the corridor now. They walked to the lift.

'Salim!'

He shook me off. And then the lift doors slid closed, and I had lost them. I ran down the stairs, but by the time I arrived in the lobby they had gone. I looked around desperately for a taxi, but today of all days there wasn't one waiting outside. I rushed back to reception but they couldn't help. A hire car would take at least half an hour, they said. So I rushed out again into the street, and a few moments later a cab arrived.

The driver went fast, perhaps he sensed something. But

when we got to South Street I could see at a glance that the house was deserted. The windows were closed; nobody was around. The children's tent-house was still on the lawn; otherwise, there was no sign of life. Outside, the street was empty. It looked wider than before.

It was two-thirty in the afternoon. I got back into the taxi and told the driver to take me to the British consulate.

It was a big old stone building, shaded by trees. I went inside. There was a Pakistani man sitting at a desk.

'I've got to speak to somebody!' I said. 'My husband's stolen my children!'

I had to wait for what seemed ages, and then I was ushered into an office. A middle-aged British woman was sitting behind a desk. When she saw my face she ushered me into an armchair. She sat down beside me. She had a heavy cold and kept sneezing.

I explained what had happened.

'Mrs Siddiqi,' she said at last. 'I'm afraid there's nothing we can do.'

I stared at her. 'What do you mean?'

'In cases like this . . .' She sneezed, and blew her nose; her handkerchief was decorated with tabby kittens. 'Sorry,' she said. 'We've just installed air conditioning.'

'You must be able to do something!'

'I'm afraid we have no extradition agreement with Pakistan,' she said. 'You'll have to go back to England and take legal advice.' She blew her nose again. 'I'm terribly sorry. We have more and more cases like this. Mixed marriages. Marriages of convenience, simply to get entry into Great Britain.'

'But you've got to get them back! They've got British passports!'

'I'm afraid they're not in Britain now.'

She looked at me again. Then she passed me a box of Kleenex.

'I'm so very sorry,' she said.

*

When I got back to my room I needed a drink so badly that I opened Sonia's champagne and drank it out of a toothmug. It was warm and tasted gluey because I was still crying. I felt dizzy and lay on my bed. I simply didn't know what to do. I rang the house but there was no answer.

It was the early evening when somebody tapped on the door. I jumped up to answer it.

A young Pakistani woman stood there. She was good-looking and smart, dressed in a turquoise *shalwar-kamize*.

'Marianne?' she said. 'I'm Aisha, Salim's sister.'

I stared at her for a moment. Then she shook my hand and came into the room.

'I recognize you from your photos,' she said.

'Where's he taken them?'

She sat down in the armchair. I sat on the bed.

'I'm so sorry about this,' she said. 'It must be dreadful for you.'

'Where have they gone?'

'I can't tell you.'

'You've got to!'

'Marianne, you'll never find them. My family is very large.'

'But they're my children!'

'I know,' she said. 'But nothing will be resolved, with you here. You'll have to go back to England. Salim is terribly angry; you've hurt him very much.'

'*I've* hurt *him*!'

'It's his pride, you see. He's always been so stubborn. He has such a temper.'

'I know.'

'When I was little, we had a fight,' she said. 'He stole my favourite doll, Teggs, and he hid her for two months. I hit him and I screamed at him, but it didn't do any good.' She paused. 'But he's an honourable man, really. He's doing what he thinks is right for the kids.'

'What, taking them away from their mother?'

'I'm trying to talk to him. You must let him simmer down – and he won't if you're still in the country. Just now he hates your guts.'

We sat there for a moment. Down in the city the wailing began again, for evening prayers.

'You must leave it to me,' she said. 'My family, they're very traditional. You know what happens here to a woman who commits adultery?'

I nodded. I didn't, but I didn't want to know.

'You're in Pakistan now,' she said. 'There's one law for men and another for women.'

'But my kids are English.'

'They're half-Pakistani. You must realize that.'

I lit my last cigarette. 'I'm going to get them back.'

'My parents, I've had to fight with them all my life,' she said. 'I couldn't see boys, I couldn't do this, I couldn't do that, I couldn't wear Western clothes. When I wanted to become an air stewardess – oh, we had such a row! "This is no job for a good Muslim girl, from a good Muslim family." But I won.'

'I can't leave them here!'

'You must. Please, trust me; I'm on your side. You'll get them back, I'm sure. But not while you're here, upsetting him.'

'They'll think I don't love them!'

'I'll speak to them. I'll see them tonight. Don't worry.'

She got up and sat beside me on the bed. I looked at her slender wrists, with their gold bracelets.

'Please,' she said. 'Think of me as a sister.'

'You don't think I'm wicked, do you?'

She smiled, and shook her head.

'Did you get your doll back?' I asked.

She nodded. 'Eventually.'

When night had fallen I went back to South Street. The house was in darkness. The children's tent had been cleared away from the lawn. It looked as if nobody had ever lived there.

I stood at the gates for a while. There was no sound but a dog barking, far away, and some insect that was making a scraping noise in the bushes.

Finally I got back into the taxi and returned to the hotel.

*

'I hope you had a pleasant stay in Karachi,' said the receptionist.

I finished paying my bill. It was breakfast time.

Just then, Donald came downstairs.

'There you are!' he said. 'Sorry I wasn't around yesterday, had to drive to Hyderabad. Any luck?'

I shook my head. 'I'm going back to England.'

'So soon? You want me to do something here? This Parsi chap I know, his uncle's chief of police.'

'It wouldn't do any good,' I said. 'But thanks all the same.'

Aisha drove me to the airport. She didn't try to talk to me in the car. She was very kind, and I don't remember if I ever thanked her. At the airport she negotiated our way through the crowds. A beggar woman came up to me.

'*Baksheesh*,' she whined.

'Oh, bugger off!' I said.

Aisha helped me at the check-in. And she got a colleague of hers, a stewardess called Muneeza, to promise to look after me on the plane.

We were going to the departure lounge when I suddenly turned back. I walked over to the beggar woman, who was by the door, and emptied all my remaining rupees into her hand. She grabbed the money. Nobody in this bloody country ever said thank you.

The last thing I remember about the airport was a little mosque, just a sort of plastic niche in the wall. Carpets were laid on the floor, and there were men in it, praying.

Fourteen

Sonia had tidied up my house. The curtains were closed and she had put a vase of flowers in the lounge.

'It looks like somebody's died,' I said. It must have hurt her feelings; I didn't seem to know what to say.

On Monday afternoon, after I had slept, she came back and made me some tea. I couldn't do anything for myself, except smoke cigarettes.

She opened my mail. 'Do you really want to hear this?' she asked. She had a letter from the building society in her hand. 'It says, that as your bankers order for your mortgage repayments has now been cancelled . . . blah blah . . . they would like you to contact them with a view to informing them how your mortgage instalments are to be paid in the future . . . blah blah . . . at your earliest convenience . . . assuring you of our . . . grovel, scrape . . . humble servants, grovel scrape. Rapacious bastards.' She put the letter down. 'Salim's stopped it. What a shit. How much money have you got?'

There was a pause. I was watching a greenfly crawling up a stalk of the chrysanths. What a monumental effort for it.

'Marianne?'

'What?'

'How much money have you got?'

'I haven't got any money.'

'Men,' said Sonia. 'They're so bloody childish. I bet Muslims are even worse. They pretend it's all these big grand words, honour, all that shit. What they really mean is – you took mine so I'll take yours. That's what he's saying. You stole my train set so I'll steal your doll.'

I remember going into the spare room, after she'd gone. There was Bobby's train set – just a simple one, don't know the name, a loop of rail and a train. Salim had played with it more than Bobby, actually.

'Choo-whoo!' he'd whistled. 'Here I come, the two-fifteen from Rawalpindi Junction!' Sometimes, when he choo-chooed, Bobby wasn't even there, he was downstairs watching the TV.

I tried to burn Salim's clothes in the garden. I took out the remaining armful of them – the painting overalls, the tailor's shirts – and heaped them onto the patio. I shoved some newspaper under them and lit it.

A dense cloud of filthy smoke came out of his clothes, seeping between the creases, but they wouldn't burn. Panting, I rushed into the house and got my lighter fluid. I poured it all over them. A blue flame leapt up, and died. The bloody things were only singed.

Furiously I bundled them into a black plastic rubbish bag, which half-melted, and dragged it through the house into the front garden. My neighbour was just coming home.

'Hello!' she said. 'Been away?'

I escaped back into the house.

Later, when I went out for some cigarettes, I met Emily and her mother. They were coming home from school. They must have known what had happened; Emily looked at me in a funny way and Jill ushered her across to the other side of the road. It was as if I had an infectious illness. Or maybe she was just embarrassed. As time went on, and more people knew, I found this often happened. It was as if my kids had been killed, and people didn't know what to say to me. Maybe they thought I'd burst into hysterics. To be on the safe side, they avoided me. They thought it was somehow my fault; that I had been a bad mother.

I hadn't discovered all this, then. Or the stages of fury and despair I was going to go through. I just sat in my empty house, jet-lagged and shell-shocked, watching the TV. The phone didn't ring, except for my parents, who had heard I'd been away. And Ray's Bikes phoned to say that Bobby's bike was mended and when was I collecting it?

I got through that night, with the help of half a bottle of

Cointreau I'd bought in Boulogne. My head ached. I slept in Yasmin's bed.

'Listen, sweetheart' said Sonia. 'I've talked to a couple of lawyers but I think this is out of their league. One was a twelve-year-old chinless wonder and the other's an old duffer who does farm conveyances. We've got to get somebody good on this.'

'I've got to go to the building society' I said. It was the next day. 'Will you wait by the phone?'

'You think they'll ring?'

'It's half-past seven' I said.

Sonia looked at her watch. 'What? It's two-thirty.'

I pointed to the clock. I had set it to Karachi time; it showed seven-thirty. 'They'll be having their dinner' I said. 'Nobody knows what they eat! What about Bobby's peanut butter? What about Yasmin's ear drops? What about school?'

'I've told the school,' she said.

'Yasmin's supposed to be in *Hansel and Gretel*' I said. Then I got up. 'I'm going to be sick.'

Upstairs, in the bathroom, I vomited into the lavatory. Afterwards, Sonia wiped my mouth.

'Why don't they ring?' I said. 'He must be stopping them.'

'You OK?'

'She's got to have her ear drops! What did you tell the school?'

'I said they were bound to be back before the end of term.'

She brushed my hair, tenderly. It hurt, because it was all tangled. I smelt of old sweat, and vomit. I wondered if she noticed.

I saw their faces, in the back of the car. Had they been taken back to the house, now I was out of the way? What on earth were they being told?

'Sure you can drive the van?' Sonia was asking.

I drove into Ashford. It was strange, going out into the real world. People were shopping, just as usual. I parked the van and got out.

'Marianne?'

I turned. There was a woman coming up to me; she looked familiar.

'Remember me?' she said. 'Estelle. I taught you French, remember? At the institute.'

She looked so neat and happy; everybody did. It was a sunny day. Soon I would be getting the children from school.

'Haven't seen you for years,' she said. 'How are the kids? I heard you had a little boy too.'

I burst into tears. She put her arm around me and led me to the Coffee Pot, just up the road. We sat down and I told her what had happened. It was worse, saying it out loud, because then I knew it was real. When I had finished she put her hand on my arm.

'Listen, dear,' she said. 'I have a friend in Lyons, the same thing happened to her. She married an Algerian man, and he has taken her daughters. He took them back on a holiday and he never returned them. It's now, since two years, I think. She belongs to an organization in France, and there is a branch in England too. I will phone her this evening and find out where they are. Shall I do that?'

I got off the train at Charing Cross. It was the next day, or perhaps the day after that. The station was crowded with people; they rushed to and fro. The loudspeaker boomed, but I couldn't hear a word. I flinched at the noise; everything was so loud. A little boy had dropped his Smarties. They had scattered over the ground and he was crying. His mother was slapping him, hard. I rushed up to her and shouted: 'Stop it! Stop it!' She looked at me strangely; people turned their heads.

I nearly went home, actually. I didn't want to see this Linda woman. I was frightened of what she was going to tell me. Her voice had sounded flat, on the phone. She ran the English group for mothers of abducted children. I had never said the word 'abducted' before. It made my kids into a statistic, like road-accident victims.

I took the tube to Kensal Rise and found her flat. It was the top floor of a house, near a street market. She let me in. She

158

was a staff nurse and this was her day off. Her ex-husband was Turkish; he had been a hospital porter, that was how they had met. When she found she was pregnant, they got married. From the start it had been a violent marriage; he used to beat her black and blue. In the end she divorced him.

She told me all this as she made the tea. She was a big, hard-looking woman, wearing a blue tracksuit. She talked in a matter-of-fact voice, as if I was writing a newspaper story and she had said this all before – lots of times. Her flat was crammed with paperwork; she said they had no proper headquarters for the group, it all had to be done here. She showed me photos of her three kids.

'This is Samantha,' she said. 'She'll be eleven now.' It was one of those school photos, in an oval frame. It showed a smiling girl in pigtails. 'This is David, he'll be nine. And this is Annabelle. She'll be six. They're old photos, of course. They've changed since then.'

She said it was four years since they'd gone. Her ex-husband took them to the zoo one Saturday and they never came home. The next thing she heard, they were in Turkey.

'David will be ten on Thursday,' she said. 'I'll send him a present, of course, but his father will throw it away. He'll never know I sent it.' She took the photos from me and put them back on top of her desk. 'They've never got any of my letters, he tears them up.' She pointed to the photo of the youngest girl. 'She can't remember any English now. They can only speak Turkish.'

She didn't tell me any more. She said it was a long story.

'Just now you need help,' she said. 'We've started this pressure group, there's five hundred of us in England, and those are just the women who've come forward for help. God knows how many more there are. And there are many more on the continent.'

'I shouldn't really be here,' I said. 'This hasn't happened to me yet.'

'I hope not,' she replied.

'I'll have mine back soon,' I said loudly. 'It's all been a stupid mistake. We just had a row!'

159

'Here's the address of our lawyer.' She passed me a piece of paper.

'He'll come to his senses soon,' I said.

'Go and see him. He specializes in these cases. He's very good. His name's Tom Wainwright.'

Her face frightened me. Later, I met a lot more women whose kids had been stolen and they all had that same look. They were polite enough – some of them were really nice – but it was like they weren't quite there. Their faces were empty; the life had drained out of them.

I hadn't stayed long. I remember walking through the street market. There was a stall selling bacon joints. They were tightly sealed; inside, they bled against the plastic. The air was frosty; someone was frying chips. I wondered when I would start to feel hungry again.

Just then, one of the stallholders whistled.

'Cheer up!' He called. 'It might never happen!'

'Why don't you spend the night with us?' said Sonia on the phone. 'The girls are cooking pizzas, God knows what the kitchen's going to look like, anchovies all over the floor, it's so blooming expensive when kids cook.' Her words seemed very far away; people's voices did, nowadays, as if they came from the end of a tunnel. 'But they'll be delicious, because it's *Top of the Pops* tonight so *I'll* end up cooking them.'

I shook my head, and told her no. Later that night I went up to my bedroom, got out my scissors and cut off my hair. It was thicker than I'd expected; it took a lot of getting through, and the scissors were blunt. I kept on seeing long bits, left. I chopped the hair off, sort of level with my chin, all the way round. I realized, halfway through, that I hadn't gone to the building society. Well, now I'd look respectable, wouldn't I? Nobody was going to wolf-whistle at me anymore. Good bloody riddance.

Don't buy a dark-blue carpet; every hair shows. I don't think I ever got them all out.

Fifteen

Reality didn't hit me until I went to see the lawyer. I was in a daze when I got back from Karachi. I wandered around as if I was sleepwalking. I didn't really register my visit to Linda, though her children's photos haunted me. I still didn't quite believe that any of it was happening. The days in Karachi seemed so jumbled and lurid that I couldn't believe I had actually gone there. It seemed utterly unreal, to connect my kids to those foreign streets; even though I had held Yasmin and Bobby in my arms, the whole memory wobbled and dissolved like a mirage. This was their home, here in Ashford. Their bedroom looked stale now, and dusty, but here were their toys, their beds – everything that was familiar to them. I still woke up in the mornings expecting to hear their thumps and squabbles through the wall.

Sometimes I still thought that Salim had just taken them to a bed-and-breakfast place along the coast. Funnily enough, I could picture it clearly – it was a house in Hythe, with a veranda facing the sea. They were playing on the beach; Salim was trying to read his newspaper, though the wind kept flapping the pages. Soon they were going to pack it in and come home. It was October now; too cold for sulking. The kids would rush in and switch on the TV; I'd go upstairs with their bags and empty the sand out of their clothes. For some reason, this seaside house was more solid than anything I had seen in Karachi; I'd fixed the kids there, in my head, and they seemed stubbornly to stay on that beach, wearing thin and unsuitable summer clothes. I suppose I had crossed-wires or something. Perhaps I was going round the bend.

The appointment was for Thursday. I borrowed the Taste Buddies van because it was cheaper than the train. I arrived in

161

London early and parked near the British Museum. Tom Wainwright's office was somewhere near there.

I had no long hair to fiddle with; my exposed neck felt chilly. I got out and walked past a church – a big, sooty, place. Suddenly I stopped. I went inside.

It was very cold and it smelt musty and unfamiliar. I had never gone to church as a kid. I'd just been to a couple of weddings. Perhaps I'd walked into the wrong place and this was a Catholic one? It seemed depressing that I didn't even know. I couldn't think what else to do, so I sat down in a pew. The place was dark; there was only one light glowing. It lit a plain wooden cross – no Jesus on it, nobody. It could have been a bit of furniture from Habitat. I squeezed my eyes shut and tried to remember some words. *The Lord's my shepherd, I shall not want.* I remembered that, from school. *He makes me down to lie. In pastures green he leadeth me. The quiet waters by.* I tried to concentrate, but all I pictured was me and Salim lying in the pastures green near Aldington; I heard the far-off voices of the kids and I knew that I was losing Salim and he was losing me. He hadn't noticed my back. It wasn't as tragic as Jesus on the cross was supposed to be, but what difference did that make?

I didn't kneel; I felt too embarrassed. I didn't really know how to do anything. I tried to pray but I couldn't find the words. I asked God to send my kids back to me, but why should He listen? I'd never listened to Him. JESUS SAVES meant as little to me as it must have meant to Salim. My husband was probably prostrating himself in some mosque right now. I looked at my watch, and added five hours. Sunset! Prayer time, as per usual. They even prayed in the blooming airport. Perhaps I was truly unworthy, and the Habitat bit of wood knew that. I'd had an abortion and I hadn't even been sorry. There could have been a child of mine walking the world; thirteen years old now – if it had been a boy, his voice would be starting to break.

I kept my eyes squeezed shut and tried to feel something – even that I was being punished. I'd been a lousy daughter – I still was. I was keeping my parents off, refusing to let them

162

comfort me because they'd say all the wrong things. They loved their grandchildren too. I'd hardly thought about *their* feelings in all this.

I tried to feel some emotion, even guilt. But I couldn't. I just felt cold and uncomfortable. I didn't belong here, and the place knew it.

Just then I heard footsteps. I jumped up. A man had come in.

'Oh,' he said. 'Sorry, I didn't know anyone was here.'

'I'm just going,' I said.

'I didn't mean . . .'

He was a curate or something, because he wore a dog-collar. He looked younger than me. I hurried to the door, blushing like a man who had been caught in a brothel. He followed me and locked the door behind us.

'We shouldn't have to do this,' he said. 'But you wouldn't believe it.'

'Believe what?'

'What people steal nowadays,' he said.

I nodded and hurried away, into the blinding sunshine.

The solicitor's office was in a big old terraced house, with a fancy doorway and railings. You could imagine a coach and horses stopping outside. I rang the bell, nervously.

Inside, though, it wasn't so posh. A black woman ushered me through a large, shabby office. Linda had said it was a radical practice, whatever that meant. There were lots of posters, anyway. And then I was in a room; a man came up and shook my hand.

'Sorry it's such a mess,' he said. 'Do sit down.'

Tom Wainwright had a nice face – dependable, I thought. Or hoped, anyway. He was tall and kind and in his late thirties; he had an educated voice but he wore an awful old corduroy jacket. It's hard to remember exactly what impression he made on me, then; I was too tense.

I sat down and he rang for some coffee. Then he sat down at his desk and took out a notebook. 'Linda sent you, didn't she?' he said. 'Now, tell me what happened.'

There was a big marble fireplace, with a tacky little electric fire shoved in front of it. I gazed at the glowing bar as I spoke.

'I've been married nine years,' I said. 'I mean, I *was* married. I've got two children, Yasmin and Bobby.' I looked up; he was writing. I lit a cigarette. 'Well, two weeks ago we split up.' I paused. 'I don't know where to begin. It started long before that.'

Suddenly, a clock chimed. It was the church nearby. I jumped.

'Sorry,' he said. 'We've got used to it.'

'Well, on the Monday Salim – that's my husband – he went to the kids' school and said he was taking them to the dentist.'

'What happened?

I told him how they had gone on the ferry to France, and then they had flown to Karachi. I told him they were staying at their grandparents' house.

'Do you think this is just temporary?' he asked.

'He's put them into a school.'

'How do you know? You've had contact . . .?'

'I went to Karachi last week,' I said. 'I tried to get them back, but I was caught. He said I had to come home and find a lawyer here.'

There was a long pause. He was writing. Then he looked up. 'How much do you know about the legal implications?'

'I don't know anything! I don't know what to do!'

'I'm here to help you,' he said. He took out a box of Kleenex and gave me a handful.

'I haven't got any money,' I muttered, blowing my nose.

'Don't worry about that now. Did you see your husband in Karachi? What did he say?'

'He said . . . I wasn't a fit mother for the children. He said he was going to bring them up now.'

'What did he mean, you weren't a fit mother?'

'I am fit!' I cried. 'I love them!'

'But did he have cause . . .?' He stopped. 'I'm sorry, but you must tell me everything if I'm going to be able to help you.'

I looked out of the window. There was a rooftop opposite; it

164

had splashes of white pigeon-droppings on it. 'I'd been seeing
. . . someone else.'

'I see.'

I glared at him. 'Don't look at me like that! He's the criminal,
not me!'

He got up and walked over to the mantelpiece. It had heaps
of papers on it; the whole place was overflowing with papers.
'Mrs Siddiqi, let me tell you how we stand. I must warn
you – '

'You've got to hurry!'

'It's a terribly difficult situation. You see, now your children
are out of the country – '

'He stole them! If he'd robbed a bank they'd get him back!'

'I do understand – '

'Have you got kids?' I asked.

He shook his head. 'You must give me the address of his
lawyer.' He paused, then he went back to his desk. 'First, we'll
issue wardship proceedings over here. Your children will then
be in the court's care, but you will be given interim care and
control – '

'But they're not here!'

'I know. We'll also start divorce proceedings. Even if he has
started them there, we should do so here. We'll cite unreasonable behaviour.'

'Unreasonable!'

'If the court orders you to have care and control, which is
likely, we'll take out a court order for the return of Yasmin and
Bobby. If he doesn't honour it, we can take out an application
for his arrest for contempt.'

'How long will this take? So he'll have to bring them back?'

'Legally, yes.'

He got up and went over to the window. He was one of
those tall men who are never comfortable sitting down, their
legs are too long. I looked at the leather patches on his elbows;
one of them was half falling off. How could I trust a man whose
clothes were falling to bits?

'He will have to, won't he?' I asked. 'If the courts make
him?'

He stayed looking at the pigeon-droppings. 'What sort of man is Salim?'

'He will, won't he?'

'Describe him to me. I need to know what we're up against.'

There was a silence. The clock chimed again. Then I said: 'He once said that if I left him he would kill me.' I paused. 'That's what he's trying to do.'

It hit me, that day. I drove home blankly. Now the lawyer had given me the official words, it had become real. Me and my kids, we were a case now. I had a solicitor, and a file. It had all been taken out of my hands. I couldn't remember exactly what he had said; I couldn't think straight, these days. He had talked about extradition agreements, and how there weren't any. He'd said something about the Foreign Office being no help in cases like this, though the group was campaigning about it. Something like that. He had said that now the children were out of the country it was a very difficult situation. How difficult?

Five hundred cases, Linda had said. I hadn't really been concentrating then, either. I hadn't wanted to hear these things, any of them. I had to use every ounce of concentration, just to keep the van on the road.

I don't remember much about the next few days. I went to Taste Buddies but I was in no fit state to work; I kept dropping things and getting measurements wrong. On the Friday I broke a whole bowl of fruit salad. Sonia kept on saying it didn't matter; she was trying to be kind too. Everybody was being kind but what could they do?

I was drinking a lot now – tumblers of white wine from those two-litre bottles. In the evenings I stayed at home, listening for the phone. I missed my children so much I can't start to describe it. I never knew anything could hurt so much. I felt physically ill for them all the time, though it was worse at night. I tried to tidy their room one evening. When I moved their chest of drawers I found a lot of sweet-wrappers squashed down the back, where they had hidden them. They weren't supposed to eat sweets in bed; I didn't know they had. For some reason, that undid me.

I wrote to them, of course. I said I missed them, and that I wasn't sending them lots of things because soon they would be back home with me. I tried to phone them, but each time I got a man's voice speaking in Urdu. He put the phone down on me.

Sonia said that Salim would come to his senses soon; he'd swallow his pride. But I kept remembering things – things I hadn't thought much about, at the time. Once, for instance, I'd bought some electric hair rollers and they kept going wrong. He'd had a terrific battle with the manufacturers; in the end he'd threatened them with court.

'They can't get away with this!' he'd said. 'I'm going to see that justice is done.'

At the time his stubborn anger had pleased me because it was on my behalf – he was defending me. But he wasn't thinking of me, was he? Not really. He was thinking of his own fucking pride.

That's why they shoved their wives into *purdah*, that's why they did all those things I'd never understood. Stupid, infantile, male, fucking pride. Now he was thousands of miles away from me, I suddenly realized how foreign he was – how foreign he had always been. When you live with somebody they're too close – too blurred – for you to see them in perspective. Then you break up and you suddenly see this alien man. It's petrifying.

And yet sometimes, ridiculously enough, I missed him. When I opened the fridge and saw his chocolate-chip ice cream – its box swollen and furry because I hadn't defrosted the freezer – just for a split-second, I missed him. And when I wanted to bore somebody about the kids, and what had happened – just for a moment, I missed him . . . until I realized it was all his fault.

And just sometimes, when I lay awake in our big bed and

the whole world was asleep – just sometimes, I missed him then.

Sonia came round with her daughters, and hoovered the house for me. I heard the clunk of my bottles as they put them into rubbish bags in the kitchen. Her kids even cleaned out the guinea-pig hutch. I sat, smoking, waiting for them all to go. They were being so nice but I didn't want anybody around. It was too much of an effort, to thank them.

And then, on the Sunday night, the phone rang. It was Aisha, Salim's sister. She said she was flying to London the next day and she had a stopover; could we meet at the airport?

I went to Heathrow and waited at Arrivals. My heart pounded, like a lover's. Finally Aisha came out, in her PIA uniform. I pushed through the people and threw my arms around her. We went to sit in the café part, though neither of us could be bothered to get anything to drink.

'They send their love, of course,' she said, unpacking her carrier bag.

'Are they really all right?'

She nodded. 'They're back at my parents' house. They did these for you at school.'

She took out some pieces of paper. They had crayon drawings on them. There was a picture of a camel, and one of a girl in Pakistani dress. Each drawing had a careful, decorative border around it – Islamic-type patterns.

'It's so neat!' I said, looking at the camel. 'Did Bobby do it?'

She nodded. Already my kids were learning things without me. At the bottom of one of the drawings was a message: 'I miss you. Love from Yasmin.' Aisha unpacked a small, embroidered pouch.

'Yas and I made you this,' she said, giving it to me. 'She did the stitching.'

I opened it. Inside were some sweets. They had crumbled during the flight; they fell out on to the table.

'Oh, dear,' said Aisha. 'She put too much marzipan in.' She gave me another packet. 'Bobby's given you some sherbert.'

The sherbert fell out too, powdering the table.

'And this is from Yas,' she said. She took out a small bottle of perfume and sniffed it, doubtfully. 'Ugh. She got it from the supermarket.'

She gave it to me; I sniffed it too. Then she produced her final gift. It was a shrivelled carrot.

'That's for the guinea-pig. They've been going on and on about him. Why's he called Toulouse? Because he's got tiny little legs?'

'What?' I took the carrot. 'I don't know. I think they saw it on a map. Did they say anything else? Any messages?'

'Oh, yes. Bobby says he left three weeks' pocket money in his Robotman box, and can he have it?'

I gave her a carrier bag of things I had collected for them.

'That's the ear drops for Yasmin,' I said, taking them out. 'That's her koala bear, and this is Bobby's green teddy.' I had decided to bring them, at the last moment; the kids might as well have them for a bit. Anyway, it was something to send them. 'Here's some peanut butter for Bobby.'

'Don't worry, we've bought some.'

I paused, and put the jar back into my bag. Then I gave her a letter I'd written.

'This is for them,' I said. 'Make sure they get it, won't you? I've written them some other ones, but will you put this into their hands?'

She nodded.

'When will you see them?'

'In three days.'

'Give them my love,' I said.

'Of course I will.'

'Say I'll see them soon! They'll be coming back soon, I know they will! Tell them that all their friends are missing them at school; tell them I'm doing everything I can to get them back! Tell them everything's waiting, just as they left it! Tell Bobby his bike's ready!'

I paused for breath. Aisha was looking at me. She had a serene, smooth, beautiful face; I couldn't tell what she was thinking.

When she left, I walked back to the Underground. All around me, people were carrying luggage. There was one woman pushing a trolley; her two kids sat on it, on top of the suitcases. I looked at her. Three weeks ago, I had been somebody like that.

Sixteen

'He took them to Buenos Aires,' the woman was saying, 'and I hired a private detective to try and find them.'

'How long have they been gone?' asked the reporter.

'Five years. He was spotted once, in a supermarket, with one of the boys, but he saw the detective and got out the back. It's like the earth has swallowed them up.'

The lights were dark in Linda's flat. It was suffocatingly hot. The woman went on talking in her flat Scottish voice. It was two weeks later, and the group was holding some sort of press meeting. There were a lot of mothers there, women I'd never seen before. All their faces had that hard, drained look. Slides came on a screen in quick succession. They showed children – school photos, holiday snapshots. All the children were smiling. They flashed on the screen, one by one. A little boy flashed on, upside-down. I was jammed between two newspaper reporters, who were writing notes.

'These are some of our lost children,' Linda was saying. 'And there are many, many more. The number of them is growing, as there are more and more mixed marriages, and as the divorce rate throughout the world rises . . .'

Tom was somewhere, the other side of the room. He had made me come here.

'. . . there are children abducted to thirty-two countries,' Linda was saying. 'Many of them are truly lost, their fathers have kept them hidden. The problem is greatest in male-dominated, Muslim societies where fathers have all the rights. In some cases, they have already married their daughters off. Many of these children can no longer speak English. Some of them haven't seen their mothers in ten years. Some of them think their mothers have died. One father showed his little girl a photo of a tombstone and said it was her mother's . . .'

Her voice echoed, down the end of a tunnel. Still the slides flashed on. My heart was palpitating; I was getting these panic attacks nowadays. They mostly happened when I was alone. Sometimes I couldn't breathe.

'. . . nobody can guess the damage done to these children. We must realize that we're talking about children's rights here, not just the rights of parents. Nobody consults the children in these cases; they are just used as pawns. It's an international problem. Our group is putting pressure on the Foreign Office. We urgently need a special mediator to negotiate these cases. We need a fund set up, because these mothers become crippled, financially, and they cannot even get Legal Aid. And we need closer legal liaison between countries, and more pressure at diplomatic level . . .'

I struggled to my feet and pushed past the bodies. Somehow, I got to the door.

Down in the street, I took deep gulps of air. It was a grey, clammy day. My lungs were clogged up. I wished I hadn't left my Valium at home. I started walking down the road, towards the tube.

Then I heard footsteps behind me.

'Marianne!'

It was Tom Wainwright.

'My phone's ringing!'

'What?' he asked.

'I know my phone's ringing!' I looked at my watch. 'I must go home!'

'Come back.'

'Why did you make me go?' I cried. 'That's not going to happen to me! What sort of lawyer are you? You haven't got any of their kids back!'

'For God's sake!' He ran his hands through his hair. 'Look, I've got to go back. Meet me in my office in an hour. I've got something to tell you.'

He left me. I walked on through the market. One of the stalls was already selling Christmas decorations – loops of tinsel. They glinted in the grey air.

*

'Don't you understand?' he said. 'We're trying to drum up publicity.'

We were back in his office. I looked at all the hopeless piles of paper, heaped up on his desk.

'It's nearly Christmas!' I said. 'They've got to be back for Christmas!'

'Let's have a drink.'

He opened a cupboard and brought out a bottle of sherry.

'I don't see what you're doing,' I said. 'Whenever I phone, you just say wait, wait, it's very delicate.' I watched him rubbing two glasses with a piece of Kleenex. 'It's two weeks now!'

'You got through to them yesterday, you said. What happened?'

'They kept asking about Toulouse.'

'What happened in Toulouse?' he asked.

'It's the guinea-pig.' I took the glass of sherry and drank some. 'They care more about their blooming guinea-pig than me. Then they started talking about their new friends at school.' I took another sip. 'He was listening on the other line; I heard him breathing. Then they were cut off. They must think I've abandoned them!'

'Of course they don't.' He paused. 'Look, Pakistan is like these other countries, it hasn't agreed to honour wardship orders. We're mounting a campaign to put pressure on all these countries, Algeria, Tuniaia – '

'I don't care about that! Just get them back!'

'I'm trying.'

'You don't understand. You're just a man.'

'Marianne!' Suddenly he got up, went to some shelves and pulled out a load of files. He flung them down on his desk, one by one. 'Look, there are children here in Dubai, Nigeria, India . . .' They thumped on to his desk. 'America, Brazil, Cyprus, Hong Kong!' His voice rose. 'What do you think I'm *doing*?'

There was a silence. Then I said: 'They're probably ringing me now.'

The church clock chimed; it was so loud it seemed to be

inside the room. Tom gazed at the pile of files on his desk, then he looked up.

'Listen,' he said. 'I'm going to Karachi on Friday.'

I stared at him. 'What?'

'I'm flying out there.'

'Will you see them?'

He nodded. 'I'll try. I need to talk to this Mr Hussein face to face.'

'But . . .' I stopped. 'What about the money?'

'The fund'll pay my fare.'

'But what about the rest?' I asked. 'All this stuff?'

'Don't worry about that now.'

'I haven't got any money!' I cried. 'Do you know what that means? They're coming to turn off my gas!'

'Half my clients haven't got any money. That's why nobody else wants to take them on. That's why the other half has to be mega-settlements in SW3, and who's going to have the house in Tuscany.'

'Bugger your other clients!' I cried. 'Give me the money, and I'll go out there!'

'You mustn't – not just now,' he said. 'I haven't gone out on one of these cases before, I'm going to write a report on it.'

'Don't let me be a report, please! You'll put him against me, you'll say the wrong thing!'

He stood up. 'Marianne, do you want me to act for you or not?'

There was a silence. 'I don't know,' I said. 'I'm sorry. I just sit there. And then I try to go to work and mess it all up, and I know my phone's ringing.'

'You've got to trust me,' he said.

'People look at me as if it's my fault,' I said. 'Like I've been a lousy mother.' I stood up. 'Or else they say I told you so, what do you expect if you marry a Paki?'

'They say that?'

I shook my head. 'Not really.' It was me who said that. I went to the door. 'I see women with kids, and I'm starting to hate them. They complain about them, you see. I suppose *I* did, once.'

He opened the door for me. 'I'll be back on Tuesday. Please trust me.'

I went down into the street. It was lunchtime, and secretaries clattered along the pavement in their high heels. A man, sitting parked in a plumber's van, threw a Kentucky Fried Chicken carton out of the window. Everyone's jaws were working. The sherry had made my head swim, and when I heard my name I didn't register it.

Tom ran up beside me. 'Take this,' he said, breathlessly.

He had something in his arms. 'What is it?' I asked.

'An answerphone. We're getting a new one.' He passed me the machine. 'Do you know how to work it? Here's its little book.'

I put the machine under my arm. 'Are you sure?'

He nodded. 'Now you can know if they've rung.'

'Thanks,' I said.

We stood there for a moment, in the chilly street.

'What're you going to do after work?' I asked him.

'Me?'

'I don't know what people do anymore.' I pointed to the passers-by. 'Where are they all going?'

'I'm going to have my cello lesson,' he said. 'Then I'm going to try and work but I'll fall asleep instead, in front of the TV. My wife left me because I was always falling asleep. Especially in her concerts.'

I smiled. 'Thanks for this,' I said.

My house was emptying. I'd sold Salim's hi-fi, and now his books had gone too. A dealer came and took them all away, in boxes. He paid me cash in grubby notes. The empty shelves made the lounge look larger and colder. With the books gone, I saw the places in the wall where Salim had misdrilled the holes. He had set up our home so painstakingly. There was not a lot else I could sell; it all costs so much to buy, doesn't it, but once you've brought it home nobody wants to take it away. It's just junk.

I was taking Valium, heavily, for my panic attacks. What with those and the booze, sometimes I didn't know if it was

175

day or night. The different times on my clocks didn't help either. At night I lay in bed, listening to that dog barking far away, beyond the houses. Sometimes I thought that he and I were the only things alive in the world. I lay there, looking at my two illuminated clocks. One said one-thirty-five and the other, the digital one, said six-thirty-five. England was sleeping but six thousand miles away my children would be stirring. I didn't even know what they ate for breakfast.

They put up the Christmas lights in Ashford High Street – three strings of them, the same every year, looping between Boots and Kwality Discount Furnishings. There were a few plastic Father Christmases on the street lamps, too; the kids used to love them. Some of them were lit, inside, but most of them didn't work. They hadn't worked when I was a kid either. But the toy shop was blazing with lights, and I was standing inside it. The shelves were piled with robots and monsters, their red eyes glaring from their blister packs. People pushed past me and something electronic was playing 'Oh come, all ye faithful.' I was stroking the ears of a fluffy rabbit. I don't know how I got there. I found myself in all sorts of places nowadays. I must have been there for ages, because an assistant came up to me.

'Can I help you?' she asked.

I went on stroking. 'Got such nice soft ears,' I said.

The toys swelled and shrank; maybe I was drunk. I must have been behaving strangely, because people turned to stare.

Outside it was dark. I walked down the street with my carrier bags. Christmas shoppers passed me – mothers with kids, fathers burdened with boxes of Toshiba equipment. What did they do with it all? Where did it all go?

A car stopped beside me, and I heard my name. For a moment I thought it was Tom again – he always seemed to be trying to catch me up. But it was the Ford Granada, and Terry climbing out.

'Didn't recognize you!' he said.

'What?'

'The hair.' He looked at me. 'Any news, love?'

I didn't know who he was, for a moment. I couldn't

remember when I had met him. Then I shook my head. He opened the passenger door of his car.

'Come in a minute,' he said.

I must have paused, because he touched my arm.

'Come on, Marianne.'

I hadn't seen him for weeks. I got into the car, and he sat down beside me in the driver's seat.

'Sonia told me you went out there.'

I nodded.

'Don't be angry with me, darling,' he said. 'I didn't mean this to happen, did I?'

'No.'

We sat there for a moment. The car smelt of cigarettes; it was very stuffy. Beside us, people walked along the pavement.

'Neither of us did,' he said. 'Come on, let's be honest.'

I said: 'I hated you.'

'It's not my fault. We were in it together, love. I didn't force you to do anything, did I?'

'No,' I said. 'I know.'

There was a silence. In front of us, someone was unpacking TV sets from a lorry.

'We just wanted a few laughs,' he said. 'It would've happened, sooner or later. You know that. If it wasn't me, it'd be somebody else.'

On the floor lay his Country and Western cassettes, and an empty Marlboro packet. It was surprising that anyone even got into a minicab this messy.

'I've missed you,' he said. 'Something chronic. Is there anything I can do?'

I shook my head.

'I'm moving to Maidstone,' he said. 'Mate of mine's opening a driving school there. But I'll stay.'

'What?'

'If you want me to.'

It took me a moment to realize what he meant. I shook my head.

'Sure?' he asked.

I nodded. Now they were unpacking hi-fis. Salim had bought

his from that shop, Lonnie's Electrics. There was a holly frieze around its window. I watched the man trundling the hi-fis across the pavement.

'I've missed your little elbows,' Terry said.

I looked at my watch. 'Better go,' I said, and opened the door.

'I'll give you a lift home.'

I shook my head. 'Thanks, anyway.'

He got out, came round my side and held the door open for me.

'Bye, Terry,' I said.

'Suits you.'

'What?'

'The hair.'

'Oh,' I said. 'Thanks.'

When I got home my answerphone said 'O'. Sometimes it said '1' but that was usually Sonia. It was never my mum or dad because the machine frightened them and they put the receiver down.

I don't remember what I did that night. The next morning I went up to London, to give the toys I'd bought to Tom. But when I got to the office they said he was in court all day, so I left them on his desk. He was flying to Karachi the next morning. I felt ridiculously disappointed that I had missed him.

It was a busy time at Taste Buddies, what with all the Christmas parties. Hours passed in a blur of red faces and paper hats. Office managers tried to chat us up but Sonia kept them away from me. I plunged sticks into little cocktail sausages, deaf to the din from hospitality suites. I had lost so much weight that my skirt was loose. At a Radio Rentals buffet a bloke I'd been at school with didn't recognize me, and asked me the way to the little boys' room. I tipped gnawed chicken bones into the bin and wondered where Tom could be. Had he seen my children yet? In my mind they were forever playing on that lawn, squabbling under their homemade tent like a rerunning film.

I went to collect my family allowance from the post office. The Indian man stamped my book and passed me the money.

'And how are the kiddies, Mrs Siddiqi?' he asked.

I smiled at him. 'Little terrors, as usual,' I said. 'Always squabbling.'

'They do, don't they?' he said. 'At that age.'

'They've been making a house on the lawn,' I said, and went out into the slush. The night before, it had been snowing.

Carol singers came to the house. They sang 'Little Jesus Sweetly Sleep' outside my front door. I was sitting in the dark, watching TV.

I climbed to my feet, closed the curtains and sat down again. They rang the bell twice and then they gave up.

Over the years, I've come to know Heathrow Airport pretty well. Terminal 3, anyway – the International Flights one. Ten years ago, though, I was just a newcomer. The noise and the tannoy announcements unnerved me, then. I always felt I was standing in the wrong place or that I was going to miss the flight.

On the Tuesday I waited for Tom. Next to me was a man with dandruff speckling his shoulders; he held up a cardboard placard that said 'Mr Yumitsu'. I wondered if I should hold up a cardboard placard for Tom; he wasn't expecting me to meet him. I had tried to smarten myself up. Brushing my hair that morning, I noticed that my bleached bits had nearly grown out; I'd become mousy again, like I had been as a child. My heart thumped. I scanned the faces of the people who were coming out of Arrivals; a man, loaded with Christmas presents, was greeted by his wife and kids. He lifted his daughter and twirled her around till she squealed. The Karachi flight said 'Baggage in Hall'.

Finally Tom came out. I waved at him and called out. He stared at me, then he smiled. He wore a khaki bush shirt, like an explorer; he even had a slight tan. He rushed over to me.

*

We sat in the bar.

'How did you get to see them?' I asked.

'I said I had to make sure they were well cared for.'

'And they were?' I insisted. 'You're sure?'

He nodded. 'They seemed fine.'

'Did they talk about me? What did they say? Tell me what they were doing again.'

He smiled. 'I told you. Playing in the garden with some other kids.' He paused. 'My God, I wish women always looked at me like this.'

I smiled. 'Go on. Tell me exactly.'

'Bobby was shooting everything in sight.'

'With what?'

'A sort of Kalashnikov bit of plank. He shot me, actually.'

'Did you fall down?'

'Of course,' he said.

'He likes you to fall down. What was Yasmin doing?'

'Bossing the other little girl around,' he said.

'Sounds like Yas.'

'Making her do some skipping thing.'

'What was she wearing?' I asked eagerly. 'How had she done her hair?'

'I don't know what it's usually like,' he said. 'I think it was sort of pulled back.'

'Did you give them the stuff? Did she like her rabbit?'

'She loved it.'

'Did you tell her it wasn't a proper Christmas present?'

He paused, then he looked up at me. 'Marianne, they won't be back for Christmas. You know that.' He pushed some ice around in his glass. 'It's going to be a long haul. Your husband was very polite, very reasonable – '

'Reasonable? Whose side are you on?'

'I just mean he didn't lose his cool. He's highly intelligent, he has a formidable lawyer, they seemed absolutely intransigent.'

'What?'

'Well – bloody-minded.'

He fished in his bag and brought out an envelope.

180

'It's from your children,' he said, passing it to me. 'I've applied for an interim access visit. They're preparing the divorce papers now; they're writing to me next week.'

I was reading the letter. I froze, then I read it again.

'They're getting a puppy!'

'What?'

I read out the letter. ' "Tomorrow we are going to fetch our puppy. His mother is a pi-dog and he is called Kulfi." ' I stared at Tom, and burst into tears. 'They can't!'

He searched for a Kleenex. In the end he found one of those airline things, pre-moistened towelettes. He tore it out of its wrapper and wiped my face with it, gently. He put his arm around me and I sat there, shuddering, in a mist of eau-de-Cologne.

We stood outside in the queue, waiting for a cab.

'T. S. Eliot said April's the cruellest month,' said Tom. 'I think he forgot about Christmas.'

'What are you going to do?' I asked.

'I usually have dinner with my ex-wife but she's going to Guadalupe. So I'll have to go to my brother's instead and hear him talking about how much his house is worth and how we should all be drinking Australian wine.'

'Don't you, anyway?' I asked in a posh voice. 'The other stuff's muck.'

'He's got a Saab Turbo.'

'He's not like you, is he?' I looked up at him; he was taller than Salim and somehow more battered. Perhaps he was just tired from the flight. He had put on his tweed jacket but he still looked freezing. He was too well-bred to complain. I realized, with surprise, that he was a good-looking man, but completely unaware of it. Soft brown hair; crooked grin. He was too English to be vain. Or maybe his ex-wife had knocked the stuffing out of him.

'I wish one could just have an injection and wake up on Boxing Day,' he said.

'Yes, and then what?'

We shuffled forward in the queue. He bumped against

somebody's suitcase and apologized. I thought: I've never met such a nice man.

'I wish I could help you,' he said.

'You are. Honest.' Then I added, truthfully: 'You're the only person who understands.'

Seventeen

Christmas Day was a nightmare. Sonia had invited me to her flat. My mum and dad came too. Then there were Sonia's daughters and her mum, who said she had been praying for me. We all sat squashed in Sonia's lounge, amongst the debris of dinner. Outside it was raining; it seemed to have been dark for hours. I hadn't heard from my children.

My mum turned to me. 'I don't know what to do with their presents.'

'More port, Dot?' asked Sonia, refilling her glass.

'Pauline at the flower shop,' mum went on, 'she asked, and I didn't know what to say.'

The Two Ronnies were on the TV. Dad pointed to the set. 'I don't like this bit, when he's sitting alone in his chair.'

Zara was trying to crinkle her hair with her new electric crimper.

Sonia said: 'I smell scorching.'

Dad was looking at the TV. 'He always laughs at his own jokes.'

Sonia took the crimper from her daughter and started crimping her hair for her. 'You're going to look like an Afghan hound,' she said.

Dad frowned at the TV. 'Go on,' he said to Ronnie Corbett. 'Get on with it!'

Sonia's mum turned to me. 'I was brought up to believe that Christmas was a time of forgiveness.'

Sonia said to her sharply: 'Not with you and dad it wasn't.'

My mum turned to her mum. 'They wouldn't understand that out there. In Pakistan. They don't even have Christmas.'

'What's on the other channel?' asked dad.

Sonia's mum said to me: 'You always had a proper Christmas, didn't you?'

'Course they did!' interrupted Sonia.

Zara jerked her head. 'Mum, you're pulling!'

Kirsty pointed to her skirt. 'I just felt my button pop.'

My dad said: 'Lovely dinner, Sonia. Think I'll book in here every year.'

My mum fiddled with her hearing-aid. 'It's making that weeing noise again,' she said.

Sometimes I caught Sonia looking at me anxiously. But even she didn't understand, not really. I looked at my watch.

Zara turned to my parents. 'My dad bought me this,' she said. She showed them her new jacket. 'It's suede.'

'*He* can pay the cleaning bills,' said Sonia.

'Bill's done what?' asked my mum.

'Not Bill, bills,' said Sonia. She looked sourly at her daughter's jacket. 'Trust him to get it in beige.'

My dad got up and searched through the wrapping paper. 'Where's the newspaper?' he asked. 'What's happened to *Morecambe and Wise*?'

There was a pause. Then I heard my mum sigh. 'It's not the same without them,' she said.

'What, Morecambe and Wise?' asked my dad.

'What'll I do with his cowboy suit?' she went on. 'He'd set his little heart on it.'

Sonia tried to shut her up. 'Have a tangerine, Dot,' she said, passing her the bowl.

Kirsty found a cracker joke amongst the rubbish. 'What's green and goes camping?' she asked.

'A Brussels scout, dickhead,' said Zara.

'Zara!' said her grandmother. She turned to Sonia. 'Where's she learnt to speak like that?'

'Her dad,' said Sonia.

My dad turned to me. 'You say you couldn't get through?'

I shook my head. 'All the lines were engaged.'

'Operator's probably gone home to put on her sprouts,' he said.

'They had that nice Russell Harty on last night,' said mum. 'Such a nice boy.'

'Lovely drop of wine, Sonia,' said my dad. 'What was it?'

'Californian,' she said.

'You must come and try some of mine,' he said.

Suddenly I couldn't bear it anymore. I stood up.

'I'm off.'

'Already?' asked Sonia.

I nodded. 'Thanks for everything.' I paused. 'Can I borrow your van?'

My dad asked: 'Where're you off to?'

'Just going home,' I said.

Sonia smiled at me. 'Course you can. Sure you'll be OK?'

I nodded.

I drove towards London, fast, the windscreen wipers slewing to and fro. Crates rattled in the back of the van. Tom had given me his home address; it was somewhere in Islington. Blurred lights loomed up; I veered to avoid them. It was eight-thirty on Christmas night and everybody else was pissed, too.

It was a miracle I didn't crash that night. I didn't mind if I lived or died. I was so drunk that I don't remember much about the journey. I must have driven up the M20. Sonia had an A–Z in her van, though I don't recall finding Tom's street in it. I must have parked. There were these tall, terraced houses looming up in the dark – posh, of course, Georgian or something; some of them had fairy-lights in their windows. What happened if he wasn't there? He'd said he was going to have lunch with his brother, and then he wasn't doing anything. Or was it dinner? When was Christmas dinner – lunch or dinner? I willed myself not to sober up and work anything out. It would be too embarrassing to go on. I pushed the bell saying 'Wainwright'.

He was in. A light came on above the door, and I heard footsteps coming down the stairs. And then the door opened and he stood there. He looked rumpled and surprised. Perhaps he had a girl with him.

'Marianne!' He put his arms around me. 'Happy Christmas.'

Now I was there, I couldn't think what to say. He took me in and we went upstairs to his flat. It was a big, messy room, with wooden shutters and lots of pictures. I didn't notice much, that first time. But I remember a fire in the grate and piano music playing.

'Have a brandy,' he said. 'I've had about eight.'

I sat down on the settee.

'I didn't know what to do,' I said.

He sat beside me and put his arm around me. 'That bad, was it?'

I nodded. He put a glass to my lips and helped me sip, as if I were a child.

'Was yours awful too?' I asked.

'Yep.'

'Should've had an injection,' I said.

He poured some more brandy. 'This is nicer,' he said. 'I'm working on it.'

He smiled at me. He was wearing a crumpled, striped shirt. Being drunk suited him. Unlike most men, it made him seem boyish and vulnerable. There was something companionable about him sitting next to me in front of the fire.

'I couldn't go home,' I said.

'I'm glad you've come.' He nodded. Then he put down his glass and kissed my forehead, tenderly.

I put down my glass and wrapped my arms around him.

'I'm so cold,' I said.

He undressed me in front of the fire. I was as limp as a doll. He took his clothes off, too, and we went hand-in-hand into his bedroom. His bed was warm; he'd put on the electric blanket. We climbed in and pulled up the duvet, right over our heads.

For a long time we just lay there, stroking each other. I'd been freezing in the van; he sandwiched my feet between his, to heat them up. Piano music came from the next room. He held me against his skin.

'We can just go to sleep,' he said.

He smelt wonderful — warm and male and slightly peppery. Muffled by the duvet, a car revved up in the street outside. Under my hands, his body grew familiar. I closed my eyes in the darkness, and stroked the smooth inside of his arms and

186

his harder, hairier thighs. I didn't feel aroused; I didn't think I could ever feel lust for a man again. But this was comforting.

Then he started kissing me – deep kisses that tasted of brandy. Our mouths blurred and explored; something stirred inside me. I squeezed my eyes shut and we rolled over.

'I must warn you,' he said. 'I'm pretty rusty.'

'Feel all right to me,' I said.

At last my brain clicked and the blackness flooded in. We made love slowly, scarcely moving, as if we both might break. When he came, he sobbed.

Now comes the difficult bit. I'm so ashamed, even now. It makes me blush to think about it. Blame it on my state of mind, or the drink.

Afterwards we lay still for a long time. His cock dwindled inside me. He stroked my cheek and pulled strands of hair out of my mouth. In the other room, the piano had stopped. Most men fall asleep afterwards but he stayed awake, gazing at me tenderly. The street light filtered through the curtains.

Then he asked: 'Are you all right? Shall I do something?'

I hadn't come, that's why. 'It doesn't matter,' I lied. Suddenly I felt terribly depressed. It was even worse than before. Nothing had worked; I just felt damp.

'Highly unethical,' he said. 'However, I can honestly conclude that after this close consultation I have discovered – ' He smiled at me – 'that you're an amazing woman.'

'I'm not!' I said suddenly.

'You are.'

Then I said: 'Anyway, perhaps it'll help pay my bill.'

He jerked back, as if I'd stung him.

'What?'

'I didn't mean it,' I said.

'What did you say?'

I was so stupid; I repeated it.

'That's disgusting!'

'I was only joking.'

He pushed me away, and sat up. 'So that's why you came here!' He looked horribly hurt.

'No!'

'No wonder he called you a whore!'

'Tom!'

'He was right. You're just a slut – '

'Tom – '

He struggled out of bed, dragging the duvet with him.

'Get out!' he said.

I got up, slowly. I didn't have any feelings, except foolishness at being naked. It was awful. He stood there, holding the duvet against himself.

'You really want me to go?' I asked.

'Get out.'

I went into the other room.

'Shut the door behind you!' he yelled.

I shut the bedroom door. The record was going round and round, with a click. My clothes were lying in a heap beside the embers of the fire. I put them on slowly. My head was throbbing and my eyeballs ached. He didn't come out of the bedroom.

I couldn't think what to say to him, so I let myself out of the flat. Down in the street it was cold and damp. The van wouldn't start for ages. As the engine turned over, groaning, I half-expected him to appear. But he didn't.

Finally the engine coughed into life, and I drove home to Ashford.

I don't know what time it was when I got to the house. The whole world seemed dead. It was the early hours of Boxing Day.

I let myself in. The answerphone said '1'. I pressed the button.

It was Yasmin's voice. She was so faint, I could hardly hear her.

'Hello, mummy,' she said. 'Where have you gone? We wanted to say Happy Christmas.'

Eighteen

Three months passed. I gave up my job at Taste Buddies; I couldn't manage it anymore. Even Sonia's patience had started to wear thin. I didn't have the concentration to work properly; because she was my friend, it made it worse when I made mistakes.

And then there were lots of little things. Kirsty was fourteen now and becoming obnoxious. Sonia would start to complain about her, and then stop. I suppose it seemed trivial, compared to what had happened to me. 'Why don't you go and live with your bloody father!' she shouted at her once. Then Kirsty shut her up and they both looked to see if I'd heard. It was weird, seeing Sonia embarrassed. She wasn't the sort.

I was becoming a liability. Our old jokiness had long since gone; we couldn't think what to say to each other anymore. I kept burning things. You can't cook when you're unhappy. You can't really do anything. I knew she was only keeping me on because she was sorry for me and I needed the money. The breaking-point came when I forgot to lock up one night and somebody broke in and nicked our petty cash. Sonia kept on saying it wasn't my fault – which was such a blatant lie that we both blushed.

So I left, and got a job at Burger Heaven. It was a new, plasticky place in the shopping centre. For some reason, it was easier to work with people who didn't know what had happened. They didn't feel sorry for me. There was a leery manager called Melvyn but he didn't impinge; he was like a gnat buzzing around out of sight. I wore a frilly apron and got through the days in a haze of frying, serving at tables and mopping up ketchup. I didn't tell anybody where I was working, not even Sonia. I sort of withdrew from the world, I suppose.

I spoke to the kids on the phone. At least they were alive, but it was almost worse, to hear their voices and not be able to

189

see them. They were full of news about school and their puppy; they sounded quite happy. I tried to keep my voice bright and not to upset them. They never asked when they were going to see me again. I wondered what Salim had told them. I never spoke to him, though I was sure he was listening on the other line.

I was getting seriously into debt. I owed Sonia a lot of money by now, and I couldn't run the house on my wages. I still collected my family allowance, the post office didn't know that there were no children anymore. But I couldn't manage, and the panic attacks were getting worse. At night I sat in front of the TV, my stomach churning. I had the runs most of the time nowadays; my insides had become very strange.

Funnily enough, the only person I did want to see was Linda, who ran the group. As the winter weeks passed I realized, with a sinking heart, that I was officially one of her lot now: a mother of abducted children. I had struggled against it but now I succumbed. I went up to London a couple of times and she made me hot, sweet tea, as if she were admitting me into hospital. In normal life we would never have been mates – she wasn't my type – but now I felt bound to her. She told me about her marriage and I told her about mine. We said how young and stupid we had been. My marriage was more complicated than I said; they all are – I'm sure hers was, too. But we didn't want to analyse that now. Her case was worse because she had no contact with her kids at all – she couldn't even speak to them on the phone. They were just a dot on the map. Her ex-husband was a simple, violent man. But he was a Muslim, like Salim, and he hated her.

I met some other mothers whose kids had been stolen. I even did some translating for a French mother called Claudine, who came over to give an interview. For a moment, I felt a small spurt of pride that I could do something. None of us had anything in common except this one event. It was like the way you feel about other mothers in the maternity ward when you've all just given birth. This time, though, we weren't united in joy but in despair.

And then one day in March there was a message on my

answering machine. It was Tom's voice. He asked me to make an appointment to see him.

I dressed carefully. I had an almighty hangover and my hands were shaking. I was noticing that, in the mornings. I took the train up to London to see him.

He was wearing the same corduroy jacket he'd worn at our first meeting, but he looked more tired. This time I noticed the paintings; he had them hanging everywhere in his office, he must be loaded. There was one of a lady in a Victorian dress, sitting winsomely at a window. Waiting for her lawyer's bill, I decided. I didn't look at Tom.

He shuffled through his papers. 'You know I had a letter from Mr Hussein,' he said. There was a pause. We were both very awkward and polite. 'It's about money. Now I know you haven't got any.' He looked up and said, bitterly: 'You've made that quite clear enough. What they mean, of course, is the house. They're demanding that you sell it and give half the proceeds to your husband.' He cleared his throat and looked out at the pigeon-droppings, splashed like paint on the roof. 'Now, I would strongly advise you against putting it on the market. If you sell your house and buy a smaller flat, then you will have a less adequate home to offer your children, and this will tell against you.'

'It's up for sale,' I said.

There was a silence. 'What?' he said.

'My house. I've got to do what he says. I don't want him to get angry.'

He looked upset. 'As your lawyer, I must advise you against it –'

'You don't know Salim. I've got to butter him up. I'm in his power, don't you see?'

'But –'

'He took away her doll, you know.'

'Who did?'

I looked at the lady in the dress. The paint glinted in the watery sunshine. There was even a taste of spring in the air. 'But he gave it back in the end.'

191

'What do you mean?' he asked.

Was it last spring we'd had that picnic? The grass was so warm when I buried my face in it. Far off I heard the sound of the children shouting. All that sunshine; all that terrible waste. 'She was called Teggs.'

'Look, I think that in your state you shouldn't take an irreversible decision – '

'What do you mean, my state?' I glared at him.

'You're obviously highly disturbed – '

'I'm not!'

'Come on, Marianne.' His voice changed. 'You won't speak to me. You've become very strange.' He half-rose, and then sat down again. 'I want to talk to you.'

'You are talking to me.'

'Don't be stupid.' He stopped, and pushed his hand through his hair. He needed a haircut; I wondered if there was anyone who would do it for him. We had lain naked together under his blue duvet – wasn't it weird? 'Look, I know it's terrible for you, all this – '

'You haven't a clue!' I pointed to the Victorian lady. 'I can't be like one of your bleeding paintings, sitting there in a crinoline or whatever, looking sad. It's not like that, not in real life.' I glared at him. 'Want to know what it's like? I don't wash, I'm horrible to everybody – even Sonia – all I think about is me, me, me!' I paused to catch my breath. 'It hasn't made me into a better person; it's made me much, much worse! Sometimes I even hate my kids, sometimes I wish they'd never been born! I got a letter from them last week and they sounded so happy I wanted to strangle them! My own kids!' I got up. 'Don't tell me what to feel, see? You haven't got a clue, you and your nice flat and your nice paintings and your nice, civilized, gorgeous ex-wife you even have Christmas with!'

He stood up. 'But I had Christmas with bloody you! Don't you remember?'

I left, and he didn't follow. I wasn't fit for anybody.

*

192

A couple came round to look at the house. They had two boys with them; they filled up the rooms. I felt I was getting in their way; they owned it already.

'Oh, look,' said the woman, standing in the lounge. 'Our curtains would fit.' She touched her husband's arm. 'Nice lot of shelves, Neville.'

I watched them in the garden, prodding around. One of the boys stood on Yasmin's flowerbed. I was going to shout at him but then I realized it was so overgrown he couldn't see the difference. Last year's flowers had gone; it was covered with weeds now. Why do they always grow faster?

I showed them the kids' bedroom. One of the boys climbed up on to Bobby's bunk.

'Bags me have this one!' he cried.

'Come down!' said his mother. She looked around the room and turned to her kids. 'Just look at that! Why can't you be like that?' She turned to me. 'You are lucky! Don't they keep it tidy!'

It was then that something snapped. When they had gone I phoned up the estate agents, and told them to take the house off the market. I just couldn't sell it.

'Wakey-wakey!' Melvyn snapped his fingers in front of my face. 'Now I know we might have had a heavy night last night – some people have all the luck. I know our mind is on something far more stimulating than this, Angel Drawers – perhaps you can share it with me later. However, in the meantime I'd appreciate it if you pulled a finger out as there happens to be three tables need clearing, as they have been for the last half hour.'

He patted my bottom. I moved sluggishly across the floor. Nowadays I seemed to be pushing my way through water. Everything took such a long time.

'Where's the vinegar, miss?' Three blokes sat at a table. I recognized them; they were the ones who had shouted at me and Salim. *Does it rub off?* Years and years ago.

I rubbed the table. Blobs of brown sauce, scattered ash – they rubbed off. I felt quite proud sometimes when I'd given a table a good old rub. I could just stand there looking at it for hours.

Tonight I pretended I was rubbing Salim out. If I rubbed hard enough, he would disappear and then the children would love me again and come home. How could they be so happy without me? I stood up straight; my temples throbbed. In the corner seat sat one of our regulars, a bloke with a toupee who worked at Barclays Bank. He was probing his nostril; he was doing it with a corner of handkerchief, rolled into a point.

And then the door opened and Tom came in. It was raining; his hair was wet.

'I've been looking for you everywhere!' he said.

'What's happened?'

'When do you get off?' He was wearing jeans, so it must have been the weekend. I'd lost track of the days of the week.

I looked at my watch. 'Midnight.'

He went over to Melvyn. 'I'm taking her home. She's not well.' His voice was authoritative; Melvyn stared at him. He said to me: 'Get your coat.'

I fetched my coat. He put his arm through mine and steered me to the door.

'Where're we going?' I asked.

'London. You impossible bloody woman.'

It was better this time. I suppose I like them rough. For such a well-behaved man he was surprisingly violent; I could hardly recognize him. He manhandled me under the duvet, yanking up my legs around him, pushing back my arms the way he wanted. He bit my ear till it hurt.

He shook me alive, waking me up from my long torpor. Though he later became the most considerate of husbands, that night he was angry with me and I deserved it. I flared up, with him; we made love in a sort of lather of desperation.

The next morning he made us breakfast in his living room. He was hopelessly inept but I let him get on with it. Something with violins was playing; I wandered around the room, looking at things.

'That's gorgeous,' I said. 'What is it?'

'Brahms. Want to borrow it?'

I shook my head. 'Flogged the stereo.' I surveyed the room. 'I've never been in a place like this before.'

The room was cluttered with things; he was a real collector. There were old Dinky cars along the mantelpiece, and postcards from abroad, and a school cup for rowing.

He cleared a pile of papers from the table and put down two cups and saucers. 'I didn't mean it,' he said. 'About you being a slut.'

'Oh, you should've seen me in my heyday,' I replied. 'Had these white boots and my leather miniskirt, and the junk I put on my eyes! Ashford's answer to Dusty Springfield. I never washed it off, just loaded on more mascara each day. Got quite archaeological.'

He groaned. 'Oh, I used to see girls like you. Did you have a charm bracelet?'

'Uh-huh.' I nodded. 'And a little gold anklet.'

'I can't bear it.'

'Dunno what you see in me now,' I said.

'Nor do I.' He laid out the plates. 'All you do is shout at me and use my body.' He fetched the knives. 'They all do, of course. My secretary, my assistants, my clients. All those mothers. It's terribly tiring.'

I went up to him and stroked his hair. 'Poor diddums. At least you can claim damages.'

I sat down on the settee. It was one of those things with a raised, curly end. I didn't know what they were called. It was upholstered in faded purple and it smelt fusty. It had probably belonged to an aged relative. The whole place looked like an auction room – and there he stood, boyishly, in the middle of it. He was scratching his head, wondering what he'd forgotten. Perhaps he wasn't used to company. It was odd to think that a few hours earlier he'd grabbed my hair in his fist and pulled my head back, to kiss me.

I got up and went over to a glass case. It was full of pottery figures; they looked ever so ancient.

'What's these?' I asked.

195

'My uncle brought them back from Syria. He was a collector.'

I opened the door and lifted one out. It was a woman with little pointed breasts. 'What's your family like?' I asked.

'They live in this freezing house in Wiltshire. Everyone huddles in the kitchen, around the Aga. The dogs always bag the best armchairs.'

I stroked the pottery woman's belly; it bulged like a pear. 'My family's dead boring,' I said. 'Biggest thrill for my dad is when he gets Herne Bay on his CB.'

'What's that?'

'A dump. One ginormous bus shelter.'

'No,' he said. 'A CB.'

'Citizens' Band radio. He does it in his shed, to get away from my mum. She tells the TV all her secrets. They're a wonderful advertisement for marriage.' I put the woman away and closed the door. 'When Salim came along he seemed so romantic. He used to read me Wordsworth in Wimpy Bars.'

He slapped his head. 'Marmalade!' He fetched it and put it on the table. 'Where did you meet?'

'Evening classes. I was learning French so I could read recipe books. I had this dream, you see.'

'What of?'

'I'd open my own restaurant.'

'You might, one day,' he said.

'Oh, yeah?'

He was standing in his kitchenette, looking inside his fridge. 'Wish I had some eggs for you. How have your parents been, over this?'

'It's almost worse when they're trying to be helpful.' I picked at a hole in his settee. Inside there were black, wiry hairs. 'I know they're upset but I haven't got room for that. It's all I can do to get on the bus in the morning.'

'I wish you didn't have to work in that place,' he said.

'Well, wish away.'

He put some bread into the toaster. I got up and crossed the room. There were two black plastic bags in the corner.

'What's this?' I asked, lifting out a dress.

He turned. 'My ex-wife's running-away clothes.'

196

'But she's run away.'

'I know, but she's living with this volatile chap and it might explode at any moment.'

I pictured him yanking back a woman's head and exposing her smooth white throat. I inspected the dress. 'It's gorgeous. Who did she run away with?'

'An Israeli conductor.'

'On the buses?'

He laughed. 'London Philharmonic. It's an orchestra.'

'I know!' I said irritably.

The toast popped up.

'Come and sit down, he said. He pulled out a chair for me, and sighed. 'Why do women always go for dark, fiery foreigners?'

'Because we're stupid.' I stuffed the dress back into the bag.

He nodded. 'I'm sure it's a sign of sexual immaturity.'

I sat down. He poured me some tea. I had to have it without sugar because he hadn't got any. We munched our toast. He was wearing a red striped shirt and corduroy trousers, he looked rumpled and Sundayish.

'Me and my friends,' I said, 'we used to dress up for blokes like going into battle. "Get on the warpaint", we said. Stilettos and all that.' I sipped my sugarless tea. 'And we were right, weren't we? They were bastards.'

'All of us?'

I swallowed my toast. 'Why did she leave you?'

'I wasn't glamorous enough for her. There she was, flying off to Milan, and I was going to the Lewisham Claimants' Centre.'

'She good-looking?'

He shrugged. 'In a thoroughbred sort of way.'

'Not like me.'

He smiled. 'Not like you.'

'Well, she didn't have kids, did she?'

'She didn't want any,' he said.

'Did you?' I asked.

He nodded. There was a silence. The violins ended with a flourish.

'It all changes, when you have kids,' I said. 'You don't know

197

when it happens, but it happens all right. In the end. Suddenly you look at this bloke and he's talking about Dulux colour cards.'

'You sound so old!' he said.

'Thanks a bunch,' I said sarcastically. I looked at my watch. 'You don't know anything, really.' I felt prickly and restless. 'I think it's tacky, staying friends. A sign of sexual immaturity.' I stood up. 'Thanks for this,' I said, indicating the breakfast. 'Must just hop on the old Concorde back to Ashford.'

He jumped up and put his arms around me. 'She doesn't mean anything, anymore!'

'Salim and me were never friends.'

He turned my face round. 'I don't want to be your friend. I love you!'

'Search me why,' I said.

April arrived, warm and sunny. Out in the garden the grass grew on the carpet squares. In the evenings the kids came out to play in the street again, like hibernating animals emerging after their long winter. A new little girl had moved in down the road; she had become Emily's friend now. They both had roller skates, the new sort like boots, which they wore with patterned tights. I didn't even know the little girl's name; I wasn't part of the family scene anymore, I was a lone woman. I presumed that my neighbours knew what had happened, but nobody liked to talk about it. The grass and weeds smothered Yasmin's flowerbed, and soon I couldn't see where it had been.

Tom came down sometimes and stayed the night. It was strange, sleeping with him in my marital bed; neither of us liked it. I had got rid of every trace of Salim but we still couldn't make love, not the first few times. Once we went out for a walk; I found a pair of Salim's wellington boots for Tom to wear. But they were too small; Salim had narrow, delicate feet and Tom's were enormous. So we ceremoniously flung them into the canal.

He said he wasn't jealous of Salim, just angry with him. But I was bloody jealous of Monica, his ex. She was horribly beautiful – I found some old press cuttings in Tom's flat, while he was out fetching our pizzas. Her Grace Kelly features made me seethe with jealousy; also, in some strange way, it made Tom seem more attractive. What made it worse was her success. She was a concert singer. She had achieved so much in her life and I'd achieved bugger all. I couldn't even manage to be a mother.

I rebleached my hair, for Tom, but I couldn't understand what he saw in me. He said I made him feel alive, which was odd when I felt half-dead most of the time. He found me fascinating, like another species. That seemed to excite him. All the other women he'd known had been well-behaved and middle-class, with Gucci shoes. Most English women, he said, had frigidity bred into them. He said I wasn't like that. Once he compared me to a minor Country and Western singer who'd fallen on hard times. He made up a cowboy song about my smudged mascara and I hit him.

Maybe he felt sorry for me. He had an over-developed sense of responsibility, and I was in need. Oh, I don't know what it was between us. We were both frail, I suppose, and battered. He had emerged, blinking, from his divorce like the kids coming out into the sunshine. For two years he had been ever so lonely, and had buried himself in his work. In the beginning we came together for comfort. But then it grew more complicated.

I didn't tell him I loved him; I couldn't imagine ever loving anyone again. But I was deeply fond of him — so tall and crumpled, with his big feet and his big hands and his total unawareness of his own good looks. I loved giving him pleasure in bed; he was so appreciative. Sometimes I worried that I was relying on him too much because he was so kind. That I felt close to him because he was my lawyer; when he rang, did my heart leap because it was him or because he might have news of my kids?

I didn't like to think about that. All I knew was that I was in no fit state for any man but he seemed to put up with it. And that when I saw his battered Volkswagen, my spirits rose. Just for a while, anyway.

*

199

I had to get a lodger. I didn't want anybody else in the house but I needed the money. So one day, when I was feeling well enough, I cleared out the spare room. Tom helped me take the top bunk in there, which left the kids' room looking denuded and adult. I dragged in the chest of drawers from my bedroom, and a chair, and put an advertisement in the *Kentish Messenger*.

The first person who came was an Indian. When I opened the front door I stared at him. He was younger than Salim, but very similar. He looked like a student.

'I've come about the room,' he said.

For a moment I couldn't speak. And then I said: 'Sorry, it's taken.'

He went away. He probably thought I was a racist bitch.

The next person who came was a travel agent called Anne. She was mousy and quiet and she moved in the next week. I worked most evenings so I hardly saw her, which suited us both.

And then, at the end of the month, I got a phone call from Tom. He said I could go to Pakistan; he had fixed me an access visit to see my kids.

I rushed around to Sonia's flat and we celebrated with a bottle of Martini.

'So when're you going?' she asked, pouring out the drinks.

'Next week,' I said. 'I've got to give up my passport when I get there.'

'They think you're going to kidnap them back?' she smiled. 'Now who put that idea into their heads?'

I lit a cigarette. 'I feel so nervous.'

'Don't be an eejit! They're your kids!'

'They haven't seen me for four months. I don't know how to behave.'

'Just be your own sweet self, silly,' she said.

'What, burst into tears? Some visit that'll be. Loads of laughs.' I drew in a lungful of smoke. 'But if I pretend to be cheerful, that it's all right, then they'll think I don't care.'

'They'll never think that.'

Zara and Kirsty were watching TV. I looked at them, hunched in front of the screen. Bruce Forsyth was on it, wagging his long chin. 'Know the worst thing?' I asked.

'What?'

'That I've got to work out how to behave in front of my own kids.' I took a gulp of Martini. 'What'll I wear?' I paused. 'Know something? I'm almost dreading it.'

'Marianne!' She refilled my glass. I hadn't seen her for some time; I didn't know anything about her life anymore. 'Who's paying the fare? Your new boyfriend?' she asked.

'Me. I've borrowed a bit from the fund and a bit from my parents and I've taken a lodger. She's a travel agent and she's got me a cheap flight.'

'Anyway, you've landed on your feet now,' she said.

'What do you mean?'

'From what you've said, there's a touch of the old private incomes about Tom.'

'He's ever so nice!'

She smiled. 'Exactly.'

'It's not like that!'

'No. Of course not.'

She had cropped her hair short again, and now she had three gold studs in one ear. I wondered what had happened to Raymond, her last bloke. He bred Alsatian dogs and sold them to security firms; I had never trusted him. I missed the old carefree Sonia, with her filthy jokes and high-heeled boots. We had both changed.

'You've got to meet him' I said.

'If I'm allowed,' she answered.

'Don't be stupid.'

She sighed. 'Wish I knew how you did it. You ought to bottle what you've got, and sell it back to poor schmucks like me.' She sloshed some more Martini into our glasses. 'Just don't get too hoity-toity. Just remember who sat beside your phone, day after day, and poured brandy down your throat. What bloke would do that?' She glared at me. 'And don't say Tom.'

*

201

Tom came with me to Heathrow. I was going away for a week. We stood amongst the crowds in the departure hall. I was wearing my most respectable clothes – a midiskirt I'd found at the back of my cupboard, a jacket and cream high heels.

'Do I look all right?' I asked him.

'You look scrumptious.'

'I don't mean that!' I said. I was really tense.

'I know.' He kissed me. 'You look fine.'

I looked around. 'It's more familiar, this place, than my own bleeding home. Funny, isn't it?'

'You've joined the jet-set now.'

I tried to smile, and looked at my watch.

'Promise you'll come back to me,' he said.

'Of course I will!'

'I'm not just talking about the kids.'

I stared at him. 'I hate him!'

'Women are always saying that. And look what happens.' He gave me his camera. 'Now, do you remember how to work it?'

I nodded, and put my arms around him. 'Oh, Tom, I'll miss you.'

'I should hope so.' He smoothed down my hair. 'Good luck, darling.'

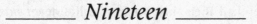

Nineteen

The flight wasn't so terrible this time. I was nervous, of course, but at least I knew what to expect, I wasn't flying into the unknown like some science-fiction film. And this time I knew I was going to see my kids; it was all arranged. I wondered if I would be allowed to see them alone, and what we were going to do. It seemed so strange, to have them for a week but with no home to be in. Would I endlessly take them to the zoo, like divorced fathers on TV? Did Karachi have a zoo?

There was no Donald next to me on this plane, only a portly Pakistani businessman unrolling reams of computer printout. For the first time in months I wondered about Donald. He had been so kind to me, and I'd hardly thanked him. I wondered if his wife was still having it off with her chippie. Stupid bitch.

Suspended above the world in my motionless seat, I tried to see it all in perspective. My marriage had dwindled to a brief interlude; speedily, it had been swallowed up, like the fleeting day we had flown through. Outside the windows, it was already black. I wondered what would have happened if I'd never seen Salim, sitting studiously in his classroom. If I'd gone to the Tuesday class instead, there would be no Yasmin and Bobby alive on the earth, even in distant Karachi. I might have married a motor mechanic and had three boys. I might have married somebody in frozen food and gone to live in Wolverhampton. Uncreated children would be munching their crisps now, and squabbling in front of the TV.

This made me dizzy so I ordered another drink. This was a BA flight, so thank God there was booze.

I had steeled myself for the faces, this time. I wasn't wearing such stupid clothes either. In my long skirt and jacket I felt like somebody's mother. I *was* somebody's mother.

Aisha met me at the airport and took me to the Rehana

Hotel. The same receptionist was there; he greeted me politely. The same people were always there, I discovered as the years went by. There was always the same old man selling *pan* at the corner of Empress Market, the same legless beggar at the traffic lights. They had their tiny patch, and life never progressed. I didn't know that then. I thought I was a seasoned traveller already, but I had no idea how seasoned I would get. If I had known, God knows what I would have done.

It was the middle of the night. Aisha said she didn't mind. She said people in Karachi spent their whole time going to the airport at unearthly hours. Rich Pakistanis jetted all over the world; it was only the poor ones who stayed put.

She took my passport. 'I'm sorry about this,' she said. 'I've got to give it to Mr Hussein's office in the morning.'

'When will I see them?'

'I'll bring them here after breakfast. You can have them to yourself each day, and I'll collect them in the evening.'

'I won't have to see him, will I?'

She shook her head. 'Of course not.'

I had a different room this time, on the third floor. The city seemed closer, here. My children seemed closer. I went to bed but I couldn't sleep. I was as jumpy as somebody on a first date.

At nine-thirty the next morning there was a tap at the door. I rushed over and opened it. Yasmin and Bobby stood there. They were dressed in traditional Muslim clothes, the embroidered *shalwar-kamizes* the tailor had been making for them last time. They looked very tidy, like somebody else's children.

'Yasmin! Bobby!' I cried, kissing them. Bobby squirmed in my arms and wriggled out.

Aisha had come with them. She said: 'I'll see you later.'

I smiled at her gratefully; she left, closing the door behind her.

I stood back from the children. 'Wow! You've grown!'

There was a pause. My voice sounded artificial, like a school teacher addressing a new class. I rushed over to the bed and picked up my carrier bags.

'Look what I've got!'

I emptied a heap of sweets – Smarties, Crunchie bars, lemon sherberts – over the bedcovers.

Yasmin said: 'We're not allowed to eat sweets, except after supper.'

'Don't be daft!' I cried. 'Come on.'

I gave Bobby a Crunchie bar. He looked anxiously at Yasmin. Finally, she nodded and he took it. I patted the bed. They paused; then they sat down next to me.

'You look a bit thin,' I said to Yas. 'How's school? How have you been? I don't know where to start!'

'Who's looking after Toulouse?' Bobby asked.

'Annie. She's my lodger. She's staying in the spare room, the one that you were going to have.'

'Our puppy ate a rat this morning,' said Bobby. 'I hope he's all right.'

'I'm sure he is,' I said.

'He doesn't like it when we go away.'

'He can do without you for a bit!' I said.

There was a silence. I sounded so bright and hectic, I couldn't recognize myself. The children sat stiffly on either side of me. Bobby didn't eat his Crunchie bar; he held it like a relay stick.

They looked the same, but different. I can't quite describe it. Maybe it was because they were three months older. Maybe it was the clothes. Yasmin's hair was pulled back in a new way, with a tortoiseshell clip.

'What are we going to do?' asked Bobby.

'Are you pleased to see me?' I asked.

They nodded. I put my arms around them.

'I've missed you so much,' I said. 'Have you missed me?'

They nodded again, politely. Bobby wriggled his feet, restlessly. He wore new white plimsolls. I rummaged in another carrier bag and brought out some Barbie clothes. I gave them to Yasmin.

'Look what I've got!' I cried. 'For Celeste.' Celeste was her Barbie doll.

'Thank you,' said Yasmin, taking them.

I took out a marine land-cruiser for Bobby, and a load of letters and drawings.

'I went to your class at school, and they did you these.' I gave a picture to Yasmin; it showed an elephant with Yasmin on its back. The elephant's trunk sort of came out of its mouth; kids never got it right. 'That's from Emily. They got a new teacher after Christmas, Miss Monson left to have a baby.' The children took the pictures, one by one, and looked at them. I gave one to Bobby. 'Darren did that. Quite artistic, for Darren.' I spoke in a rush. 'Nan and grandad send their love, of course. So do lots of people. Stacey's had her hair cut short. There's new people moved in down the road – there's a little girl your age, she looks ever so nice. Oh, Sonia bought you these.' I took a pair of fancy sandals out of the carrier bag. They had red glass jewels on the straps. 'Kirsty had some, remember? And you said you liked them.'

Yasmin took off her sandals, and tried them on.

'They're too small,' she said.

'No they're not!' I suddenly felt desperate.

We struggled to get them on, but the straps wouldn't reach around her foot.

'I'm a five now,' said Yasmin.

There was another silence. We sat there in a row. Then I put the sandals back in the carrier bag.

'What are we going to do?' asked Bobby.

I looked at them in despair.

Their school was a crumbling, yellow-stone building. It was shut because it was a holiday that week. There was a high wall around it, and an empty, dusty playground. It was shaded by huge trees with black pods hanging from them. Strange birds made hoarse cries in the branches. An old man with a snowy beard sat dozing at the gate. I tried to imagine my children spending their days in there, behind the thick, stony walls. The whole building was pitted, like nibbled cheese; it looked like a prison.

We stood outside the gate. 'Do they teach you in English?' I asked Yasmin. 'I've never asked. I don't know anything.'

'We have Islamiat Written,' she drawled. 'Islamiat Oral, English Dictation, English Recitation, Urdu Text . . .'

'What's it like?' I asked. 'Do you like the food?'

'Jalal makes us a packed lunch,' said Bobby. 'It's called tiffin.'

'Who's Jalal?' I asked.

'Our cook-bearer.'

'Oh,' I said. 'Him. I remember.'

'He's nice,' said Bobby.

'Very nice,' I said bitterly. 'Terrific left hook. Come on, I'll take your photo.'

'At school?' said Bobby. 'Ugh!'

I went up to the old man. 'Can we go in?' I asked. 'Just for a photo?'

He opened his eyes and shook his head. Or did he shake it? Yasmin stepped forward and said something in Urdu. He shrugged again, and indicated that we could go in.

'That's Urdu?' I asked Yasmin.

'*Abba-ji* teaches me too,' she said.

'Who's *Abba-ji*?'

'Daddy,' she said.

We went into the playground and I stood them against the wall. They posed stiffly, like prisoners in front of a firing squad.

'Come on, big smile,' I said. 'What's green and goes camping?'

'What?'

'A Brussels scout,' I said.

'What's that?' said Bobby.

'Oh, forget it,' I said.

We got back into the taxi and drove through the streets. It was suffocatingly hot, even worse than the autumn. The radio played the theme from *Goldfinger*. We passed prosperous-looking houses, set behind high white walls.

Suddenly, Yasmin pointed. 'That's Sharine's house! Oh, let's stop!'

'Come on,' I said. 'You've got me now.'

She turned, pressing her face to the window. 'She's there! I can see her!'

'Go on,' I said to the driver.

We drove on. Yasmin swung round and gazed longingly out of the back window.

I couldn't think where we could go for lunch. I suggested the hotel, but Bobby said it was boring. So we stopped at an outside café, it was just a collection of tables and chairs, set beside the road, with lightbulbs strung up around it like that tea-stall I'd been to with Donald. Men sat at the tables, dusty cloths wrapped around their heads. A lorry passed, blaring its horn.

'We can't have lunch here,' said Yasmin. 'Daddy'll go mad!'

'Listen, Yas,' I said, sitting down. 'We can eat wherever we blooming well like.'

'It's so dirty,' she said.

'I think it's fun!' I told her.

A man brought us a menu. I looked at it.

'I can't read it,' I said.

Yasmin took it from me. 'It's in script,' she said.

'Can you?'

'Bobby can't yet,' she said. 'But I can. A bit.' She frowned, looking at the greasy sheet of plastic. 'That's . . . mutton tikka, I think . . .' She pointed to the hieroglyphics. 'That's mutton kofta. But today's a meatless day. That's kulfi cone . . .' She pointed. 'It's a sort of ice cream.'

'That's what your puppy's called,' I said.

'It's yummy,' said Bobby.

'It's yukky,' she said.

She frowned at the menu like a mathematician. I thought of all the things inside her head that I would never know. And she would learn more each day. For a moment she didn't seem like my child at all.

A rickshaw stopped nearby. The driver switched off the engine and went to a table.

I pointed to the rickshaw. 'Let's jump in!'

'Mum!' said Yasmin.

I sighed. 'Only joking.'

Bobby said: '*Ayah* won't let us go in those.'

I turned to him. 'You and your blessed chinsel. If it wasn't for that . . .'

208

'I don't have my chinsel anymore,' he said. 'I'm a big boy now.'

'You're not!' said Yasmin. 'You're a baby!'

I pulled a face. 'No more chinsel?'

A fly was crawling across the plastic tablecloth. Bobby squashed it with his finger.

We sat in my hotel room watching TV. There was a film with Rex Harrison in it, but when he spoke Urdu came out in a gruff, low voice. It wasn't quite in time with his lips. We switched channels and watched a game show for a while, two men were bouncing balls around and laughing at themselves. Then that ended and a man's head came on, talking to another man in a studio. The children fidgeted. I sat there, sunk in gloom. I had run out of things to say.

At five-thirty there was a knock at the door and Aisha came in to collect the kids. They jumped up eagerly and went over to her.

'Have you had a lovely day?' she asked them brightly.

They nodded politely.

'Bye,' she said to me. 'See you tomorrow.'

'Bye,' said the kids. They barged into each other in their hurry to get away. I heard them racing to the lift.

'Bags me press it!' came Bobby's faint voice.

I sat on the bed, alone. Somebody had cleaned the room. All their sweets and toys had been put in a neat pile on the table.

I tried to phone Tom that night but I couldn't get through. So I lay on my bed, eating Kit-Kat. I would have killed for a drink. Drenched in sweat, I thought: What a fucking awful country.

The days dragged on, hot and dispiriting. There was a zoo, so I took the children there. Mangy animals stood in cages, gazing at us through the bars. They needed rescuing. Didn't we all?

We seemed to spend a lot of time standing on street corners, waiting for a taxi. That took care of an hour or so. We sat in the Holiday Inn coffee shop and the kids drank milkshakes. That seemed to be the only thing they had missed, apart from

209

the guinea-pig. If I sent Toulouse over, they would be perfectly happy.

They were bored in the hotel. After the first day or so they'd sussed the place out. They'd raced along the identical corridors and gone up and down in the lift. They had explored the newspaper-stand and the little shop next to the restaurant which sold green marble lamp bases and ivory bangles. They had teased the staff.

There was a tiny, dusty garden at the back. It had an empty concrete swimming pool in it, with a notice in English and Urdu saying 'Management Accepts No Responsibility for Loss of Life'. They had chased each other around the pool a few times, unsettling a couple of Air France stewardesses who were sunbathing and trying to read *Marie-Claire*. They knew every item on the menu and ordered lavishly from room service; God knew what my bill was going to be like.

Even then, there was another six hours of the day left. But when we went outside, everyone stared. I took them to a sort of playground place but there weren't any kids there. It was full of young blokes with radios. They crowded around us, jostling to get a better view.

'Bugger off!' I shouted. Misery had made me bolder.

'I don't like it here,' said Yasmin.

I snarled at the men: 'Leave us alone!'

Wherever we went, we had an audience of thousands. The whole of Asia had turned out to watch the pitiful spectacle of me trying to entertain my kids. They should have asked for their money back.

'When are we going home?' asked Bobby.

Yasmin glared at him. 'Bobby!'

'Not yet,' I said.

We were sitting in the hotel room. The TV was on. It was showing a sewing demonstration. We had spent the afternoon walking up and down Elphinstone Street, looking at the shoe shops. We had nearly died in the heat.

Then I remembered the Ludo. I darted to my suitcase and took it out.

'Forgot this,' I said, laying out the board. 'Remember? We used to love it. Bags be red.'

The kids started helping me. My spirits rose.

'You can be yellow,' I said to Yas, 'your favourite colour.'

'It's green now,' she said, picking up the green counter.

'Don't know how to play it,' said Bobby.

'Course you do!' I told him.

'Where's the dice?' asked Yasmin. She started rummaging in the box. 'It's not here.'

'It must be,' I said.

We scrabbled through the box, and then we looked in my suitcase.

'It's not here,' said Yasmin.

'We've got to have the dice!' Frantically, I flung clothes out of my suitcase. 'We've got to!'

The dice wasn't there. For some reason this was the last straw. I burst into tears.

And soon, down in the city, the wailing started. Every evening, when the wailing came from the mosques, it was time for my kids to leave. It was like the factory hooter at the end of the day.

Up in the sky the black vultures wheeled round and round, lazily, waiting for the moment to pick our bones clean.

That night I took a taxi to the house in South Street. The road was dark. I got out of the taxi. There was no sound except the scrape-scrape of some insect in the bushes. I stood in the dust, and looked through the wrought-iron of the gate.

There was a new climbing-frame in the garden. Aisha's and Salim's cars were parked in the drive. I looked up at the house. In the ground-floor window, a light glowed through the closed curtains. I stood still, hardly breathing, trying to catch some sound.

Then, upstairs, a window lit up. Somebody had switched on a light in one of the bedrooms. Just for a moment I saw Yasmin, silhouetted against the window. A woman's head moved past her; it must be the *ayah*. I heard Bobby's voice, faintly, and then a muffled laugh. Then the *ayah* drew the curtains closed.

211

I stood there for a while. Behind me, I heard the scrape of a match as the taxi-driver lit a cigarette. The climbing-frame gleamed in the faint light from the house. I tried to imagine my children's lives there. It had nothing to do with me at all.

I was just about to leave when the front door opened. A rectangle of light lay across the drive. Salim came out. Something scampered out; I heard the faint scuffle of claws on the concrete. It was the puppy. I moved back behind the wall. Salim glimmered in his pale clothes; he was wearing *shalwar-kamize* pyjamas. It was shocking, to see him in Pakistani clothes. His shiny hair caught the light.

He picked up a toy or something from the lawn. I realized for the first time how graceful he was. The breeze caught his loose trousers; they flapped around his legs as he straightened up. I couldn't believe that I had once been married to this man. We had actually spent nine years together, sleeping in the same bed.

He paused for a moment. Perhaps he was breathing in the perfumed air; there was some bush nearby that had such a strong scent it made me queasy.

He looked around. The light fell on his face.

'Kulfi!' he called. His voice was low and caressing; a voice he had sometimes used with me.

He was looking in my direction; I sank away into the shadows.

'Kulfi!'

I stood behind the gatepost, a few yards from my children. A few yards from the man I feared more than anyone on earth. I hardly dared breathe.

The dog ran up to him. He patted it and went back into the house. The dog followed; it was quite big, it wasn't a puppy anymore. There was the murmur of voices, then Salim closed the door and the garden was dark again.

I turned away, and took the cab back to my hotel. That night I lay awake, scratching my mosquito bites.

'They're so polite!' I said to Aisha. It was the next day; the kids were in the corridor, playing with the lift buttons. 'It's like . . .

like I'm some distant aunt or something; like . . . it's a duty. Each day, they look as if they're longing for you to take them home.'

'Of course they're not,' she said.

'He's set them against me.'

'He hasn't,' said Aisha. 'He doesn't talk about you; honestly, he doesn't.'

'Doesn't he?'

'He doesn't speak about you at all.'

'Never?' I asked.

She shook her head.

'Not even to you?' I asked.

She shook her head again.

We sat for a moment, sipping Bubble-Up. She was wearing an orange chiffon *shalwar-kamize*, with a matching scarf around her head. Bracelets shifted at her wrist. She seemed as exotic and foreign as a humming-bird. I pictured her chattering in Urdu to my kids, and them answering her in a language I didn't understand.

'You've got to give them time,' she said.

'I haven't got any time!'

'To get used to you.'

'Used to me? I'm their mother!' I paused and lit another cigarette. My room stank of fags, no wonder my kids wanted to get the hell out of it. There were only two more days left. 'They seem so . . . happy, and settled. They go on about their school and their *ayah* and their friends and their ruddy dog. They seem to have forgotten all about England, and me.'

'They haven't. They talk about you a lot.'

'Do they?'

She nodded. 'To me.' She put down her drink. 'It's just . . . they've been very upset.'

'They don't seem upset,' I said. 'They just seem bored. I don't know where to take them, there's nowhere to go. There aren't any parks. Everywhere's full of these berks, staring at us. Where do kids go here? What do they bloody do?'

'You see, they usually go and play with their friends.'

'I hate Karachi,' I said. 'There's not even anything on the TV.'

'We all watch videos at home.'

'We're not at home, are we?' I glared at her. My face heated up; I was going to cry again.

She put her hand on my knee. 'Listen, Marianne. I've got this . . . well, this friend.' She smiled, bashfully. 'He's got a beach hut; it belongs to his family. Let's go there, to the beach. We'll all go. I'll ring him tomorrow.'

I'll never forget that day at the beach. Suddenly, everything was all right – just for a while. The kids and I clicked together, like the old days. There's something about the seaside, isn't there? I had felt it back in England, on the beach at Hythe. You feel free. Whatever has been happening at home, you're liberated by the sun and the waves. Perhaps we all become kids again, that's why.

Freed from their strict grandparents' home, the children giggled and became silly again. The beach was way outside the city. We drove there, our crates of soft drinks jangling in the boot. Yusuf, Aisha's boyfriend, was driving. He was a nice bloke, with brilliantined hair and a moustache. We drove across the grey scrub desert, singing.

The beach was a stretch of sand lined with concrete beach huts. There was hardly anybody around, which was a relief. The wind blew hot air at us, like one of those furnaces you get in garages. Bobby found a congealed jellyfish and prodded it with a stick. We opened the shutters of the beach hut and unpacked the picnic.

'He's nice, your friend Yusuf,' I said to Aisha.

She smiled, shyly. 'This is where we meet.'

'Ah-hah,' I grinned.

Just for a few hours we were all outside the law. We felt like escaped convicts. Sod the others; sod the lot of them.

Aisha turned to Yas, who was unpacking chapattis. They were rolled up like tea-towels. 'Don't tell them about Yusuf,' she said. 'This is our day, our secret. Promise?'

Yasmin nodded. 'Cross my heart and hope to die.' She turned to me. 'What's the other bit?'

'Stick a finger in your eye,' I chanted.

'Stick a finger in your eye!' she chanted back.

A camel appeared, plodding along the beach towards us. It wobbled in the heat, elongated, and tinked with bells.

I rode on the camel with the kids. We swayed from side to side, shrieking. Aisha took our photo.

Bobby was sitting in front of me. I put my arms around him and spoke into his hair. 'When you come back we'll go to Hythe.'

'Hythe's boring.'

'We'll go to Brighton. You can ride those little cars.'

Groaning, the camel sank to its knees. We tumbled off. The camel-*wallah*, a wizened old man, put out his hand.

'*Bis rupea*,' he said.

I calculated in my head, and gave him the money. '*Acha-tikka*,' I said.

'*Shoukriah.*'

Yasmin looked at me. 'You're learning,' she said. Then she asked: 'Why didn't we speak Urdu when we were little?'

I knelt in the sand and rebuckled her sandal. 'I suppose dad wanted you to be British, then. I don't know.' I stood up, dusting the sand off her leg. 'I never asked.'

When I turned round, the camel had gone. There was just the shimmering hills, way inland, as unlikely as theatre scenery.

But I still have that photo. Ten years later, it's still hanging on my wall.

Bobby splashed in the water, getting himself wet.

'Bobby!' Yasmin called. '*Ayah* will be mad!'

'*Ayah*'s a silly belly-button!' Pleased with this, he splashed around more wildly. Foam flew around him. 'Silly belly-button! Silly belly-button!'

Suddenly, Yasmin started giggling. She rolled up the legs of

215

her pyjama trousers and rushed into the sea. We all started dancing in the waves, shouting until we were hoarse.

We lay beside the embers of the barbecue. Lunch was over; Aisha and Yusuf had left us. They were walking along the beach, hand-in-hand. Far away I heard a dog barking. There was a fishing village, way beyond the huts; it was a tangle of nets and subsiding wooden shacks. Just for a moment I felt like a Pakistani housewife on a day outing.

We sat in the shade of the hut. Bobby piled up pebbles in the sand. I brushed Yasmin's hair and started to plait it, the way it used to be done. A plait on either side of her face. The way they did it, one plait at the back, made her look too grown-up.

'Who reads to you at bedtime?' I asked.

'Ouch!' she said. 'Daddy does sometimes.'

'He's reading us *Three Men in a Boat*,' said Bobby. 'But it's really boring.'

'Remember I used to make you up stories about Horace the Hedgehog?' I said.

'Only about twice,' said Yasmin.

'It was lots of times!' I said.

'You were always going out,' she said.

'I wasn't!' I yanked her plait into a rubber band.

'You did this funny face when you put on your mascara,' said Yasmin, and pulled a grimace.

'Like this?' I grimaced too.

'You shaved your legs with daddy's razor,' she said.

'Ssh,' I replied. 'He never found out.'

'He did,' said Bobby, throwing stones at a Pepsi can.

'Only once,' I said. 'That's why we split up, actually.'

The Pepsi can pinged. 'Was it?' asked Yasmin.

'Not really,' I said.

'Why did you?' she asked, turning her head around.

I pushed her head back and wound a rubber hand around her second plait. 'It's hard to explain,' I said. 'We just realized we were different from each other. One day you'll understand.'

'I wish he laughed more,' said Yasmin. 'It's more fun with you.'

I spoke to the back of her head. 'Is it, darling?' Her parting wasn't straight; I'd never been able to get it straight.

Bobby said: 'I could hear you coming when you fetched us from school.'

'How?' I asked.

'Your bracelets jangled.'

I smiled. 'Did they?'

There was a pause. I had finished Yasmin's hair. Now it was done, I could hardly bear it.

'Listen,' I said to them both. 'I've got to go back tomorrow.'

'Don't go!' said Bobby. He flung another stone; it missed the Pepsi can.

I got up and sat beside him, putting my arms around him.

'I don't want to,' I said. 'Oh, Bobby. Think I want to?'

There was a silence. We sat there for a moment, listening to the sigh of the waves.

'Listen carefully, you two,' I said. 'You must realize, I love you more than anything else in the world. I'm doing everything I can to get you back. We'll be together again, soon.'

Suddenly Bobby blurted out: 'I want to go home!'

'Which home?' I asked.

'With you,' he said.

That evening, when they had gone, I went back to Bohri Bazaar. It was still crowded. Shot-gold saris hung in the alleys; brass pots shone in the light from kerosene lamps. This place held no terrors for me now. I had bought an embroidered blouse; it chafed my sunburnt arms. Around my head I had wound my *dupatta* veil. For a moment I felt a part of this bazaar, which had held my dearest secret for me.

The tailor was sitting there at his machine. He looked as if he hadn't moved all these months. Maybe he's still sitting there now.

He must have recognized me because he nodded and said, '*Salaam, aleicum.*' I shook his bony hand.

The T-shirt man was wrapping something for a customer. She went away and he turned around.

'Well, hi!' he said.

217

I gave him the carrier bag I'd brought from England. He opened it, and took out *Classic Kinks*.

'It's a present,' I said.

He gazed at the LP, turning it over in his hand and reading the sleeve notes.

'Wow,' he said. 'Thanks.'

'Have you got it?' I asked.

He shook his head.

This time he did buy me a cold drink. He pulled out his stool and I sat there, nibbling peanuts and sipping Fanta through a straw.

'You're dead lucky,' he said, 'going back to England.'

The children came with me to the airport. I wish they hadn't; we had really said our goodbyes the day before, at the beach, and it was too painful to see them again. School was starting that morning and they were dressed in their uniform – maroon cardigans over beige, traditional baggy trousers. Yasmin had a skirt over her trousers and looked pinched and unfamiliar. Her hair had been tied back in that plait again, with the tortoiseshell clip. In the harsh light they both looked pale.

Weeping, I kissed them goodbye. They both clung to me. A long time passed, and then Aisha beckoned them away. Bobby had his chinsel with him again; he sucked it furiously.

I turned away and hurried blindly through the crowd. I didn't look back.

Of all my flights, that one was the worst. I can't even describe it to you. When I got to Heathrow, Tom was there to meet me. He didn't speak. I stood, rigid in his arms, like a piece of wood.

Twenty

Two years passed. The divorce had come through and I was granted access, twice a year. I had to go to Karachi to see the kids; they weren't allowed out of Pakistan. I watched them growing up at intervals; they startled me with their changes. It was like watching one of those speeded-up Disney films – do you remember? – flowers unfolding in the desert.

Tom and I got married. I kept saying we shouldn't, but he didn't listen. He had never liked London, so he sold his flat and I sold the house and we went to live in the country. We stayed in a rented place for a while, then we found this wonderful cottage just outside Ashford. It was a real picture-postcard place – inglenook fireplace, beams, all that; Tom kept bumping his head on the ceiling. It had an orchard, a barn, and what the estate agent called 'panoramic farmland views'. It was covered in roses and things. In fact, it was just the sort of place Salim must have imagined when he came to England all those years ago. Ironic, really.

I looked out over our panoramic farmland views and thought: This is where he would have liked to bring up our kids. Even when we moved to the cottage I still woke up at night, alarmed, and thought they were asleep in the next room. Why hadn't I got their school stuff ready? Had I bought any Rice Krispies? I thought it would stop, but it didn't. When someone has their leg amputated, apparently, it can still hurt years later. They can still feel their phantom foot aching.

In the daytime it caught me too, at odd moments, like a missed heartbeat. I'd be shopping in Ashford and suddenly I'd feel panicky – where had I left them? In another shop? It was a draughty, bereft sensation, the sort all mothers feel. It's like thinking you've forgotten your wallet, and patting your pockets. In a split-second, of course, it was over.

Sometimes, it wasn't too terrible. I came awake like a normal person. Over the months, in fact, I slowly got better. It must have been difficult for Tom, like living with an invalid who must be nursed back to health.

He taught me lots of things. He taught me how to make proper espresso coffee on his incredibly complicated machine. He taught me about the countryside. He wanted to divert my energies. Neither of us had a clue about gardening, but he knew the names of birds and he took me on long, therapeutic walks. He wore an old fisherman's sweater and grew ruddy in the sun.

I became quite cultured. I started to talk better, I used more interesting words. He taught me how to play the piano. I wasn't much good but I did learn a Chopin thing by heart. When he came home I pretended I'd practised, but he found me out one day when he tied a thread of cotton to the piano lid, like a detective, and it was still there in the evening.

I started listening to music, classical music, for the first time in my life. I didn't go for it all, but I began to love things with masses of people singing. It was so sweetly painful that tears came into my eyes. One evening, when he was late home, I listened to some requiem and forgot about the kids for two whole hours. Well, I remembered them, but in an enlarged, noble way; the swelling voices sang of everybody's children and everyone's losses.

I just tried to take each day at a time. Donald had told me that, back at the hotel in Karachi. When his wife left him he had to put himself together again, very slowly, one piece and then another. Just taking his clothes to the launderette had been a small triumph. 'You may have lost the battle,' he'd told me. 'But you haven't lost the war.'

Tom took me to Venice but being abroad, for some reason, made it worse. I lay awake at night; the water lapped outside and I felt utterly adrift from my kids. The panic attacks came back. It was like two steps forward, those years, and one step back. I kept wondering what the children's bedrooms looked like, what their friends were like. I hadn't cooked them a meal for two years. I hadn't tucked them up at night.

I hung photos of the kids all over the bedroom wall at

Chestnut Cottage. There were photos from my visits – Yasmin sitting on a beach pony, Bobby bunder-boating in the harbour. Endless shots of them screwing their eyes against the glare of the sun, sitting on the hotel balcony, sitting beside the pool where the management accepted no responsibility for loss of life. I had hung up some Pakistani stuff, too – pieces of antique embroidery from Bohri Bazaar. When I put on the light the mirrorwork glittered. It was like a souk, our bedroom; or a shrine.

Tom commuted to London each day. I drove him to Ashford Station and kissed him goodbye, feeling like a wife on a stage. Sometimes I didn't feel married to him at all. I never told him, of course. Then I went to work at the Riverside Restaurant, which was a new place next to the canal. It was between the abattoir and the Ashford Industrial Park. I served lunch to businessmen. That *nouvelle* stuff had just come in; people had discovered kiwi fruit. I couldn't cook anymore. I'd lost the heart, or the appetite – you have to be greedy to cook well. Whatever it was, the libido had gone. It was another casualty of all this. So I waited at tables. Some days, it was all I could do, to remember who had ordered what. Sometimes I slipped right back, down into the pit.

Poor Tom. He was the only person who kept me sane. God knows what I was doing to him. There were so many casualties.

I'm sitting here, wondering about Tom. Somehow it's easier on a plane. The guilt doesn't disappear. It just recedes a bit, like the tide going out and the pebbles hissing. You see the glittering expanse of the sea, and you can jump in or not jump in, just as you like.

The little Pakistani boy has told me his name. It's Mohammed Sohail Something-or-other. I've given him my watch to play with. It's got a stretchy strap, and he's pushed it right up his arm, right above the elbow, like a newspaper reporter in an old film. When I get it back I'll wind it on to Karachi time. I usually do it at the beginning of these flights, but this time I was so excited I forgot.

*

One day in April Aisha phoned, saying she was coming on a stopover. We had only just moved into Chestnut Cottage; it was 1982.

My mind worked fast. I met her at Heathrow and drove her through the lush green countryside. She was coming to stay with us for a night. I was in high spirits; I had this plan, you see. I had it all worked out.

Squeezing past the piano, I showed her the living room. It was cluttered with our things – Tom's paintings, stacked against the walls, my embroideries from the bazaars. There were lots of books, too – Tom was a reader, like Salim. I had been frantically getting it ready. I had even picked some flowers and put them into old marmalade jars.

'How are they, really?' I asked her. 'Tell me everything.'

It was strange, seeing her in this new setting. In her PIA uniform she looked like a large costume doll. She had this calm face and sheeny skin.

She opened a bag and took out some drawings. 'Yas did you these. Her teacher says she's very talented, for eleven.' She gave me a painting of a decorated tent full of people; it was mounted on card. 'This was pinned up for Parents' Day.'

Which parent? I thought bitterly. My stomach always tightened, seeing their drawings. 'Do they talk about me?' I asked.

'Of course they do! You're their mother.'

I shook my head. 'I'm just a sort of visiting relative. We only warm up towards the end.'

'It wasn't too bad last time. We had that lovely day at Thatta.'

'What, all those old tombs? I've learnt more about Pakistan, now, than I ever learnt when I was married to one.'

'Perhaps that was part of the trouble.'

'When you're married you don't talk about blooming Islam,' I said. 'You talk about grouting the bathroom. You'll see, one day.'

She got up, and went to the window. 'Is it different, this time?'

'I don't have kids, do I?' There was a silence. 'It's different,' I said. One of Tom's clocks pinged the quarter hour; it was always wrong.

'Lovely garden.'

'I keep digging up the wrong things. Tom's mother came down last week to show me how to do it. She went through the compost heap like a policeman.'

'What's his family like?'

'Posh. That's why he feels he ought to work for law centres and things. And marry me.'

'Marianne!' she smiled.

'*I* wouldn't marry me,' I said.

She just smiled; she hadn't a clue.

Yasmin's room was all arranged, upstairs. The window looked over our paddock, with the gnarled old apple trees she would one day climb. I had set out her toys on the shelves. It seemed as if she had just stepped out for a moment.

It was chilly. Aisha sat down on the bed and I dragged in an electric fire.

She took off her high heels. 'It was an awful flight,' she said. 'One of the girls had a migraine and two of the loos were blocked.' She lay down on the bed.

'I'll wake you in time for supper,' I said. Then I took a breath. 'Aisha?'

'Mmm?'

'When you go back, you will talk to Salim, won't you?'

She nodded.

'Tell him about this place,' I said urgently. 'Tell him how much the kids would love it. We've got a stream and a paddock! They've got a room each! Tell him things are different now. Tell him this is the England he always loved, and shouldn't they see it too?' I paused, breathlessly. 'Tell him he can trust me. Be sure to tell him that.' I looked down at her face. 'Promise!'

She smiled. 'Of course I will.' She took a piece of paper out of her pocket. 'Here's their list.'

I took the piece of paper. 'Sleep well,' I said, and left.

I went into Ashford, to Ed's Record Mart. It had given me a jolt, that Yas wanted Spandau Ballet. Up until now she'd asked for Storyteller cassettes. I felt shifted forward, with a jolt. My God, she was almost a teenager. Her hormones were stirring.

After all these years Ed still recognized me. 'You used to come in with your mates,' he said. 'Saturday morning, you settled down in my booths. Practically brought your bleeding thermoses in.'

'I'm getting these for my daughter,' I said, giving him the list of records.

He gallantly raised his eyebrows. 'You don't say!' He fetched the records and I paid for them. His booths had long since gone. Passing me the carrier bag, he said, 'Well, you won't be having any peace now.'

'Not kidding,' I sighed.

'One minute they're kids, the next thing they're socking great . . .'

'I know,' I sighed, the put-upon mother.

It was easier to pretend. Friends knew, of course. But with other people it was easier to carry on as usual. I even collected my family allowance from the post office each month. Well, why not?

I went to C&A and bought Yasmin a Snoopy nightshirt, also on her list. I didn't know what size she was; I had to hold it up against another little girl who was shopping with her mother.

'How old are you?' I asked.

'Nearly twelve,' she said.

I held the nightshirt against her. The world was full of growing children. I felt dislocated, that afternoon. I always did, when I was shopping for my kids. I felt like an aunt who has to phone up first to check what age to write on a birthday card.

We were having supper that night. Tom had put candles on the table, lots of candles in saucers. He was more artistic than me.

'France needs Algerian oil,' he told Aisha. 'But the Algerians won't hand back any of these kidnapped children till the French hand over some political prisoners being held there. It's terribly delicate, especially with Muslim countries where women have so little power.'

'We want a law passed that makes your brother a criminal,' I said.

'Marianne!' He turned to me.

'He is, anyway,' I said.

'He's trying to be a good father!' said Aisha. 'He's never looked at another woman.'

'Hasn't he?' I asked, with interest.

'Never. He spends every spare minute with the children; he even takes them on site with him sometimes.'

'Maybe somebody'll drop a block of concrete on him,' I said.

'Darling . . .' said Tom.

I turned to him. 'I hate him! Don't you understand? You've never hated anybody in your life. Everybody's been so nice to you, with your labradors and your public school . . .'

He laughed. 'Nice to me, in public school?'

I said to Aisha: 'He's even best friends with his ex, so frightfully civilized! He's had it easy.'

Tom said: 'Well, you're sure making up for it now.'

Tom was in bed when I tiptoed in later that night.

'Funny having someone else here,' I whispered. The mattress sighed as I sat down and took off my shoes.

'It's nice, this,' he said. I was wearing a turquoise, silky dress. He stroked my slippery flank. 'Aisha brought it with her?'

I nodded. 'I was fitted for it, last time.'

He chuckled and pulled the duvet up to his chin. 'Now who's sounding posh?' He put on a silly voice. 'My wife goes to Karachi for her frocks. My dear, they have darling little tailors there, and so hysterically cheap.'

I looked at the photos on the wall. Tom had lit a candle in here, too; all that wine had made him romantic. In the flickering light the framed faces looked ancestral, as if they were in somebody else's house. Did they really belong to me?

'Bobby had measles last week,' I said. 'Nobody told me. When he writes to me it's about three lines long.'

'I was like that, when I wrote to my parents from school.' He pushed down the duvet. 'Let's forget about them, mmm?' His hand felt round my side, and found the zip. He pulled it open. 'You look absolutely gorgeous.'

He pulled me down beside him. I lay, awkwardly, on top of the duvet. He stroked my stomach, the only part of me he could reach.

I sat up and pulled the dress over my head. I thought: Yasmin will start her periods without me. Who was she going to tell? Suddenly my eyes filled with tears.

'Keep your stockings on,' he whispered. He lifted up the edge of the duvet, and finally I slid in.

The next morning I got up early to drive Aisha to Heathrow. We sat drinking coffee in the kitchen.

'I can get a cab,' she said. 'Honestly.'

'I don't mind,' I said. 'I don't sleep well, anyway.' I looked out of the window; the garden was knee-high in mist. 'I love the dawn,' I said. 'I thought I'd be bored here, but things change all the time. It's much noisier than Ashford.'

'I'm thinking of coming to live here.'

I stared at her. 'What?'

'PIA have offered me a desk job in London.'

'But you can't!'

'I can't stand it in Karachi anymore.' She sipped her coffee. 'It's so restricting, it's impossible for women. Nobody seems to realize that I've been all over the world. Yusuf wants to come, too. We're going to get married.'

'But what about the kids?'

'Oh, we won't have any for a while.'

'No,' I said. 'I mean *my* kids!'

There was a silence. Aisha looked at me, puzzled.

'You can't leave Karachi!' I cried.

'Ah. Look, I know, but . . .'

'You bring me things from them! You tell me what's happening! You can't leave!'

'Marianne, I've got to have my own life.'

'But what about me?' I wailed.

Tom came in, wearing his dressing-gown. He stared at me. 'What's happened?' he asked.

Aisha pulled off some kitchen roll and gave it to me. 'I can't say anything right,' she said.

When she had gone I felt bereft, as I always did. My phantom children had departed with her. Now all I had to wait for was her next visit. And how long were her visits going to last? I knew I'd behaved selfishly, but I *was* selfish. She was all I had.

Things came to a head on the Saturday. I was hoovering in the living room, listening to Radio 1. When I turned off the hoover there was a pause in the patter, and I heard the sound of typing upstairs.

I went up. Tom was sitting in Bobby's bedroom. He was sitting at the desk I had bought Bobby to do his homework on. Papers were piled up around him.

'This isn't an office, you know,' I said, standing in the doorway.

'Couldn't hear myself think down there.'

I gestured round the room. 'It's getting all cluttered up.'

'I don't know where to put all this stuff.'

'This is Bobby's room.'

He switched off the typewriter. 'I know,' he said. 'But Bobby isn't here.'

'He's coming, I know he is!'

He got up, and sat down on the bed. 'Listen. You must face up to it . . .'

'Face up to what?'

'They might never come here.'

'They will!' I cried. 'Of course they're coming!'

'You'll make yourself ill again.'

'Look – I'm married now, I've got a lovely house . . .'

'Know something?' he said. 'Sometimes I think you just married me for this.'

I stared at him. 'For what?'

'You've always known how to use men, haven't you? You and your warpaint.' He looked out of the window; there was a block of blue sky; it was as solid as a child's play brick. 'I think you only married me to get your children back.'

'That's not true!'

227

'Bobby, Yasmin; Yasmin, Bobby. You're getting obsessed. It's like living with ghosts. No — it's like *I'm* the ghost, and *they're* real. They can't do anything wrong, can they, when they're not here? If they were, they'd probably be driving you round the bend . . .'

'They wouldn't!'

'Sometimes I wish you had a lover.'

'What?'

'At least I could get angry.' He sat, a large man on the narrow bed. The duvet was printed with Garfield cartoons. I had gone up to London and bought it in John Lewis. For the first time, I noticed some threads of grey in Tom's hair. 'It's hard, competing with your kids.' He nodded towards our bedroom, next door. 'Especially in there. Children shouldn't be in grown-ups' bedrooms, you know. Real children aren't.'

'Mine are real!'

Suddenly he got up, grabbed my hand and pulled me to the door. 'Let's get out of this bloody house!'

We sat on the Downs. It was very hot, the first day of summer. Tiny birds trilled, way up above us — maybe they were larks. Below us lay Kent, shimmering in the heat. Way beyond lay the sea.

Tom pushed me down on the grass. 'Oh, let's have a baby!' He rolled on top of me. 'Come on, let me get traumatized too! Oh, let's; it's my turn!' He glared down at me. 'Old misery guts.'

I struggled, giggling, underneath him. Men are really heavy, aren't they, when they want to be? He lay on me like a porpoise.

'*I've* been married too, you know,' he snarled.

He rolled me over; we rolled, bumping, down the hill a few yards, and came to a stop.

'Shall we really?' I asked.

He nodded. I lay on top of him, pinioning his arms.

'Let's think about me, me, me,' he said.

'You, you, you!' I flopped down and pressed my face against

his cheek. His skin smelt like shortbread, warmed by the sun. 'I do love you,' I murmured.

'Well, blooming well show it.'

He pushed me; we started rolling again, bumping down the hill. When we stopped, I was underneath.

'Ouch!' I yelled.

He pulled me over, roughly, and looked underneath.

'Trust *you* to get the bloody thistle,' he said.

I hit him. He held my arms; I struggled, laughing and shouting. We grappled like kids, tussling and pulling at each other's clothes. Suddenly, desire rose up in me; it stopped my breath. It was like feeling hungry again, after you'd thought you'd lost interest in food. Flushed, we gazed at each other. We sat up and looked around at the expanse of hillside. There were cars parked down in the lane, and families picnicking

He stood up and pulled me to my feet. 'Come on.'

He drove us home with one hand on the wheel, the other down the front of my shorts. I slobbered over his ear and stroked his crotch. He drove home fast. The gravel spurted as he braked outside the cottage. We stumbled out.

The phone was ringing. We could hear it as he searched for his keys. It went on ringing; the answerphone had packed in. He fumbled in his pocket.

'Oh, quick!' I gasped.

The phone was still ringing. We could hear it faintly, inside the house. At last he found the keys and opened the door. I rushed in, bumping past him, and hurried into the living room.

I lifted the receiver, my heart thumping.

'Marianne?'

It was Salim.

'I've thought about it for a long time,' he said. 'I've given it very careful consideration.' The crackling on the line was so loud I could hardly hear his voice. It sounded thin and very formal. It was two years since I had heard it, and I could hardly connect it with Salim. His accent sounded more Pakistani now. He said something about Aisha, I couldn't hear, and then I caught the words, 'now you're a respectable married woman' – or something like that. Then I heard the children's names.

'What?' I yelled down the receiver.

'For their next access visit,' he said, and then something about England.'

'What?'

'I have given my permission,' he shouted, 'for them to come to England!' then he said something about giving my word of honour that I wouldn't do something.

'Do what?' I yelled.

'That you don't pull any tricks on me,' he yelled. 'I am trusting you, Marianne. I know I can trust your husband.'

He meant, of course, that I was not to try and keep them. After two weeks, I must put them on a plane back to Pakistan.

My plan had worked. I put down the phone and looked at Tom. He had come in and sat down on the settee.

For a moment I couldn't speak. Then I said: 'Isn't that fantastic?'

He smiled, and nodded.

'They're coming here!' I said. 'Next month!'

'Fantastic.' He stood up. 'Better get my stuff out of his room.'

And he went upstairs.

Twenty-one

Suddenly, everything was transformed. Now it was going to happen I could hardly believe it; I had to catch up with myself. For months I had imagined my kids coming home, climbing the apple trees and damming the stream. But I had imagined it in a vague, pastel-tinted way. It was like waking in the morning and trying to remember what your dream has been about. I couldn't connect them to solid kids, really being here. Perhaps it was because they had never seen this house. I couldn't dare to believe that they would really sit down on the kitchen chairs, eating my food; that the ceiling would creak as they moved around their bedrooms.

After all these years, two long years, they were coming! I felt shy and excited, like a bride before her wedding day. I rushed around, rigging up a tyre on a rope in the garden and bulk-buying crisps. Would they like their rooms? Would they get bored in the country? Sometimes I snapped at Tom and sometimes I flung my arms around him and practically throttled him. I was just as impossible as before, but in a different way.

I spent a long time standing in their bedrooms – those two silent rooms, museums to my kids' childhoods. I thought: I'm going to put my children to bed, I'm actually going to tuck them in at night. I could tell them the next instalment of Horace the Hedgehog, if I could remember how the blooming thing went. Maybe they were too old for that now. Yasmin's dolls sat on the shelf like an audience waiting for a long-delayed show to begin.

I told Sonia, of course, and my mum and dad. I went back to my old estate and knocked on Emily's door. She opened it.

'Wow, you've grown!' I said. 'I like the hair. Yasmin's coming back! Can you come to tea?'

She had a friend with her, another girl. I felt stupidly hurt; it was like asking an old flame out for a date, and finding he's got married.

Jill came out. 'You'd like to see Yasmin, wouldn't you?' she said to her daughter. Emily looked at the other girl, and went on eating cashew nuts. I fixed a date.

On the way back I walked past my old house in Harebell Close. A family called Pewsley had moved in. There were new curtains at the windows and a kid's trike in the front garden. New children were growing up there now, but today I didn't mind.

I cleared up the cottage and stuck up posters in their bedrooms. I restocked the freezer. Sonia came round and helped me to calm down. I was already dreading them leaving, before they had even arrived. At night I lay awake, my heart racing.

What if they didn't come? Perhaps Salim had only done this to trick me? Once again, the bastard was trying to pay me back. Or perhaps he'd had second thoughts. He had acted on impulse, during some rare good mood, and now he regretted it. My husband was a lawyer and my mother-in-law was a magistrate, but he still didn't trust me. He didn't trust me to send them back.

But he did. A week before they were due to arrive he phoned Tom's office with their flight number.

He did trust me.

I met them at Heathrow after their long flight. They wore 'Unaccompanied Minors' labels around their necks; it made them look thin and defenceless, like evacuees. They had grown taller, and wore *shalwar-kamize*. They stood stiffly as I hugged them. Each time we met, I had to start from the beginning again. Oh, it took so long!

I drove them back to the cottage. It was a cool, grey day for June. I cursed the English weather. I wanted it all to look great for them.

'Are you cold? Are you hungry?'

Wittering like a madwoman, I gave them a conducted tour.

'Isn't it lovely?' I jabbered as we walked across the garden.

232

'I've taken the whole week off! Darren's coming round tomorrow, and Emily . . .'

'Ugh,' said Yasmin, daintily lifting her foot.

'It's only mud,' I said. 'Good old English mud. Kirsty and Zara are coming for tea – they're huge now – and look at our stream! I thought we could dam it together.'

But the kids weren't listening. They had rushed over to the guinea-pig's hutch.

'Where's Toulouse?' demanded Yasmin.

I paused. 'Er, he died.'

'Why didn't you tell us?'

'I've got you another one.' I pointed at Toulouse's replacement, a tufted, beige female cowering in the corner. 'Isn't she sweet? We can think up a name for her together!'

They looked at the hutch, doubtfully.

The days passed. The children were happy, I was sure of it. I bought them English clothes; they looked more like my own kids then. Their old friends came to visit, awkwardly at first but they warmed up. Tom was ever so nice; he played with the kids in the garden and fell over each time Bobby shot him, again and again. He seemed genuinely fond of them. They said they liked him.

I gave them smoky bacon crisps. 'Bet you don't get these in Pakistan,' I said.

Bobby replied: 'We only get boring ones there.'

'Do you like the cottage?' I asked.

They nodded, obediently.

'If you lived here,' I said, 'we could buy a pony and put it in the orchard.'

I tucked them up in bed each night and hugged their firm little bodies. I tried to tell them a story but I felt as stagey as an actress who had forgotten her lines. Sometimes I couldn't believe they were actually there; it seemed so unlikely, after the years of longing for it to happen. The days were going by so quickly; some wicked clock was speeding up. I thought of Salim, counting the hours till they came home. Not home – to *his* home. What right had he to take them back?

233

They were settling in, I was sure of it. After five days they even stopped talking about their bloody dog. By this time, though, I could hardly concentrate. My mind was racing; my plan was thickening up. Sometimes I caught them looking at me oddly, but that was probably because they were trying to get used to having a mother again. They were connecting me up to Tom and the new cottage. They were trying to get their bearings.

Or perhaps they guessed. I don't know, now. To tell the truth, I can't remember much about that first week. My mind was busy, but something inside me had locked. I didn't let myself feel anything.

Sonia came round. We sat in the kitchen drinking white wine.

'Blokes and spots,' she said. 'That's all they talk about. I had to take Zara to buy her first bra last week.' She put on a mock voice. "Oh, mum, you can't come, you're so embarrassing!" God, they're driving me round the bend. Why can't we send mine back to Pakistan and keep yours?'

I didn't laugh. 'They love it here now,' I said. 'I know they do. Bobby hasn't talked about his computer for three days.'

'Marianne . . .'

'Mmm?'

'What're you going to do?'

There was a pause. I was watching Bobby in the garden, scuffing the grass and eating Twiglets.

'I used to know, once,' she said. 'We were such mates.' She lit a cigarette. 'Christ, I'm not blaming you. It's just . . . you've changed.' She gestured around the kitchen. 'All this. Everything that's happened.'

I turned to her. 'You know exactly what I'm going to do.'

That night, for the first time, Bobby let me dry him. We stood in the steamy bathroom. I wrapped the towel around him and squeezed him so tightly he squealed.

'Got you!' I breathed.

Just then the phone rang. I went downstairs. Tom had answered it.

'I'm afraid they've gone to sleep now,' he was saying. He put the receiver back.

'Him again?' I asked.

He nodded. It had been Salim.

'That's five times since they've been here!'

'He's very jittery,' he said.

'So am I.'

He looked at me sharply. 'What do you mean?'

'Nothing.'

For the first time in my life I lay awake for the whole night. I heard the house sighing and creaking as it settled down. I heard the sound of some bird outside, making a cry like steel being sharpened. Tom's clocks downstairs chimed the hours, and the half hours, and the quarters. Down in the kitchen my Karachi-time clock, a digital one, must have flipped luminously from minute to minute. Beside me, Tom turned over and exhaled breath, with a quiet, rubbery sound – even in sleep he was well-behaved. He murmured my name, once, and cupped his hand around my buttock. I heard the bed creaking in the next room as Bobby turned over. The old beams arched over us like a church and held us safe; just for now. I lay, flat on my back; I thought of the wicked being punished, and my children growing up amongst men who bowed on carpets at airports. Sometimes my head span and I thought I was going mad. I got up and fetched a drink of water, just to prove I was still in working order.

'Ghastly day today,' said Tom at breakfast. 'Court all morning, then the dreaded Mrs Molyneux. Lucy's off sick. Then I've got a case conference on baby battering. Sometimes it seems that the whole world has either lost their kids or else is beating them up.' He sighed. 'Why didn't I get into conveyancing?' He looked at me. 'You OK?'

I looked at my watch. 'You'll miss your train.'

*

When Tom had gone, I left the kids with my parents and went up to London. When I came back, my dad was playing hide-and-seek with them in the garden. I watched him walk down his row of sheds, opening one after another.

'Coming!' he called. 'Coming to get you!'

I turned to my mum. We were standing in the kitchen, looking out. 'If I sat very still, I thought nobody could find me.'

'What's that?' she asked, fiddling with her hearing-aid.

I looked at the sheds. 'I could hide there for ever. If I sat very still.'

'Oh, I'll miss them,' she said. 'When're they going back? Thursday?'

I looked at dad's chrysanths, stout bushy plants at this time of the year, yoked to their stakes. 'No,' I said.

'What?' she asked.

'No, they're not.'

'Or is it Friday?' she asked.

I shook my head, but she didn't notice.

That night I went into the bedroom. Tom was undressing. I watched his shadow behind him, moving against the beams.

'Did you turn off the lights?' he asked.

I nodded.

'I'm taking Wednesday off,' he said, loosening his tie and pulling it over his head. 'I thought we'd all go to Brighton.'

'They're not going back,' I said.

'What?'

'The kids. They're not going back to Pakistan.'

He stood still, his shadow huge behind him. The bedside light was on but I couldn't see his face, he was standing in front of it.

'I'm keeping them,' I said.

There was a pause. That bird started up again, outside.

'Marianne,' he said, 'I told you – '

'They're staying here with me.'

'You can't!'

'I'm keeping them!'

'Ssh.' He walked across the room and closed the door. 'Look, we've been through all this – '

'He stole them; well, I'm going to steal them back. Why the hell can't I?'

'Because it's madness – '

'Tomorrow I'm going up to London. I'm going to make them wards of court. I've got it all worked out – '

'Marianne, he trusted you – '

'*I* trusted *him*!'

'You mustn't do this,' he whispered.

'Don't be so feeble.'

'I'm being realistic.'

'He's not getting them back. If you won't act for me, I'll get another lawyer.'

He patted the bed. 'Sit down,' he said. 'Listen.' He sat down. I looked at him in his shirt, with his two long, bare legs. 'I told you,' he said. 'If you do this, we'll have to go to court to try and prove that you should have care and control – '

'I know, I know!'

'It's a huge, huge risk. Salim'll fly over, he'll give evidence against you. The children have been living in Pakistan for two years, they're settled there now – '

'They're not settled!'

'Ssh!' He glanced at the door. 'Every month, every *day* they've been there has weakened our case, don't you see?'

'This is their home.'

He pushed his hand through his hair. We both gazed down at his big, bare feet.

'Oh, Tom,' I said. 'Help me, please.'

He raised his head; his face was still in shadow. 'In the end, it'll be up to the children themselves, and the judge.'

I sat down on the bed. We sat side by side, with a gap in between us. For a moment, he didn't speak.

Then he said: 'If you lose, you'll lose them for good.'

'I won't lose!'

'If you lose, Salim will take them away. And do you think he'll ever let you see them again?'

'I won't lose! I'm their mother!'

He didn't reply. We both sat there, staring at his toes.

Twenty-two

The next morning Sonia came round, early, to look after the kids. Tom and I dashed out to the car and drove to London. On the way he told me that he couldn't possibly act for me, it would be unethical; as my husband, he couldn't give me independent advice. Besides, he would probably be called as a witness. This was a shock but he told me not to worry, we would get Bella instead; she worked for him and she was very good.

We parked on a yellow line and dashed into his office. He got us some coffee and buzzed for Bella.

'Now, when she comes, you're going to Somerset House, right?'

I nodded.

He sat me down on a chair and lit my cigarette. My hands were shaking.

'It's just a formality, to issue the originating summons. She'll explain in the car.'

'Then what? I've got all muddled.'

'Then she'll get leave to serve papers on Salim.'

'When'll he come?' I asked.

'Fast.'

There was a pause. I looked at a row of pigeons, sleeping on the roof outside. My throat was so dry I could hardly swallow.

'Once the summons has been issued,' he said, 'you'll have to file an affidavit. You'll have to give details of schools, day-to-day arrangements and so on.'

'They'll come and check me out, won't they?'

He nodded. 'The court will direct a welfare officer to prepare a report.' He buzzed again. 'Is she there?' He turned back to me. He spoke at high speed; now he was at work, he was suddenly impressive. 'They'll visit you, they'll interview you, they'll talk to the kids, alone and with you, they'll watch you together. You'll have to arrange something about your job. Are you prepared for this?'

I nodded. 'Then we go to court?'

'Yes. It'll all take some time.' He came over to me. 'Listen, darling. This is your last chance. You can still pull out.'

I shook my head.

'It's very dangerous. You know what you're letting yourself in for?'

Suddenly I felt as if I was in a wartime drama, and he was priming me for an undercover operation. None of it seemed real. It was all being taken out of my hands.

I nodded and stood up. He put his arms around me. We hugged each other. At that moment, I loved him very much.

Just then, the door opened and Bella came in. She was black, and smart, and businesslike. Tom and I sprang apart.

Tom drove Bella and me to Somerset House. I wished we had a siren for the car. He left us outside and sped off. We waited impatiently, then we saw a man in an office. It seemed odd that a scrap of paper connected this stranger to my children. I suddenly missed Bobby and Yasmin, painfully. As we clattered down the stairs I realized that I felt like a mother again. I hadn't for such a long time.

The rest of the morning passed in a daze. Tom was on the phone most of the time; he had to set a whole system in motion. He didn't question me again about going through with it. He had made up his mind to help me. I sat there, knotting my fingers together and gazing at him with devotion.

Bella got through to Karachi, to Mr Hussein's office. Tom gave me a sherry. Then Lucy, his secretary, got me a taxi and I took the train back to Kent.

'Come and sit down,' I said to the children. 'I've got something to tell you.'

They were in their pyjamas, ready for bed. We were in Yasmin's room that night. They sat down on either side of me. I took a breath.

239

'Listen, darlings, very carefully.' I put my arms around their shoulders. 'How would you like to stay here, with me and Tom?'

They turned to look at me, puzzled.

'For ever,' I said. 'This would be your home. Our home. How would you like that?'

For a moment, neither of them spoke. Then Yasmin said: 'What about daddy?'

'You'd still see him. Sometimes.'

Suddenly Bobby wailed: 'What about Kulfi?'

'What?' I asked.

'What about my dog?'

'We can get another one!' I said, desperately. 'I'll get you anything. But we can be together. For ever. Wouldn't you like that?'

They nodded. I'm sure they did.

'I'll tell you what's going to happen,' I said, and told them.

Events moved fast. It was a week or so later. Salim had flown over to London, as Tom had predicted. I was sitting in the lounge, talking to Tom on the phone. I'd tidied up the house; it was unrecognizably clean. I had even dusted the books and washed the kitchen floor. Out in the garden, the welfare officer was chatting to the kids. I had bought a tent and put it up on the lawn. Bobby was lifting the guinea-pig out of its hutch and showing it to the woman.

'. . . She's been here for hours,' I said. 'No, not bad. We had our little talk. Bobby's shown her his tent, he's so proud of it. He tried to make her go inside but she's too big.'

The woman looked up at the cottage; I ducked behind the window. Then I heard her voice, talking to the children, and their chattery replies. I couldn't hear what they were saying.

When she came in I was just taking some cakes out of the oven. I was wearing an apron and looking very housewifely. I'm a respectable mother, I thought, baking for my children.

'Mmmm,' she said. 'Smells nice.'

I pointed to the cakes. 'They're my children's favourites.' I took off my oven gloves. 'Would you like some tea?'

'No, thanks.' She looked at her watch. She was a portly woman with a big mole on her cheek. I hoped Bobby hadn't remarked on it. 'Must be pushing off.' She looked at her notes. 'Now, Mrs Wainwright, I'd like to see the children with their father. He's staying at . . .' She looked at her notes again. 'Oh, yes, the Kensington Hotel. But I'll see them in my office. Probably Thursday. Can you make sure they're there? I'll give you a ring when I know the time.'

'Yes, of course,' I said unctuously. If we were in Pakistan, I thought, I could slip her five hundred rupees.

I nearly started giggling then; I was feeling so pent-up I was almost hysterical. Then I thought: Why the hell should I prove I'm a good bloody mother?

We waved goodbye to the welfare officer, the three of us at the door. I kept my arms around my kids, and we watched her drive away in her mini. When we went back into the kitchen Bobby stared at the cakes.

'What's that?' he asked, surprised.

'Just some cup-cakes,' I said casually. 'What did she ask you?'

Yasmin said: 'She asked if I wanted to go to the big school.'

'You do, don't you?' I said.

'Emily's not going.'

'But Mandy is,' I said. 'You like her.'

Bobby was greedily eating a cake; crumbs scattered on the floor.

'She's best friends with Carol now,' said Yasmin.

I turned to Bobby. 'I showed her your new computer. She was ever so impressed. I showed her all your computer games.'

Bobby didn't answer. He was stuffing himself with another cake.

When Tom came home that evening he closed his eyes dreamily.

'Ah . . . that Proustian smell of Pledge . . . I'm a boy again, everything's safe . . . the snip-snip of secateurs . . .' He looked around the living room. 'Why can't it always be like this?'

'He hasn't got a chance in hell,' I said. 'He'll just sit there in

241

the welfare office, he won't look like a father at all. The kids'll be bored out of their minds.'

Tom went to the drinks cupboard and poured us Cinzanos. 'Don't underestimate your ex.'

'But what can he do?'

'He'll show her photos.'

'Photos!' I laughed. 'What, compared to this?' I gestured round at the cottage. He didn't reply. He just sipped his drink.

'We're going to win, aren't we?' I said.

'You expect a lawyer to tell you that?'

I said: 'I expect a husband to.'

He smiled. 'Even a husband wouldn't be *that* stupid.'

As time passed, I felt more and more optimistic. The weather was beautiful; down in the village they played cricket on the green. The countryside was bathed in sunshine; it was the dreamy England people feel homesick for, when they live abroad. I knew my kids wanted to live here with me. They didn't talk about Pakistan anymore, not at all, and seemed quite calm about the whole business. In fact, I think Bobby enjoyed being the centre of attention, with strangers asking him questions and his mother spoiling him. Yasmin started taking riding lessons and I promised her a pony. Their primary school took them back for the rest of the summer term. I ferried them to and fro and became a much more diligent mother than I had ever been before, like one of those mothers in a Ladybird book. During the weeks before the court hearing, in fact, we settled down into a strangely normal routine. I arrived from work and chatted to the other mothers at the school gates, as if the last two years had just been a temporary setback. A couple of new babies had arrived, but otherwise everything seemed weirdly the same. Everyone told me I was bound to win.

Looking back, the days had a golden, timeless feel to them. They resembled the photos of that summer before the First World War broke out. One day, when I was driving the children home, Bobby turned to me.

'When dad came, he said we were going to the dentist.'

242

Yasmin said: 'Then he said we were going on the ferry. He said we'd see you soon.'

'He told a lie,' said Bobby. 'He says we can't lie, but he told one.'

The presence of Salim, only sixty miles away, was like the rumbling of artillery, massing for the assault. The kids saw him a couple of times at the welfare place, but I never did. I didn't even know if he stayed in London all those weeks, while we waited for a date for the court hearing. But I could almost feel his anger, like an electro-magnetic force. At night I barred and bolted the doors and lay in bed, tense for the sound of a car arriving.

I told the children we were fighting like this because we both loved them so much. I said that whoever won, we would both love them for ever. This often happened after a divorce, I said. It had happened with Bill and Sonia; we were just like them, only a bit more so. Quite a bit more so. I spoke with a kind of tender exhilaration, because I knew I would win. I think Tom secretly thought so, too. Sometimes, just occasionally, I almost felt sorry for Salim. He was going to lose them. We had divided the world between us, East and West, and now never the twain would meet. How could my kids possibly want to grow up in their grandparents' house, going to their strict, boring school each day to learn chunks of the Koran by heart? How could they possibly want to grow up motherless?

There was just no competition.

'We've got you a barrister,' said Tom one evening when he came home from work. 'You're lucky. We've managed to get Henry Allen. He looks a bit of a queen – well, he *is* a bit of a queen – but he's terrific. Bella's arranged a conference for next week.'

I went up to London and met him. He was large and florid and reassuring. He asked me a lot of questions and told me not to worry if the odd tear flowed in court. It wouldn't do us any harm.

Then I went to Fenwick's and bought myself a suit – dark-blue, tailored, straight skirt.

243

'I look like an IBM executive!' I wailed that night.

Tom shook his head. 'You look like a respectable, responsible mother,' he said. 'Power dressing for parents.'

A few nights later, when Bobby was having his bath, I went into his room to straighten his bed. Underneath the pillow I found some photos. He must have hidden them there.

I took them out. They were all of Kulfi, his dog – Kulfi lying on the dusty lawn; Kulfi curled up on Bobby's bed; Kulfi jumping up – blurred – at a pair of unknown legs.

I looked at them for a moment. Then I put them back under the pillow. They didn't mean anything.

The next week we got a date for the hearing. It was July 15.

I remember the night before. My new suit lay over the chair. Outside, it was a heavy, starless night. The whole world seemed to be holding its breath. In the next rooms my children lay sleeping.

I thought of my kids growing up tall and strong here. I could almost hear the pony, snorting and stamping in the orchard. I thought of us all being together, down the years. I would take Yasmin into Ashford to buy her first bra. We'd make autumn bonfires together. Oh, I don't know what we'd do. Everything. My stomach ached; my head throbbed.

'You awake,' whispered Tom. 'Want one of your pills?'

I shook my head. I needed my wits about me for the next day.

'I won't have to speak to him, will I?' I asked.

'You won't even be sitting with him.'

We lay side by side, stiff as knights in armour. Downstairs, one of his clocks chimed twice.

'Do you hate him?' I asked.

'I hate what he's done to you.'

I turned to looked at him; his face in darkness. 'Have you ever been jealous?'

'No,' he said. Downstairs, another clock struck two. 'Of course I have,' he said. Then he kissed my forehead. 'Better get some sleep.'

Twenty-three

We left the children at home, with my mum and dad, and drove up to London. We didn't say a word all the way.

We collected Bella from the office and took a cab to the Law Courts. We walked along miles of corridor, our footsteps echoing. I was wearing new high heels, which pinched. Barristers passed us, chatting and laughing as if the whole thing was just a game. Their gowns billowed behind them. Tom held my slippery hand.

The family courts were in a modern part of the building, at the back. Some people were standing around in the corridor, smoking. I searched their faces for Salim, but he hadn't arrived yet. It was eleven-twenty-five.

There was a row of doors leading to numbered courtrooms. Lists were pinned up beside them. We stopped outside 43. Tom helped me light a cigarette.

Henry Allen, our barrister, arrived and shook my hand.

'We're in luck,' he said. 'We've got Jenner.'

'Who's he?' I asked. 'What's he like?'

'She.'

'What?'

He smiled down at me. 'She's a woman.'

I stared at him; he smiled back. I knew, then, that it was going to be all right. She was probably a mother too. She would understand.

When I turned round, Salim had arrived. He was standing at a distance from us, talking in a low voice to Mr Hussein and their barrister. He didn't meet my eye. He was wearing a pale-grey suit; he looked grave and expressionless.

Everyone looked at their watches. Henry murmured a few words to Bella; I couldn't hear what he said. I needed to go to the toilet, yet again, but suddenly it was too late because an usher came out of room 43 and looked at her piece of paper.

'Siddiqi!' she called, looking around.

Henry bent down to me. 'You're going to be fine, my dear,' he said.

Tom squeezed my hand, and let it go. We walked into the courtoom. Salim and his counsel followed us.

It was a modern room, very plain. The usher showed us to our seats. Tom had told me exactly what would happen; I felt I was replaying a dream. I sat down next to Bella. Out of the corner of my eye I saw Salim sitting down next to Mr Hussein. Tom sat behind me, in the next row.

There was nobody else there, except somebody writing. Tom had said that was the clerk.

'All stand!' said the usher.

We stood. The judge came in. She was a kind-looking, middle-aged woman. She smiled at us, slightly. She had a generous mouth. She bowed; everyone bowed. Then she sat. We sat.

The clerk rose and read out from a piece of paper: 'In the matter of Yasmin and Robert Siddiqi.'

Henry stood up. He cleared his throat and spoke to the judge.

'May it please your Ladyship. I appear on behalf of Marianne Wainwright, the plaintiff, and my learned friend Mr Forbes appears on behalf of the defendant, Salim Siddiqi.' He paused. When he spoke, his voice had changed. It was full of emotion. 'My Lady, this is one of the most distressing and disturbing cases I have come across in my twenty years at the Bar. What you see here today is a young mother whose children have been forcibly removed from her.' He glanced at me, then back to the judge. 'Let us go back two years, to 1978. The plaintiff, then Marianne Siddiqi, was a young married woman. She had two small children, Yasmin and Bobby, then aged eight and six. She lived with her then husband, the defendant, in a house in Ashford, Kent, her home town, where she was bringing up her children in a happy and secure environment. Mother and children were exceptionally close.' He paused and cleared his throat. I looked at his profile – large nose, fleshy neck. He looked strong and eloquent. 'It was around this time that the marriage began to break down. They agreed to separate.

246

'On Monday, 11 September, my client took her children to school, totally unaware of what her husband was plotting. She went to work. At midday, her husband took the children from school, telling them that he was taking them on a day-trip to France. They were bundled into a train to Paris, and thence to the airport where he had tickets to take them to Pakistan, a country completely unknown to them.' He paused for breath. When he spoke again, his voice had risen. 'Imagine what went through the mind of their mother when she arrived at the school gates, that afternoon, to find them gone.' He glanced at me again.

'She promptly alerted the police, but it was not until two days later that a short phone call from the defendant informed her that her children were at least alive. With considerable courage she managed to track them down to Karachi – she had not been told their address. However, she was unable to get them out of the country and had to return to England. Eventually, by agreement, an access visit was granted her, of a meagre fortnight twice a year, during which time she had to sit in a hotel room in Karachi, her passport impounded, and try to make contact again with the children who had been lost to her.' There was a silence. In the room, nobody stirred.

'It will be my client's case, my Lady, that it was deeply wrong of the defendant to take the children from their mother, in the most distressing circumstances, and uproot them from their home, their country, their friends, their grandparents, their school and security, and that their rightful place is at home, where they belong.'

I had listened, spellbound. He was like an orator, or a wonderful actor. Salim was a blur in the corner of my eye.

They asked me to stand in the witness box. It took ages walking across the floor to it. I was sworn in and asked my name and address. Henry turned to me, kindly, and spoke in a gentler voice.

'Mrs Wainwright,' he said, 'in the years you were married to the defendant, could you describe him as a father?'

I hesitated. When my voice came, it was squeaky. 'Well . . .

he was like a lot of fathers, I suppose. He was always doing something else.'

'Can you explain?' He indicated that I should answer to the judge, not to him. I turned to her. She was so near that I could see her little gold earrings.

'He was always busy. He worked very hard, he usually left before they went to school, and when he got home he put on his overalls and did up the house. Days went by and he hardly spoke to them.'

Across the room, Salim stirred angrily. I ignored him.

'Can you give an example?' asked Henry.

'One Saturday I was out shopping, and Bobby fell over in the garden. Salim didn't hear him crying because his Black and Decker was on. His drill. Our neighbour had to ring the doorbell but he didn't hear that, either. Bobby had to have six stitches.' I was speaking more fluently now; the words poured out of my mouth like coins. Tom and I had rehearsed this so many times. 'I mean, he loved them, really, I suppose. But he didn't really bring them up. Most fathers don't. They give them treats. It's the mothers who do the ordinary stuff. He didn't even know where their clothes were kept.'

'That's a lie!' Salim shouted.

The judge frowned at him. 'Mr Siddiqi!'

'Your parents,' said Henry, looking at his paper, ''er, Frank and Dorothy Simpson, they lived nearby, did they not?'

I nodded. 'Half a mile.'

'As grandparents, did they also have a part in the children's upbringing?'

I nodded obediently. 'Oh, yes. The kids used to go there for tea all the time. They loved them. They sometimes stayed the night.'

'And were the children happy at school?'

'Oh, yes,' I said. 'Bobby adored his teacher, and he was starting Cubs. Yasmin was going to be in *Hansel and Gretel*.' I stopped; my eyes blurred with tears. Suddenly I missed them, terribly. What had this place got to do with us?

'And friends?' Henry asked, gently.

'Her best friend, Emily, lived three doors away. They were always in and out of each other's houses.'

He smiled at me encouragingly. 'They were happy, normal children?'

'Oh, yes.' I nodded.

'Outgoing?'

'Yes.'

'Over the past two years,' he said, 'have you noticed any change, during your visits, in their behaviour?'

I nodded. 'They seem . . . shut off. Frightened. They don't let me cuddle them.'

'Now, for the past two months the children have been living with you and your husband, Thomas Wainwright. He is a solicitor, am I right?'

'Yes.'

'He runs his own practice?'

'Yes. He works in London and commutes.'

'Can you describe your home?'

I reeled it off, eagerly: 'It's got a paddock and a garden. It's an old cottage, five miles from Ashford – they've always wanted to live in the country. They've got a bedroom each, and we're going to buy them a pony . . .'

'Yes.' He smiled, slightly. 'Any financial worries?'

'No.'

'Have the children changed, over the past few weeks they've been staying with you?'

'Oh, yes!' I said. 'They're happier. Bobby lets me dry him now. It's getting better every day, but these things take time. They've been hurt so badly.'

He nodded. 'If they came to live with you, on a permanent basis, can you tell the court the day-to-day arrangements? Let's take school.'

I turned to the judge; I kept forgetting. I spoke to her wide, understanding face. 'Yasmin, she's got into a secondary school, St Hilda's.'

'I believe that's a private day school?' said Henry.

I nodded. 'It's very good. She's lucky to get in. She starts in September.'

'And Bobby?'

'We've arranged for him to go back to his old primary school, to his old class. He adored it there.'

'In fact, they've both been back at school these past three weeks?'

I nodded. 'They settled back in really quickly.'

He nodded. 'Now, you're working, I believe, at the Riverside Restaurant?'

'Yes.'

He smiled slightly. 'Two stars, isn't it?'

'What?' I asked. 'Oh, yes.' I turned to the judge. 'I do the lunches there, but that's just in school hours. I'm out in time to collect them each day. And in the holidays, Dennis – that's the owner – he's giving me leave; he's taking a student then. It's all arranged.'

'And is your present husband happy for the children to come and live with you on a permanent basis?'

I looked across the room at Tom. He smiled at me. 'Oh, yes,' I said.

Henry said to the judge: 'My Lady, we'll be calling Mr Wainwright later.' He turned back to me. 'One final question, Mrs Wainwright – and, I suppose, the obvious one . . . but the most important. Do you think your children would be happier living in England with you, rather than in Pakistan with their father?'

'Of course they would!' I cried. 'I'm their mother!'

He smiled. 'Thank you.'

I was just about to leave but he motioned me to stay standing. I was breathing heavily; I felt I had just run ten miles. I was so exhausted that all I wanted to do was go home and go to bed. Even with Henry on my side, it was exhausting.

Charles Forbes took his time standing up. He had a dry, papery face – narrow nose, pale skin. He looked at me pleasantly.

'Mrs Wainwright,' he said, 'you've been painting a very cosy picture of yourself and your children, but it's not quite the whole picture, is it?' He paused. 'Can you describe, to the court, your relationship with a certain Terence Gilby?'

For a moment, I couldn't recognize his full name. 'He was . . .' I stopped.

'Yes?' he asked. 'Can't quite hear.'

I glared at him. 'We had a, you know . . .'

'Yes?'

'Relationship,' I snapped.

'Can you be more specific? An adulterous relationship, was it not?'

I nodded. 'But it wasn't important!'

'Come, come, Mrs Wainwright. Important enough for you to lie to your husband and neglect your children – '

'No!' I shouted.

'He was your lover, was he not, from June to September 1980. During this period, on numerous occasions, you made an alibi of your work – '

'Not that numerous!' I said.

He ignored me. 'When in fact you were having an assignation with your lover. I have some dates here.' He put on his glasses, slowly, and looked at his sheaf of paper.

'That doesn't matter!' I cried.

He looked up, over his glasses. 'It mattered to your husband. Not perhaps surprisingly. I put it to you that it also had a direct effect on your responsibility as a parent – '

'It didn't!'

'Let's take an example.' He looked at the paper. 'On August 15, with the help of your employer, Sonia Turnbull, you fabricated a story about a crisis at work. Your children were left in the care of a non-registered childminder, one Tracey Smith, who had a previous criminal conviction – '

'I didn't know that then!'

' – whilst you spent the day with your lover, returning home so inebriated that when parking your car you caused £250 worth of damage – '

'It was only a little dent!'

He adjusted his glasses, and looked at the papers. 'On September 2, you had all arranged an end-of-holiday treat for the children, a day-trip to Brighton. At the last minute, however, you said you couldn't go with them, am I right?'

I glanced at Tom. He frowned, slightly. I nodded.

'Your reason being a lunch for a group of Environmental Health Officers,' said Charles Forbes. He raised his eyebrows. 'Were you speaking the truth?'

I didn't reply. I gripped the wooden ledge of the witness box.

'Mrs Wainwright, were you speaking the truth to your husband and children?'

'No.'

'Where did you in fact spend the day?'

'It was good for them to go to Brighton together! He hardly ever saw them alone, I told you – they had a lovely day!'

'Mrs Wainwright, did you spend the day with your lover?'

'You know I did! That's why you're bloody well asking!'

Across the room, Tom shifted in his seat.

Charles Forbes looked unperturbed. He went on, still pleasantly. 'Let's get on to your parents. You say you are very close?'

I was trying to calm down. I breathed deeply, and nodded.

'Closeness, I suggest, is not the first word I would use to describe a young lady of sixteen who ran away from home to set up in a squat with a registered heroin addict.'

'That was years ago!'

'Of course,' he smiled. 'Er, carefree young girls do grow up to be responsible parents – but, in this case, I suggest that such a transformation didn't take place.'

'It did!'

'Far from being close to your parents, you seldom saw them during the period of your marriage.' He smiled a wintry smile. 'Except to collect your children from their house.' He paused. 'Your mother's health is somewhat frail, I believe?'

'She's got a bit of arthritis, that's all.'

'She has trouble with her hearing, too?'

'Only a bit.'

'A bit?' he asked.

'She's not really deaf, when she takes her hearing-aid out.'

There was a stirring across the room. He smiled, as if I had made a joke.

'And yet you used her as a childminder, for sometimes a day at a time,' he said. 'To suit your own convenience.'

'It was hardly ever when I was with Terry; it was when I was at work!'

'I see,' said Charles Forbes. 'When you were at work.'

'I mean – '

'Far from those cosy teas, she was simply a convenient – though elderly and unsafe – person upon whom you could dump your children . . .'

Henry stood up and spoke to the judge. 'I really don't see the relevance of this, my Lady.'

She said: 'Mr Forbes, how much longer do you propose to follow this line of questioning?'

'I'm just trying to suggest, my Lady, that her children's safety and well-being were not the plaintiff's first consideration during the latter years of her marriage.' He paused, and took off his glasses. Turning to me, he said: 'Mrs Wainwright. We have seen that you are no stranger to deceit. Let's move forward to recent events. Did Mr Siddiqi trust you, when he agreed that this last access visit should take place here, in Britain?'

'I suppose so,' I said.

'Did he?'

'Yes.'

'What were the conditions?'

'That I didn't make the children wards of court.'

'That you didn't take proceedings? And what did you do?'

'He lied to me!' I shouted. 'He took them in the first place! How could I bear to let them go!' My voice rose. 'You wouldn't have! Nobody would! Stop asking me these stupid questions! I'm not a criminal – I'm their mother!'

The court was adjourned for lunch. I stumbled out. Salim walked away, briskly, with his counsel. Tom lit a cigarette for me.

'What's he trying to do?' I asked.

'His job,' he said.

'It's disgusting!'

Tom nodded. 'I know.'

'I bet he's been screwing his secretaries for years, and going back home to his wife.' I drew in the smoke, deeply. My voice shook. 'I feel so . . . You didn't tell me it would be like this.'

'I did.'

'Not like this.'

'Nobody knows it's like this,' he said, 'till it happens.' He took my arm. 'Let's have some lunch.'

'I want to phone my kids,' I said. 'I need a drink.'

We went back after lunch. Tom gave evidence, very eloquently. He told them about his job and his income; he told them about the kids, and how he thought they were settling in.

Then Salim's barrister did his opening spiel, and finally Salim stood up. He looked calm and composed, standing in the witness box in his grey suit. It seemed unbelievable that I had ever touched him.

They gave him a book. 'I take this oath on the Koran,' he said, 'believing in the Koran as God's true word, believing in the true God above us, and that everything whatsoever I tell the court shall be the truth.'

The clerk said: 'Would you please give the court your full name and address.'

'Salim Mohammed Siddiqi, 55 South 4th Street, Karachi, Pakistan.'

Charles Forbes smiled at him, gravely. 'Mr Siddiqi, the court has heard about the events of September 11, 1980. Could you tell us why you took your children to Pakistan?'

'Because their mother was an unfit parent.'

'Why was that?'

Salim spoke to the judge, calm as calm. 'She abused everything I felt was vital for their moral and spiritual welfare.'

The judge asked: 'Could you be specific, Mr Siddiqi?'

He paused, sorrowfully, as if the whole thing was regrettable. 'She swore and drank in front of them, she spent their family allowance on clothes for herself, she neglected them – '

'I didn't!' I cried. 'You weren't at home with them all day!'

The judge frowned at me. 'Mrs Wainwright!'

254

'Some women are natural mothers,' said Salim. 'With some disappointment, I saw, quite early on, that she was not a woman who found total fulfilment in her children – '

'I did!' I shouted.

'She preferred to leave them in other people's care while she went out to work – '

'I would've gone round the bend otherwise!' I cried. I glared at the court. 'Any of you would!'

'Please, Mrs Wainwright!' said the judge.

Salim went on. 'And that is quite apart, of course, from her extramarital activity.' He spoke the words as if he had found a slug under his shoe. 'I deeply regret the way I had to take them. Please understand this. But it was for the sake of my children. Believe me, there was no other way.'

His barrister asked: 'Mr Siddiqi, was there any other reason that you felt an upbringing in Pakistan was more suitable for your children?'

Salim nodded. 'They had been subject to racial harassment in Britain.'

'Can you give an example?'

Salim turned to the judge. 'They are dark-skinned, my Lady, and there are very few Asian families in Ashford. On one occasion, I was in the shopping precinct with my children when some boys came up and called them . . .' He stopped, for effect.

His barrister asked him gently: 'Yes?'

Salim paused. 'Dirty Pakis. They said, "Why don't you go back to your own country?"' He sighed. 'On another occasion, a year later, I took them to see Buckingham Palace and we were . . . insulted in a restaurant.'

'What happened, exactly?' asked Charles Forbes.

'They said, "Kit-e-Kat not good enough for you?"' He shrugged, sorrowfully. 'My children didn't understand, at the time. But any older, and they would. I couldn't bear that to happen. They were already asking me about news items on the TV – items about the National Front and events in East London. They asked me what it meant, and I tried to explain.' He looked around the court, distressed. The bastard. 'They couldn't believe that it meant *them.*'

Charles Forbes nodded, kindly. 'Thank you. Now, we've seen details as to the children's life in Karachi in your affidavit. For the benefit of the court, could we just run through the essential details now? The children are living with whom?'

'They are living in my father's house, with myself, my parents and my sister. And, of course, the servants.'

'What other relatives do they have in Karachi?'

'We are a large, close family,' said Salim. 'They have six cousins, living locally, their age. And two uncles and another, unmarried aunt. Plus more relatives in Lahore.'

'Your father is a businessman, I think?'

Salim nodded. 'He has a prosperous building and contracting company. He is also chairman of the local Rotary Club.'

'And their grandmother, your mother?'

'She is active in charitable work,' said Salim. 'She is also on the board of the Quaid'I'Azam Hospital and is a governor of the Grammar School.'

'I see,' said Forbes. 'She also looks after the children at home?'

'Yes,' said Salim.

'Who else looks after them?'

'Myself, my sister when she is at home, and their *ayah.*'

'Have they both settled down at school?'

'Oh, yes,' said Salim obediently. 'They're very happy there. Yasmin has joined the Girl Guides.'

Charles Forbes turned to the judge. 'You've seen their school reports, my Lady.'

She nodded.

'Yasmin is already top of her class,' said Salim, 'and has been entered for our National Junior Art Competition.'

Suddenly I missed them so much. What were we doing here? Were we all mad?

'Mr Siddiqi, in your opinion, as their father, are they truly happy and settled?'

'Yes,' he said. 'It is their home.'

'Have they ever, in your presence, expressed any wish to be living back in Britain?'

'No,' he said.

'Thank you.' Charles Forbes turned to the judge. 'No more questions, my Lady.'

It's a funny thing, with trials. At times I thought I was in *Perry Mason* or something. I drifted off. That might seem odd when it mattered more than anything in the world, but it seemed to have no connection with me. This judge, this dumpy clerk, this plain wooden room – none of them had anything to do with me wiping my kids' noses or brushing the tangles from Yasmin's hair. What did they know? Even Salim didn't really know. Their voices echoed irrelevantly, they hadn't a clue. And yet, ridiculously, I was in their hands. I should have been concentrating but I kept wondering what the children were doing and if Sonia had found the Swiss rolls for their tea. Why had I bought them Swiss rolls? I'd just seen them in the supermarket. I hadn't eaten them since I was little.

Henry was standing up now. He was talking to Salim.

'Mr Siddiqi,' he was saying, 'do you consider that your children trust you?'

'Yes,' said Salim.

'Let's go back to that day two years ago, when you took them from school.' He looked at Salim, innocently. 'Did they ask where they were going?'

'Yes.'

'And what did you tell them?'

Salim hesitated. 'At first, I told them we were going to France.'

'For the day?'

'Yes.'

'You didn't tell them you were taking them to Karachi?'

Salim paused. 'Not at first.'

'In other words,' he said, pleasantly, 'you lied to them.'

'Only for a few hours. It was for their sake.'

'But you lied to them.'

Salim said: 'Yes.'

'Did they ask about their mother?'

Salim stood there stiffly. 'Yes.'

'And what did you tell them?'

'That they would see her later.'

'Was that a lie?'

They were on the ferry, with the wind blowing. It was sunny that day. Salim was standing on the deck with the suitcases. For two years I had imagined them – but now, for the first time, I saw them. Yasmin was starting to get anxious. She was pulling at his sleeve, asking him questions.

'Mr Siddiqi, was it a lie?'

'Yes,' said Salim.

'I see,' said Henry. He scratched his big, flushed nose.

'I did it for their own good!' said Salim. 'They might have been upset!'

'Upset?' He raised his eyebrows. 'Yes, I imagine they might.'

'I didn't mean . . .' said Salim, and stopped.

'When did you tell them you had lied – that, in fact, you were taking them to Pakistan?'

'At Charles de Gaulle Airport.'

Passengers, with their trolleys, were pushing past them. The tannoy sounded; the children cocked their heads, like animals. But it was already a foreign language.

'I see,' said Henry. 'And what was their reaction, these young children, when they discovered that their father had lied to them?'

Salim shrugged, a higher-class version of the taxi-drivers in Karachi. How dared he? 'They were surprised. But then they were excited, to see their new family.'

He suddenly looked so foreign. It seemed amazing that I had once been married to him. Surely nobody could believe him?

'Ah, yes,' said Henry. 'Their family.' He looked at Salim, pleasantly. 'Let's get on to them. Would you say you were close to your family in Karachi?'

'Yes,' said Salim.

'And you'd been married – how long?'

'Nine years.'

'What surprises me, Mr Siddiqi, is why, if you were so close, you had never bothered to bring either your wife or your children on a visit before.' He smiled. 'If you were such a close, happy family.'

Salim shifted slightly, as if his collar was too tight. 'I had arranged to bring the children over three years before, but Bobby developed whooping cough and so we had to cancel the tickets.'

'I see,' said Henry. 'And that was the only time?'

'I myself had visited twice.'

'But they had never seen either your wife or your children? Their grandchildren?'

Salim paused. Finally he said: 'No.'

'Mr Siddiqi, did they approve of your marriage?'

Salim didn't answer.

'Did they?' Henry repeated.

Salim still didn't reply.

'I put it to you, Mr Siddiqi, that they deeply disapproved of your marrying an English girl.'

Suddenly, Salim's voice rose. 'Well, they were right, weren't they?'

He stopped. His barrister turned to look at him. There was a silence in the room. For the first time, Salim looked uncomfortable.

Henry cleared his throat. 'Your family, as you say, is wealthy and influential. Relations were all but cut off when you eloped with a working-class English girl. Your father wanted you to go back, years ago, marry a suitable Pakistani girl and join the family firm. Am I right?'

Salim didn't reply.

Henry's voice rose. 'I put it to you, Mr Siddiqi, that you do not in fact have your children's best interests at heart. When your wife fell in love with another man, you were motivated entirely by pride and revenge.' His voice throbbed. I sat there, transfixed. 'It was for those reasons that you stole your children and took them to a strange country – '

'That's not true!' Salim shouted.

' – to your alienated parents – '

'That's a lie!'

' – and to the care of a hired *ayah* who cannot even speak their native English tongue!'

He stopped, breathing heavily, and sat down.

It took us all a moment to recover from this. Under my suit, my blouse was wringing wet. Henry was blowing his nose. He suddenly looked like a normal man again – shrunken and quite ordinary, like a TV actor you happen to see in the street.

The judge was speaking. 'I think this is a convenient moment at which to break. I will adjourn this hearing until tomorrow.' She paused. 'This is a very delicate case and I need some time to think about it. Could I please see the children, Yasmin and Robert, in my chambers at ten-fifteen tomorrow morning? And then I should be able to give my judgment. Thank you.'

She got up to leave.

'All stand!' said the clerk.

Twenty-four

That evening I spoke to the kids. I told them that the judge wanted to talk to them, alone. It would all be very informal. Bobby was ever so disappointed; he wanted the works — wigs, gowns, the lot.

I told them that the judge would ask them where they wanted to live — with their dad or with me? That, in the end, it was up to them to choose.

'And you know what to tell her, don't you?' I asked.

We were sitting in the garden, after supper. Yasmin was making a daisy-chain. Most kids get bored after a few stalks split but she had always been persistent; she was making a whole necklace.

'Don't worry,' I said. 'Tomorrow night we'll have spaghetti and watch *Dr Who*, and it'll all be over.'

I put them to bed early, so they would be fresh for their big day. I had ironed their smartest clothes. Bobby snuggled down; I kissed his shiny black hair. The photos of his dog had long since disappeared from under his pillow. He must have found somewhere safer to hide them.

I went next door. Yasmin had always been tidier than Bobby; her room was so neat, it still seemed like she was a visitor. I bent down to kiss her but she turned her face away.

'What's the matter?' I whispered.

'Nothing.'

'Don't worry,' I said. 'She's ever so nice. You'll like her. And Tom and I'll be waiting outside.'

She didn't reply, but she let me kiss her. Over the years her skin had changed. When she was a baby, her cheeks were plump and soft. Now her skin was firm and elastic. She smelt so young, with a whiff of Colgate toothpaste. I sat there for a moment, stroking her arm. She was hairier than any of her friends; she'd be borrowing my razor soon.

When she had gone to sleep I went downstairs. Tom was sitting in front of the TV, drinking brandy. I joined him, and we finished the bottle. We didn't speak. Other topics seemed too trivial, but neither did we want to talk about the kids. We both knew we were going to win, though we were too superstitious to admit it. I had secretly bought a bottle of champagne, and I found out later that he had, too. His was vintage, of course.

The next morning we dressed in our suits again and took the kids to London so early that we had to hang around for ages. We wandered along Fleet Street and sat in a café. The children had milkshakes, but even they didn't finish them. We bought them comics – *Beano* for Bobby and a teenage pop-music one for Yasmin.

Then we went into the Law Courts. When we arrived outside the courtroom we were still early – it was only five-past ten. Bella and Henry were there. We greeted each other, tensely. There was no sign of Salim. I smoked a cigarette.

At ten-fifteen, on the dot, the usher came out of another door – the judge's private room.

'Yasmin and Bobby?' she smiled, holding the door open. 'Would you like to come with me?'

The children looked at me. I kissed them. Just then Salim arrived with Mr Hussein and Charles Forbes. They stood along the corridor, at a distance.

The children went into the room and the door was closed behind them. We waited.

Ten-twenty . . . ten-twenty-five – I tried not to look at Salim. Instead, I concentrated on the other people waiting for their cases to be heard. There was a young couple who had been there the day before. They stood a few yards from each other; the girl kept blowing her nose. She had a ladder in her tights. Another couple arrived; they had a kid with them. Everyone here had come for divorce or custody hearings.

Ten-twenty-seven. Two barristers walked breezily past in their gowns. They greeted Salim's barrister, laughing. Tom said something to me but I didn't hear him. Bella looked at her watch. I didn't really like her; she was too cool and impersonal. She was the only person who hadn't been encouraging.

I was just about to light another cigarette when the door opened and Yasmin and Bobby came out. They hesitated; they had seen Salim. I rushed up to them.

'Was it all right?' I asked, breathlessly.

They nodded.

'What did you say?'

But they didn't have time to answer. The usher was calling us all in.

'This way, please,' she said, holding open the door of court 43.

Tom was going to wait with the children in the corridor. He fished in his pocket.

'I've got your comics,' he said.

'It's not a comic,' said Yasmin. 'It's a magazine.'

'All stand!' said the clerk.

We stood up. The judge came in. She was wearing a bright-blue suit today, like Mrs Thatcher. I searched her face for a clue.

I was so busy wondering what the children had said that I didn't hear her for a while. She was talking slowly, with emotion.

'. . . In my years as a lawyer, I've heard many cases as tragic as this, and they increase year by year. When a marriage breaks down it is the children who are the victims, and in no case I've known has it been more difficult than this to come to a fair judgment. If, indeed, any judgment can be fair in a case of this sort. For here we have two children who are pulled, not just between two warring parents, but between two cultures and two continents . . .'

I could see Salim out of the corner of my eye. Beside me, Bella recrossed her legs.

'. . . I have thought long and hard about this case,' said the judge. 'It has caused me considerable heart-searching, and before I give my judgment I want you to remember that, above

263

all, the welfare of the children must be the paramount consideration . . .'

She paused, and glanced at us all in turn.

'I've heard evidence from both the parents and the welfare officer, and I've talked to the children themselves, who have been remarkably mature and helpful.' She paused again. 'There is no doubt that to be uprooted from their home, their friends and, above all, their mother, was deeply traumatic for them. And, indeed, for their mother.' She looked at me, kindly. 'In abducting his children, the defendant acted improperly and I doubt if the scars will ever be healed, or trust completely restored . . .'

She fell silent. The room held its breath. I looked at Salim; he was gazing at the judge intently. In a moment I was going to take the children home. Yasmin had a riding lesson booked for five o'clock. I suddenly realized I had to buy a present for Darren's birthday party.

'Having said that, I must repeat that my principal concern must be the welfare of the children themselves. Two years is a long time in a young life.' She cleared her throat. 'I am aware of how much distress this will cause but, having heard the evidence, I am satisfied that these children are, by now, so settled in their new home, and with their new family, that, on balance, and after very careful deliberation, I have decided that their best interests would be served by allowing them to return to Pakistan.'

I hadn't heard it right. I stared at her. What had she said?

I swung round to Bella. 'What did she say?'

I stared at the judge, numbly.

'You can't!' I yelled. 'You *can't*!'

And then I started shouting.

The doors were opened and we went out into the corridor. The children were sitting on the floor. I pushed past everyone and rushed up to them. They climbed to their feet.

Tom grabbed me. Then he looked at Henry, who shook his head.

'*What*?' Tom demanded, staring. He had honestly thought we were going to win.

Suddenly Mr Hussein was beside me. He approached the children, his hand outstretched.

'Say goodbye to mummy,' he said.

'You can't take them now!' said Tom.

'I'm sorry,' he said, 'but – '

'They haven't even packed!' said Tom. 'Surely they can spend one last night – '

'I'm sorry,' he said, 'but we're booked on the evening flight.' He looked at his watch.

I grabbed Bobby, pulling his T-shirt towards me. Yasmin was standing still, looking at me. Her face was pale and utterly blank. Mr Hussein took her hand and she turned away.

'Yasmin!' I yelled. 'Bobby!'

I tried to yank Bobby back. His comic slipped to the floor; we skidded on it. I pulled at his shoulders but he ducked out of my grasp and ran away. Salim was waiting for them at the stairs.

I rushed after them, screaming. I pushed past a whole lot of people who were in the way.

'*Yasmin! Bobby*!'

Yasmin turned to look at me. She had started to cry. I tried to get hold of her but Mr Hussein held me back. Salim put his arms around my children and they clattered down the stairs. I pushed Mr Hussein off and stumbled down the stairs after them, yelling, shoving people aside.

'*YASMIN*!' I yelled. '*BOBBY*!'

But they were swallowed up in the crowd.

PART TWO

PART TWO

Twenty-five

People are stirring, now. We'll be landing soon. The business-men across the aisle are closing their briefcases, click-click-click. They do it in unison, like a music-hall routine.

The little boy has woken up. He's jabbering excitedly to his mother. Perhaps he's going home. It's been ten years since my children were taken away but I still don't know what he's saying. He's talking too fast. Kids who speak in a foreign language, they seem so experienced, don't they? Even little ones like him.

I can speak well enough to bargain in a bazaar, though. Mr Ajazuddin, one of the people I do business with, we rattle along. 'That's not your last price!' I cry in Urdu, throwing up my hands orientally. '*Bahut! Bahut repea*!' It's a ritual we both enjoy, a sort of Pakistani foreplay before I produce my wallet and we climax in a flurry of paper-signing. 'Ah,' he sighs. 'What a bargain you have, *memsahib* Wainwright.' He snaps his fingers for a cold drink; exhausted, we sip our Pepsis.

My neighbour, the little boy's mother, fishes for her high-heeled sandals and wriggles her feet into them. Then she turns to me and starts chatting. People always do, don't they, near the end of a flight? If you talk earlier, you feel obliged to make conversation all the way. So you come awake at the end, and talk, and then you disembark, and at the luggage carousel you feel slightly shy, meeting each other standing up, like you feel when you've been swimming next to somebody in the public baths and you meet them later in the street, fully-dressed.

'So you've visited Karachi before?' she asks.

I nod. 'Lots of times.' I don't mention my kids. I tell her the other reason. 'I've got a little business in Kent. A shop. I import stuff from Pakistan.'

'How interesting,' she says, in a cocktail-party sort of way.

She's one of these well-bred Pakistanis you never really get to know, shiny and closed as a conker. 'What goods?'

'Old embroidery. Clothes. Wedding pieces from Sind and Baluchistan. Mirrorwork *kurtas*, that sort of thing. Brassware. *Pan* boxes.'

'People want these things, in England?'

'If you lived in England, you'd want them,' I reply. 'If you lived in Ashford.'

'Ashford's a dump.' I said to Salim, all those years ago. Well, it was a bigger one now. They call it the boom town of the Southeast, and you know what boom town means.

'A bit short on oriental mystery,' I say.

'*Agar tum mujhe chorogi*,' said Salim, '*main tumhe maar doonga aur phir apney aap ko*.' He had touched my cheek, his face close to mine. 'If you ever left me, I'd kill, first you, and then myself.'

He'd had a good try, I'll give him that. And left me for dead.

Funnily enough, now we're about to arrive I feel quite calm. Numb, in fact. For hours my stomach has been churning. Stupid, isn't it, when I'm going to see my own flesh and blood?

My darlings.

My own flesh and blood, who betrayed me.

There's thousands of questions I want to ask them, but one especially. I'll never dare. And anyway, haven't I betrayed them too?

I wish I knew what they thought, these two great strangers. Smooth and closed as conkers. I'm getting nervous again. 'Don't be an eejit,' Sonia would say.

Sonia's had a baby, did I tell you? Four months ago. She fucked a big black Radio Rentals bloke, who came to deliver her video. And, hey presto!

Easy, isn't it? Easy-peasy.

I've got a video too, now. So many things have changed since my kids have been in England. People have got videos and phone cards. They've build a Texas Homecare where Stacey's dad used to keep his pigs. I've given up smoking. More sorts of crisps have been invented, but my kids are probably too old to mind. Pot Noodles have come and gone. My dad – their grandad – has died from lung cancer. Russell Harty's dead too; my mum loved him as well. But Mrs Thatcher's still here. She'll always be here. And I'm still married to Tom. Just about.

After the court case Salim wouldn't let me see the children for a long, long time. Tom was right about his reaction. It was a gamble, and I lost. Terrible damage was done, to all of us. I won't tell you what I went through, because you can imagine that.

Tom battled on with all the other cases, as well as mine. In the end, though, he despaired too. He felt he'd failed us. I told him it wasn't his fault, it was mine, but we both knew the damage was done. Neither of us admitted it, of course. In the end he gave up his practice in London and set up an office in Ashford. It's near Talacre Road, where Salim and I had our flat. But I haven't told him that.

In a dream I'm digging a trench. Above me is a row of kids in yellow T-shirts. They're standing on the rim. They're black kids – West Indian black, I think. I don't recognize any of them. And then, as I go on digging, the edge of the trench starts to crumble. I try to shout, to warn them, but no sound comes out of my mouth.

The trench walls collapse. But instead of falling in, the kids take to the air. Off they all fly, with a curious noise as if somebody's shaking silver foil. They're making that noise in their throats, helping themselves along.

And then I realize that the earth is falling in on me, where I'm standing in the ditch. But it doesn't hurt at all.

There's so much to tell you. There's so much stuff. About when I started up the business, for instance, and came to Karachi. I hadn't seen the kids for nearly two years by then. But when I arrived in Pakistan I worked on Salim's mother, I appealed to her as a woman; it took a long time but I managed to fix a visit.

271

I didn't see Salim – I never saw him – but from then onwards I came to Karachi twice a year and saw Yasmin and Bobby. In hotel rooms, those sorts of places. It was the only thing that kept me going. I hope it meant something to them, too. I could never ask them. There was so much I couldn't ask. Practically everything. Every question was too painful. So you end up asking, 'What did you have for dinner last night?'

Once, when I phoned from England, this gruff voice came on the line. For a moment I thought I was speaking to a stranger. Then I realized it was Bobby, and his voice had broken, without me.

There's so much to say. I don't know what you want to hear. What can I say about all those years? They passed. I'll tell you how this whole thing started, why I'm flying to Karachi tonight.

Yasmin has grown up, that's why. It was her eighteenth birthday a few months ago. I had been waiting for this moment for ten long years, the only light at the end of our tunnel. I knew I had to wait until my children were old enough to come back, of their own free will. Once you're eighteen you can do what you like, you've come of age. That was my only hope.

Yasmin has grown up artistic. Heaven knows where she got her talent – not from either of us, that's for sure. She had done a diploma course in Karachi, but she wanted to go on to do Graphics, like her Uncle Aziz. I had investigated Canterbury College of Art – they had a good Graphics department there. I had got them to send her a prospectus; I had got her to send them her portfolio. I told her not to let her father know – not until her birthday. This was my plan, my gamble, and this time I was determined to win.

Shortly after her birthday, Salim phoned. I remember exactly what we were doing, that evening. I was squatting on the living-room floor of the cottage, unpacking a bale of *kurtas* – sort of tunic things.

'Phew,' said Tom. 'Bit whiffy, aren't they?'

'They're antiques!' I said.

'Something's certainly authentic.'

The doorbell rang. It was Marjorie Something, a loud, horsey woman. She ran the East Kent Rural Trust, and she wanted him to chair some meeting about a new development – some new housing estate or something. Probably Salim's old firm was building it.

'We've got the facts on the threatened pondlife,' she whinnied. 'Great Crested Newt and so on.'

'I'm in court all morning,' he said. 'Why don't you drop in after lunch? You know where I am – between Tescos and Allied Carpets.'

She brayed. 'Sounds like one of the circles of *Purgatorio* Dante forgot about.' Pretentious old bat.

'The whole of Kent will be soon,' he said, 'if we don't get a move on.'

She gleamed at him, showing her teeth. 'You're a treasure!'

He saw her out. When he came back, I said, 'It's the Great Crested Tom she's got her eye on.'

'She hasn't!'

'It's you who's an endangered species. Nice heterosexual bloke, all in working order, under sixty, does the washing-up. Half the women in Kent are pretending the High Speed Rail Link's going through their back garden, just to get you round.'

He sighed. 'Wish you felt like that.' He poured us a drink. 'Trouble is, your mother likes me. Women's mothers have always liked me. It's a death knell.'

I remember everything we said that evening. My senses were alert; my skin tingled. I knew something was going to happen; it was only a matter of time. I remember looking at Tom, as he sipped his whiskey. He was ageing well; good stock, of course. A distinguished touch of grey around his temples, but not an ounce more flesh on him. There was just a strained look around his eyes, as if he was squinting against the sun, searching the horizon for a train that never came.

He put down his glass. I knew he wanted to talk but I didn't want to hear it. And just then the phone rang.

I rushed over and picked it up. It was Salim.

'Marianne?' he said.

My heart thumped. I hadn't heard his voice for years.

'How are you?' he asked.

What the hell did he expect me to answer? 'Fine,' I said.

'I'm flying to London on Thursday,' he said. 'Do you think we could meet?'

I dreamed that night that I was trying to board a bunder boat in Karachi harbour. The plank kept rocking. Bobby was sitting on the boat, with his back to me. He was wearing dirty white *shalwar-kamize* pyjamas, and smoke drifted up from his cigarette. When had my son started smoking? Behind him the sky was stained red; the oily water swelled and subsided. I tried to call his name but no sound came.

And then he turned around and looked at me. He wasn't Bobby at all; he was the pock-marked man who sold nuts in Empress Market. I woke. I'd stuffed the edge of the duvet into my mouth, and I was sucking it like a baby.

'And tell Elaine I don't know when I'll be back,' I said, flustered. Elaine was the girl who ran the shop for me. 'Does this look all right?'

It was early Thursday morning. Tom was sitting in bed, and I was opening the wardrobe and trying on various clothes.

'Why do you have to go?' he asked.

'And that woman – forgotten her name, split veins – she's coming for her cushions ... oh, I think I'll wear my black skirt.' I zipped it on, hopping on one leg. I was dead nervous. 'Oh, and that bloke's delivering the lawnmower – '

'Why can't you just talk on the phone?'

'But he's mended it, he's got to deliver it – '

'Not him,' said Tom. 'Salim. Don't see why he's got to summon you like this. Bloody cheek.'

'Something's wrong,' I said. 'Perhaps he's going to get married again. He's going to marry a marine biologist and they're all going to live in Australia and the kids'll love her better than me.'

'You'll make yourself ill again,' he said. 'Doesn't he understand what he's doing? Still, he's always been an impulsive chap, hasn't he?'

'Wonder what he'll look like?' I said, pausing in front of the mirror. My face was flushed.

'Fatter,' said Tom. 'All those curries.'

And then I heard the crunch of gravel outside; my cab had arrived.

I went to the station and took the train up to London. The moment I stepped into the carriage everything was wiped from my mind — my husband, the cottage, the past eight years. It was as if they had never happened. It scared me rigid. I tried to concentrate on the face of my kids, like you concentrate on the face of some beloved pet before you go to have your teeth drilled. Trouble was, I could only picture them when they were young. Their teenage faces were confused with my dreams — I dreamed about them most nights, and usually in some unlikely setting. They kept dissolving back into the kids I'd brought up, back in Harebell Close.

I arrived in London, and took a taxi to Salim's hotel. It's better, arriving in a cab; it gives you confidence. The Kensington Hotel was a white, stucco cliff above me, rearing up. Was he watching from one of the windows? It was chilly for June. I shivered in my pink sweater. I told myself: I'm thirty-eight, I'm a mature woman. What can he do to me now?

I went into the lobby. My guts had turned to water and I had to use their toilet. Shaking, I stood in the cloakroom. I tried to reapply my lipstick but my hand wouldn't stay still. I looked in the mirror. My bleached hair had grown out a lifetime ago; I had a brown bob, to my shoulders. Maybe he wouldn't recognize me. How could he possibly harm me? What else was left for him to do?

'Come in,' his voice said. I opened the door and went into his room.

He was standing at the window, with his back to me. He looked like a stranger. He could be a consultant who was about to tell me that the growth was malignant.

He turned. 'Hello,' he said, stepping forward.

'Hello.'

For a moment we hesitated. Were we going to shake hands? We paused, and stood there awkwardly.

Two things jolted me. How handsome he was – beautiful, really, the bastard – and how little he had changed. His shiny black hair had receded, that was all. More of his polished forehead showed. He wore a blue, open-necked shirt and pale trousers; he looked quite casual, for Salim. But then I didn't know him anymore, did I?

'Sorry it's early,' he said, 'but . . .'

'It doesn't matter.'

'I'm going to visit Aisha and I've got a bit of business to do. Then I have to go back to Karachi.'

'When?'

'Tomorrow,' he said.

I sat down on a chair. 'They're great,' I said.

'What?'

'Her kids. Aisha's. I saw them last month.'

'Ah.'

There was a silence. Then he said: 'Would you like some coffee?'

'Yes, please.'

He went to the phone. I got up and looked around the room.

'Coffee for two,' he was saying. 'Room 607. Thank you.'

He put the phone down. I stood beside the TV, fiddling with a leaflet. It had a list of video films on it.

'Wow, you can get films and everything,' I wittered. '*Arthur 2. Roger Rabbit*. You seen it?'

He shook his head. There was a pause.

Then I asked: 'How are they?'

'Fine.'

'I spoke to Yasmin last week, but Bobby was out.'

'He's in the junior tennis team at the Gymkhana Club,' he said. 'Did he tell you?'

I shook my head.

'When he can spare time from his beloved computer,' said Salim. 'A real video-age kid.'

'Not a kid anymore,' I said.

'No.'

276

There was another pause. I went on fiddling with the leaflet.

'I heard your father died,' I said.

He nodded.

'So has mine,' I told him.

'Oh,' he said. 'Good old Frank. I'm sorry.'

'They didn't tell you?'

He shook his head.

'Well,' I said, 'they hadn't seen him for years.'

'No.' Salim cleared his throat. 'I really wanted to talk to you about Yasmin.'

'What's happened?' I asked, alarmed.

'I just wanted to ask your advice.'

'My advice!'

He sat down on a chair. I stayed standing. 'You see, she's being very . . .' He stopped. 'Bobby's easy, he's just a chap. We understand each other. But Yas.' He pushed the ashtray away. 'She doesn't know what she wants.'

'What does she want?' I asked.

He looked up. 'I think *you* know that. You wrote to her about the art school.'

'What about it?'

'She's so confused. One minute she wants to stay in Karachi, the next minute she wants to come here. Something's up.'

'Well, I wouldn't know, would I?' I said. 'I haven't seen her since October.'

'I think she ought to stay in Karachi.'

'Look, she's half-English!'

'She's happy there,' he said. 'She's lots of friends. Since Benazir Bhutto, it's a transformed country; it's much more liberal – '

'*She* obviously doesn't think so.' I took a breath, trying to gather my strength. My plan had worked, but now I was here in this feminine bedroom, with its flounced, flowery curtains and Salim sitting there, I needed to concentrate. I sat down on the other side of the table. 'Look, why do you make her feel guilty?' I asked him. 'Hasn't she had enough of that?' I took another breath. 'Salim. She's grown up. Look, *you* can't paint,

I can't paint. She can. She's separate. Let her do what she wants!'

He looked up. 'You've been influencing her.'

'What the hell do you mean?' I shouted. 'Eight years and I've hardly bloody seen her, you stole her from me – '

'I didn't! The court decided that – '

'I've lost their whole childhood, my own kids! You stole their childhood from me!' My voice rose, I couldn't stop myself. 'Can you imagine what it's been like? Never putting them to bed, never taking them to school, never knowing their friends, never making their supper, never even quarrelling with them? Never touching them? *Never touching them*? My own kids? God, I've hated you!'

There was a frozen silence. Just then there was a tap at the door.

'Come in,' said Salim.

A maid came in with a tray of coffee things.

'Thank you,' said Salim.

She put them down on the table; we moved back politely, to give her room. Then she went out.

There was a long pause. We didn't touch the coffee.

Then I spoke, more gently. 'Please let her come.'

I gazed at him. I had to try a new tack; I had to unlock something in him, something I unlocked all those years ago.

'Don't you remember?' I said. 'Can you remember? You were young and rebellious once. You said your parents were stuffy and old-fashioned, you longed to get away. They disapproved, just like you're disapproving now.'

He nodded. 'Of course I remember.'

'I thought you would.'

We sat there in silence. I was breathing heavily. The room was so stuffy; I was sweating like a pig.

Finally he spoke. 'I've tried to be a good father,' he said.

'I'm sure you have.'

'I didn't want to live at home. Not really.' He turned the sugar bowl round and round in his hand. We weren't looking at each other. 'I could've got married,' he said. 'There've been,

278

well, lots of friends, family friends; they brought their daughters for tea . . .'

'I bet they did.'

'But I thought it would be bad for the kids. Confusing for them.' He stroked the rim of the sugar bowl. Down in the street, a car hooted. The double-glazing made it seem a long way off. 'All these years,' he said, 'I've been looking after my parents, and the kids . . . The way my father lived – the Rotary Club, the Sind Club, the dinners . . . oh, those dinners! I seem to have spent my whole life at the Holiday Inn, shaking hands with somebody's uncle who wants a bit of business put his way.' He looked at me. 'It's so boring!'

There was a silence. 'You want your kids to only know that?' I asked. Then I took a breath, and spoke urgently. 'Let them come! Let Bobby come too.'

'Bobby?'

'He'll keep her company, he'll keep an eye on her. He'll love it. *You* loved England – well, let them find out for themselves! He can come to a sixth-form college for a year – just a year!' I looked at him, breathlessly. He was gazing at me. 'Let them come, Salim. But let them come freely. With your blessing.'

He didn't reply. We sat there, on either side of the table, gazing at each other over the cooling coffee pot.

That night in bed I put my arms around Tom, pulling him against my bare skin. I squeezed my eyes shut and wrapped my leg around his thigh. He grunted with surprise; we hadn't made love for weeks. I slid my tongue into his mouth.

The mattress creaked as I moved him over. I slid my hand down, under the duvet, and cupped his balls. They felt loose and cool. I held his cock, and stroked it. It stayed soft in my hand.

He spoke into the darkness. 'Seems like you've fallen in love with him all over again.'

I jerked back. 'I haven't!' Then I said: 'I only want to get my kids back.' He didn't reply. I rolled off him, and we lay there in the blackness.

*

It worked. Now she was eighteen, Yasmin could legally come anyway – but I knew she wouldn't come without her father's blessing. She'd been brought up as a dutiful Pakistani daughter. She'd needed him to approve. And he had. I had persuaded him.

There was a phone call and some letters. The arrangements were made. Two months later, and I'm coming to fetch them home.

The 'No Smoking' sign has come on. I look out of the window, into the black night. With a bump, we land on Pakistani tarmac.

'Please keep your seat-belts fastened,' says the pilot's voice, 'until the plane has come to a complete standstill.' He has a faultless British accent.

You might wonder why I've come all this way to fetch them. If you were the Pakistani woman I'd just say it was a buying trip.

I'm coming to fetch them because, now I've got them, I can't bear to be a moment without them. I want to be with them, freely, in Karachi. I want us to spend one more day in this hot, dusty city that I've grown to know so well. That I've hated so violently, but that has become more dear to me than anywhere on earth.

I want to help them with their suitcases, like a real parent, and I want to sit next to them on the plane all the way back to England. We can talk, or we needn't talk at all. We can sit side by side, the three of us, with our plastic dinner trays. I can fiddle with their headphone dials so they can hear the film. I can be a mother.

Twenty-six

Except, of course, they can fiddle with the dials themselves. It shocks me, how large and capable they are, especially Bobby who has grown huge, taller than Salim. On the plane he reads the *Amstrad Users' Monthly* all the way. It's hieroglyphics to me. He's got two pimples on his forehead.

Yasmin has grown up incredibly beautiful. I've realized this, more and more each visit; but now I've got her, I'm awestruck. She smells of honeysuckle perfume, classier than the stuff she bought for me once in a supermarket. Around her long, slender wrists the bangles tinkle, like Aisha's. It seems impossible that I ever gave birth to her. Do all mothers feel like this? I don't know what mothers feel; real ones.

She seems nervy and excited. It must be because she's coming to England. She's like a young filly, shying at a sudden noise.

She's too old for me to buy her a pony now. We've missed all that. I can't ask her mother-and-daughter things, either. Somebody else must have bought her first bra with her. Does she use Tampax, or does she have some strange, Pakistani arrangement?

The bitterness – it lies in my stomach, a sediment. It dissolves my guts, eating away like acid.

Tom has been nice and welcoming. The sun is shining. I feel like a stage mother as I open the cottage door; I can't connect this to my past at all. I've longed for this for so long, I've played it in my head so often, that now it's happening I can't believe it's real. I take Bobby upstairs to his bedroom. He's hardly said a word to me yet, except 'It's OK. No problem' when I tried to carry his suitcase. He sounded like the sunglasses man in Bohri Bazaar.

I gesture, slightly hysterically, around the room.

'Remember this?' I cry. 'I've painted it. Your old stuff's in

281

the cupboard. Nice, isn't it? You can bring your friends back to play.'

'Play?' He raises his eyebrows.

'I mean, records and things.'

When I come downstairs Yasmin is on the phone. She puts the receiver back, quickly, when she sees me.

'Just phoning Emily,' she says.

'Oh, good!' I say, pleased as anything.

'She's not there.'

'She's just started horticultural college. So you still write to her?'

Yasmin pauses, then nods.

My shop is just up the lane. It's in this sort of complex of old farm buildings; they've been converted into retail outlets. There's a pine-furniture shop, and a tea shop, and an art gallery run by an old dear called Lily, who sells paintings of blue-tits sitting on twigs of pussy willow. There's my shop, which Tom calls Calcutta Corner even though I've told him Calcutta's in India. It's real name is the Magic Carpet, because when you step inside and close your eyes you could be in Karachi. It even smells the same. I bring the kids in and introduce them to Elaine, who is plump and sixteen and can't tell a *kelim* from a *kurta*. When Bobby sees her he takes his Walkman headphones off. 'Hi,' she says, eyeing him. Yasmin yawns; she says she is jet-lagged.

So we cross the yard and I take them into the farm shop. It sells fruit and vegetables and dinky little jars of Country Pantry jam, which they make in a factory in Ilford and then cover with gingham mob caps. Sonia supplies the farm shop with cooked stuff; Taste Buddies has expanded, she's become ever so successful.

I lead the kids along the aisles, chattering brightly. 'Remember Kirsty? She's into hypnotherapy. Zara's living with a town planner in Dundee.' I point to the rows of food. 'Steak and kidney pud! When did you last have that, eh? Kent's grown all these yuppies now. They shove this stuff into their microwaves and pretend they cooked it themselves.' I point at the glass cases. 'Go on, choose! Chicken pies, sausages?'

Yasmin says: 'We don't really eat pork.'

'Oh, no.' Then I babble on: 'Well, what shall we have for supper?'

Yasmin yawns.

I put my arm around her. 'It's great, having you here. You warm enough?' I turn to Bobby. 'You OK?'

But his Walkman is plugged into his ears.

I turn to Yasmin. 'Tomorrow we'll give you your birthday present. Better late than never.'

The next morning, Sunday, Tom and I get up early and fetch the mini from where it's been hidden, up the lane. We tie yards and yards of red ribbon around it. The birds are singing in the garden; beyond the fields, church bells are ringing in the village.

When Yasmin comes downstairs we blindfold her and lead her outside, singing 'Happy birthday to you'.

I untie the blindfold and she stares at the car. It's white and shiny. She turns, her face radiant, and hugs me.

'You can drive to college tomorrow,' I say.

'It's beautiful!' she breathes, and turns to hug Tom. Just for a moment we seem like a *pukka* family. Somebody ought to take our snapshot.

'Bit old, I'm afraid,' says Tom. 'It belonged to somebody in my choir. One loud lady owner, mezzo-soprano.'

Yasmin takes the keys and gets into the car.

Beside me, Bobby says: '*Abba-ji* gave her a car too.'

I stare at him. 'What?'

'Daddy gave her a Toyota. He had it all covered with garlands and tinsel. For her birthday. But then she said she wanted to come to England, so he sold it.'

Yasmin is so excited about the car. It's Sunday afternoon now and she's driving off to meet Emily for tea. I'm glad that she seems to be settling in so quickly. She can't decide what to

283

wear, and she's come into my bedroom to try on my clothes. We feel quite giggly.

'What about this?' I hold up my yellow fluffy jumper against her.

'Not with my colouring,' she grimaces.

'Come on, you'd look great. Much better than me.'

She tries it on doubtfully, and looks at herself in the mirror. We frown, and laugh.

'I look like an Easter chick,' she says.

'I made you an Easter egg hunt once, remember?'

She nods. 'Bobby ate all his in one go.'

'He was sick.'

She rummages in the wardrobe. She's certainly going to a lot of trouble for Emily. She pulls out another sweater, with rhinestones around the collar.

She holds it up. 'You've always had . . . well . . .'

'Dead vulgar taste – '

'No! You just didn't dress . . .' she pauses. 'Like other people's mothers.'

'In my heyday, Yas, I was something of a raver. Known to the roadies as Spangles.'

'What's a roadie?'

'Big fat blokes at rock gigs. Wore purple velvet bellbottoms much, much too small for them.' I take out a lurex top. 'Haven't worn this for yonks. Not ideal for weeding the herbaceous border.'

Happiness sweeps over me. We're like a bona fide mother and daughter. Isn't it a miracle?

Yasmin rummages in the wardrobe and pulls out my white leather miniskirt.

'You can't!' I laugh.

'The sixties are back. I read it in *Harpers*.'

I smile. 'If that skirt could talk . . .'

She's putting the skirt on. She turns away modestly, and then shows herself to me. She is transformed – pink sweater, white skirt, long brown legs. Suddenly she turns her back to me and starts caressing herself, running her hands over her back, lasciviously, just as I did all those years ago in C&A. A lifetime ago, when I wore that fateful jumper.

'You used to do this . . .' she says.

I laugh. 'You watch out, in that.'

'I won't get it dirty.'

'I don't mean the skirt,' I warn her. 'I mean you.'

I hug her, and then draw back. She's like myself, starting out all over again.

'It's so weird,' I say.

'What is?'

I just smile, and shrug.

When she's driven off I start to feel anxious. I don't know why. She hasn't even told me where she's meeting Emily. I go out to Tom, who is digging in his beloved vegetable garden.

'Hope she's all right,' I say to him.

'It's just had its MOT.'

'She's not used to English roads.'

'You mean, she's not used to people driving in the right direction,' he says.

'What's the matter with you?'

'Nothing.' He pulls out a string of couch grass, and flings it away.

Bobby is in the lounge, watching TV. His stuff is spread all over the floor – tapes, his sweater, an empty can of Coke. At least he seems to be settling in.

I'm taking some clothes from the washing machine in the kitchen. I pause on the stairs. 'It's dead boring there, isn't it?'

'What?' He looks up.

'TV. In Pakistan.'

'We get lots of videos,' he says.

'Got.'

'What?'

'You *got* lots.' I pause, one foot on the stairs. 'Are you bored? Want to go for a walk?'

'It's OK.'

I show him his shirt. 'I'll iron this and you can wear it

285

tomorrow, for your first day, and then we'll go shopping and buy you lots of clobber.'

'Clobber?'

'Clothes. Gear.'

'It's OK,' he says, turning back to the TV. 'I've brought lots.'

'I want to!'

'OK.'

When Yasmin comes home she spends hours in the bathroom, soaking. I used to do that. I tell her through the door where my avocado bubble bath is, but she doesn't reply.

Later, when she's come out, I tap on her bedroom door and go in. She still hasn't unpacked all her stuff, but she's put aside a pile of clothes for tomorrow.

'How was Emily?' I ask.

'Fine.'

'Where did you meet?'

She is rubbing moisturiser into her shins. 'Oh, some tea shop.'

'Where?'

'How do I know?' She suddenly glares at me. 'I don't know this place!'

I back away, hurt. She yawns. She must still be jet-lagged.

We're all getting edgy. Tom says I'm smothering them. I'm only mothering them. What's in an 's'? Smother-mother, mother-smother. At night I lie, smothered by the duvet, and dream about them even though they're lying in the rooms next door. In my dreams they are always little kids.

Elaine and I are in the shop, pricing goods.

'They liking college then?' she asks.

I nod. 'Bobby's even met up with an old mate of his, Darren Beasley. You know him?'

'Mmm,' she says. 'He's really dishy, isn't he?'

'Elaine! His skin!'

'It's gorgeous,' she says, dreamily.

'What, covered in acne?'

'Not Darren. Bobby. He's gorgeous. All smouldering.'

I glare at her. That's my son she's talking about.

I look at my watch. 'You can knock off now.'

She gazes into space. 'His dad's got a Merc, he says. And a driver.'

When she's gone I sit down, heavily, on a mirrorwork cushion. Besides, she shouldn't go fancying Pakistani blokes. They're nothing but trouble.

Sonia drops in, on her way to the farm shop. She flops down on the mirrorwork cushion, unbuttons her blouse and plugs Archie, her baby, to her breast. She's come from the clinic.

'So weird,' she says, 'going there again. There're all these little bimbos half my age, discussing Milton.'

'Milton?'

'Not the poet. The sterilizing tablets.' She chuckles, and tells me about this boardroom lunch she did yesterday. 'A bloke kept saying, "You got a cat out there in the kitchen?"'

She squeezes Archie, smother-mother.

'Got to comfort myself, haven't I? Honestly, Marianne, it's all over so quickly. One minute they're little girls, then they're on the bloody phone all the time, and suddenly they've gone. As if they've never happened.'

I don't reply. She's got fine lines around her eyes and the corners of her mouth; laughter-lines, really, not wrinkles. Can it really have been the same for both of us?

She kisses Archie's black, damp hair. 'What's it all about, eh? There's this John Updike book I read. He says, "What's it all about? A few laughs, a few babies."'

I look at her breast. It's huge; under the skin, there's raised, blue veins.

Tom comes in from the garden and looks around the lounge. The floor is strewn with computer magazines, a sock, a pair of trainers and a half-eaten bowl of Weetabix. Upstairs, there's pop music coming from Bobby's stereo.

'We're not his servants, you know,' says Tom. 'Your son's got a very oriental attitude to this place.'

'It's not oriental. It's adolescent.'

'Same thing, really,' he replies. 'When you've got to clear it up.'

'He's been working hard.'

'So have I,' says Tom. 'In many ways.'

'What do you mean?'

He doesn't reply. I look at my watch. 'She's late again.'

Yasmin hardly seems to be here, nowadays. She stays late at college, and she's often out in the evenings. Today, Saturday, she's gone off sketching at the seaside with a girl called Belinda.

'I wonder if I could possibly book the bathroom for later?' asks Tom.

'He's not in it. He's in his room.'

'Ah, but will he stay there?'

They've been here five weeks now. Tom's trying to be a stepfather; I'm trying to be a mother. What are they trying to be? Grown up? Sooner or later, I'm sure, we're bound to click. At the moment we feel like four people who happened to have been stranded in a lift together. No, it's not always as bad as that. Sometimes Bobby and I watch *Eastenders* together, and we're quite companionable. And he's been showing Tom how to work a computer – we've bought him an Amstrad. Once or twice he's even brought his mates back, Darren and Tony, and they've played warbling computer games upstairs. Yasmin doesn't really feel like my daughter but sometimes, when we're washing up together, we feel close, I'm sure we do. More like sisters. It's nice when she borrows my clothes.

We haven't heard much from Salim, thank God. Now he's let go of his kids he's gone off somewhere on holiday. The kids had a postcard from him, postmarked Kashmir. He's having some male menopausal jaunt in the Himalayas. Perhaps he'll meet a hippie and go through a life-change. Good bloody riddance. I can have the kids to myself; it's my bloody turn now.

Except it's too late. That's what I suspect when I'm lying awake at night. They're poised for flight: both of them. Now that I've finally got them in my nest, they're ready to leave it.

Oh, I don't know. I just wish they'd *talk* to me. They never say that they've missed me, all these years. Is the damage too deep? And they're too old, now, for me to kiss them goodnight.

Yasmin comes home and runs up to her room. I hear her door slam shut. She looks so radiant, as if there's a light under her skin. She's so excited to have escaped from her stultifying grandparents and to come here. She's a real college kid now, with her striped scarf and muddy car. She's always on the phone to her friends. I wish she'd bring some of them home. She must seem like a bird of paradise amongst all those pasty faces. I went to the art school once and all the girls were dressed in black, with clumpy black shoes; they looked like old Greek grandmothers. Except for their punky hair. All the blokes must be falling in love with my exotic daughter. I want to guard her against them, she looks so innocent; she's been practically brought up in *purdah*. But when I ask her, she says she doesn't fancy any of them – they're so young. She's devoting herself to her art.

One Thursday I've been shopping at Sainsbury's. When I come out it's four o'clock so I drive to Bobby's sixth-form college and park outside. I see him with some of his mates. When he spots me he comes over to the car.

'It's all right,' he says. 'I can take the bus.'

'Don't be silly. I'll give you a lift.'

I often do this. I like giving him a lift home. He looks at his friends, and hesitates. Then he climbs into the car. I've got to pick up something in Charing, on the way home; there's an old woman there, Mrs Albright, who sews my embroidered cloth into cushions.

I start the engine. 'So what did you do today?'

'English.'

'What – novels?' I ask. 'Poetry?'

'Shelley and things.'

'Your dad used to love Shelley,' I say, driving into the traffic.

'Did he?'

'Didn't he ever read it to you?'

Bobby shakes his head.

'That's sad,' I say.

He plugs in his Walkman. We drive out of Ashford.

It's a wet, thundery afternoon in late October. As we drive along the country road the wind blows yellow leaves across the windscreen. Some of them get plastered to the glass. I switch on the wiper and slew them away. For some reason, I'm feeling jumpy today and irritable. Tom and I have not been getting on too well. He's finding it difficult, sharing the cottage with these two great teenagers. He doesn't snap at them, though; he snaps at me instead. He stomps around. That's all it is; nothing else. We're fine, really. He hasn't talked about the other thing for months now.

The hedges are thinner now, on either side of the road. Winter will be here soon. For some reason I'm thinking about Terry. I sometimes do when I'm driving. 'You wouldn't believe what people get up to,' he had said. 'Just 'cos I'm driving a minicab, they think I'm invisible.' According to Terry, Kent's a hotbed of adultery. I feel nostalgic for him sometimes, and wonder what he's doing. We were mates, Terry and me. We were familiar, in a way I've never been with Tom or Salim. We had the same sort of upbringing; we spoke the same language. Tom's posh, and Salim was Pakistani.

I'm thinking all this as I drive up Charing High Street. It's a picturesque place, ever so photogenic. Tea shops, all that.

And then I see Yasmin's car. It's parked outside the Oast House Hotel. I look at it, puzzled, and slow down. What's she doing here?

I park further along the street, and I'm just about to get out of the car when I stop.

Yasmin is coming out of the hotel. She is with a man – a tall bloke, late twenties, with curly, light-brown hair. He's wearing a leather jacket. Their arms are around each other, and they stop on the pavement and kiss. Then she looks at her watch, kisses him again and gets into her car. I watch them in my rearview mirror. She winds down the window and he says something to her, laughing. Then he kisses her again, through the window. He walks to his car and gets in. Yasmin drives off; he starts his engine and drives off in the opposite direction.

I sit there for a moment, my heart racing. Bobby hasn't seen anything; he's sitting there with his eyes closed, his Walkman in his ears. The disco-beat sounds like mice scratching against my brain.

Twenty-seven

It's a quarter of an hour later. I'm sitting on Yasmin's bed, in her room. She hasn't come home yet. Sonia's words keep going around my head. 'He must be blind,' she'd said. 'You're lit up like a frigging lightbulb.'

Why hasn't Yasmin told me? I'm her frigging mother. I sit there on her embroidered counterpane, burning with hurt feelings. They weren't just having a cream tea in there, either. No way. I'm not stupid.

There's the crunch of gravel outside. A few minutes later she comes in. She stares at me.

'Hi,' she says.

'You're late.'

She looks at her watch. 'Am I?'

'How was college?'

'Fine. We did typography this morning.'

She puts her portfolio down with a weary sigh.

'You're lying,' I say.

She stares at me. 'What?'

'What are you up to?'

'What do you mean?'

'You haven't been to college today.'

'I have!' she cries.

'You haven't.'

She pauses. 'I did go.'

'When?'

She stands, fiddling with the make-up tubes on her dressing table. 'This morning.'

There is a silence. Downstairs I hear the jingle of a TV commercial.

'Who was he?'

'Who?' She stares at me with her beautiful wide eyes.

'You know who. That man. I saw you in Charing.'

292

She raises her eyebrows. 'Ah.' Then she says: 'He's just . . .'

'Who is he? When did you meet him?'

'He's just . . .'

'Who?' My voice startles me, it's so loud.

'Somebody I used to know in Karachi.'

'How long have you been seeing him?'

She shrugs. 'Since . . .'

'Since when?'

'Since I came here.'

A moment passes. She bends to look in the mirror, and pushes a strand of hair out of her eye.

'You've been lying to me,' I say, 'all this time – '

'I haven't!'

'Trotting off to college – '

'I have been going to college, look at my stuff!' She darts across to her portfolio and fumbles open the ribbon. 'I just see him . . . sometimes.'

It's now that I realize. I'm so stupid, it's taken all this time. I stare at her, frozen.

'You knew him in Karachi?'

She nods, and closes her portfolio.

'When did he come here?' I ask.

'He was posted there for two years, he worked in the port, he's a surveyor – '

I interrupt her. 'When did he come here?'

'Six months ago. He came back to the London office.'

I take a breath. 'I see.'

'What?'

'You devious bitch.'

'Mum!'

'That's why you wanted to come here.'

'No!' she sits down heavily at her dressing table. 'Not really.'

'That's when you wrote to me about the art school – '

'It wasn't just that – '

'You didn't come to see me, you came to see him!'

'No!'

'It all fits.' I'm so hurt, my throat closes up. 'Christ.'

'It wasn't just – '

293

'I thought you wanted to see me!' My voice rises, shrilly.

'I did!'

'I've been a right fool, haven't I?'

'That's why I didn't tell you!' she cries, her eyes blazing. 'I thought you'd think that!'

'I thought you wanted to come back to England – '

She puts her hands over her ears. 'Stop it! Oh, I knew this would happen! I want to see him, I love him, stop bloody smothering me!'

Somebody has turned the TV off downstairs. The house is silent, listening.

'I can't believe it – ' I begin.

'I thought *you'd* be all right!' she shouts. 'You're behaving like bloody *they* would!'

'I'm your mother!'

Then she says, 'You're not, really.'

She says this sorrowfully. My blood freezes.

'What do you mean?' I ask.

'You've hardly seen me, you don't know what I'm like.'

'Who's fault is that? What do you think it's been like – '

'You don't know anything!' she cries.

'Oh, don't say that!'

She swings around on her stool and faces me. 'I can't just come here and suddenly start being your daughter. It's too late! I'm grown up now – '

'Are you sleeping with him?'

'That's none of your business.'

'Are you sleeping with him?' I ask her again.

'Don't get all priggish – you, of all people!'

I stare at her. 'What do you mean?'

She looks down at her brown leather boots. 'Nothing.'

'What the hell are you talking about?'

She pauses. 'You and that man. You know, when we were little.'

'What's your father been telling you?'

She doesn't look up. I stare at her glossy black hair, tied back in a plait. 'I just remember it,' she mumbles.

'That's nothing to do with you.'

'Oh, no,' she says, looking up. 'It only changed our lives. Nothing important.'

She gets up.

'Yasmin – '

She glares at me, her eyes bright with tears. 'At least *I'm* not bloody married!'

And she rushes out of the room.

Twenty-eight

Yasmin has run away to London. It's a week now since she's been gone. She's holed up with this bloke, somewhere. He's called Ross, he's Scottish. She'd been having an affair with him for months; Bobby knew all about it. Why didn't he tell me?

Yasmin met this Ross when they were acting in _The Importance of Being Earnest_ at the British consulate. Bobby says they used to go to the beach, to a hut, just like Aisha used to go with her secret boyfriend, Yusuf. She'd bribed Bobby not to tell their father – Christ, if Salim knew about this he'd explode.

I feel shattered and betrayed. All this time she's been borrowing my clothes and lying to me. She said she was going out with her girl friends; she said she was going to Petworth House to look at the paintings. Are there any bleeding paintings in Petworth House? She said she'd be back late. She said she was going to Brighton, to visit some printing press. What had she really done, that day? She said, she said . . . I feel like a jealous husband, piecing together his wife's adultery. Now I know what it feels like. When was she lying? When was she telling the truth?

'Did you in fact go to Brighton that day, Mrs Wainwright?' they'd asked me in court. 'Come, come, Mrs Wainwright.' You're lying, lying, lying.

My own daughter! It's so bloody hurtful. All these years I've been waiting for her, aching for her. And then, when she comes home, it's not for her mother, it's for a fuck.

'Listen, ducky,' says Sonia. 'She's phoned you up, she's perfectly all right – '

'I don't know where she is!'

'She's with her boyfriend, he'll look after her.' We're sitting in my shop – as usual, bereft of customers. Sonia is peeling a tangerine.

'I've lost her, all over again!' I wail. 'I'd only just got her back!'

'She'll come home, pet.' She offers me a segment. 'Just don't act the parent – you'll scare her off.'

'I *am* a parent!'

Sonia nods, munching. 'And she's being a daughter. Come on – *you* were like that once. Or have you forgotten?' She spits a pip into her hand. 'She's only being normal.'

'I can't lose her again. I've already lost Bobby.'

'What do you mean?' she asks.

'We haven't got anything in common. All he talks about is cars and computers.'

'They all do. Boys his age are the most boring creatures on God's earth.'

I look out at the courtyard and the parked cars. 'He hasn't been upset by anything. Going to Karachi – anything.' Outside, a woman opens the back of her Volvo Estate and loads in her shopping. Her son watches from his pushchair. Soon they'll be going home to a blameless tea.

'Course he has. Underneath.' Sonia crumples up her paper bag and throws it in the bin. 'Anyway, do you want him to be all traumatized?'

I pause. 'Just a bit.'

When I get home Bobby is on the phone. He's speaking in Urdu, fast.

'Who's that?' I ask.

He jumps and quickly put the receiver back. 'Nothing.'

The next day I'm coming home to the cottage when I hear the phone ringing. I fumble for my door keys, and finally get the door open. But as I rush across the lounge the phone stops.

The next afternoon I'm walking home from my shop. It's a cool, blustery day in early November; in the next field there's a tractor, ploughing. Gulls are following it, buffeted around in the wind like scraps of paper. I'm thinking about sex. Tom and

I are lying in bed, that first disastrous night. 'Perhaps that'll help pay my bill.'

I lost my children by fucking, and I fucked to get them back. Crude, isn't it? But I got them back, in the end, and I never paid my bill. 'I think you only married me to get your kids back.'

It's not as simple as that, of course; it never is.

Last night I dreamed I was back in Harebell Close. Salim was laying carpet squares of grass over the bed, turfing it. He patted them down the sides, whistling under his breath. In the end, the bed was a grassy mound, like a grave in a churchyard.

JESUS SAVES said the sign outside the chapel. Across the road, up in our bedroom, I opened my legs for Salim. 'Let one in,' he smiles, 'and they'll all come.'

Christ, what a mess.

I open the door and go into the cottage. It's empty. Tom is picking up Bobby from his college; they're going to buy some floppy disks together. They'll be back soon.

I sit down in the armchair. I'd slaughter for a cigarette. The wind rattles the window panes. It's dusk now, but I don't light the lamps. The tractor is still ploughing, beyond the garden. I can hear its engine.

I sit there, gazing at Tom's cabinet. Behind the glass stand the pottery women from Syria or wherever. I used to pick them up and feel their bellies, their petrified pregnancies from 1000 BC.

The tractor's getting louder. In fact, it's a car. I hear the gravel crunching outside. It must be Tom and Bobby.

But the doorbell rings. I sit there for a moment; I don't want to answer it. Finally I get up.

Salim is standing in the porch. A moment passes. I stare at him.

Finally, I ask: 'What are you doing here?'

'Where's Yasmin?'

He's wearing a sports jacket and dark trousers. He looks freezing cold. I move back, so he can come in.

'How did you know?' I ask.

'Bobby phoned me.' He steps inside, into my home. Perhaps he's come straight from the airport. 'I can't leave her alone for a moment, can I? Only two months and – '

'For Christ's sake!' I say.

'What sort of mother are you?'

'What sort of father are you?' I yell. 'She met him in Karachi and you didn't know a bloody thing about it!'

We're standing in the lounge, in the dark, glaring at each other like two bulls. My heart is thumping in my ears. It's such a shock, seeing him here. I try to gather my wits.

There's a car door slamming outside, and footsteps in the hall. Tom and Bobby come in. They stare at Salim. Bobby rushes up and flings himself into his father's arms.

'*Abba-ji*!' he cries.

Tom switches on the light; I flinch, blinking. Suddenly I feel ridiculously guilty.

'He's come because of Yasmin,' I tell Tom.

Salim says: 'I'm sorry to barge in. I phoned but there was no reply.'

'Quite all right,' says Tom coldly. 'Have a drink.'

I say: 'He doesn't drink.'

'Well, *I* will,' says Tom, and strides across to the cupboard. He turns to me. 'Want one?'

But I'm talking to Salim. 'All I know is, he's called Ross.'

Bobby says: 'He used to live at the Sind Club. His second name's McIntyre.'

I swing round to Bobby. 'You never told me!'

'What company did he work for?' asks Salim.

'Dunno,' replies Bobby. 'I don't know anything else.'

'What about college?' he asks.

'She hasn't been there,' I tell him.

We all stand there in the middle of the room. Then Salim speaks.

'Look, the Sind Club manager's an old friend of mine.' He turns to Tom. 'May I use your phone?'

Tom shrugs. 'Go ahead.'

Salim goes over to the phone and dials. I turn to Bobby.

'Why on earth did you tell him?' I hiss.

Bobby blurts out: 'I wanted him to come!' He suddenly looks about eleven years old.

'Why?' I ask him.

'I just did.'

'You never used to phone *me*,' I say to him.

Salim is talking in Urdu on the phone. Tom crosses the room to refill his glass. As he does so, he stumbles over an anorak.

'Will you take your bloody stuff upstairs!' he shouts, glaring at Bobby.

'Ssh!' I'm trying to listen to Salim. I turn to Bobby. 'What's he saying?'

Bobby tells me. 'He's asking him where this Ross guy works in London.'

Tom strides to the window, sipping his drink. He looks out into the darkness. Salim puts the phone down.

'It's Saville Engineering, in London,' he says. He looks at his watch. 'They'll be closed now.'

Tom turns round. 'She's not kidnapped, you know! She phones us up. She's only trying to get away from you two for a bit.'

Salim says: 'I'll go and see them in the morning.'

'I'll come with you,' I tell him, quickly. Tom shoots me a look.

Salim moves towards the door. 'I'd better get back to London.' He pauses, and clears his throat. Then he turns to Tom. 'I'm so sorry.'

'For everything?' asks Tom. 'Or just this?'

'I'm sorry,' Salim says.

He walks towards the door. Bobby follows him.

'Can I come with you?' he asks.

Salim shakes his head, and goes out.

In bed that night Tom lies very still. We lie there stiffly, side by side. Perhaps he's gone to sleep. Outside, that bird sharpens its steel, over and over.

He's not asleep. He says: 'I don't want you to go.'

'I must.'

'Marianne – '

'She's my daughter.'

He moves slightly, the mattress creaks. Perhaps he's looking at me in the darkness. I don't turn my head.

He says: 'You know perfectly well who I'm talking about.'

'I hate him!'

There is a silence. I hold my breath, silently urging him not to speak. It's going to make us too sad.

But he does. He speaks into the darkness. 'The first couple of years, you know, I thought we were going to be all right.'

I can't reply. We lie there, listening to the sounds out in the darkness.

Twenty-nine

I've taken the early train to London; there's nothing else I can do. I arrive at Salim's hotel and hurry upstairs. All along the corridor, breakfast trays have been left outside doors, like religious offerings. I remember the men, praying at Karachi Airport. Where has all that praying got Salim? To just the same place as me.

I tap on his door and go in. He's on the phone, his hair still damp from the shower. He sees me, raises his eyebrows in suprise, and nods a greeting. I wonder if he really was expecting me. I feel as if we've been on some huge voyage, across oceans, and finally we've been washed up together on some lonely beach.

The curtains in this room are blue poppies. I sit down on the bed and he put the receiver down.

'We can see the personnel officer,' he says.

He puts on his tie and fetches his shoes. It's shockingly intimate, to watch him dress. He puts on his watch, twisting his wrist to strap it up, the way he always did. It even looks like the same watch.

He looks at me for a moment, in silence. Down in the street, cars have been hooting. There's some enormous traffic jam. Then he sweeps his change off the table with the side of his hand and puts it in his pocket.

'Come on,' I say at last. 'Let's go and be parents.'

Ross is out of town today, apparently. We sit in Mr Culvert's office, at Saville Engineering. Mr Culvert is the personnel officer.

'We don't, as a rule, give out personal details of our employees,' he says. He's a skinny, colourless bloke.

Salim and I sit side by side, like we did at the kids' primary school when we went to see the head teacher.

'It's very important,' Salim says.

'It's not our policy . . .'

'I've got some important documents for Mr McIntyre,' says Salim. 'Gavin dropped them in to me, on his way to Melbourne.'

'Gavin?' asks Mr Culvert.

'His cousin,' says Salim blandly. He lies so convincingly; I shoot him a look. Suddenly, we're confederates.

Mr Culvert gets up and opens a file. 'This is his last address,' he says, writing something down. 'But he was talking of moving.'

'Where?' I ask.

He shrugs. 'He just said his circumstances had changed.' He smiles, slightly. 'You know Ross, he's a law unto himself.'

I'm so nervous that on the way out I nip into the toilet. Somebody has scrawled, on the wall: *It's 12" but I don't use it all as a rule.*

We've stopped the car in this street in Kilburn. Salim looks at the piece of paper with Ross's address on it.

'Flat 4,' he says.

Our Avis car is unnaturally tidy; its beige interior smells of air freshener. I remember our messy Vauxhall; when it came to cars, Salim was really sluttish. Everybody is contradictory, aren't they, when you get up close? For instance, he's not being that hysterical over this. I thought he'd blow his top. He must have mellowed over the years.

On the other hand he was mad enough to jump on a plane and hightail it over here, like a bat out of hell. He used to say things like that — 'a bat out of hell'. Lots of Pakistanis, their slang is like those old films you see on TV.

Neither of us, for some reason, feels like leaving the car. It's a shabby street. Some of the shops are boarded up. Even the NatWest has decamped; there's bleached stonework and little holes where its sign has been. I can't bear to think of our daughter living here. How could our beautiful Yasmin, cherished in two continents, want to come to this dump?

I know exactly why, of course.

Salim gets out and opens the car door for me. We glance at each other briefly. Then we go across to the building and ring the bell of flat 4.

The door is opened by a weedy bloke in a T-shirt.

'Excuse me,' I ask. 'Do you live in flat 4?'

He nods. His T-shirt says *I came. I saw. I took a Valium.*

'We're looking for Ross McIntyre,' says Salim. 'He lives here.'

'I live in flat 4,' says the bloke. He has a Wolverhampton accent.

'And there's a girl with him,' I say.

Salim asks: 'How long have you been living here?'

'Two weeks,' says the bloke.

We gaze at him, hopelessly.

'Did he leave a forwarding address?' asks Salim.

The bloke shrugs. I step into the hall. It smells like the place I squatted in with Lester. It smells of brussels sprouts, joss sticks and secrecy. 'You were like that, too,' Sonia had said. 'She's only doing what you did.'

There's a table piled with old letters and circulars. Dyno-Rod, 24-hour minicabs, plumbers, take-away tandooris. I sift through the letters: Willoughby . . . Kureishi . . . Ajabimi . . . There's nothing there.

'What's the address of your landlord?' asks Salim.

We've just visited the landlord. It's a socking great place in the suburbs. There's a BMW parked outside.

He didn't know where Ross had gone.

'Why should he?' says Salim, as we walk to the car. 'It's none of his business.'

It's nearly six o'clock; we seem to have been driving around for days.

I turn to Salim. 'I've done this before, you know.'

'What, living in a squat?'

I shake my head. 'Searching for my kids.' I glare at him. 'Now you know what it's like.'

Salim doesn't reply. We get into the car and sit there for a moment. The back windowsticker of the landlord's BMW says

Keep Orthopaedics in Stanmore. What on earth does that mean? I suddenly feel light-headed.

Salim says: 'What shall we do now?'

'I'm so hungry!' I blurt out.

I brush my hair and powder my nose. I sit in the car, trying to tidy myself up. It's funny how quickly you can feel like outcasts. We haven't touched base for hours; London is a huge city, and we're adrift in our hired Metro. I'm wearing my old jeans and a sweater. I turn to Salim.

'Do I look OK?'

'You look fine,' he says.

I tried to phone Tom but the box was broken, it said '999 Calls Only'. I wondered how much of an emergency this was. I meant to try another box but it's too late now.

We've come to this Italian restaurant near the British Museum. We used to eat here sometimes, when we came up to London. The same fat man, with moustache, has welcomed us in. There was a lot of *signor* and *signora* but I don't think he recognized us. He couldn't, could he, after all these years? It's strange; we've gone through all this and he's just been standing here next to his rubber-plant, beaming at customers. He hasn't changed at all.

Salim has changed; more than I realized. We've been talking about Pakistan. He's become very political. He campaigned for Benazir Bhutto, he wanted a new broom, he says, a clean sweep. The country is much more liberal now, he says. We've been talking like this, about impersonal things. I've told him what's happened to Ashford: how it's grown, just like he said it would, and how they're digging the Channel Tunnel after all these years. I tell him about people he knew, about Malcolm, his ex-colleague, who's packed it all in and started a watercress farm. About my mum, stone-deaf now, who's living in a retirement home in Hythe, chairs in a semicircle around the picture windows.

We're not exactly hostile, but we're edgy. We skirt around each other delicately, as if we're radioactive. So many topics are too painful to talk about – nearly everything, in fact. Sometimes there are long silences.

We've eaten tagliatelli. He had cassata ice cream; I'd forgotten about his sweet tooth. I've drunk a lot of wine – well, wouldn't you? Even talking about Yasmin is too painful – there's so much blame and unhappiness. I can't bear to hear her name coming out of his mouth.

Then, over coffee, he suddenly says: 'What did you see in him?'

For a moment I don't know who he's talking about.

'That man,' he says.

'Terry? But that was ten years ago!'

'What had he got that I hadn't?'

I glare at him. 'I wouldn't have done it – would I – if I'd known what was going to happen.'

'Why did you do it?'

I pause. 'He made me laugh.'

He looks at me, surprised. 'That's all?'

'It seemed a lot, at the time.' I push the pepper mill around. 'And he noticed my new sweater.'

'What sweater?'

I look up. 'Exactly.'

Then Salim says: 'To cast one's full gaze on a woman is tantamount to fornication.'

I stare at him.

'Where I come from,' he says.

I can't make out his expression. Is he half-smiling? I can't tell, in the candlelight. I suddenly feel very hot.

I turn away, and look at the other couples. The restaurant is full; I hadn't noticed.

'Oh, I don't know why,' I say. 'It's all so long ago.'

The waiter comes up and asks if we'd like some more coffee. We don't hear him; then we shake our heads. He leaves us.

Suddenly, Salim says: 'I felt so jealous of you and the kids.'

I stare at him. 'Did you?'

He nods. 'See. *You* didn't notice things, either.'

'Did you really?'

306

'You had fun with them,' he says. 'You used to dance with them in their bedroom.'

'But you said I was a bad mother!'

There is a silence. He won't reply.

'Was it just because of him?' I ask. 'Is that why you did it?'

He shifts in his seat. 'I'll get the bill.'

'Why did you do it?' I ask, desperately.

'Because of everything.' He stops. 'You don't smoke anymore?'

I shake my head. 'What do you mean, everything?'

It's his turn to fiddle with the pepper mill. 'At the time, it seemed so important.'

I lean across the table. 'What does it seem now?'

'I thought I was right,' he says. 'My God, what a mess!'

Suddenly he pushes back his chair and gets up.

I look up. 'I don't know what to do.'

'What do you want to do?' He's looking down at me, his eyes bright in the candlelight. He sits down again.

'Where's the bloody waiter?' I mutter. Abruptly, I get up. My chair scrapes across the tiles. 'I'll miss my train.'

When I get home, Tom is in bed. The lights are off. He turns over; I can hear the bedsprings.

'You're late,' he says.

'I've been looking for Yasmin!'

'All this time?'

Thirty

Tom once said: 'I've always fallen for difficult women. I blame it on my happy childhood.'

'Why?' I asked.

'I want to make it all right for everybody else. The worse they are, the more of a challenge. Makes me feel alive, you see. I'm the sort of Albert Schweitzer of matrimony.' He had looked at me. 'Trouble is, they start resenting it. They don't want somebody nice, they want somebody dark and Lawrentian who beats them up.'

'Salim never beat me up.'

'No. He had a better method.'

It's Sunday, two days after my dinner with Salim. Tom is in the lounge, surrounded by Sunday papers. One of his Brahms things is playing. I gaze at him with such guilt and tenderness. I feel myself loosening from our marriage, like a tooth rocking when you touch it. 'The first couple of years, you know, I thought we were going to be all right.'

He wanted a child so badly. More than a child – children, a family. His first wife was too neurotic and wedded to her career. I'm too fucked-up and wedded to my past. How could I trust another man, even him? How could I start the long journey, all over again?

Perhaps I've just never loved him enough.

'You only married me to get your children back.' He had said it was like living with ghosts. My kids watched from the walls as he tried to make love to me, to shake me awake. All these years I've been sleepwalking; I've only been half-here. 'No, it's like I'm the ghost, and they're real.'

Our children could be swinging on that phantom tyre, which I took down long ago. They could be splashing in the stream. Tom was born to be a father. I've done him terrible damage.

Standing there in the living room, with computer bleeps coming from upstairs, I realize quite clearly what has happened. I've stolen Tom's kids, just like Salim has stolen mine.

Tom's flipping through the *Sunday Times* colour supplement – flip-flip, Renault-Johnnie-Walker-Relative-Values-BMW-Cambodia-Sainsbury's. I know he's not concentrating. I'm just about to speak when there's the crunch of gravel outside.

A car door slams. Before I can move, Yasmin bursts in. She flings herself into my arms.

'Mum!'

'What's happened?' I disentangle myself. 'Where have you been? You OK?'

She starts crying. 'Oh, I hate them all!'

Tom moves the newspapers. She sits down on the settee, heavily. Her hair is loose and falls over her face as she fishes in her bag for a Kleenex.

'We had this fight,' she says.

I sit down beside her. 'Why?'

'Oh, he's so selfish, he's so immature! How can I spend my life with somebody like that? I want to die!'

'What happened?'

'Now I've mucked up college, I've mucked up everything!'

'Course you haven't,' I tell her.

She raises her head. Her face looks ravaged. 'First he wants to resign, then he wants to go to Rotterdam – *Rotterdam* – then he wants to chuck it all in and start a sheep farm.'

I smile at her. 'Sounds just like the rest of us.'

She blows her nose. 'Everybody's always hauled me around and told me what to do, first it was dad and now it's him, nobody asks me what *I* want!'

'What do you want?'

'Ross!' she wails. 'Then this, this *girl* phoned up – '

'Aha,' I smile. 'Now we're getting warmer.'

'He said it was over ages ago.'

'Don't you believe him?'

She raises her streaming face. 'Why should I? Why should I believe anyone? Oh, I didn't know it would feel like this!'

309

'Nobody ever does.'

'Can I have a bath?'

Bobby has phoned his father, and now Salim's arrived. Tom has gone out into the drizzle; he's digging his vegetable garden. I know I ought to go out and speak to him, but I can't. Not just now.

Yasmin, wearing my towelling bathrobe, is sitting on the floor. Her hair is wet. I've combed it for her and now I'm drying it, squatting on the rug. The cottage feels cramped; the Siddiqi family has taken it over.

'All this time, all these years, I've had to be grown up,' she says. 'I've felt like a little old lady.'

'Oh, don't say that!' I say.

She speaks over the drone of the hair-dryer. 'I had to look after Bobby. He was really upset, you know, but I couldn't let *you* see.' She turns to Salim, pulling my hand with her. 'Because then you'd be upset. All the time I've had to be so bloody careful. Trying to please you . . .' I pull her head back, and keep on drying her hair. 'Not talking about *you*,' she twists her head round, to look at me, 'not saying I missed you because then *you'd* feel guilty.' She turns to Salim; her hair slides through my hand. 'And then, when I saw *you* . . .' She twists round; she's talking to me again. 'I couldn't tell you the nice things that had happened because then you'd be upset that we weren't missing you, but we were! Oh, God! Everything I said was wrong!'

Her hair is dry now. I switch off the dryer and sit back on my haunches. 'You shouldn't have had to worry. You were just a kid.'

'Didn't feel like a kid.' She snuffles and wipes her nose with a corner of the bathrobe. 'Then I met Ross and suddenly . . . oh, we laughed all the time.' She looks at me. 'Bit like *we* did, I suppose.'

Her eyes are puffy from all the crying. She suddenly looks plain and naked and very young.

'He's at his sister's?' I ask.

She nods.

310

'Phone him up.'

'Phone him up?' says Salim. 'After everything he's done?' He's sitting there in his open-necked white shirt, glaring at her. He's cut himself shaving; there's a spot of dried blood on his cheek. 'Where did you used to meet? At the beach?'

I glare at him. 'Oh, shut up!' I turn to her. 'Phone him up.'

Yasmin stays sitting on the floor. 'Why should I?'

Wearily, I tell her: 'It's all such a bloody waste otherwise.'

She pauses; then she gets up, pulling the bathrobe around her. Salim gets up, to stop her.

'Don't!' I tell him. I climb to my feet and put my hand on his arm. Just then Tom comes in from the garden. His hair's wet from the rain. He looks at Salim and me. Then he goes into the kitchen to wash his hands.

Yasmin goes upstairs and phones Ross. The ceiling creaks as she crosses our bedroom. The phone pings, down here, as she lifts the receiver.

Salim, Bobby and I sit in silence, amongst the wreckage of Tom's Sunday papers. I'm sitting on the floor, fiddling with a hole in the rug. It's a *kelim* I bought in Karachi. One of the clocks whirrs, as if it's clearing its throat, then chimes. There's the sound of running water in the kitchen. I know I should get up and go in there.

A moment passes. Then Tom comes out of the kitchen. He doesn't look at us. He just walks across the room and stomps upstairs.

I hear the bedroom door opening, then a pause. Yasmin is in there, on the phone. The door slams shut and he comes downstairs. I climb to my feet, hastily.

'I'm sorry,' I tell him. 'She's upset.'

He glares at me. 'So am I.' Suddenly, his voice rises. 'Listen, I'm fed up to the teeth with the lot of you!'

'Ssh!' I go up to him and hold his arm.

He shakes me off. 'Why should I? This is my bloody house! Bloody hell, I can't get into my own bedroom, I can't get into my bathroom, I can't use my own phone! Everywhere I go, there's these bowls of bloody Corn Flakes!' He turns to me. 'Ten bloody years I've listened to you, I've tried to be a supportive bloody husband – kids, kids, all I've ever heard is kids. Except it's not *my* kids, is it? Oh, no! That'd be far too nice and easy! I'm not allowed anything normal like that! Oh, no! Whinge, whinge – year after year, typical bloody women, except I'm not allowed to say anything because you're a bloody woman and it's all so terribly tragic. Well, it's been tragic for me too, but nobody wants to listen to me!'

He pauses for breath. There's mud on the side of his face, and on his old gardening sweater. Yasmin is standing half-way down the stairs, listening.

'It's *your* kids,' he shouts, 'and *your* traumas! And now you've *got* your kids, with their towels all over the bathroom and their ghastly music and their dirty clothes and bits of Marmite in the butter – now you've got them all you can do is scream and row! Why on earth did you want them in the first place? Take them back – and take your horrible, smelly old thingamagigs with you!' He pulls a hanging off the wall; there's a tearing sound as it catches on the nail. 'And your bloody ex! Why don't you all go back where you belong!'

There's a long silence. I stare at him, with horror and with a sort of admiration.

I'm standing in Salim's hotel room in London. It's a couple of hours later. Yasmin is in the bathroom – Tom was right, they're always in the bathroom. She's doing up her hair.

I'm trembling; my limbs seem to have turned to water. I'm sitting in the chair and Salim is standing by the window.

He speaks to the blue poppy curtain. 'Do you want to stay here?'

I shake my head. 'I've got to go back.'

'Is this going to blow over?'

I shake my head again. 'He's right, you see.' Suddenly, I ask him: 'Why did you never marry? Really?'

He turns round. 'Why did you never have kids?'

I ignore that: 'Why didn't you marry?'

There's a thud and some muffled laughter from the next room. Salim pauses, then he says: 'Because I never wanted anyone but you.'

In the bathroom, the toilet flushes. I say: 'Weird way of showing it.'

'I didn't realize until it was too late.'

I look at him coldly. 'You were just too fucking proud. All you lot, you're so fucking rigid. You think you're right just because you're bloody Muslims! Oh, you make me sick!'

He looks at me, his face dark against the blurred daylight of the curtains. 'Why do you think I gave it all up, then, in the first place?' he says in a low voice. 'You know why? Know why I could never marry anyone else?'

'No,' I say, sulkily. My heart is thumping.

'You think I'd want a Pakistani wife who agreed with everything I said and sat there chewing betel-nut all day?' he says. 'After I'd lived with you?' He runs his hands through his hair. For a moment, neither of us speaks.

Suddenly, he looks exhausted. He sits down on the bed. 'I knew it wouldn't be easy, but at least it would be . . . exciting.'

'It was exciting, all right,' I say, bitterly.

The door opens and Yasmin comes out of the bathroom. She's piled her hair on top of her head and fixed it with silver clips.

Salim says to me: 'Why do you think we had a daughter like her?'

Yasmin pauses, and looks at us.

I get to my feet, shakily. 'Come on,' I tell her. 'I'll take you to Ross's.'

_____ *Thirty-one* _____

A marriage crumbles so fast. It's like one brick getting dislodged at the bottom of a building. Suddenly, the whole thing topples and you're standing in a heap of rubble. It's terrifying, because the rubble is so meaningless. Suddenly, you can hardly remember what the building looked like.

It was like that the last time. Once it's started, it's got this momentum. You can't stop it; anything you say – it only makes it worse. Besides, what is there to say?

Perhaps Tom should have shouted at me long ago. He might have shaken me to my senses. After all, he'd tried everything else. Perhaps, perhaps.

You're in this house – beamed ceiling, thick walls. Even thin walls; even flimsy walls like Harebell Close. But you're in there, and you think you're safe. You tuck the kids up at night and kiss them. You turn to this man, your husband, and kiss him. You draw the curtains closed; you don't dare see what's out there in the dark.

When I got back from London that Sunday, the car had gone. I knew Bobby had gone to Darren's, but the car should have been there. It was late afternoon; the drizzle had stopped and a watery sun had come out. Soon it would be dusk.

I paid the minicab-driver, unlocked the front door and went into the cottage.

'Tom?' I called.

The place was empty. I could tell, just by standing very still.

I rushed upstairs and into the bedroom. I flung open the wardrobe. Some of Tom's clothes had gone.

'*Tom*!' I yelled.

I started to cry – hoarse, ugly sobs.

*

He's gone to stay with that Marjorie woman, the newt woman. She's much more his type, the bitch. She's got this big old yeoman's hall near Canterbury; she opens her garden to the public. I've got no right to feel jealous.

I'm closing down the shop. Tom's been subsidizing it all these years. I've never told you that. I've written a 'CLEAR-ANCE SALE' notice, and stuck it on the window. Except the Pentel dried up, so it says 'CLEARANCE SA'. Bloody typical.

Bobby's just come in on his way home from college. He puts down his bags and watches me sticking 'Sale Price' labels on to *pan* boxes. *Pan* is that betel-nut stuff they chew; it's what spatters the ground red, when they spit it out. It's what Salim's wife would have chewed.

Bobby munches a Toblerone. 'Dad's looking for a flat in London,' he says. 'He wants to stay here.'

'You really want to go to college in London?' I ask.

'Ashford's a bit of a dump.'

'You could always try spitting competitions in the bus shelter.'

'What?' he asks, his mouth full.

'I used to do that.' I pause. 'You really want to be with your dad?'

'I want to be with both of you.'

There is a silence. I stack up the *pan* boxes in the window. 'There's something I've always wanted to ask you. You know when you went to court and talked to the judge?'

He nods. 'She was nice.'

'What did you tell her?'

He looks out of the window. A woman with a broken leg is coming out of the café; she hobbles across to a car. 'Can't remember.'

'She must have asked if you wanted to live with your mother or father,' I say, urgently. 'What did you say?'

Bobby takes another bite of his Toblerone. 'I said I wanted to see my dog.'

Later, in his bedroom, we sort through his stuff. In the cupboard he finds a box of his old clothes. He pulls it out and lifts up his blue anorak. It looks ridiculously shrunken, against him.

'I remember this,' he says. He inspects it. 'Still got that tear in it.'

'When you fell off your trike.'

'You were never much good at sewing, were you?' He looks at the box. 'What're we going to do with all this?'

'I think we can throw it away, now.'

He smiles at me briefly.

All of a sudden he says: 'I remember the stairs.'

'What stairs?'

'You used to leave my pushchair at the bottom, and then we'd go up and the landing light always went off at the same place, when I'd got to the broken banister.'

'That was at Talacre Road!'

'And you always hummed when you were looking for your keys.'

I stare at him. 'You were only tiny!'

He fiddles with a frayed bit on the seam of his jeans. 'Sometimes I thought you were going to come and collect me.'

'When?'

'From school,' he says. 'In Karachi.'

We sit there in silence. I want to put my arms around him but I know he'll be embarrassed. So we take out his baby clothes, instead, and burn them in the garden.

He's been talking more, these past few days. My marriage breaking up has unlocked something in him; or perhaps it's his father coming to England. I don't want to ask. But for the first time in my life I've been eating breakfast alone with my kids. Yasmin is going to college again. She sees Ross, but she's staying with me. Bobby wants to go to London but she likes it here. It's strange. Now I've got them to myself, at last, I'm in such a state I can hardly appreciate it.

'What are you thinking?' asks Salim.

I've come up to London. My excuse is that I'm buying Bobby some clothes. I left him in Carnaby Street.

We're in the hotel room. I'm fiddling with the video guide.

'Sonia says it's all over so quickly,' I say. 'A few laughs, a few babies. But then you never liked her, did you?'

316

'I'm looking for a flat.'

I nod. 'You really going to live here?'

There is a silence. I've read *Cocoon 2* about eight times.

'Will you come back to me?' he asks.

I look up. He's wearing a blue, crumpled shirt. He looks terribly tired.

'I can never forgive you,' I tell him. 'You know that.'

'Will you? If you don't want to live in London, we'll go somewhere else! Anywhere else!' He looks at me wildly. 'We can go to Karachi, we can go to Montreal – I've got cousins in Montreal – we can go anywhere! I know we can!' He pauses, breathlessly. 'Marianne?'

'I've been terrible to Tom. You've no idea. It spreads, you see.'

'Has he moved out?'

I nod.

'He'll find someone,' says Salim. 'A man like Tom.'

I lay the video guide on the table. 'He knows how to be friends. You and me, we never managed that.'

There is a silence. Then Salim says: 'We were lovers.'

He's coming towards me. He steps nearer and touches my face. I turn away quickly.

'You'd be better off without me,' I tell him. 'You all would be.'

'Marianne . . .'

'I'll call you tomorrow.'

And then I leave, closing the door behind me.

Tom and I met yesterday, just outside Ashford. It was a cold, windy day. We sat in the car. His Peggy Lee tape stuck out of the cassette-player, like a tongue jeering at me for being so stupid. All around us stretched flat grey fields. Nearby stood a sign saying 'Site Purchased by Cormorant Homes.'

'Come home,' I said.

'You really want me?'

I nodded. We sat there, side by side, looking out of the windscreen.

'Can't we park somewhere else?' he asked. 'Everywhere I look, he's bloody closing in.'

He meant Cormorant Homes. I hadn't even noticed it. 'He hasn't worked for them for ten years,' I said.

'Ten years, with you two, doesn't seem to have made any difference.'

'It has. We're all changed now.'

He spoke to the windscreen. 'Don't go with him. You've got your kids now, they're grown up, it's all over. You've all survived. Don't go with him.'

'We were lovers.' It sounds incredible after all we've been through, after all those years when I've hated Salim and wanted him dead. But it's true. I haven't fallen in love with him again – I'm not a bloody idiot. But I feel joined to him, in my blood. He answers something dark in me still, after all these years. I'm bound to him till we die. His son is my son, his daughter is my daughter. But it's more than that.

Maybe it's just unfinished business. Maybe.

Maybe I need a man to hurt me. It's the only way I can come alive. Tom said: 'You want somebody dark and Lawrentian who beats you up.' I read a book by D. H. Lawrence once, the one they did on the TV. It was all flaming loins – it was terrific. Salim reached inside me where no nice man – no reasonable man – had ever reached. Between my legs and then up, up, to my scalp and my fingertips, molten. Salim reached there. He lit me like a bonfire. No one else ever did.

Anyway, if I was Tom I wouldn't bother. I'm not worth it. He's too liberated for me; he's too nice. Maybe I just need a man who treats me like an object.

Christ, I don't know. I want Tom back, desperately. Why should I even contemplate running off with a priggish, stubborn Pakistani who's ruined my life? Tom will save me. He's saved me in the past – can't he do it again? I'll be better to him, next time. We'll start our real marriage from now.

Yasmin has just come in from college. She dumps down her bags and take out something they made in Graphics. They did

318

it for a hoot. It's one of those cards like kidney donor cards that you keep in your wallet. But this one says: *In case of accident, I do not want to be visited by Mrs Thatcher.*

I pour her a cup of tea. She says: 'I saw Tom today, in Canterbury. He was in Habitat with that woman.'

They're buying bedroom curtains. They're going to get married. They're going to sing in the choir, their voices twining together like a well-bred version of Ravi Shankar and Yehudi Menuhin. They're going to campaign against the theme park. Somebody's planning to build one just outside Ashford; they're going to build over that copse where Terry and I fucked like rabbits.

Tom read about it in the paper, when we were still together. 'Maybe we should just stay here and charge admission,' he'd said. 'A typical eighties family.'

'We're not typical!' I had said.

'Yes, we are,' he'd said. 'Just a bit more so.'

Yasmin sips her tea. 'You coming to see the flat tomorrow?'

Salim is going to buy one in Kensington.

I nod.

'What are you going to do?' she asks.

'What do *you* want?'

'It doesn't matter now,' she says. 'We're grown up.'

'Sonia's moving to Fulham,' I tell her. 'She's opening a restaurant.'

Yasmin looks at me in surprise. 'You going to move in with her?'

I don't know. I don't know anything. 'Do you really mean it, that it doesn't matter now?'

She nods. 'We're sort of together, anyway.'

'You mean we've survived?'

She nods, and sips her tea.

Tonight Tom phoned. He told me that I've got a week to make up my mind.

'I'm tired of being bloody reasonable!' he shouted. 'Why bloody should I? Where's it got me?'

He must have been in a call box, because just then his money ran out.

Yasmin, Bobby, Salim and I are hurrying across Trafalgar Square. The sun is shining and the pigeons scatter as we stride along, bickering.

'It's got three bedrooms,' says Salim. We're going to look at his flat.

'Can we move next week?' asks Bobby. He turns to me. 'Are you going to live with us?'

'I'm just going to look at it,' I tell him.

'Hurry up,' says Salim. 'We'll get a cab.'

Panting, we weave in and out of the tourists. Suddenly, I realize that we're a family. Whatever happens.

Yasmin looks at her watch. 'I've got to meet Ross at three!'

'I've got to do my homework,' says Bobby.

'Wish I'd washed my hair,' she says.

'You and your bloody hair,' I tell her, stumbling over a Coke can. I'll always be closer to Yasmin; Bobby is his father's son, but then most boys are, whether you're split up or not. I point to the National Gallery. 'I've never even been there.'

'*I* have,' says Yasmin.

Salim turns to me. 'You're really giving up the shop?'

I nod. 'Why should I go to Karachi now?'

'Will you come to London?'

'I don't know!' I bark at him.

'Why can't you make up your mind?' he asks.

'Why should I?'

Bobby says: 'You're so childish, you two.'

'Such babies!' says Yasmin.

Bobby says: 'Why don't you let *us* make up your minds?'

I wail: 'I don't know what to do!'

'Stay with me!' yells Salim. 'Please!'

'Don't shout at me!' I glare at him. We run down some steps. I've got to phone Tom; time is running out.

'You're driving me insane,' says Salim. 'You always have.'

'Oh, shut up, you two!' says Bobby. 'Come on!'

Just then, a photographer steps out.

320

'How about a smile?' he asks.

We turn, startled, and stop bickering. He clicks his camera, then he looks up. He's got a flushed, jovial face. He looks like a seaside photographer.

'Visitors, are you?' he asks.

We all reply at once, contradicting one another.

'No!' I tell him.

'Yes!' says Salim.

Yasmin and Bobby say 'No!' 'Yes!' – both at the same time.

We stand there in a row, perspiring from our walk.

'Nice smile,' he says. 'Nice smile, now.'

He clicks his camera. The four of us, standing in the middle of Trafalgar Square, freeze for him. He clicks again.

The photo's framed, now. All of us with our fixed smiles, together at last. Who could ever guess what had happened? Who could tell?

I had it framed – oh, months ago – in polished pine. It sits beside the bed. At night, when I awake, I can see it glimmering in the greenish mist that comes out of my digital alarm clock.

Whatever has happened – and you might have guessed what I did – whatever has happened nobody can steal that away from me.

Reunite

Hundreds of children are abducted from Great Britain every year and taken to countries all over the world. Precise figures do not exist but numbers range between 500 and 5000 every year.

Abduction is parental kidnapping. Children can be taken at any point during the breakdown of relations between two parents and are mostly abducted when on an access visit. Although both mothers and fathers take children, it is usually the latter who commit the crime.

Once the children have left this country, official government assistance virtually ceases. The Foreign and Commonwealth officials, both here and abroad, are limited in the help and advice they can provide by existing British law and international diplomatic etiquette. The most they can do is to ask for welfare reports and provide rooms for access visits.

Even more basic, there is no information available about what to *do* if your child is abducted, how to cope with the grief and how to get in contact with parents in the same situation. Government is patchy and ill-coordinated, resulting in an inefficient service and conflicting advice. Social services, lawyers and advice centres are often at a loss as to how to advise the increasing number of parents, in this situation, who approach them.

Reunite is an organisation, established by a group of mothers and supporters, which addresses the above issues, advises professionals and parents alike and acts as a focal point for child abduction in this country. Experience has shown that full-time workers are essential in order to run an effective and reliable service. The organisation is always happy to accept donations. The address below can also be used by people seeking advice about child abduction.

Reunite, PO Box 158, London N4 1AU.

Also by Deborah Moggach and available in paperback

SEESAW

Take an ordinary, well-off family like the Prices. Watch what happens when one Sunday seventeen-year-old Hannah disappears without a trace. See how the family rallies when a ransom note demands half a million pounds for Hannah's safe return.

But it's when Hannah comes home that the story really begins.

Now observe what happens to a family when they lose their house, their status, all their wealth. Note how they disintegrate under the pressures of guilt and poverty and are forced to confront their true selves.

And finally, wait to hear all about Hannah, who has the most shocking surprise in store of all.

'Provocative, enthralling, bang-up-to-the-minute… truly, Moggach gets better and better' Val Hennessy, *Daily Mail*

'A delight to read' *Daily Telegraph*

THE EX-WIVES

Actor Russell Buffery's voice is his most reliable organ where women are concerned, and he's got three ex-wives to prove it.

Under the weather, over the hill, and with only a dog for company, Buffy's bachelorhood is looking worryingly confirmed – until he meets Celeste, a young girl who works in the local chemist shop and who appears to hold the prescription for the elixir of Buffy's lost youth.

Dazzled by love, Buffy little suspects that Celeste is systematically resarching his ex-wives, children and step-children, and unearthing secrets that will change all their lives irrevocably.

'You'll be hooked from the first page of this original, funny book… Just delicious' *New Woman*

'*The Ex-Wives* marries comedy and canniness into a novel that's warm, tolerant, shrewd and exuberant' *Sunday Times*

PORKY

At school they called her Porky on account of the pigs her family kept outside the bungalow near Heathrow. But she felt no different – not until she realised she was losing her innocence in a way that none of her friends could possibly imagine. Only a child robbed of her childhood can know too late what it means to be loved too little and loved too much...

'Deborah Moggach conveys with chilling skill the process by which a fundamentally bright, decent child becomes infested by corruption' *Spectator*

'Illuminates with great compassion how love can so easily go off the rails' *Daily Mail*

'At once eerily exuberant and bleak, this is a compassionate, tough book' *Observer*

'Extraordinarily skilful' *Anita Brookner*

DRIVING IN THE DARK

Desmond never did have much luck with women– except in getting them through their driving tests. Now a coach driver, he is at the most crucial cross-roads of his life. His wife has thrown him out. The crisis serves only to deepen his despair over another failed liaison – until he elects to steer his coach on a spectacularly reckless quest for the son he has never seen.

'Disturbing and witty... a deftly-described odyssey that places the battle of the sexes in a new arena' *Sunday Times*

'Moggach, for the purposes of this book, has turned herself into a bloke. His monologue throughout strikes me as totally authentic, but not only does Moggach get his lingo right, she thinks through his head, dramatizing his confusion, decency, wit, pain and determination. This is not just ventriloquism, but empathy so complete as to be phenomenal' *Irish Times*

'At once acutely funny and sad... a woman's protest at the inequality thrust on men by the worst excesses of the women's movement' *Mail on Sunday*

'Poignant and funny... Deborah Moggach is brilliant at capturing just the right voice for her characters' *Cosmopolitan*

CHANGING BABIES

Changing Babies will delight both die-hard fans of Deborah Moggach's books and those readers new to her charm and wit.

In it she writes of a woman who thinks she has found the perfect man until he becomes too mysterious for words; of a rock star writing his memoirs who can't remember a thing; of harassed teenagers and harangued fathers; of opera lovers, Belgian lovers, young lovers and romance on the Costa del Sol courtesy of Sunspan Holidays.

Here are fifteen brilliant stories – all sharp, funny and painfully accurate.

'This is Moggach at her best' *Times Literary Supplement*

A QUIET DRINK

Claudia has always been independent – own flat, absorbing job, a husband so devoted he is almost a housewife. Until she finds herself an abruptly and uneasily liberated woman.

Steve Mullen deals in faces – and is perhaps too well fitted for his job as a cosmetics rep. His wife June is a perfect model for his firm's products. Yet after a year of marriage, life is proving rather less than perfect.

It is a sly stroke of chance which brings Claudia and Steve together. Yet neither could know how far the consequences of a quiet drink would reach…

'I immensely enjoyed *A Quiet Drink*… social comedy of the highest order. Ms Moggach is funny, shrewd and has an ear for dialogue that is lethally accurate' *Daily Telegraph*

'A highly intelligent, fluent comedy about the consumer society… a lot of good jokes… wonderfully readable' *Sunday Times*

'An expert and lively exploration of marital frustration… disarming in its moments of comedy and error' *Spectator*

ALSO AVAILABLE IN PAPERBACK

☐	Close Relations	Deborah Moggach	£5.99
☐	Seesaw	Deborah Moggach	£5.99
☐	You Must Be Sisters	Deborah Moggach	£5.99
☐	Driving in the Dark	Deborah Moggach	£5.99
☐	Hot Water Man	Deborah Moggach	£5.99
☐	The Ex-Wives	Deborah Moggach	£5.99
☐	Close to Home	Deborah Moggach	£5.99
☐	Porky	Deborah Moggach	£5.99
☐	The Stand-In	Deborah Moggach	£5.99
☐	Smile	Deborah Moggach	£5.99

ALL ARROW BOOKS ARE AVAILABLE THROUGH MAIL ORDER OR FROM YOUR LOCAL BOOKSHOP AND NEWS-AGENT.

PLEASE SEND CHEQUE, EUROCHEQUE, POSTAL ORDER (STERLING ONLY), ACCESS, VISA, MASTERCARD, DINERS CARD, SWITCH OR AMEX.

☐☐☐☐☐☐☐☐☐☐☐☐☐☐☐☐

EXPIRY DATE .... SIGNATURE ....

PLEASE ALLOW 75 PENCE PER BOOK FOR POST AND PACKING U.K.

OVERSEAS CUSTOMERS PLEASE ALLOW £1.00 PER COPY FOR POST AND PACKING.

ALL ORDERS TO:

ARROW BOOKS, BOOKS BY POST, TBS LIMITED, THE BOOK SERVICE, COLCHESTER ROAD, FRATING GREEN, COLCHESTER, ESSEX CO7 7DW.

TELEPHONE: (01206) 256 000
FAX: (01206) 255 914

NAME . . . .

ADDRESS . . . .

. . . .

Please allow 28 days for delivery. Please tick box if you do not wish to receive any additional information ☐
Prices and availability subject to change without notice.